DEEP-SEA DETONATION

Looking at the map of detonation locations, Kim Otsuka's anxiety increased. If *DepthFinder* was in the right area, they could maneuver into a nuclear blast at any moment. Brande and Dokey leaned forward, close to the ports, examining the solid granite ridge that had blocked their radar.

"Brande! We're showing a heavy magnetic field!" Otsuka said.

"Where?"

Otsuka tapped a finger on the monitor.

"Probably the floor crawler," Dokey said.

"He's protected himself well," Brande said. "It's down in the rocks. Oh, shit! Dive, Dokey!"

Dokey didn't ask for reasons. He slapped the stick forward and ran the electric motors up to full power, pushing the submersible toward the black ocean floor.

They'd almost reached it when the concussion wave hit them.

Otsuka heard it, a crescendo of deep-throated thunder that hit in one loud clap. Bracing herself, she closed her eyes just as the capsule went black.

OCEAN BLACK

HANK BOSTRUM

PINNACLE BOOKS
KENSINGTON PUBLISHING CORP.

*Dedicated to the memory of my grandparents,
Henry and Matilda Bostrom,
and my father,
Henry William "Hank" Bostrom*

Acknowledgment

Dr. Robert D. Ballard and his book, *The Discovery of the Titanic,* are to be credited for my pursuit of this subject, but neither is responsible for any errors on my part.

THE PEOPLE OF OCEAN BLACK

MARINE VISIONS UNLIMITED

Dane Brande, Chairman of the Board, Marine Visions

Kaylene Rae Thomas, President, Marine Visions Unlimited

Kim Otsuka, Director of Computer Systems

Maynard "Okey" Dokey, Chief Robotics Operations Engineer

Lawrence Emry, Director of Exploration

Robert Mayberry, Director of Electronic Technology

Ingrid Roskens, Chief Structural Engineer

Svetlana Navratilova Polodka, Computer Software Engineer

Orville Bull Kontas, Captain, *Mighty Moose*

Mel Sorenson, Captain, *RV Orion*

Connie Alvarez-Sorenson, First Mate, *RV Orion*

WASHINGTON

Avery Hampstead, Undersecretary of Commerce, liaison for National Oceanic and Atmospheric Administration

Mark Stebbins, Director of Central Intelligence

Carl Unruh, CIA Intelligence Directorate
Sam Porter, Commerce Department
Damon Gilliland, State Department
Marlys Anstett, Office of the Vice President
Pamela Stroh, Justice Department

UNITED STATES NAVY

Admiral Benjamin Delecourt, Chief of Naval Operations
Admiral David Potter, Commander-in-Chief, Pacific
Captain Mabry Harris, Captain, *California*
Commander George Quicken, First Mate, *California*

OTHERS

Mark Jacobs, Captain, *Arienne* (Greenpeace vessel)
Wilson Overton, *Washington Post* reporter

AQUAGEO LIMITED

Paul Deride, Chief Executive Officer
Anthony Camden, Corporate Counsel
Penelope (Penny) Glenn, Chief Corporate Geologist
Bert Conroy, Manager SeaStation AG-4, Geologist
Mac McBride, pilot of B-3, the *Melbourne*
Gary Munro, pilot of B-7, the *Sydney*
Hap Inverness, pilot of B-4, the *Perth*
Jim Dorsey, Team Three, Operator FC-9 floor crawler

JULY 8

PROLOGUE

Kaylene Thomas shouldn't have left Santa Barbara so early in the morning.

She had been awake hours before dawn, however, and it seemed a shame to waste those hours lolling around in bed. She checked out, threw her suitcase in the trunk, and fired up the big V-8. The top wouldn't go up, naturally, because some silly piston was acting up, so she braved the early morning chill with a sweater.

The wind whipped her short, platinum-blond hair in swirls and eddies at the back of her head. She didn't worry about her appearance; it was too grand a morning, and she was going to beat heavy traffic through L.A.

The throaty roar of the dual exhaust at seventy miles per hour rumbled behind her, and the heavy car hugged the pavement like syrupy glue, chasing the light cast by its headlamps. Thomas thought she knew what the attraction of the fifties had been. She had been born a couple years after the decade had disappeared, but Dane Brande's 1957 Pontiac Bonneville convertible was her time chariot. The car was Brande's pride and joy, fully restored in pristine fashion to its original white with blue trim and blue interior. He never complained about the frequent tunings required by the temperamental fuel injection or the never-ending search for scarce replacement parts.

She figured that the true demonstration of his love for her was his unflinching "Sure, why not?" when she asked to use the car for her trip to Santa Barbara. He only cautioned her about the dips into gas stations; he had recently added a Continental kit for the spare tire that extended the rear bumper by about forty yards and was prone to grabbing the asphalt.

Tuning in an L.A. oldies station, she enhanced her journey back in time with "This Diamond Ring."

Highway 101 was nearly bereft of traffic, and she luxuriated in the absence. A few faster, squirtier cars passed her before she reached Ventura. If they were driven by men, and the men were alone, they checked her out and smiled their best, toothiest smiles as they went by. She told herself that she was ambivalent about the attention a blonde in a classic convertible got, but she was still reassured by the waving hands and assessing eyes. She was fit, her figure holding its own despite being on the lean side.

And she was fairly certain it wasn't the car that they were interested in.

By the time she saw the exit for Thousand Oaks, she was aware of a black Camaro that had passed her, subsequently been repassed, and was staying in place behind her. The man driving appeared innocuous enough in the beginning light of day, but he wasn't anyone she wanted to meet anywhere in the world, much less on a lonely highway.

She thought instead of the two-day meeting in Santa Barbara. As the President of Marine Visions

Unlimited, she felt that the sessions had been rewarding. Kaylene Rae Thomas had especially enjoyed the keynote address in the general assembly meeting by Nick Masters, the man who had been her mentor during her two years at the Scripps Institute of Oceanography. He was still a friend, even though Dane Brande had lured her away from the Institute with intriguing promises. Her elevation to the presidency of MVU had come as an unpromised surprise, and her stature among her colleagues at the conference was certainly not diminished by it. A large number of her colleagues, who wouldn't have done it two years before, had sought her out for her opinions. That was satisfying, and she had learned a few things in the seminars that she could pass on to her colleagues.

Her only disappointment was that her father had not shown up, as he had promised. Admiral Thomas, retired from the Navy, kept a time-share condo in Palm Springs, though he lived most of the year in Aspen, Colorado. He had planned on moving down to the Springs for some golf, detouring to spend time with her, then changed his mind at the last minute. She hadn't seen him in seven months and was sorry that he had become so fickle in the last few years.

The guy in the black Camaro was still behind her as she went by Encino, and she stayed in the ongoing 101 lane. It was getting much lighter now, and in the rearview mirror, she saw him grinning at her.

He crept up behind her.

Without signalling, she cut off her headlights and taillights, pretended a last-minute change of mind, and whipped into the off-ramp lane for the 405 with only yards to spare. Easing on the brakes to bleed off speed, she watched the startled Camaro driver flash past in her rearview mirror.

Goodbye, Camaro.

On the San Diego freeway now, headed south through the Hollywood Hills, she moved the speedometer needle back up to sixty-five and listened to Jack Scott singing "Midnight Special."

Then Herman's Hermits broke into "Can't You Hear My Heart Beat?"

Kaylene Thomas was about four miles south of the junction with Highway 101 when the earth convulsed.

The heavy Pontiac, wailing along at sixty-five, went sideways.

About two feet to the left side.

Abruptly shaken out of her reverie with the sixties, Thomas gripped the steering wheel with both hands, straightened her back, and wondered what the hell was going on.

Suspension?

She was stepping on the brakes when a bridge joint ahead of her opened up. It was a smooth, straight line of asphalt one moment, and in the next moment, a jagged ridge erupted across the full width of the highway.

A dull crack sounded in her ears as the fissure appeared. The asphalt wrenched upward in torn chunks.

With both feet on the brake pedal, she pressed hard.

Her knuckles went white with the pressure of her grip on the wheel.

The car slewed from side to side, rolling heavily, a barge at sea.

Then slammed into the ramped asphalt.

The front end of the Pontiac leaped into the air, the right fender rising faster than the left.

The heavy rear end, with the Continental kit, smashed into the ramp, throwing the front end downward.

There were no seat belts.

Thomas was catapulted upward, her thighs banging into the steering wheel, then slapped back into the seat.

The left front wheel smashed into the ground.

And the earth coughed again.

The front wheel lost its hubcap and folded under as the A-frame snapped.

The convertible went up on its left side, skidding along, grinding the bodywork against the pavement, at over fifty miles an hour.

The ground rumbled and belched.

The right side started coming over.

Thomas, leaning hard to the right, attempting to stay upright as the car rolled, grabbed the underside of the dashboard and pulled herself to the floor.

And the Pontiac went onto its top, ripping the windshield away, scattering glass and bits of chrome in its wake.

Slid sideways and came to a stop.

Shaking like an aspen leaf, Thomas lowered herself from her grip on the instrument panel to the asphalt.

It was dark, with the morning sun peeking in at the juncture of road and car. The earth rumbled.

My God! Dane's going to kill me!

The engine had died, but her safety training told her to fumble about until she found the ignition key and turned it off.

She tried to open the driver's door, but couldn't get it to budge.

The right door wouldn't move, either. The door handle stayed in the open position when she tried it.

Twisting herself around, she primed her legs and kicked at the door, stinging her feet through her running shoes.

On the third kick, the door gaped open, and she was able to force it far enough to crawl out from under the hulk.

She stood up, trembling, took a deep breath, and walked around the car.

Totally destroyed.

Dane's going to kill me twice.

Her purse was lying next to the car, the fawn leather deeply lacerated. She picked it up.

The engine creaked and groaned as it cooled. Fluids—gas, oil, and coolant—dripped onto the roadway.

She rotated to survey the hills to either side of the freeway. They appeared normal. A mile to the south, a pickup and a car in the northbound lanes had come to a stop.

Earthquake.

She had shuddered her way through perhaps a dozen small quakes over the years, but nothing like this.

After taking one more look at the car, and seeing no others on her horizon to the north, Thomas started walking south. Her upper legs were sore, and she knew she would have massive bruises on her thighs.

Checking herself with her hands, she found only one small cut on her temple, but the bleeding had already stopped.

She hadn't reached the cars on the other side of the highway when she heard the wail of a car coming behind her. She turned to see the flashing lights of a squad car. The deputy sheriff squealed to a stop, told her to get in, and wrote himself a note on her accident as he sped on south. He paused to ask the people in the northbound lane if they were all right. They were.

At Sunset Boulevard he rolled off the interstate to block traffic onto the freeway.

"Sorry, ma'am. This is as far as I can take you."

"Thanks, Deputy."

She got out of the car as the radio chattered with emergency calls, and she was aware that the dispatchers had run out of people and vehicles to respond to all of the requests.

She could see smoke rising over the hills, though certainly not like the smoke of last year's fires. She opted to walk toward Beverly Hills, looking for a phone.

When she reached buildings, she peered inside. Supermarkets had their inventory spread across the floors. A liquor store reeked of mixed spirits. There was broken glass everywhere. Some people were crying. A woman sat in the middle of a parking lot with a sinkhole in one corner, consoling two small children who were bawling their heads off. The woman was wearing a torn denim jacket and white slacks with the knees ripped out.

There were cracks in the asphalt of the streets, a

few trees fallen onto cars, a few more trees uprooted, people sitting on the curbs as they were tended by friends and family. Primitive first aid was being applied by well-meaning neighbors with deficient first aid kits. A small redheaded girl, maybe eight or nine, passed out paper cups of red Kool-Aid.

Sirens wailed. An ambulance worked its way down the street, bypassing stalled cars and structural debris.

This could be a war zone, she imagined. Worse than the physical carnage was the shell-shocked appearance of the people. Happy, normal lives had been shattered in an instant. She felt shattered herself until she saw two ambulance attendants escorting a gurney with a fully draped body; then she felt lucky.

She could smell the odor of natural gas, as well as that of ruptured sewer lines. There didn't seem to be any electricity, and when she found a phone booth, she wasn't surprised when the phone would not give her a dial tone.

So she sat on the floor of the booth and cried.

NOVEMBER 11

Nuclear Detonation:
32° 39′ 26″ North, 137° 32′ 16″ West

ONE

"She's just too damned pretty for my likes, Chief."

Orville "Bull" Kontas, captain of the *Mighty Moose,* didn't care for the new paint scheme on his workboat, an ex-tugboat converted to new uses by the Marine Visions Unlimited crews.

Kaylene Thomas had sold the other two workboats, *Priscilla* and *Cockamamie,* and used the proceeds to dry-dock and fully refit the *Mighty Moose.* In addition to her new engines and refurbished living and working spaces, she sported the company's recognizable theme of white paint with a yellow stripe rising diagonally on each side of the pilothouse.

"You've sailed prettier, Bull," Dane Brande told him.

"Maybe. But not on a damned tugboat."

Brande had to cede the point. The workboat's captain had probably sailed every classification of boat and ship in every available sea and ocean. Kontas was over seventy, with no documented evidence of his true age. His black-market-purchased papers—birth certificate and passport—reported that he had been born in Shanghai of a Greek father and a Chinese mother, but the data was based primarily on hearsay. His bald pate had a rusty-edged fringe of white hair, and the lines of his weather- and sea-beaten face were deep. His ears were huge and blistered. Whatever his age, his strength seemed undiminished, and his loyalty would never be faulted. He had been with MVU from soon after the start-up.

It wasn't until after the *Moose* came out of dry dock that Brande realized how much pride Kontas had taken as master of a boat that didn't fit into a corporate scheme. Her decrepit state of repair had not meshed with the MVU ideology, but it had meshed perfectly with Bull Kontas.

"Would you like it better without the yellow stripe, Bull?"

"Ah, Chief. . . ."

"Go ahead and paint it out."

"Well, shit. I mean, it's your boat and all."

"I don't care, Bull. I just like to come and ride with you."

And that was true. He liked almost any form of marine transport. After Brande's parents died in an automobile accident, and while he was being raised on the farm by his grandparents, Sven and Bridgette, he had learned to like more water than wheat farmers generally appreciated. With his fifteen-foot aluminum boat, he had sought adventure on Tenmile Lake, then Leech Lake, then Lake Superior. Obtaining scholarships where he could and working the summer wheat harvests, Brande had accumulated enough cash to get him to the University of California at San Diego, then on to graduate schools.

Though he had left the wheat farm, Brande carried much of his Swedish heritage with him. Henning Sven Brande's wide shoulders and barrel chest were apparent in Dane, disguising the fact that he weighed 215 pounds. He was six four, and that too was a reflection of both Sven and his father, Stephen. Henning Sven's antecedents, confused by the tradition of differing surnames—Brandeson, Svenson, Petterson—all had identifiable blue eyes, and Brande carried that trait forward. He had been unable, or unwilling, however, to continue plowing the ground that Henning Sven had broken in Minnesota in 1917.

Brande sported the hands of his grandfather, large with blunt fingers, but they displayed the scars of contact with coral reef and sharp-edged equipment rather than John Deere tractors and harrows. His blond hair was bleached to near whiteness by sun and salt water, and his face was deep-sea tanned and weathered, with early crow's-feet at the corners of his blue eyes.

Keeping his private life private wasn't an obsession, but it was a habit. While his professional successes were the fodder of boasting, he didn't bother. Brande's quiet demeanor and self-confidence gave outsiders the impression of arrogance, but his employees, whom he considered more as colleagues than hired staff, accepted his indirect style of leadership without question. Except, perhaps, for Bull Kontas.

Stepping to the back of the pilothouse, Brande poured two mugs full of coffee from the cradled pot and took one forward to Kontas.

Keeping one gnarled hand on the helm, Kontas accepted his mug with the other and said, "Miss Kaylene, she won't like that."

"You take care of the paint, Bull. I'll take care of Rae."

In the nearly five years that she had worked for him, Brande had always called Kaylene Rae Thomas by her middle name. He knew it was an avoidance trait. His wife, Janelle Kay, had died on their honeymoon trip to the azure depths of the Caribbean, pinned beneath the broken crane boom of a sunken Liberty ship. His frantic and unsuccessful attempts to free her before her oxygen ran out had partially set the course of his career.

He preferred to call the president of his company, for which he was still chairman of the board, Rae.

Brande stood next to Kontas and watched the endless blue sea rolling toward them. The waters off Southern California were calm and smooth. Off the stern, North Island disappeared behind Point Loma, and San Diego Bay faded.

Two hours later, the chronically taciturn Kontas, after a silence of nearly an hour, said, "There she is, Chief."

Brande scanned the sea and found the buoy. It was a beat-up, steel concoction emplaced for the duration of the construction phase of Ocean Deep, which was two hundred feet straight down. They had come today to replace it.

Bending toward the low-placed PA microphone on the side bulkhead, Brande pressed the switch and yelled, "Both hands on deck!"

Several minutes later, Darby Jones appeared. He was Bull Kontas's entire crew.

A minute later, Maynard Dokey followed him into the pilothouse, still rubbing the sleep from his eyes. "Okey" Dokey was short of stature and hated dentists so much that he went through life with a chipped front tooth. At sea he rarely combed his hair, which was a tangled mass of dark curls. He was wearing cutoff jeans and a bright yellow T-shirt with the boldly printed legend, Save the Mammals? I Thought You Said Mammaries.

Dokey designed his own shirts and coffee mugs, in addition to intricately plotted electronic circuits and massively complicated software programs. When he felt like it, he could be a genius with a machine tool, fabricating intricate components for mechanical monsters. Despite his sea-bum appearance, he was a graduate of Massachusetts Institute of Technology, and he carried the Marine Visions Unlimited title of Chief Robotics Operations Engineer. Robots being the prime concern of the company, Dokey and Brande were frequently in one another's company.

He clomped into the pilothouse and stopped in front of Brande. "The next time, Chief . . ."

Kontas had learned to call Brande, "Chief," as a result of Dokey's example.

". . . I prefer to be awakened gently, preferably by someone with long, blond hair, swishing it lightly across my face. There should be coffee at hand, perhaps a warm croissant. . . ."

"Coffee's on the hot plate," Brande grinned at him. "Maybe Darby has a croissant in the galley."

"What's a croissant?" Jones asked.

"God," Dokey complained, "there's got to be a better outfit somewhere, like the Navy."

"The Navy didn't have croissants," Jones told him. He had retired as a chief petty officer.

Kontas reduced speed as he neared the buoy, saying, "Let's hop to it."

"I didn't get my coffee," Dokey said.

"Get up earlier," Kontas told him.

Dokey grinned and headed for the afterdeck, followed by Jones.

Brande moved to the rear bulkhead, now outfitted with state-of-the-art radar, sonar, and radio equipment, including an acoustic phone. Radio waves tended to bend in the wrong directions in water, and most of their subsurface communications were accomplished with acoustic transmissions.

Lifting the phone from its cradle, Brande said, "Ocean Deep, anyone listening? This is the *Mighty Moose.*"

"*Voyager Two* here, Dane. I'm surfacing."

The captain of *Voyager II* was Ron Zendl. Eventually, there would be six *Voyager* submarines, passenger-carrying vessels accommodating thirty-two tourists. That was two more subs than originally planned, but expectations had risen. They were designed to operate at depths of less than two thousand feet, carrying visitors from San Diego and Los Angeles to Ocean Deep.

"We're watching for you, Ron. How about Dot?"

"They're loading her up now," Zendl said.

"Dot" was short for *Neptune's Daughter,* a two-man minisub utilized for undersea chores. Her sisters were *Neptune's Niece* and *Neptune's Wife,* known as "Nice" and "Wifey," and the three subs, like the *Voy-*

ager-class, were designed for relatively shallow waters.

"All right. We'll have a package for her in about twenty minutes," Brande said.

He replaced the telephone, slipped out onto the side-deck, and walked aft to join Dokey and Jones.

Dokey had pulled the tarpaulin from the new buoy. It was, naturally, finished in white and yellow. It was eight feet in diameter, and it was not intended to serve any useful purpose for seafarers. Rather, it was Ocean Deep's communication link. On top of the globular buoy was a fiberglass housing protecting a wide array of antennas and a video camera. A small radar dish provided a twenty-mile scan of the area around it, triggering radio warnings to ships that might collide with the buoy.

Microwave antennas connected Ocean Deep with the mainland, and a satellite uplink provided a route for more heavenly communications. Rae Thomas frequently complained about the cost of MVU's satellite communications subscription.

Another set of sensors—for wave motion, wind direction and speed, temperature, salinity, and the like—in addition to the video, provided inputs to the consoles on board Ocean Deep. The technicians and the tourists could monitor conditions on the surface. Those conditions were often a stark contrast to the seemingly motionless serenity at depth.

Dokey and Brande released the tie-downs, then Brande signalled Jones, who was operating the controls of the crane. The boom's line went taut, stretched a tad, then eased the buoy from its cradle on the deck. When it was six feet above the deck,

Jones stopped the lift, and Brande took some strain on a guideline to steady it. He studied all of the lines and cables, looking for undue stresses before he nodded an okay to Dokey.

Dokey slipped beneath the buoy with the end of a thick umbilical cable that was coiled high on the deck and began to fasten the connector in place. The cable was Kevlar-shielded, strong as steel and contained as an inner core a bundle of fiber-optic filaments.

Marine Visions utilized a cable of the single-mode fiber type. The diameter of the filament was small enough to force a single beam of light to stay on a direct path. Lasers generated light signals in binary code—pulsing on for 1 and off for 0—that zipped along the fiber at tremendous speeds. The high frequency of light waves allowed the transmission of thousands of times more information than was permitted by current flowing in a copper wire. The speed and data capacity of fiber-optic cables reduced immensely the thickness of the cable required. A quarter-inch-thick fiber-optic cable could handle telecommunications, computer data transfer, electronic mail, and image transfer with ease, and with space left over. This cable, because it would also anchor the buoy, was two inches in diameter, the additional bulk made up of carbon-reinforced strands of fiberglass.

The laser-light generators and receivers on both ends of the cable had to be correctly aligned. A cable inserted into a connector with a 1/64-inch twist off alignment would scramble all communications between the host vehicle and the sensors and antennas. Dokey inserted the male connector into the female receptor, levered the locking ring into place, and bolted it down. Or up, since he was working on the bottom of the buoy.

Backing out from beneath the slightly swinging buoy, he said, "I must have designed this, Chief. It fit."

Dokey had helped, but the team had also included Kim Otsuka and Bob Mayberry, the respective directors of computer systems and electronic technology.

Brande released his guideline, disconnected it from the buoy, then waved at Jones.

The crane boom moved outboard, carrying the buoy with it, dragging its cable behind, and lowered the sphere to the sea.

As Jones released the crane line's lift hook remotely, Dokey said, "I'll be damned. It floats."

"This stuff won't," Brande said, referring to the coil of cable. It was six hundred feet long, with a fitting 250 feet from the buoy which would fasten to the concrete anchor pier embedded in the seabed. The remaining length would snake across the seafloor and be attached to an exterior connector on the dome.

With Jones's assistance on the crane, they lifted the coil from the deck, swung it over the side, and lowered it to water level.

Then they waited for the subs. When both Dot and *Voyager II* popped their sails above the surface, out of harm's way, Jones released the coil from the crane line.

Brande watched as it began to unfurl, disappearing into the depths.

Dot immediately submerged again, chasing after the fitting she would attach to the pier.

Zendl cautiously brought *Voyager II* alongside the workboat, and Brande and Dokey leaped from the low gunwale to the tower of the sub, which was located well forward on the hull. The sail tilted back and forth in the wave action, and Brande kept a firm grip on the exposed handrail. The access hatch popped open, and Zendl stuck his head out. Boyish and charming, the thirty-year-old had an adolescent's cowlick at the back of his head, completely uncontrollable.

"Going my way?" he asked.

"Forgot our tickets," Dokey told him.

"We'll bill you."

Brande followed Dokey through the hatch, then closed and dogged it tight. Descending an eleven-foot-long ladder brought him to the main deck of the sub, in the control cabin. The smooth, well-illuminated sea was visible through the four large ports over the instrument panel, which was a Boeing 747 pilot's dream. Red, green, and blue digital readouts monitored the submarine's performance and position. There were two comfortable seats for the pilot and his assistant, though Zendl was the only operator on board just now. When they started carrying passengers, they would have a full crew of two operators and two stewards.

The first *Voyager* was already back in dry dock, her interior being fitted for the expectations of the travelling public—airline-type seats, carpeting, laminated bulkhead panelling. *Voyager III* and *IV* were in the final stages of construction in Bremerton, and *III* would undergo sea trials within the month.

Zendl offered Brande the pilot's seat, but he shook his head, and the captain settled into his seat.

Brande often felt the pangs of jealousy in such encounters. He had been the primary designer of this sub, which was based on the configuration of the submersible *Ben Franklin,* but he was reticent about taking the controls from the people he had designated as captains of his vessels, whether it was Bull Kontas or Ron Zendl.

Voyager II was seventy feet long, and almost all of her operating systems were below the passenger deck. Water, trim, ballast, and waste tanks took up the most space, followed by the four gigantic sets of battery banks which powered the twin electric motors. The liquid-oxygen tanks and the electronic components were mounted in an aft compartment.

He dipped his head and passed through the hatchway into the main cabin, which could seat thirty-two people. Each pair of seats had its own porthole, the better to view the trip through Southern California seas. The *Voyager* craft had been given much thinner hulls than other submersibles since they would travel in shallower water. Additionally, they had sleeker shapes in order to increase speed. The interior of *Voyager II* had exposed electrical and hydraulic conduits along the sides and ceiling. The floor was steel, and the seats were covered in canvas. The utilitarian decor, finished in gray-speckled paint, did not bother the work crews who were transported daily to Ocean Deep.

The submarines made their way out of San Diego Bay on the surface, and the first leg was generally rough. Once into open sea, and submerged to a level of one hundred feet, most impressions of motion disappeared. The submersibles could make almost thirty knots subsurface, and the trip to Ocean Deep was usually accomplished in about an hour. Out of Los Angeles, whenever they arranged for porting facilities, it would be seventy minutes.

He and Dokey flopped into seats on the opposite sides of the narrow aisle as Zendl took on ballast and the sub began to settle into the sea. The relatively mild wave motion decreased, and *Voyager II* felt increasingly stable.

"The trouble with this job," Dokey said, "is the more we accomplish, the less we get to do."

"Agreed, Okey. Figure out another project for us."

"Done."

Dokey liked to get his hands dirty, delving into the innards of robots or diving on the sea's treasures. In that respect, he and Brande were exactly alike. Brande had, at one time or another, fulfilled his wish list for skydiving, race-car driving, scuba diving, and a few other adrenaline-producing pursuits.

One of the benefits, he had learned, of relinquishing the president's position in favor of Rae Thomas was more freedom to pursue the on-site activities of MVU's mining, agricultural, and seabed-living experiments. Still, many of those projects were manned by experts in the fields, and Brande didn't want to encroach on their territories.

The deck tilted forward, and the sunlight filtering through the water dimmed. Humming lightly, the electric motors drove them downward as Zendl added to his ballast load.

Voyager II descended in a wide spiral, finding the sea bottom several minutes later.

Zendl called back through the open hatchway, "They've deployed 'Turtle.' "

"Give us a look, will you, Ron?" Brande said.

The submarine drifted to a stop, and Brande leaned close to his porthole. Dokey crossed the aisle to the seat behind him.

Neptune's Daughter was just rising from the sandy seabed after deploying the robot from the sheath beneath her hull. A gaggle of silver-and-orange fish darted across her path, and a lazy sea bass looked on with disapproval.

The two-man minisubmarine, devised and built in MVU's San Diego shops, was intended only for tasks that could be accomplished at depths of less than one thousand feet. In side-by-side lounge seats, her two operators had a fair view of their environment from within an aircraftlike canopy. Less than twenty feet long, the sub was normally used as the control platform for tethered robots, in this case, Turtle.

Turtle had never been given a more exotic title. Like "Gargantua," the heavy mover, Turtle had come to be known by a male appellation. Most seacraft were provided with feminine pronouns, but Turtle had always been Turtle, possibly in deference to his squat, solid physique.

He had a heavy metal body and two sets of rubber-cleated tracks, giving him the image of a downsized battlefield tank. Guided by the operator in the sub through the Kevlar-shielded fiber-optic cable, he crawled along the bottom, waving his hands in front of him. A small rotatable housing on the top of the body contained cameras for remote viewing of the work performed by his three manipulator arms, also attached to the movable housing. Each arm had a reach of twelve feet and a specific duty—cutting and welding operations, gripping and lifting, and spinning. The spinnable wrist simplified the task of installing bolts and nuts. Seabed-crawling robots had leverage; they had footing. Robots suspended in the water relied on the power of their thrusters for leverage, and frequently they were found wanting.

Leverage was a basic principle that Brande had learned, or relearned, in agony when he had been unable to pry the crane boom away from Janelle and had been forced to watch her drown.

Now he watched Turtle trundle across the uneven seabed, skirting some deep depressions and swirling the leaves of a clump of seaweed as he passed. His control tether trailed after him like an exotic sea snake, and his three manipulator arms were folded in front of him like those of a mutant praying mantis.

When he reached the anchor fitting attached midway down the buoy's line, he stopped, and his central arm extended. The hand, composed of two curving fingers at the top and one opposed thumb at the bottom, gently closed on the fitting and raised it from the seafloor. The tracks dug in and began to spin, raising a minicloud of particulates. Turtle started moving again, dragging the fitting and its attached cable toward the anchoring pier, which was seventy yards away.

The minisub trailed along behind the robot, providing the brains and the guidance for the operation.

"Love that guy," Dokey said.

Brande did, too. Now, after two years of nearly glitch-free trials with Turtle, the San Diego shops were producing his brothers on order for sale to mining and drilling operations. The cost of his development had already been recovered, and the profit column on that particular project was beginning to show positive numbers.

Revenue production was one of Marine Visions' shortfalls. In the nearly nine years of their existence, they hadn't yet reported a profit on total operations.

They watched Turtle at work for a few more minutes, then Brande called to Zendl, "Take us on in, Ron."

"On the way, Chief."

Voyager II slipped into forward motion, and Brande leaned closer to the porthole to get a glimpse of what Rae Thomas called Disneyland West. Brande thought of it as a revenue producer, designed and built solely to compete with tourist attractions like Sea World and Universal Studios. He didn't particularly want to be in the entertainment business, and he thought of the project as one that, first, demonstrated MVU's capabilities and, second, created income to support the loftier goals of exploration and scientific experimentation.

The domes came into view.

There were three of them, oversized and connected by twelve-foot-long cylindrical tunnels. Each of the domes rose one hundred feet above steel piers embedded in the seafloor, and each was two hundred feet in diameter. The two end domes had airlocks and docking facilities on their lower sides, between the stabilizing legs.

Kim Otsuka had told him that she thought they looked like spider plants. An olive-colored plastic embedded with carbon fiber made up the hub, at the top of each dome. The superstrong carbon fiber was also used in the curved beams that radiated from the tops down to the bases of the domes. There were four horizontal rows of thinner structural beams, and the spaces between the structural members were filled with a translucent plastic that had also been strengthened with carbon.

The design, the construction, and the materials used had been tested for over four years on Harbor One, MVU's first sea lab, and Brande had utter confidence in the reliability of the engineering.

The official name of the complex, a separate corporation owned by Marine Visions, was Ocean Deep, though it was not actually very deep. Located thirty miles west of San Diego and about thirty-five miles south-southwest of Los Angeles, the complex was two hundred feet below the surface, its foundation legs embedded in the Patton Escarpment. The tourists were to be given a thrill, not put at extreme risk.

The domes had been designed for specific functions. One would house marine-theme amusement rides aimed at youngsters, one would contain museums and galleries, and one would focus on marine life. And still, Brande would avoid direct contact with the entertainment aspects. The company would own the complex, the transportation system, and the operating systems, but subcontractors would operate the internal businesses. The subleases were slowly being finalized, since the insurance underwriters had agreed to terms two months before.

As the submarine closed in, the interior lighting made the domes stand out prominently against the darkness of the sea.

Zendl dove beneath the western dome and slowed to approach the mating collar. The base of the dome was sixty feet above the seabed, allowing ample room for the submersible to wend its way to the interlock on the floor of the dome. The captain could look directly up through a port in the sail, line up a red painted cross, and blow ballast to rise to meet the collar.

A solid clunk reverberating through the hull told Brande the connection had been made. He waited while technicians above checked the seals, then equalized pressures. A hiss and a swirling movement of air inside the submarine indicated that the hatches had been opened, and he rose from his seat.

Dokey followed him forward to the ladder, and as Brande stepped up on the first rung, he had a thought.

"Okey."

"Yo."

"Here's a project for you. We want a system, probably in *Voyager Five,* for embarking wheelchairs. We don't want to exclude anyone."

"Good idea, Chief. I'll talk to Ingrid about it."

Ingrid Roskens was the chief structural engineer for MVU.

Brande climbed the ladder and emerged into the wide central corridor of the dome's first level. Engineering and life-support systems were hidden behind bulkheads. Two escalators, not yet operating, would move people to the upper level where variants on traditional amusement-park rides were in the final stages of construction by the subcontractor. There would be Davy Jones's Locker, Shark Spree, and Orca's Revenge, among the attractions that Brande didn't intend to visit.

Along this corridor, souvenir booths and fast-food enterprises were getting their final touches. T-Shirts by Dokey was located in a ten-by-ten stall, a business commissioned by Okey Dokey, but operated by someone else. He liked to use ideas, ink, and paint, not credit-card machines.

"You want to stop by Jack's Galley?" Dokey asked.

"It's not open yet."

"Damn. And here I am, hungry again."

"My grandma Bridgette always told me to eat a big breakfast," Brande said.

"Yeah, but your grandma probably knew how to make a big breakfast. You've never seen me with a mixer and pancake batter."

"And let's keep it that way," Brande told him.

1447 Hours Local
Washington, D.C.

Avery Hampstead was a scion of the Hampsteads of Philadelphia, but outside the pale of Hampstead appearance. His father's handsome good looks had been wasted on others in the family, like his sister Adrienne.

Hampstead was identifiable from a block away by his protruding and overlobed ears which, if he were not a proper Undersecretary of Commerce, he would have disguised with a 1960s' Ringo Starr styling of his dark hair. He had horsey, square teeth that were often revealed in a smile on his elongated face.

While he didn't fit the Hampstead image, he did mesh with the family's tradition of public service, joining two brothers and a sister in the nation's bureaucracy. His youngest sister, Adrienne, detested the foppish, intriguish ways of the Capitol, and she had found her calling in promotion, from wrestling matches to fund-raising. Like the rest of his siblings, Avery Hampstead earned his living. There was steel and railroad money in the family, but his father had other, unknown designs for it. Beyond education and a single automobile for each of his offspring, the elder Hampstead had provided only the philosophy that work was good for the soul and the psyche.

Fortunately, Hampstead enjoyed his work. He was the Department of Commerce's liaison with the National Oceanic and Atmospheric Administration, overseeing the administration's contracts and projects in the marine sector. He worked frequently with other agencies conducting research and surveys in the ocean depths. While NOAA had twenty-one specialized vessels in its inventory, Transportation, Interior, and the National Science Foundation could account for another three. The Navy dedicated eight ships to subsurface missions, and the academic institutions controlled another sixty vessels. Then there were the private firms which obtained federal subsidies for exploration.

It was a challenging position, and it kept him from aspiring to higher rank. Hampstead was quite happy where he was.

He liked his office, also, which to the disgust of Angie, his secretary, was decorated with framed posters of some of the wrestling matches Adrienne had promoted. They were garish, and the captions were filled with hyperbole, and he personally found the sport revolting, but they gave him a sense of balance with the real world.

Sometimes he needed that when working so closely with academics.

Culling through a foot-high stack of contracts, which had adorned his desk for a week, Hampstead was deep into goals and objectives and the dollars necessary to fulfill them when his intercom buzzed.

"Yes, Angie?"

"The Secretary's on line one, boss."

"Thank you." He punched the button. "Yes, sir?"

"Avery, I'd like to have you fly out to Golden."

"Colorado?"

"That's the one."

"Right away?"

"I don't think there's any great rush," the Secretary said, "but the seismic people have an anomaly they think you might be interested in."

"I can't imagine that. I don't know the first, or the last, thing about earthquakes."

"This one's out in the Pacific somewhere. That's your bailiwick."

After the Secretary rang off, Hampstead looked at the pile of paper in front of him. He thought that his prospects for the afternoon were dismal.

He pressed the intercom bar. "Angie, would you call Alicia and tell her I won't be home tonight."

His favorite women were all A's. Alicia, Adrienne, Angie. He couldn't have designed it better himself.

"Me? Why me? You always saddle me with these messages."

"Because if I call her, I can't come home tomorrow night."

"That's possible, I suppose. Do I tell her where you'll be?"

"I'll be in Colorado."

"You never take me to these exotic places."

"Someday, I promise."

"When are you going?" she asked.

"I don't know. You haven't made my reservations yet."

1520 Hours Local
San Diego, California

Paul Deride was a big, blustery man with a red face, penetrating green eyes, and a spreading halo of thick, blond hair. He was fond of wearing sunglasses with lenses smoked so black that his eyes were indiscernible until he whipped them off and stabbed his quarry with those bright eyes.

His torso maintained the same diameter from chest to hips, a solid cylinder of muscle and sinew. At six foot five inches of height, with wide shoulders and heavy arms, Deride plowed through crowds on the street or in airport terminals like an ultralarge crude carrier. His determination and momentum were difficult to arrest, and he went through life with the same singleness of purpose. Many years before he had plowed his way through the University of Sydney in record time, then repeated the feat at Oxford. Both of his degrees had been obtained on scholarship for he had been stone broke, right off a sheep ranch in the outback of New South Wales.

Deride drove his rented Buick through the Rose-ville area of San Diego, on the western side of the bay. The streets were all named for people he didn't care about—Emile Zola, Louisa May Alcott, Lord Byron. They were all poets and writers who hadn't contributed much to the world's gross product.

He found the headquarters of Marine Visions Un-limited by its small sign on the side of an ancient, red-brick warehouse off Dickens Street. The offices were apparently on the second floor, accessed from a street-level glass door facing a stairway. The ground floor was devoted to their experimental endeavors, he supposed.

Parking the Buick at the curb, Deride got out and straightened the tail of his suit coat. He had expended a thousand dollars U.S. for the suit, but like almost anything else of a personal nature, he didn't pay much attention to it. If someone asked him what color he was wearing, he would have to look down before saying "gray."

On one end of the building was a small loading dock, backed by an overhead door which was closed. He crossed the street, pulled open the glass door, and stepped inside. Another sign told him he was wel-come, just climb the stairs. A door on the right was labelled for Authorized Personnel Only, and he twisted the handle and pushed it open. Deride quite often went where he wasn't invited.

Stepping inside the large, open space, Deride took a slow look around. Shoved into one corner were the remains of an old American convertible. It had been badly damaged in a turnover, and he couldn't understand why it was there. He would have sent it off to the landfill.

The rest of the room was something of a lunatic asylum. Tools and welding equipment littered the concrete floor; worktables and steel lockers were shoved against the walls. Schematic diagrams and blueprints were taped to walls and lockers. Out in the center of the floor were a half dozen big worktables, and the odd shapes, electronic boards, and electric motors scattered on them suggested that six or seven differing projects were under way at the same time.

There were fourteen people in the lab, and not one of them took notice of him. They were bent intently over their work, six of them gathered together at one table.

He didn't take notice of them, either. His attention was drawn to another corner, opposite the damaged automobile.

Sitting on a four-wheeled trailer was an oblong monstrosity that Deride knew from experience was the result of practical design. It was about—staying in American measurements—twelve feet long and eight feet wide, perhaps two-and-a-half feet tall. The corners and edges were all rounded. Deride had understood that there were legs, but they were apparently retracted, and the body rested on the bed of the trailer on four one-foot diameter steel pads.

He walked slowly toward the trailer, studying the creature.

The forward end was slightly bulged and featured large round floodlights on stalks, giving the monster a bug-eyed appearance. Below the lights were projections that Deride assumed to be the lenses for video and seventy-millimeter cameras. Between the floodlights was an upright, circular housing that contained a fan. A similar housing and fan on the stern, combined with the forward unit, controlled the side-to-side movement and the horizontal plane rotation. A single propeller in a protective housing on the aft end provided forward propulsion.

Three rounded wells, two of them forward and one aft, passed completely through the body and contained three more turbine blades. Powered by electric motors, those blades would provide up-and-down movement, and judging by their size, Deride expected a massive lift capability.

In addition to the apparent lift capacity, Deride was also intrigued by the manipulator arms. There were three of them, mounted just below the floodlights, and though they were folded back in repose, he estimated a reach of around eight feet. Each had elbow and wrist joints and were probably capable of the seven axes of movement he had heard about.

Two of the arms were fitted with two-fingered, one-thumbed hands which appeared extremely strong. The third arm was outfitted with a cutting torch at the moment.

The whole apparatus was painted a virginal white, and diagonal yellow stripes—the corporate identification of Marine Visions Unlimited—ran up the sides from bow to stern. At the stern terminus of the yellow stripe was the legend, in black letters, *Celebes*.

From the newspaper accounts of the Soviet rocket retrieval, Deride also knew that the unofficial name of the robot was Gargantua.

"Mr. Deride?"

He turned away from the robot to find a stunning young woman looking at him. She was tall, with platinum-blond hair and pale blue eyes that didn't waver from his own. Definitely a bird of another feather, he decided. Most women demonstrated a large degree of timidity when they faced him. His reputation, his physique, or his money accounted for that, but he did not know, nor care, which of those attributes was responsible for the subservience of women. Or of most men.

Pulling his glasses off, he folded the temples and dropped them in his breast pocket.

"You know me?" he asked.

"I've seen your picture. You aren't authorized to be in this area, Mr. Deride. I'll have to ask you to leave."

"I'm here to see Dr. Brande."

"Dr. Brande is out of the country. Perhaps I can help you?"

"And you are?"

"Kaylene Thomas."

"I need to meet someone in authority," he said.

"I'm president of the company."

He had known that. Deride always knew everything about any mission he took for his own. He even had a copy of her picture in his dossier on MVU. Still, it never hurt to put people down a little, keep them off-balance.

"I see. Well, I want to buy that thing." He pointed back at *Celebes*.

"He's not for sale."

"Oh, I think it is." Deride produced his wallet from his inside jacket pocket and extracted a cashier's check. Handing it to her, he said, "That's made out for two-and-a-half million dollars. I believe it covers your development, as well as a tidy profit."

She looked at the check.

Deride also knew that Thomas was a pragmatist when it came to dollars and cents. He preferred dealing with her over negotiating with Brande.

Unexpectedly, she shoved the check back at him. "Not for sale."

Deride held up both of his hands, palms toward her, rejecting the check.

"Why don't you discuss it with Dr. Brande? Keep the check for the time being."

He turned and walked out of the laboratory, carefully taking time to don his sunglasses and set them squarely and precisely on his nose.

TWO

Rae Thomas called it "Hoboville," for the transient nature of the employees as well as for the junkyard accumulation of furnishings, but Brande kind of liked the homey and relaxed decor of the Marine Visions headquarters on the second floor of the warehouse off Dickens.

Except for the prerequisite spaces for rest rooms, storage, and a kitchenette, the entire floor was open, providing an expansive feeling, Brande thought. Thomas objected to the furnishings, but she couldn't fault the cost. The desks, file cabinets, and chairs were mostly Navy surplus. The computer terminals were generally purchased from the newspaper want ads and refurbished and upgraded by Dokey and Ot-suka. Their cables dangled from the false ceiling, and above the ceiling was a snake's nest of gray and color-coded cabling that would defy the logic of most mortals. Fortunately, MVU had a plethora of electri-cal engineers and computer-literate folks who found the maze intriguing.

Brande admitted to himself—though not to anyone

else—that the color schemes prevalent in the office
might be a trifle jangled. The metal pieces were black,
gray, or beige, depending on what was on sale at the
time. The woods and fabrics ranged from walnut to
oak and yellow or blue to orange and red. Then again,
he reminded himself, it wasn't a perfect world. One
didn't order the angel fish to stand in that corner of
the ocean, and the silver grunion to move over there.

Thomas, whose father was a retired admiral, also
thought the desks and cabinets should be lined up in
neat, shipshape rows. She didn't care for the seemingly random placements—three desks angled together here, five circled there. The blueprints and
schematics taped to the walls and to the windows
bothered her. Brande was all for ship-shape aboard
a ship, but in his office, in the workroom on the first
floor, or in the dockside building on the Commercial
Basin a half-block away, he was more interested in
creative output. The people who formed the various
project teams kept shifting with the projects, or
worked on multiple tasks, and he didn't care if they
moved their desks to the roof.

The disciplinary specialties—oceanography, biol-
ogy, computer science, civil and structural engineering,
environmental engineering, robotics, and propulsion—
interacted with each other by shouts across the room,
by telephone calls from one desk to another, and by
computer conversations.

Downstairs, the same kind of controlled confusion
existed. The birth of a new concept resulted in the components of one project being shunted to one side while
the new idea was formed into brass, stainless steel, reinforced carbon-carbon, fiberglass, or fiber optics.

It was all very reassuring to Brande. It meant that creation was taking place.

He was never bothered by the fluorescent light that buzzed nor the ceiling-mounted air conditioner that shivered loudly from time to time.

To the northeast, San Diego International Airport was busy, a file of United, Continental, and Quantas passenger liners taking to the skies. From where he sat, Brande could view the U.S. Naval Air Station on North Island, relatively quiet this evening.

Where he sat was in Larry Emry's high-backed, blue Naugahyde chair, with his feet up on one of the pulled-out drawers of Emry's scarred gray metal desk. He would have used the Formica walnut desktop for his feet, but it was piled high with geographical reports, charts, maps, paper cups, and the remnants of two large pepperoni, black olive, green pepper, and onion pizzas.

In the far corner, in a quiet buzz of their own, Okey Dokey and Ingrid Roskens were ideating submarine entrance and exit hatches for the physically challenged.

Across from him, sitting cross-legged in the middle of Mayberry's green blotter with a huge slice of pizza in one hand and a can of Coke in the other, was Kim Otsuka. In the chair at her own desk, to his left, was Rae Thomas.

"I think," Otsuka said, "that Dane ought to endorse the check, then give it to the American Cancer Society or to one of the AIDS projects."

"That would be called theft. Or fraud, or something," Thomas said.

"That's justice," Otsuka countered.

Neither of the women liked Paul Deride any better than Brande did.

Thomas waved the check in the air. "It's a cashier's check."

"Hell," Brande said, "let's cash it then. We could maybe pay off a couple notes, and there's this forty-foot ketch I saw over at the marina. . . ."

"Dane," Thomas said.

"My grandma Bridgette used that very same tone with me all too often."

"There is no doubt in my mind that she probably had a right to use it," Thomas said.

"We could," Otsuka mused, "actually sell him Gargantua. Or a copy of Gargantua."

Brande went along with the musing for the moment. "What have we got invested in him?"

Thomas turned to her computer terminal and played with the keys. Since she had taken over the presidency, a number of things had become organized. Project costs, for example. In the past, if it wasn't required by some federal or institutional grant, Brande had never worried unduly about the efforts and dollars put into a contract. Scientists were happy to boast about their accuracy in research and development, but many of them were slippery when it came to how much of the government's, or their own, money they were pouring into some hole in the ocean. Rae Thomas preferred a more exact accounting than "give or take a few hundred thousand."

"*Celebes,*" she said, "has consumed two-point-two-six million to date."

"Nah," Brande said.

"Yes."

"Can't be."

"But it is."

"How?" he asked.

"You never allocated the salary and fringe benefits costs of the people working the project."

"I didn't?"

"You didn't."

She was correct, of course. Brande hadn't worried about such things as fringe benefits. His people got salaries and were happy with what they were doing. Sometimes, they got an insurance program thrown in, if they asked for it, but Brande wasn't big on administration. Now, Thomas had standardized life, health, dental, and retirement programs in place. They cost money, and the cost was allocated to the various projects.

"So, a second Gargantua, with all the research and development costs taken care of, would cost us how much, Rae?"

She scrolled through her numbers, finding the materials section. "Nine hundred thousand, roughly, allowing for inflation, for the bits and pieces, and maybe another three hundred thousand in personnel costs."

"That would give us a one-point-three mil profit," he said, trying to be practical.

"Except that we want to recapture some of our R and D costs," Thomas said. "Call it a half-million profit. On a second copy of the robot."

Brande looked at the check. "It's damned tempting, isn't it?"

"Look what happened the last time," Otsuka said, "with 'Sneaky Pete.' "

Sneaky Pete was a small tethered robot for use in

exploration. Controlled from a submersible or from surface craft, Sneaky's still cameras and video lens assisted deep-sea searches. While beginning life with a more exotic name, the robot had become Sneaky Pete as a result of a graduate student intern's use of the robot's video system to survey naked female scuba divers.

Copies of the robot were in general and occasional production out of the workroom and, while not sold outright, had been leased to a number of research and salvage concerns.

Paul Deride's AquaGeo Limited had leased four of them, and a couple years later, when Brande tried to get them back, he found that Deride's superattorney, Anthony Camden, had written the lease agreement in such a way that MVU would never get the robots back, so long as the lease fees were paid. On top of which, MVU was required by law to maintain the robots. At controlled maintenance fee levels. The way he had been snookered still rankled.

Brande, accustomed to working with fairly reliable government offices and relatively standard forms, had learned a valuable lesson in legal maneuvering. He no longer relied on the clients' legal firms.

"Tear it up," Brande said.

"Mail it back," Otsuka said. "Put it in a big box and send it third class, to the wrong address, so that it takes a couple weeks."

"We can use the money," Thomas reminded them.

"From Deride?" Brande asked.

"I'll mail it back."

"God, I'm glad that's settled," Otsuka said. "I'm going home."

She slid off the desk and started for the door. Seeing Dokey and Roskens still at work, she changed her mind and dodged around desks and filing cabinets to join them.

"Are you ready to go home?" Brande asked Thomas.

"I'm ready, but since we're suddenly out a couple million, I'd better review Adrienne's latest proposal." Thomas tapped a thick sheaf of paper resting on the corner of her desk.

Adrienne Hampstead was a whiz at raising money. She tapped into the foundations, institutes, and institutions, scrounging research funds. She arranged dinners for Brande, so he could meet people and convince them that the future for minerals and food could be found beneath the sea. Since Avery Hampstead was her brother, all federal contracts through the Commerce Department were left to Brande, to avoid a conflict of interest.

"Do it tomorrow," he said. "I'll take you to dinner."

"We just had dinner."

"I'll take you home then."

"Let's go."

1940 Hours Local
San Diego, California

The Director of Computer Systems for Marine Visions Unlimited braked her Oldsmobile Festiva in front of the main entrance of the Sea View Tower.

The Chief Structural Engineer pushed open the passenger door. "Thanks for the ride, Kim."

"You know, Ingrid, I was thinking," Otsuka said.

Roskens brought her legs back inside the car. "That's a problem with most of the people I work with. What are you thinking?"

In her midforties, Roskens was the only member of the MVU team who did not know how to swim, and she had no intention of doing so. Her auburn hair was peppered with gray, and she had large green eyes, the kind that saw beyond lines and shadows into the underlying foundations. She was responsible for the basic design of the structures for Harbor One, the mining and agricultural complexes, and Ocean Deep. Her husband, Jake, ran a student-counselling center at San Diego State University.

"I was thinking about the visually impaired. The museum at Ocean Deep could be adapted for the sense of touch."

"You could do that landward, Kim."

"Ah, but you could not capture the feeling of depth, the smell of salt water, the sense of detachment from the dry land."

"The clamminess, you mean?"

Otsuka laughed. "All right, the clamminess."

"But you're right, Kim. We'll have to convince the museum subcontractor to deal with it. He might just go along, if Dane gives him an incentive in his lease."

"We will need to adapt the submersible and perhaps the domes. Braille signs will be necessary, for one thing."

"Okey and I will put it in our proposal. Dane and Kaylene will buy it, and Adrienne can find the bucks somewhere."

"We ought to hire a consultant who is blind."

"Dane loves adding people to the roster," Roskens laughed as she slipped out of the car and hurried up to her building entrance.

Otsuka slipped the shift lever into drive and pulled away from the curb.

There were currently eighty-seven people working for MVU, in one capacity or another, at one site or another. There might even be more; Otsuka found it difficult to keep up with all of the new operations Brande founded. Graduate students from Georgetown University, San Diego State, Rice, Miami, Washington, and other institutions spent a semester's internship with MVU, swelling the employment rolls, then ebbing. People appeared, shifted to new endeavors, or disappeared.

Otsuka was part of the cadre of the company, as were the boat crews and most of the fabrication personnel. Others came and went in proportion to the contracts they were working on, but she was permanent, and she was grateful for it. She was a Japanese national, having been raised and schooled in Tokyo. Stanford University had admitted her to its doctoral program, and after she obtained the degree, she had assumed she would work as one of the computer science cogs in a giant conglomerate, a Sony, or an IBM. Indeed, that had been her goal until Dane Brande showed up at her apartment in Palo Alto the day after she graduated. Now, she had over nine years with the company, conducted largely in jeans and swimsuits, as often below the surface as above it. The business suits of an IBM had never materialized for her, and she did not miss them at all.

The atmosphere of MVU was so casual and so bereft of infighting and job competitiveness that she had learned to laugh. Humor in her family had been in short supply as she and her siblings devoted their teenage years to study, to achieving coveted positions in school.

With short blue-black hair that was frequently damp and crusted with salt, Otsuka was tiny at five two. She was agile and peppy, and she could take thirty-hour stretches of work without blinking her brown eyes.

It frequently happened that way. A project on deadline, or just one of intense interest, might demand days-long effort. No one complained about it, and no one punched a clock, and no one drew overtime pay.

Which was another reason she was happy; she liked her colleagues.

When she arrived at her home in Bay Park, she left the Oldsmobile in the carport and unlocked the side door into the house. It was a small house, but it was hers, a possession she had never dreamed of owning.

She dropped her purse on the counter in the kitchen and went through the house turning on lights. From her living room windows, she could see the lights of the developments around Mission Bay. In the front bedroom, which she used as her home office, she also had a view of the Bay. She also had three computer systems, one of them dedicated solely to the design of computer systems. In her backyard, a satellite dish gave her instantaneous access through communications satellites to some of the world's finest supercomputers. She had hard disk drives, CD-ROMs, and tape drives stacked in banks against the back wall, and they contained encyclopedias of information, ranging from atlases to oceanographic maps to arcane electronics reference works.

Otsuka loved her work, and her work was also her hobby.

She crossed the room to the wide conference table she used as a desk and flicked the switch to turn on the monitor. She did not have to initiate the computers since they operated twenty-four hours a day.

Using the keyboard, which she could switch between the three computers, she first called up her stock portfolio and updated it with the stock quotes that had been collected at the closing bell in New York. Otsuka was trying to learn the stock business. In six months, she was twenty-four dollars down on an investment of two hundred dollars.

She was not trying to learn the business of investment the hard way.

Then she checked her incoming messages and found one from Dokey:

YOU GET HOME OKAY? I'M WORKING UNTIL AROUND MIDNIGHT, THEN I'LL GET A COUPLE HOURS' SLEEP. CAN I PICK YOU UP IN THE MORNING? SAY AROUND FOUR A.M.?

Otsuka keyed in the automatic dialer, selected the number for Dokey's home computer, and typed in the response:

YES. YES.

She felt like Molly, in James Joyce's *Ulysses,* starting with "yes," and ending with "yes," but avoiding the forty-five substantial pages in between.

But then, she had a new hobby in Maynard Dokey, and she would learn the new pages, one by one.

2035 Hours Local
San Diego, California

Thomas and Brande stopped for a drink at a neighborhood bar they had come to like. She had wine, and he had a Black Label with a whisper of water.

She didn't want to rush him, but she was eager to get him home.

"Is something bothering you, Rae?"

"Bothering me? No. Why?"

"You seem fidgety."

"I'm always fidgety," she said.

He shook his head, like he always did when she mystified him. His eyes were dark, drawing her in. His smile was a minor lift of one corner of his mouth. She could imagine him at ten years of age, smiling that way for Bridgette, probably after he had broken a prize vase.

He finally finished his drink, left some bills on the table, and they slid out of the booth. Outside, the air was balmy, and they walked down the quiet street to her Grand Am. He opened the door for her, then took the driver's side.

Brande was a bit on the old-fashioned side, she thought. Bridgette had taught him to open doors for women, and he never failed to do so. Whenever he was in a car, he wanted to drive. She had to force herself to picture him driving a race car, as he used to do in road rallies, because on the streets of the city, he was a cautious driver.

Brande's condo was in Crown Point, on Mission Bay. He had offered to flip a coin when they decided they might as well share their quarters, but she had readily given up her apartment. His place was spacious, even if a bit sparse on decoration. What there was was too masculine, anyway, but she was working on it. His condo also boasted a two-car garage, and the car he had leased since losing the Pontiac was sitting in one of the stalls because they had driven her car to work together that morning.

He left the Ingraham Street causeway crossing the bay, passed La Cima Drive, and turned into the driveway.

Thomas pushed the button on the remote control.

The garage door came up and the light went on.

Revealing Brande's leased Mercury.

And a 1957 Thunderbird roadster in bright red for which she had paid $27,000.

He was rolling up the drive at a fair clip, and the tires chirped on the concrete when he slammed the brakes on.

"What the hell?"

"What do you think?" she asked.

Brande slapped the shift lever into park and got out. She followed him into the garage as he made a complete circuit of the Thunderbird. His fingers trailed over the smooth finish, and in the dim glow of the door-opener light, his eyes sparkled. Thomas thought that if she ever had a child, Christmas would be like this.

He bent and peered in through the driver's-side window, then stood up and looked across the top at her.

"Where did it come from?"

"I don't know. Okey helped me pick it out. It's supposed to be a first-class restoration."

"When did you decide to collect cars?"

"Me? Oh, it's not mine, Dane."

"What?"

"It's yours."

"Rae, this is crazy."

"I broke your Bonneville."

"Not your fault. And I'm fixing it."

"You've found what? Two fenders and a hood? What about the windshield frame?"

"That's a little tough," he admitted, moving around to the front of the T-Bird. "But I'll find it."

She moved up to meet him at the front fender. "In the meantime, you need something to drive."

Brande slipped his arms around her waist. "It's lovely, Rae, though not as lovely as you."

She kissed him. There was still some salt tang from the sea on his lips.

His hands moved up her back, caressing.

"Got something in mind, sailor?" she asked.

"I can get the top off, and we can go for a ride."

"Let's."

Then she realized that he meant the car.

NOVEMBER 12

Nuclear Detonation:
32° 45′ 15″ North, 137° 50′ 34″ West

THREE

Avery Hampstead had landed at Denver International Airport late in the afternoon the previous day, so he had rented a car and then checked into a Holiday Inn off Interstate 25. He had a leisurely dinner of Rocky Mountain Oysters, imported from Bruce's Bar in Severance, Colorado. The deep-fried bull's testicles lived up to their international reputation for excellence, and he recalled reading a piece of trivia: The entrance to Severance had a sign that read: Where the Geese Fly, and the Bulls Cry.

The area was known for its fine goose hunting, also.

After dinner, he had a glass of Chablis in the lounge and listened to Lannie Garrett. Despite his lack of company, he had an enjoyable evening.

And he felt a little guilty about it. The taxpayers were footing the bill.

So he rose at six in the morning to put in a couple extra hours for the taxpayers. After his wake-up call, he had breakfast in the coffee shop, tossed his carryall in the rented car, and drove west on Interstate

70 until a sign told him that it was time to turn off the freeway. He drove slowly into the foothills of the Rocky Mountains, enjoying the scenery. The north sides of the mountains, protected from sunlight, still had traces of the last snow clinging stubbornly to cold ground.

He was early enough to take a spin around the Coors brewery to examine the basis of that fortune and still be present when the doors opened at the National Center for Earthquake Information. Dr. Emmett Shaefer was waiting for him.

Shaefer was a shock-haired, tiny bit of energy. His eyelids and his hands moved in rapid flutters. Hampstead had the feeling that almost everyone around the man, Hampstead especially, was slowing him down.

They introduced themselves to each other, and Shaefer found them cups of coffee. Hampstead didn't think the man needed stimulants beyond what was self-generated.

In Shaefer's office, which was a jumble of charts, diagrams, and printouts, the seismologist directed him to a chair at a small conference table.

"Are you familiar with our operations, Mr. Undersecretary?"

"Let's speed things up, Doctor. I can get by on Avery, rather than a title; and yes, I know that you monitor disturbances in the earth's crust. Every time we have an earthquake in California, the media flock here to interview the experts."

"Would you like to see the monitoring room?"

"I think I've seen it on TV."

Shaefer smiled a thin smile and spread a long sheet of paper out on the tabletop. Hampstead recognized it as the paper fed from a roll through the automatic ink pens that provided a graphic record of one thing or another. By his eye, the squiggle of ink lines that worked their way down the center of the paper appeared consistent.

Shaefer unrolled two more long sheets, then aligned the three sheets on the table.

"We have an anomaly," he said, "which we could have lived with. In fact, however, we have three of them, and that's what makes them out of the ordinary."

He ran his forefinger along the squiggle on one sheet and tapped a neatly clipped fingernail against the dried ink.

Hampstead leaned forward and stared at the indicated point. It didn't appear much different to him. The points of several lines were perhaps a couple millimeters out of line with the other points.

"And here," Shaefer said.

He tapped the next sheet.

"And here."

"Yes, I see that, Doctor. What do you suppose it means?"

"This first one occurred six hundred and twenty-two miles off the coast. It measured one-point-two on the Richter scale. Nothing to be concerned about, really. There's a small fracture zone in the area. It could have been simply a mild shift. It happens all the time."

"Uh-huh," Hampstead said to fill in the gap of silence when Shaefer looked up at him.

"Then, some twenty-seven hours later, and thirty

miles farther to the west, there was another disturbance, this one measuring one-point-one."

"Aftershock?" Hampstead asked, trying to be
knowledgeable.

"No, no. It's in what we believe to be completely
another structure."

"Believe to be?"

"It is nearly twenty thousand feet below the surface. The area hasn't been fully explored."

"I see."

"The third movement occurred thirty-two hours after the second, some thirty miles northwest."

"I see," Hampstead said again. "It's moving away
from the coast."

"Yes. That appears to be the case." Shaefer abruptly
stood up, uncollapsed a collapsible pointer, and moved
to a chart on the wall. The head of the chart said
Pacific Ocean Floor, and Hampstead recognized a few
of the seabed features from the charts he used himself.

"In the grander scheme of things," Shaefer said,
"the disturbances are located between the Murray
Fracture Zone on the south, here, and the Pioneer
Fracture Zone on the north."

The two zones were formed along east-west lines,
their ends abutting the North American continent. The
Pioneer Zone was some three hundred miles north of
San Francisco, and the Murray Zone petered out offshore directly west of Los Angeles.

Shaefer continued, "The pattern. . . ."

"Three events lead you to a pattern, Doctor?"

"Perhaps. We shall see. In any case, I believe a
pattern is developing, with the events moving to the
northwest, approaching the Pioneer Fracture Zone."

"All right. I see the picture you're painting, Doctor. You want a closer look."

"Exactly."

"And, at those depths, only deep-diving submersibles will do the job."

"Which the National Oceanic and Atmospheric Administration has at its disposal," Shaefer said.

"It's not quite that easy," Hampstead told him. "Every vessel in the inventory is currently on assignment, and most of them are in southern waters at this time of year. Perhaps in the spring. . . ."

"The spring! Look, Mr. Und . . . look, Avery. This could be catastrophic. It can't wait for spring!"

"You're pretty certain of yourself," Hampstead said.

"Certainty is relative in this profession. Let's say I'm concerned enough that I think a closer surveillance is warranted."

How in the hell do I sell that to my boss? Hampstead wondered.

"You mentioned catastrophic?"

"Should this pattern continue, in a curving line leading to the north, it would intersect some sensitive structures in the Pioneer Fracture Zone."

"All right."

"If a major event took place in the Zone, there might well be subsequent shifts in faults that we should not like to see."

"Faults such as?"

"The San Andreas Fault," Shaefer said.

"Right down the state of California."

"Exactly."

"The Big One," Hampstead said.

"Not a precise title, but the connotations are well publicized."

"What would cause these disturbances?" Hampstead asked. "Doesn't Mother Nature kind of balance herself?"

His casual use of "Mother Nature" didn't impress the scientist.

"I thought I was clear on that, Avery. I don't believe these are natural at all. Very certainly, they are man-made."

0950 Hours Local, AquaGeo Canadair CL-215
34° 50′ 27″ North, 124° 46′ 10″ West

Paul Deride was a "hands-on" businessman. He was not content sitting at a desk, watching the numbers change. He frequently circled the globe, checking personally on the hundreds of operations taking place within the twenty-four separate companies that comprised AquaGeo Limited.

Some of the sites were difficult to reach, especially since in the last decade, most of his projects had moved offshore. The AquaGeo navy that supported his operations had grown to immense proportions for a private owner. Discounting the smaller craft, there were fifty-three major vessels under ownership or lease by his various companies.

Deride usually travelled alone. Outside of his attorney or his chief geologist, who might accompany him from time to time, he had no desire for a coterie of attendants and assistants. If he had dictation for one of the seven secretaries that served him worldwide, he had a telephone.

This morning, he flew aboard one of his own aircraft, a Canadair CL-215 normally utilized for transferring work crews. It was a reliable amphibian, powered by twin 2100-horsepower Pratt and Whitney radial engines. While the airplane could carry twenty-six passengers, he was the sole occupant of the cabin. The two pilots and the flight engineer were partitioned off from him.

When he heard the throb of the engines decrease and felt the airplane bank to the right, Deride sat up in his seat and peered through the window next to him. As the plane circled, he saw only the sun reflecting off minor whitecaps on the blue sea. Then he saw the conning tower of a gray submarine. Two men standing atop it waved at his plane.

The pilot levelled out, flew east a few miles, then turned back to the west. The seat belt sign flashed on, but there were no oral reminders over the public-address system. The pilot knew that Deride detested receiving anything that sounded like an order.

His seat belt was already fastened, but he tightened it another inch. Through the window, he could see the ocean surface rising toward him. It was a calm day, the seas running perhaps two or three feet in elongated swells. There were no clouds in his sky.

The engines idled, and the hull of the amphibian touched a wave top, then skidded into the sea. He saw the outboard pontoon dip downward, jetting white foam and water behind it. The hull sang with the vibrations of friction and the creaks of joints.

The Canadair slowed rapidly, rising and falling

with the sea, and the engines picked up tempo again as the pilot closed on the submarine.

Deride released his belt and stood up. He was wearing rubber-soled deck shoes, chinos, and a short-sleeved tan safari shirt, his typical uniform. He found it preferable, and certainly more practical, to the suits he was compelled to wear when interacting with other businessmen.

With a wide stance, he maintained his balance on the pitching deck of the cabin. Picking up his brief-case from the empty seat next to his, he walked forward to meet the flight engineer, who emerged from the cockpit to open the port hatch.

The engine died on that side as the tang of salt air poured into the cabin. The starboard engine idled back, then also died. The Canadair would float about on the surface until he was ready to return.

A yellow rubber dinghy dispatched from the submarine appeared outside the hatch, and Deride stepped through the hatchway and down into it. The dinghy rose and fell with the waves, and maintaining his balance was difficult. He sat down athwart in the bow.

"Good morning, sir," the helmsman said.

"Morning. Let's go."

The small outboard motor shrieked, and the dinghy backed away from the amphibian. Two minutes later, Deride was aboard the submarine. His bulk was a challenge for the deck hatch, but he descended the ladder with practiced familiarity. The captain, a man named Keller, met him.

"Good morning, Mr. Deride."

"Captain. How's the timing?"

"Very good, sir. The first barge is loaded, and the second is prepared for transfer."

"Let's get down there then."

Deride followed the captain forward to the control room. Like others in the fleet, the *Troubadour* was constructed along the lines of the U.S. Navy's Skipjack-class submarines. At 3100 tons of surface displacement, it was 250 feet long with a beam of 34 feet. There was no armament, of course, and the crew complement was minimal at seventeen. The nuclear reactor was modelled on the S5W2, powering two De Laval steam turbines. Two propeller shafts could raise her speed to thirty knots, but speed was not her purpose.

The *Troubadour* was a tow boat.

The spartan control room was manned by five people, all of whom had gained subsurface experience in one navy or another around the world. Whatever the nationality of his employees, Deride expected them to speak, or to learn, English. He did not have time, personally, to bother with other languages.

As soon as the crewmen aft reported that the dinghy was aboard and the hatch secured, Captain Keller said, "First Officer, take her down. All ahead one-third. We want twelve hundred feet and a heading of two-four-five."

"Aye, aye, sir," the first mate responded.

As the submarine submerged, the rolling motion created by the waves disappeared.

Deride felt the loss.

He was totally claustrophobic. Being confined in a steel can beneath an oppressive and frequently angry sea stirred heavy fears in him, probably the only fears he had ever acknowledged to himself. The irony was that so much of what he had achieved was created out of an environment which frightened him almost irrationally.

He always told himself it was irrational, and he faced the challenge each time with intrepidation and stoic silence. He would not let the fear best him, and he would never tell another about it.

As the deck inclined by about ten degrees, he stepped aft to watch at the video console. Cameras secured at various spots on the submarine's hull fed their image to six monitors on the console. The forward camera captured only bluish-green water, seemingly without life, and dimming rapidly as they descended. The aft camera's image was marred by a white flurry created by churning propellers. A school of silvery bluefish was caught briefly in the view from the port camera.

The two screens which displayed images from the remote-controlled cameras mounted on the conning tower were currently dark.

"Depth, sir!" called the planesman, and the deck began to level.

The man tending the video console activated the movable cameras.

Two dark blobs appeared in the forward-view screen.

"All stop," Keller ordered.

"Aye, aye, sir. All stop."

The propellers stopped spinning, but the submarine continued to coast forward, closing on the blobs, which evolved into dark gray, cylindrical capsules.

Exactly like the capsules that contained cold medicine, Deride thought. He had never taken a drug or an aspirin in his life voluntarily. Only the governmental requirements for visas or ingress to a country had forced him to keep his vaccinations current.

These capsules, however, contained something far more valuable than amphetamines. They could be engorged with sixty thousand barrels of crude oil. The bullet nose housed pumps for egesting ballast as oil was sucked aboard. The exchange was carefully controlled by a computer so as to maintain the proper neutral buoyancy of the capsules.

The second capsule was connected to the first by a thirty-foot-long steel cable, and both capsules had four tiny fins on the aft ends, to stabilize their flight through the water.

Each capsule was, simply, a barge. Neither had motive power. Propulsion was provided by the submarine, which would tow these barges to an offshore pipeline near Ecuador.

Once the submarine train was under way, it could maintain eighteen knots of speed, and unlike surface tankers, it was not affected by the weather or sea conditions. While AquaGeo also kept a surface tanker fleet, the submarine transports proved fast and invaluable, and the sub-trains were gaining dominance in the fleet.

The subsurface freighters were especially valuable when loading or unloading in privacy was desirable.

Keller ordered engines astern briefly to halt their forward movement.

The console operator increased the magnification on one of the cameras, focusing in on a small submarine. Deride likened them to worker bees. Large enough to embark three men, the miniature submarines were used for drudge work and were not named. As he watched, this one rose from the seabed several hundred feet below, trailing an eight-inch-diameter hose. The other end of the hose was connected to the pumping station on the seafloor which gathered the output from six wells. All of them had been drilled nearly four years before, and all of them continued to produce copious amounts of crude oil.

His start-up costs on these subsurface wells had been enormous, but more importantly, Deride did not have direct or indirect, general or limited, partners. Drilled outside of any nation's territorial waters, he paid no land leases, no royalties, and no royalty overrides to another living soul. When the oil was sold in relative privacy, as this batch would be, he also paid no taxes to any government. Compared to his land-based oil production, the offshore wells produced more than three times the income.

Payback on the drilling costs came three times faster.

The rest was gravy.

Keller came back to stand alongside him. The captain had watched this operation many hundreds of times, but part of his well-paid job was to humor the boss, though not too obviously.

"Mechaum," Keller said to the console operator, "let's monitor the audio channel."

"Aye, aye, sir."

He flicked a switch, and the dialogue between this worker submarine and another one operating the pumping station came over the speaker. The acoustic telephone gave voices a hollow quality.

"How you doing, Snake?" the submarine on the seabed asked.

"Another five minutes, Gorgi. Let's not rush it."

Time was money, but Deride refrained from saying anything about it. His head felt compressed, and the old, standard headache was coming back. It always went away when he returned to the surface.

Deride had grown up in oil fields. From his teenage years to his midtwenties, he had worked as roustabout, roughneck, and tool pusher. He had worked the deck in snowstorms and blazing heat, and he had enjoyed every minute of it. This remote control manipulation of the earth's treasures was not as enticing, but it was the way of technology, and he was astute enough to use the technology.

On the primary video screen, assisted by the halogen light cast by the camera's floodlights, he saw the small sub approach the second barge. It slowed, moving gently, its manipulator arm reaching forward to plug the hose connection into the barge's receptacle.

"Got it, Snake?"

"Hold on a—"

Abruptly, a cloud of blue-black spurted from the incomplete connection.

"Goddamn it, Gorgi!" Snake yelled. "Shut her down!"

The oil ceased to flow, but Deride watched the cloud of escaped crude slowly rise above the barge and disappear into higher waters. He estimated that four barrels—about 176 gallons—had been released. It would rise to the surface and create a small slick.

He was not concerned about that. If it was spotted,

someone would attribute it to the offshore wells near Santa Barbara.

He turned to Keller. "Captain, you will see to it that Gorgi Whatever-his-name-might-be is charged for four barrels of crude at the spot-market rate."

"Of course, Mr. Deride."

1032 Hours Local, Harbor One
31° 48' 12" North, 118° 12' 36" West

Harbor One, at six hundred feet of depth, where the light of the sun was almost totally diminished, was one of Svetlana Polodka's favorite places on earth.

Her favorite place also was America, generally, and California, specifically. From the day she had arrived in San Diego to complete postgraduate work at the Scripps Institute of Oceanography in La Jolla, she had been enamored of America and all that it meant. After she joined Marine Visions, Dane Brande had periodically assured that hers and Valeri Dankelov's visas were extended whenever they came due. She and Valeri had enjoyed a brief affair, but he was a true Russian, homesick, and he had returned to the *Rodina,* the motherland.

Polodka carried a Russian surname, but not many of the other stereotypical Russian traits. She was barely five feet tall, petite, and with curves that Valeri had modestly called "exponential." Dark-haired and dark-eyed, she did not try to emphasize either with elaborate hairstyling or makeup. Like the other women of MVU, she was so often in the sun or in the water that the expenditures would have been wasted.

She was a computer software engineer for MVU, with a special interest in fiber optics, and when Brande had told her that he wanted her to stay as long as she wanted, she had applied for American citizenship. Dankelov, she thought, had been dismayed at that news, hoping to rekindle their relationship, but he was tied to St. Petersburg, and she had new ties.

The special bond was Harbor One.

The prototype for Ocean Deep, it was emplaced on steel pillars eighty feet above the seabed, and the inverted bowl design had a diameter of one hundred feet. The lowest deck of three decks within the bowl contained engineering spaces, including the highly important electrolysis components which extracted oxygen from seawater for the atmosphere. Chemical filters cleaned the air, and a very efficient distilling plant provided pure drinking water.

The atmospheric and water-generation units, in addition to the turbine farm on the seabed which produced electricity from ocean currents, made the sea laboratory nearly self-sufficient, which was Brande's eventual goal. He had shunned the thought of bringing electrical power from the mainland to the station via cable.

As it was, even with the recent installation of an additional turbine generator, the electrical heat tapes applied around the dome only kept the temperature at sixty-five degrees. It was never comfortably warm, and the silica gel filters and high pressure of the atmosphere could not quite cope with the interior moisture.

Polodka did not mind. The whole concept was too fascinating to worry about the mundane details.

In the drive toward the eventual self-sufficiency of Harbor One, as well as toward developing new products to ease world demands for food and energy, two smaller domes had been constructed to the northwest, both within a quarter-mile. The mining project and the agricultural project domes were linked to Harbor One by Kevlar-shielded cables and tubing providing them with electrical power and communications. Each of the dependent domes did have their own atmospheric and water-distillation plants.

On the engineering deck in the main dome were a dozen doorless cubicles in which resident or visiting MVU staff members worked, and where Polodka and Robert Mayberry now worked at side-by-side computers.

There was also a large reception chamber on the main deck which doubled as a workshop, with tools and benches lining two of the fiberglass walls. An airlock large enough to accept a minisub or the larger robots was also located in the reception chamber.

"Damn!" Mayberry said.

"What? What's wrong?"

"We've almost missed our coffee break, Svet. Come on, let's get a move on."

Robert Mayberry, who was Director of Electronic Technology, uncoiled from his armless castered chair. He was over six feet tall and so thin that Dokey called him "Shadowless." His ash-blond hair was unruly, and unnoticed, as far as Mayberry was concerned.

They left the lab and climbed the spiral staircase to the second deck where the residential, recreational, sanitary, and eating facilities were located. The aluminum railing felt cool and sweaty under her hand.

"Tea or coffee?" Mayberry asked as they stepped into the self-serve kitchen.

"Hot chocolate, please, Robert."

Polodka had been working in the United States for over six years now, and she was still not accustomed to the largesse in foodstuffs. In Russia, she had never had to watch her weight; here, she was almost grateful that she feared blossoming into a 150-pound gorilla. But she adored chocolate.

They went back to the stairs and climbed to the top deck. It was an open-space laboratory, with dozens of experiments under way in hydroponic tanks, pressure chambers, and controlled seawater chambers. Sensors and computers monitored biological, psychological, engineering, and oceanographic projects. Seventeen people, supported by federal and state funding through universities around the United States, were currently in residence. Additionally, seven full-time MVU people maintained the dome and conducted company-sponsored probes into undersea life.

The top deck, some twenty feet below the highest point of the dome, was a working environment rather than a tourist attraction, but Polodka always enjoyed it anyway. The view was almost unobstructed for 360 degrees. Only the rib and crossbar structural members of the curved clear acrylic dome detracted from the sensation that the viewer was one with the sea.

Little of the exterior could be seen at the moment since the exterior lights were extinguished and the interior lights were at full brilliance. Above, through the bluish-gray light, she could see Charlie, the blue-fin tuna that had adopted the colony, making his rounds.

To the south, she saw the anchor point and thick umbilical of the Kevlar-shielded fiber-optic cable that rose to the buoy on the surface. She had designed the computer interfaces for the fiber optics, an achievement that gave her some pride.

In the very center of the deck was a large round conference table surrounded by a dozen castered chairs. It was used for the impromptu scientific debriefings when the experts in residence shared their progress, failures, and successes with their colleagues.

Andy Colgate, who had taken over as director of Harbor One when Kaylene Thomas became president of the company, was already there, nursing a big mug of coffee.

Mayberry pulled out chairs for them and they sat down. Charlie stopped his "finnish" pacing and took up a station where he could keep an eye on them.

"Have you found my problem yet?" Colgate asked.

"We've narrowed it down," Mayberry said. "It's somewhere between the antenna buoy and the engineering deck."

"Gee, thanks, Bob. You're a big help."

"Do not look so crestfallen, Andy," she said. "We have also determined that the fiber-optic system is not at fault."

"You're only saying that because it's your system," Mayberry said.

"I am not."

"Don't be so literal, Svet. I'm teasing."

"It is difficult to tell with you, Robert."

"Actually, Andy," Mayberry said, "our best guess right now is the secondary data relay. I'll open it up in a little while and take a look for salt."

"The damned maintenance is going to overwhelm us," Colgate said.

Mechanical and electrical systems subjected to the sea environment, whether on the surface or below it, were always sensitive to moisture and salt. Though every primary component was normally contained within a sealed compartment, the insidious fingers of the sea seemed to find their way within, depositing corrosive elements which eventually brought on system failures.

Because of it, and because of Dane Brande's almost obsessive insistence on safety, all communication and life-support systems had redundancy built in. Additionally, most systems had monitoring devices of some kind. In the current problem, a backup system for transferring data between the mainland and the dome had begun to act up, occasionally spitting out gibberish.

"The more complicated we get," Mayberry said, "the more likely we'll have a failure now and then. I don't think we're going to get around the maintenance chore, Andy."

"If you two were any kind of engineers at all, you'd make the systems simpler," Colgate said. "Fewer components, fewer problems."

"That is funny," Polodka said. "My psychic consultant said I should make my life simpler."

"Your what!" Mayberry said. His mouth had dropped in total surprise.

"My consultant," she backed off.

"Yeah, I heard that part. What kind of consultant?"

"Uh, psychic."

"Where'd you find him?"

"Her."

"Where'd you find her?"

"I called this nine-hundred number. . . ."

"Svet, my love. You and I have to have a long talk."

"After you fix my data relay," Colgate said.

"Talk about what?" she asked.

"About consultants."

"Why? It helps to talk sometimes."

"Sure, but have you seen your telephone bill yet?"

"No. Is there a problem?"

"Not until you get the bill."

1145 Hours Local
San Francisco, California

Mark Jacobs slid out of his cab and entered the Francis Drake precisely fifteen minutes before the luncheon was to begin. He prided himself on his punctuality.

He felt a little uncomfortable in a suit and tie. For all he knew, he was five or ten years out of style. Accustomed to Levi's and nylon windbreakers, he didn't keep up with *GQ,* and he had no desire to start doing so.

Jacobs captained the *Arienne,* a sixty-eight-foot Bertram cruiser whose hull sides were festooned with

the swooping rainbow stripes and large green letter-
ing of Greenpeace. He was also proud of the role he
was playing in the service of mankind.

A Frenchman by virtue of his mother's heritage,
Jacobs had grown up in the South of France and had
obtained a degree in international law from a pres-
tigious French university. Now in his early forties, he
had never practiced law, but his knowledge of it,
combined with the substantial trust fund settled on
him by his American father, served him well. The
income from his trust allowed him to call the *Arienne*
his own boat.

His ancestry was apparent in his dark coloring, his
very white and even teeth, and his tightly curled
black hair. One unruly forelock dripped over his
smooth brow. He was a careful estimator of probabilities, and when he mounted a commando-style as-
sault on environmental polluters, the odds were that
he would come out of the confrontation with a successful attraction of media attention on, not only himself, but the ecological felonies being perpetrated by
the industries he hated.

His media-generated persona had evolved to the
point where he was constantly being invited to address groups such as the one today, the Northern
California Sierra Club. He never turned down such
invitations if they fit into his schedule because he
was ever prepared to discuss the impending environmental death of the planet and to offer his solutions
toward countering the threat.

He just hated dressing up to do it.

He also found himself disenchanted with some
kinds of people, the ones who were willing to talk

about the problem from sunup to sundown, but un-willing to take personal, effective action. Still, those people quite often donated to the cause, sometimes substantially, and he was careful not to antagonize anyone.

Inside the front entrance of the hotel, Jacobs paused to orient himself. He was looking for an an-nouncement board pinpointing the meeting room when a man in a three-piece blue suit and paisley tie approached him.

"Mr. Jacobs, I'm Dave Argosy."

They shook hands.

"How extemporaneous are you, Mr. Jacobs?"

Jacobs raised an eyebrow. "Do you want to change my topic?"

"If you prefer to speak on sewage dumping, that will be fine," Argosy said. "But we just got word about an oil spill in the North Sea."

"My favorite subject," Jacobs told him.

1350 Hours Local
San Diego, California

Orion appeared ungainly out of her habitat. Be-cause of her twin hulls, she was perched on a dual set of cradles at the end of the slipway. Out of the water, she seemed taller than one would expect, and Brande had the disconcerting notion that a mild wind would topple her from her roost.

Like her sister research ship, *Gemini*, which plied the Caribbean and Atlantic, the 240-foot *Orion* was the result of Brande's design. The foredecks of the twin hulls were short, and the main deck stopped short of the end of the twin sterns, creating a space between the hulls for deploying and recovering submersibles.

The interior of each of the hulls was large enough to provide cabin accommodations for the normal crew of sixteen plus a couple extra beds when necessary. The main deck superstructure contained the large laboratory, fitted with workbenches, test equipment, and computers. It could be accessed by a large, centered door from the stern deck, by side hatches, and by a hatchway into a forward cross-corridor. On the other side of the corridor, on the bow end of the superstructure, was located the combination galley/wardroom/lounge.

The top deck contained the bridge, the sonar and radar spaces, the captain's and executive officer's accommodations, and four small guest cabins. The exposed deck behind the cabins was dominated by two Boston Whaler-type boats. A mind-numbing array of antennas topped the bridge, the result of Brande's shopping sprees.

Rae Thomas called him incorrigible when it came to electronics gadgets and wizardry. The radio compartments of the *Orion* and the *Gemini* had been spacious in the design stage. Now they were cramped because the bulkheads were hung with radios spanning low to very high frequencies, satellite communications transmitters and receivers, ship-to-shore sets, and acoustic transceivers. There were tape recording decks and computers. The compact disc players delivered music throughout the ship. CD-ROMs (Compact Disc-Read Only Memory) gave instant access to encyclopedias, almanacs, atlases, and other research materials. Telex and fax machines required their own space. The overflow of navigation system black boxes which would take up too much room in the chart/sonar/radar compartment were also bolted to the radio shack's bulkheads.

Thomas complained about the cost, but that didn't stop Brande from poring through the catalogs and picking up the phone while digging for his credit card.

The cost of this overhaul was going to run to about a hundred thousand dollars, and Brande expected to hear from Thomas about that, too.

He walked slowly beneath the hulls, examining the fresh white paint and the dark red antifouling coats that had been applied to the hulls.

Connie Alvarez-Sorenson walked with him. She was first mate and executive officer of the ship, as well as the wife of the captain, Mel Sorenson. A dusky and tiny beauty, she could match sea-developed vocabularies with any sailor in the Western Hemisphere. Bull Kontas had given up trying to impress her with his knowledge of curses.

"They've done a nice job, Dane."

"Looks that way," he agreed.

"Once the cycloidals are finished, probably tomorrow, we can put her back in the water to finish the topside chores."

"You're in a hurry, Connie?"

"She belongs in the water."

"True."

Brande ducked his head to peer up through one of the open panels in the hull. The flush panels could be retracted, allowing the cycloidal propellers, which appeared to be giant eggbeaters, to extend downward.

Modelled on the propulsion system used by the oceanographic research vessel *Knorr*, the four propellers—fore and aft on each hull—were linked to the two diesel engines and controlled by computer. The helmsman could dance the ship forward, aft, sideways, or in circles with precision. Using the NavStar Global Positioning Satellite system as the navigation aid, the computer could maintain the *Orion*'s almost exact position in both calm and heavy seas.

In the hull cavity above him, Brande noted the absence of the propeller.

"We didn't lose it, I hope."

"No way," Alvarez-Sorenson said. "They're straightening a couple dings while it's out for the bearing replacement."

He backed out from under the hull and looked up again at the gleaming white paint. The superstructure still required repainting of its coat of white and its diagonal yellow stripe.

She was still a beautiful ship, despite her stubby look and her functional hatches and cranes—the submersible lift was a gigantic yoke spanning the distance between the stern hulls. He was proud of his ownership, though less impressed with his $28,000-a-month finance payments for both ships.

That number seemed high, but was considerably less than the $232,000 a month spent on crew salaries, maintenance, and supplies. Brande used to think it was less, but Rae Thomas, who had a way with numbers, was getting a better grasp on the allocation of costs.

"So, how much longer do you think, Connie?"

"Back in the water the day after tomorrow, so we can stop paying the slipway charges. . . ."

"You're getting to be just like Rae."

"Nothing wrong with that," she said. "Then, we're looking at another two weeks for the topside finish and the systems maintenance."

"Two weeks."

"Right. Have you got something lined up for us?"

"Adrienne might have a project, if we can get right on it. A luxury yacht, *Committee of One,* ninety-six feet, went down in fifteen thousand feet of water off Mexico. The owner wants her back."

"Warm waters," she said. "I like that. Mel will, too. This guy can afford us?"

"According to Adrienne, he'll foot the bills up to half a million to get his boat back. As long as we're idle, we might as well cover the overhead."

"I'll stock up on margarita mix."

"This isn't a vacation, my dear."

"Not for you, maybe. Every day I'm on the job, though, it's vacation for me."

She smiled up at him, and Brande smiled back.

He loved it, too, and he was trying to think of an excuse to avoid a trip to Washington in search of government funding. He would rather dive in Mexican waters.

1730 Hours Local
Langley, Virginia

Carl Unruh was Deputy Director for Intelligence for the Central Intelligence Agency. Though six of his twenty-eight years with the Agency had been devoted to the operations directorate, he felt much more comfortable dealing with the cerebral exercises of analysis and prediction than with the action-orientation of field work.

On a personal level, he was relatively comfortable with his midfifties, the sagginess below his green eyes, and the desire for more sleep. He had given up trying to hide the gray at the temples of his dark-brown hair. In the past four years, he had smoked nine packs of cigarettes, all during the Russian missile crisis. In the past year, he hadn't smoked at all, but he carried a still-sealed pack of Marlboros in his jacket pocket where he could caress it from time to time, and where it was available if necessary.

Since the missile problem, when he had reestablished contact with Avery Hampstead at the Commerce Department, with whom he had attended graduate school in international affairs at Princeton, Unruh and Hampstead had developed a lunch-and-occasional-dinner relationship. He wasn't surprised when his secretary told him on the intercom that Hampstead was on the line.

He picked up the receiver. "Are you buying dinner?"

"Sure," Hampstead said. "You want to meet me?"

"Where?"

"Let's try the Brown Palace."

"Where in the hell is it?"

"Denver."

"Christ. You're not even in town. That means you want something, probably top secret."

Hampstead told him about his meeting with Dr. Shaefer at the Earthquake Information Center.

"We're talking anomalies, Avery?"

"You do recognize an anomaly when you see one, don't you, Carl?"

"At least once a day. Where is this going?"

"Shaefer thinks his problem is rooted in man's evil design. And he may be right. I'm going to see about running a survey in the area, but something occurred to me."

"What's that?" Unruh asked.

"I wondered if our esteemed colleagues across the river in the Department of Defense might be conducting some kind of supersecret, arcane experimentation. I would hate to send a submersible down there, only to be attacked by friendly twenty-first century weaponry."

"And you want me to ask them?"

"That would be my preference," Hampstead said. "First of all, DOD doesn't talk to Commerce about its weapons system development. Secondly, they don't talk to us about their classified weapons systems. Thirdly, refer to the first two points."

"I'll ask," Unruh said, "but I'll probably regret getting involved."

NOVEMBER 13

Nuclear Detonation:
32° 52′ 42″ North, 138° 8′ 23″ West

FOUR

The station, with the nondescript name of AG-4, rested on three stiltlike legs thirty feet above the uneven seabed. It was a globe, seventy feet in diameter, and it was divided into three decks. For the fifteen people in residence, it was not spacious or luxurious, but then it was not designed to be either. It was a working habitat, and Penny Glenn, who was accustomed to working, did not even notice the lack of amenities.

The station was globular because it was a pressure hull, designed to resist the immense pressure of water three miles below the surface of the sea. All of the vehicles attending AG-4 were based on the same, life-preserving design, including two deep-submergence submarines for transport to the surface and four tracked crawlers for crossing the seafloor.

The deep-diving submersible *Sydney* accommodated five people, but in an emergency, could cram eight bodies within its cramped interior. The crawlers were composed of twelve-foot-diameter pressure hulls, manipulator arms, and dual sets of four-foot-wide, ribbed steel tracks. The normal work team in a crawler was made up of two people, though an additional two passengers could be transported. Passengers, however, created an increased draw on the life-support system, reducing the excursion time. With a relatively level seabed, the crawlers could manage twelve to fifteen miles an hour.

As with all of AquaGeo's subsurface vessels and vehicles, the designs allowed for the mating of entrance hatches to facilitate the transfer of people from one type of transport to another.

Penelope Glenn had boarded AG-4 from a crawler three hours before, after taking a tour of the manganese test site. She had been less than impressed with the progress made at Site C, but had still been effusive in her praise of the crews working the site. It was difficult to find capable people willing to work in the conditions imposed by the sea, despite the impressive salaries they were paid. Little words of encouragement did much to maintain morale.

Frequently, she had to chastise Deride—as much as he could be chastised—about the terse manner in which he treated his people. Deride was a firm believer in the concept that the large amounts of money he paid his employees entitled him to treat them like stray dogs that were kickable simply because he bothered to feed them.

Some people thought Deride's demeanor was the direct result of his wealth, but Glenn had known him all her life. Back when he was nearly penniless, his interactions with others had been exactly the same. A few billion dollars did not make a bit of difference in his personality.

She did not think another billion dollars—if this trail she was on developed into the world-class manganese deposit she thought was possible—would change Paul Deride one whit. By her own estimates, he controlled fifty billion dollars' worth of resources, and he had at least a $2.5 billion net personal worth. A year from now, all going well, he would be personally worth another billion.

Because of her commission arrangement with AquaGeo, Glenn expected to have another ten or twelve million in her own accounts, but then she already had seventeen million dollars invested around the world. It was just another number; it did not mean much to her since she rarely took the time to spend any of it.

Her passions were directed along paths not particularly associated with money or power. She did not care unduly about travel, except that it was necessary in her work and in the occasional holiday she forced on herself just to remain sane. If she wanted, she could call up the transportation necessary to get her to the surface and then to San Francisco, just over a thousand miles away. If she wanted, she could build a ten-thousand-square-foot house anywhere in the world. What she owned was a modest apartment in a high-rise in Melbourne.

She also owned a comparatively modest fifty-foot motor yacht, the Phantom Lode, which was somewhere above, awaiting her. She had ordered the yacht into these waters since, after her inspection of AG-4 and a meeting with Deride, she intended to take a few days off and perhaps visit San Francisco.

With her looks—reddish-tinted blond hair, high

classic cheekbones, smooth and long Egyptian throat, blue eyes with a trace of aquamarine fire in them, and slightly busty well-trimmed figure, she could compete in any jet-setting society in Europe, America, or Australia.

She preferred being bundled up in a thick jumpsuit, with an additional sweater to combat the cold at depth, hunched over a computer terminal, seeking the solutions to geological jigsaw puzzles.

The earth and its secrets had forever been her challenge.

And her reward.

She was not dismayed by the road she had taken. It would lead her to her most cherished prize.

Which was the passion she left unspoken. It was nameless, and yet, she knew it by many names.

1340 Hours Local
Washington, D.C.

Carl Unruh needed sixteen minutes to find a parking place for his Taurus, and he had only planned for five. A few years earlier, the delay would have elevated his frustration to the upper reaches of tolerance, but now he took it as a matter of course. The Washington gridlock was everywhere: traffic, bureaucracy, minds.

Automatically scanning faces and body language as he weaved his way along the congested sidewalk—an operations habit holdover—he made his way to the corner of G Street, turned onto it, and then found the entrance to Reeves.

The luncheon crowd was noisy, and much of it was gathered into a mob at the bakery counter at the front of the restaurant, clamoring for pie, pie, pie. The place had a turn-of-the-century feel to it, a nice patina of age on the varnish, a warm-hued glow from the Tiffany lamps.

He found Hampstead halfway down one of the long counters, his folded top coat reserving a seat for Unruh. He picked it up and tucked it into his lap as Unruh shrugged out of his own coat and settled down at the counter. All of the coat hooks on the mirrored wall were already in use.

"I might have known you'd go cheap, Avery, when it's your turn to buy."

"Nonsense, Carl. The menu is what draws me."

The elderly waitress paused in front of them for a few seconds.

"I would like," Hampstead told her, "the peanut butter and jelly sandwich. With mayonnaise, please."

The waitress didn't even wince.

"And a tall, tall glass of cold, cold milk."

"Mayonnaise?" Unruh asked.

"They make their own."

"I know that, but with peanut butter?"

"It keeps the peanut butter from sticking to the roof of your mouth."

"I'll pass." Unruh ordered a ham sandwich on rye and potato salad.

The waitress slid away, and Hampstead said, "Where else in this town can you order peanut butter?"

"I imagine supply meets demand."

"You just remember that from economics class."

"It's about all I remember," Unruh said.

"Did you remember to ask my question?"

"I did. The boys in white uniforms are doing lots of magical things they don't want to talk about, but they're not doing them in the area you specified, Avery."

"Hmmm. I don't know whether that's good or bad."

"It would have been nice to have a simple, possibly logical answer without having to go take a look," Unruh said.

They were having to speak loudly, and somewhat cryptically, because of the raucous diners around them.

"However," Unruh went on, "because of our sudden interest, the boys in white are now intrigued."

"Good. They can go look."

"Actually, they said they'd pick up part of your cost."

"Amazing!" Hampstead said. "And how about your shop?"

"Maybe we can spring a few bucks. I'll have to talk to the elders."

"Why this display of largesse, Carl?"

"It seems the admirals had already had a report of two anomalies."

"From whom?"

"Some seismologist at Scripps."

The Scripps Institute of Oceanography at La Jolla was a unit of the University of California at San Diego, operating on both public and private funds. It was the counterpart to the East Coast's Woods Hole, Massachusetts.

"All right, then," Hampstead said. "I'll see what I can arrange."

"Use Brande."

Hampstead raised a bushy eyebrow and revealed his horsey teeth in a grin.

Unruh had never met Brande, and he suspected that Brande didn't like him much after the decisioning processes that had taken place during the Russian missile fiasco.

In response to the questioning eyebrow, he said, "While we had some differences of opinion, I still respect ability, Avery. However, you might not mention my name."

"I'll avoid it like the plague."

1410 Hours Local
San Diego, California

Adrienne Hampstead didn't in the least mind asking people for money, and lots of it, and if for no other reason, that made Kaylene Thomas appreciate her. Since Adrienne had signed on with MVU as the Director of Development—hired personally by Thomas, Brande's workload on the fund-raising circuit had been reduced substantially.

There were still institutional and salvage groups who wanted to meet the boss personally, and Brande accommodated them, but Adrienne did all the preparatory work. And in direct negotiations with units of the Commerce Department, it was Brande who did all the work. They would not taint Avery Hampstead with even the shadow of a conflict of interest.

Adrienne was taller than Thomas by three or four inches and svelte. Her coloring was several shades darker, and a mild resemblance to Avery was apparent in the slightly elongated shape of her face. With happy green eyes and a nearly permanent smile, she was an instant friend to nearly everyone she met.

The two of them had taken chairs in a corner of the office, trying to get away from the buzz of technical jargon spouted by fifteen scientists and researchers dotted around the room. One intern from the University of Colorado had commandeered the telephone on Thomas's desk. Adrienne didn't have a desk; she worked out of a briefcase.

En route to a meeting in Portland, Oregon, Adrienne was wearing a pale green travelling suit with a lacy-cuffed white-on-white blouse. Thomas was in her typical jeans, running shoes, and a blue-and-gray-striped blouse.

"Devlin Gerrard has nearly four and a half million invested in the *Committee of One*," Hampstead said, leaning against the front of someone's desk. "He's willing to put another mil into her—half to raise her and half to refit her."

"Where did you meet him?" Thomas asked.

"Corpus Christi. A charity bash."

"He could take the insurance and run."

"I think he loves the boat. I also think he'll get the insurance people to put up the recovery cash. They'd prefer to take only a partial hit on this one."

Marine Visions had worked with insurance companies before on recoveries. They had also worked with the Department of Defense in the salvage of downed aircraft and supersecret components from aircraft and ships. Their search robots and retrieval robots could operate freely at depth while reducing the risk to human beings.

"The primary factor is speed," Adrienne said. "The longer she's down there, the greater the damage to interior fittings. He'd like to have her on the surface tomorrow."

"Dane says two weeks, minimum, before *Orion*'s available."

"I'll see what I can do with the man."

"Anything you want, I'm sure," Thomas told her. "What's in Portland?"

"A rumor I heard about. There's a maritime museum teaming up with an environmental group to take on projects to help the coastal environment. There might be some way in which we can contribute."

"Plus?"

"Plus, Ricky's going to be in Seattle for a match. I'm going to run up and see him."

Ricky Kidd was a professional wrestler with whom Adrienne was involved. She had been a wrestling promoter working out of New York prior to joining MVU.

"Do you miss the promotions?" Thomas asked.

"A little. It was all hype and hyperactivity. There was something going on all the time—telephones, meetings, negotiations. The money was good."

"Did Avery talk you out of it?"

"Avery's my favorite brother—don't you tell him that—and we talk at least once a week. I can't remember a time that he's given me advice, but he often asks for advice for himself in such a way that it starts me thinking."

"And you thought?"

"I thought I could be doing just a little more than making money in, and for, the entertainment business. I like the fact that we're doing some things that may benefit fellow humans. I feel less selfish."

"Me too," Thomas said.

1525 Hours Local, SeaStation AG-4
33° 16′ 50″ North, 141° 15′ 19″ West

Paul Deride transferred from the deep-submergence vehicle to SeaStation AG-4 with the same shortness of breath and the same high anxiety level that he experienced any time the sky and the free atmosphere were out of his reach.

Penny Glenn was waiting for him, leaning in the hatchway of the damp reception chamber. She wore the impish grin that he thought she reserved specifically for him.

Since he had taken on her guardianship—never formalized in any legal sense, when she was twelve years old, he had learned her moods and her motivations almost completely. He thought he knew how much she was devoted to him, and though it was not in him to say as much, he was certain that she knew how deep his love ran.

"Welcome aboard, Uncle Paul."

He glanced at the steel walls, which appeared to be oozing moisture. "Isn't it colder than usual, Penny?"

"It's perfectly normal," she said. "Come on. I've got coffee going, and that'll help."

He followed her through the hatchway and up the spiral staircase to the main deck. Someone on the upper bunkhouse deck was snoring loudly. When he looked up through the opening to the top level, Penny said, "Geoffrey takes his sleep periods seriously. You'll have to ignore him."

"That might be difficult."

One half of the main level was devoted to creature comforts in a rustic way. The open lounge contained a small galley and three tables surrounded by chairs. In front of a large sofa and three cushioned chairs, an entertainment center was stacked against the curved wall, its shelves crammed with cassettes, CDs, and videotapes. Deride could be certain that the X-rated films had been stashed elsewhere for the duration of Penny Glenn's visit to the sea station.

She poured two mugs of coffee at the galley, handed him one, and then led him into the other half of the deck. Here, the curved wall was fitted with mystifying consoles, and a big worktable dominated the open area. Six castered chairs could be drawn up to the table or scooted over to workstations. The interior wall was fitted with cabinets and bookshelves, and the reading matter was devoted to geological subjects. Deride had read most of the books.

Above the consoles, video monitors and computer screens lit the space with flickering images. Two men wearing headsets were at work, communicating with crews operating crawlers or one of the submersibles. He had just arrived on *Sydney,* so they must be talking to Melbourne.

Penny pulled two chairs up to the table, and they sat down. Deride sipped at his coffee. It was hot, and the warmth raced through him, but was inadequate. He felt as if he were on the verge of breaking into uncontrolled shivering.

"So," she said, "you toured Oil Field Twenty-two this morning?"

"How did you know?"

"I tried to reach you earlier."

"For something important?"

"Important enough. How was Twenty-two?"

"Fine. Production's holding. What's important?"

She gave him that special grin again. "The production at Twenty-two is excellent. I was there two weeks ago, and we were hitting seven hundred barrels a day. That's world-class, Paul."

"Well, don't tell anyone," he said.

"Who would I tell?"

Deride turned his head to look at the two technicians. With their headsets in place, they probably could not hear the conversation at the table. A great deal of AquaGeo's business data resided only in his head, but he had slowly been doling it out to Penny. As his chief geologist, she roamed the world much as he himself did, keeping an eye on all of the operations. He was sure she had learned more about the company and its subsidiaries than she told him, but that was all right. In fact, it was good. The man—or woman—with the most information held the most power.

He was grooming her to one day assume control of the company. He knew that, and she knew that, and neither of them had ever spoken of it.

"Are you going to tell me about this fabulous discovery you've made?" he asked.

"You're sure it's a discovery?"

"You said it was important. What else would it be?"

"Over here," she said, pushing her chair backward and rolling across the carpeted deck to a console.

Deride stood and followed her. The excitement in her eyes was transferring to him, and he nearly forgot about the several thousand pounds of water pressure outside the fragile hull attempting to reach him.

She spun around in her chair and began tapping at the keyboard. He stood behind her and peered over the top of her head. He was aware that she smelled of gardenias. It was not a normal aroma in his sea stations.

The screen came to life. There was a blue grid overlay on parchment white, scaled to minutes of latitude and longitude. The position of AG-4 at 33° 16' 50" North, 141° 15' 19" West was indicated by an orange rectangle. The station was secured to the seabed at a depth of 2.2 miles, resting on top of a flat mountain that would have been called a mesa in New Mexico.

Prominent geologic structures—seamounts, peaks, canyons, dormant volcanoes—were indicated in shaded grays, the shade representing varying depths. Some canyons were completely flat, dark gray, suggesting unexplored and unknown depths in excess of three and a half miles.

To the east, some forty miles away, was a red circle, indicating the site of the drilling rig.

Farther east, over two hundred miles away, were three yellow circles, labelled on the screen as A, B, and C.

Penny tapped the red circle with a clear-polished fingernail. "That's the fourth drilling site."

"And you've found signs?"

"There are some indications of oil, yes. I'm going to go down another five hundred feet and see if it gets better. If not, we'll come west a couple miles and try again."

Her finger slid across the screen toward the east, and her nail click-clicked on the yellow circles.

"That's manganese, Paul."

He leaned closer, as if the screen would show him a true picture, or the atomic number—25, of the metallic element. It was used primarily in alloy with steel to increase hardness and wear resistance. With other metals, it formed highly ferromagnetic materials.

"When we drilled the first test well in this region, I found a high concentration of pyrolusite ore, in which manganese occurs, so I sent a crawler north and punched another hole. That's Site A."

"It's a good find?" he asked, his excitement growing. Deride liked nothing better than discovering what others had failed to locate.

"Very good. I've got samples in the lab. What's better, at Sites B and C, the concentrations are even denser. See the dotted lines?"

The A, B, and C positions on the screen formed a short, slight arc aimed to the northwest. From Site C, Glenn had projected three different courses, indicated by lavender, purple, and green dotted lines. All of them continued to the northwest, but followed differing curves.

"I see them."

"I think the green line is our best bet, but we've got to test along the other lines anyway, to define the vein."

"And you think this is going to be worthwhile? Better than the petroleum?"

"The way it's taking shape, Paul, there won't be another vein in the world like it. We'll have a single source of cheap, readily available manganese."

"It's not a particularly precious element," he said, though he was already forming a strategy.

She pushed back from the console and swung around to face him. "What counts is what we do with it."

He stepped back and sat on the edge of the table, quite interested in what she had to say.

"And what would you do with it, Penny?"

"You own seventy-five percent of Matsumoto Steel Industries."

He was amazed that she knew about that, and as a reward, he would not ask her how she had found out.

"Sixty-five percent."

She shrugged. "Whatever. It's a controlling interest."

"What would you control?"

"We could put the manganese on the market and do very well. Or we could channel it all into Matsumoto and flood the world with high-grade hardened steel."

"That would drive prices down steeply."

"And drive how many international companies out of business?" she asked.

Deride was happy. She was thinking along the same lines of the strategy he had just formulated.

"Most of them, if not all," he admitted.

"If we passed on the short-term, low-profit angle," she said, "in five years, we would control the world market for hardened steel. Providing that governments did not step in and subsidize their steel industries."

"Yes, we'd have to be careful."

"You'd give up a billion dollars in assured profit?" she asked.

"For fifty or sixty billion down the road? What would you do, Penny?"

"I'm patient."

"Do you want to negotiate a new commission structure?" Deride asked.

"I'm not worried about it."

He looked past her to the colorful symbols on the computer screen. Little dashes of color that defined a fortune surpassing the gross national product of most Third World nations.

"Are there any hitches in this scenario?" he asked.

"The vein is fairly deep," she said.

"How deep?"

"So far, it varies between thirty and seventy feet below the seabed."

"We're drilling for it?"

"That takes too long. We're blasting. In a week or two, once I've defined the drift, I'm going to need to start moving in conveyors and separators. I'll want six submarine freighters in the beginning. You'll have to start working on the Japanese end, preparing Matsumoto for the influx and securing sources of steel."

"You're using conventional explosives?"

"Nuclear. It's much more cost-efficient, Paul."

"That's what counts," he said.

1540 Hours Local
San Diego, California

The red Thunderbird drew admiring glances everywhere it went, and it went everywhere Brande could think of. He had removed the hard top and hung it in the garage, and the soft top was rarely raised. The bright finish gleamed under the Southern California sun, and he parked in the far reaches of parking lots—away from adolescent door swinging, hoping to keep it that way. He had ordered a replica of the original Continental spare-tire kit for it.

And he had insisted on giving Rae the proceeds of his insurance payment for the Pontiac. It amounted to $18,000, but she wouldn't accept more than that. Her nurturing of his obsession for old and expensive automobiles amazed him since she had complained about the Bonneville's nagging little deficiencies—power windows inoperative or hydraulic top cylinders leaking—as much as Okey did. It made him love her all the more.

And the decade-old vision of Janelle Kay Brande became just a little blurrier, and he allowed it to do so. The memory of her hand squeezing his as she lay pinned beneath the broken boom of a sunken Liberty ship on their honeymoon diving expedition was a little less insistent. As she sipped the last of the air from Brande's scuba tank, Janelle had known she was going to die that day. And she had smiled at him and mouthed the words, "I love you."

And the smile had stayed with him for a long, long time.

"Won't this sucker do better than fifty?" Dokey asked. He was slumped in the passenger seat, completely bored with his day.

Brande levered the accelerator pedal, and the speed picked up, the needle moving to sixty-five, which was about what the other Californians were averaging. The breeze whipping around the windshield stirred his hair.

He and Dokey had just left the U.S. Naval Station where they had sat through an interminable briefing on the Navy's goals for subsurface research in the second half of the fiscal year. These briefings tended to be superficial, dealing with only the non-secret stuff. Still, they had to be endured because they frequently led to side-room discussions, like today, of how MVU might assist the Navy in some of its remotely operated vehicle development. In a matter of only months or years—the way the military operated—they might land a development or consulting contract.

He and the 'Bird flowed with the Interstate 5 traffic through the downtown area, rounded the curve to the west, and rolled beneath the series of overpasses carrying the numbered avenues. Departing the freeway for Laurel Street, and then North Harbor Drive, Brande crossed the northern end of the bay. San Francisco International Airport was on his right, and Roseville was dead ahead.

"I think," Dokey said, "that since the afternoon's shot anyway, I might as well go home. Uncap a bottle of *Dos Equis* and see if it helps me absorb the sun. Create a new T-shirt or something."

"You aren't running out of ideas?"

"I'll run out of shirts first."

Brande glanced at his friend, who was, in deference to possible Navy contracts, wearing a nicely tailored blue suit and a Republican tie of blended red and gray stripes. He looked like an MIT grad, which he was. If he were to guess, Brande would guess that beneath the facade was a T-shirt blaring, in big red letters, "The Navy Sucks Eggs!"

He dodged over a lane to the left as a battered Renault decided at the last possible minute to grab the exit for the east terminal of the airport.

The telephone buzzed, barely heard in the slip-stream of wind rushing off the windshield.

"Where in hell is the phone?" Dokey asked.

"The glove compartment?"

Dokey tried it.

"Nope."

The phone rang again.

"Try under the seat."

He found the cellular unit, tapped the On button, and said, "T-Bird Lounge. I don't know who you're looking for, but he went home an hour ago."

He listened for a moment, said, "Damned sure, Avery," then handed the phone to Brande. "This guy speaks a foreign language. East Coast, I think."

Brande pressed the set close to his mouth, to overcome the wind noise. "Afternoon, Avery."

"Are you real busy, Dane?"

"If I say I'm not, the price goes down, right?"

"There's some people around here who would like to have you take a little trip."

"Where?"

"North and west a bit. About three miles down."

"We looking for something interesting?"

Hampstead told him about the little tremors spooking the earthquake people.

It sounded intriguing. All mysteries and all unknowns below the sea intrigued Brande. The fact that Hampstead was passing the data over an unsecured, scannable cellular telephone suggested to Brande that the project, while it was mysterious, wouldn't carry some of the bureaucratic and mostly unnecessary security classifications he hated.

"There's a little problem, Avery. *Orion*'s drydocked for maintenance."

"Damn. How soon will she be ready?"

"Connie tells me a couple weeks."

"There's no chance you could go earlier?"

"Who's backing this little foray?" Brande asked.

"Navy, CIA, and myself, I guess."

"That's quite a crowd you've put together. Is someone worried about something?"

"I don't know that worry is the right word, Dane. We'd like to satisfy some minds."

"I guess we could hold off on a few of the topside chores for a while."

"It could be worth a nice bonus, on top of your regular fee."

"Could be?"

"Will be."

"I'll have to check with Mel Sorenson and Connie,

but we could take off a couple days from now, maybe."

Dokey sat up tall in his seat, finally showing some interest in his day.

"Plan on it then," Hampstead said. "This shouldn't take you more than a day or two, I think."

NOVEMBER 14

FIVE

Sarscan II was almost identical to her predecessor, SARSCAN, and had been given the name instead of the acronym for Search and Rescue Scanner.

The sonar search vehicle was twelve feet long and almost four feet wide—a fiberglass box with rounded corners, but she did not have robotic arms. *Sarscan II* was an improvement over her predecessor in that she mounted floodlights and cameras, combining the sonar and visual search functions. Because of her size, she was not a total replacement for the much smaller Sneaky Pete, who could maneuver his cameras into some very tight places, but on search or research missions with a scale grander than the pilothouse or cargo hold of a sunken ship, she precluded the requirement to operate two separate ROVs—remotely operated vehicles.

She was still a towed vehicle utilizing rudders and planes for stability and limited guidance, but unable to move on her own. Brande anticipated that the next generation of *Sarscan* would also have a self-contained propulsion system. If developments that were showing promise in the Loudspeaker acoustical system proved out, she might also operate without the hindrance of a tether.

Dressed in the corporate colors and resting on a trailer parked next to the Commercial Basin warehouse, *Sarscan II* appeared simplistic. Her innards, as Dokey called them, were considerably more complex, however. An open gridwork supported the exterior streamlining panels as well as the interior sonar antennas and miniature pressure hulls containing computers, batteries, and transducers. One reinforced ball housed the solenoids that controlled the stubby rudder and the diving planes on the aft end. The heavy-duty connector that coupled her, via a Kevlar-shielded fiber-optic cable, to the tow vehicle was mounted on the top surface of the forward end. On either side of the coupling connection were fairings that housed the floodlights and two cameras. One was a seventy-millimeter still camera, and the other was a video camera that had a limited forty-degree range of travel from side to side, as well as up and down.

Designed for intensive bottom searching, the sonar did not have a lot of range, but it was very powerful and very accurate downward for a thousand feet and sideways for three thousand feet. The images it picked up were transmitted through the optical fibers of the towing cable and displayed on screens aboard the towing vehicle. *Sarscan II*'s functions were a great deal more complex than her appearance sitting on a trailer on a San Diego dock in the early morning.

The sun was well above the horizon and a light fog was burning off as Brande waited on the dock for the arrival of *Orion*. It promised to be a blue-sky day, typically balmy, and a great substantiation of his rationale for headquartering MVU in San Diego.

Waiting with him was Kenji Nagasaka, one of *Orion*'s helmsmen, who had helped him move *Sarscan II* to the dock from the workshop. Nagasaka had obtained his degree from the University of Southern California the previous spring, but his year of internship on board the research vessel was one factor that had convinced him that he wanted to stay near the water. Brande knew the obsession.

Nagasaka was short and slim, with lanky black hair under little control. He was also madly in love with Kim Otsuka, who was eight years his senior and, Brande thought, bound to frustrate him. She had other interests.

Nagasaka sat on one of the trailer's fenders. He said, "This was a sudden decision, wasn't it, Dr. Brande?"

At sea, Nagasaka was given to calling him "Chief," as most everyone did, but his innate politeness prevailed ashore.

"Someone is in a hurry, Kenji. It kind of filters down to us."

"What are we looking for?"

"That's the fun part," Brande said. "We don't know."

"Well, I'm happy to be doing something. Waiting around for *Orion* to be overhauled is nerve-wracking."

Brande remembered his youth on the Minnesota wheat farm as filled with the same inaction. The highlight of every year occurred during harvest when the unruly custom combine crews came through. Their long, hard days and their brawling nights had made his life seem lazy by comparison. Those indolent years occasionally seemed desirable now, but they had driven him to skiing, scuba diving, automobile racing, and skydiving. Action in any form.

A dark-blue Buick Park Avenue turned in from the street and parked in the cramped parking lot at the side of the building. Lawrence Emry got out, locked the door, and headed toward them carrying a small duffel bag.

Emry was tiny at five five. He sported a full, gray moustache in compensation for his baldness. At sixty-four, he was the oldest employee of MVU, but his experience went far beyond his doctorate in geophysics toward making him a wise man. He was the Director of Exploration.

"Where's the damned boat?" he asked.

"Good morning to you, too," Brande said.

"Kaylene caught me last night, two hours before I was to take off for Tahiti. My morning was supposed to be quite different from this." Emry waved a hand at the freighters docked around the basin.

"Well, hell, Larry. I forgot about your vacation," Brande grinned at him. "Tell you what. You reschedule your flight, and I'll handle the mapping."

"And no doubt get yourself lost, Dane. No, I'd better go along this time."

Emry wouldn't pass up an intriguing expedition for anything in the world, Tahiti included.

"Here she comes," Nagasaka said, scrambling up from his seat on the trailer fender.

Brande looked east to see *Orion* turning into the

basin. As Connie Alvarez-Sorenson had said, she appeared much more natural in the water.

The topside's paint still looked a little dingy, but a fresh coat could wait. They had things to do and places to go, and Brande was almost as excited about the prospects as he had been the day he left the farm.

When the research vessel drew near, the tone of her diesel engines ebbing, he could see Mel Sorenson's face behind the safety-glass windscreen of the bridge. Fred Boberg, the other helmsman was on the wheel, and Frank Vogl, the chief and only engineer, was standing next to Sorenson.

Bucky Sanders and Paco Suarez, the two communications specialists, were leaning against the railing on the main deck, alongside the superstructure. They shared the chores in the radio shack, but the ability to turn a knob was not an adequate job description anymore. Both men were engineering students, completely familiar with all of the electronic wizardry that filled the communications and chart compartments. Nothing made them happier than when Brande had made a finger-walking tour through a marine electronics catalog.

Sorenson issued the orders, and *Orion* slowed, turned, and began to back into the pier. Normally, she was docked abeam of the pier, but loading *DepthFinder* required that she be stern-on to the pier.

Seamen and women appeared on the deck to handle lines, and Nagasaka ran forward to help.

Twenty minutes later, the ship was snugged up against her fenders, and Emry had carried his charts and CD-ROMs aboard to begin setting up his computers.

This expedition was one of search, rather than re-covery, and Brande had selected his deep-submer-gence vehicles with that objective in mind. *Sarscan II* was wheeled forward onto the dock, and a marine biologist switched hats and became a crane operator, maneuvering the starboard-aft crane into position to lift the sonar search vehicle aboard. She would be tied down on the starboard, stern hull.

Dokey arrived by the time they had opened the big sliding doors to the warehouse. He was wearing a gray sweatshirt with the one-foot-high red letters spelling, YES! emblazoned on the back. Dokey and the women of MVU were fighting a sexual innuendo battle through decorative shirts. The female version was NO!

He was also working his way through breakfast burritos and a tall cup of coffee.

"Hell, Chief," he said. "I thought you'd be loaded by now. I was ready to go aboard and climb into my bunk."

Brande looked him over carefully. "I think you're getting old, Okey. Little more gray at the temples. Timing's way off. I'm going to be worried about your reflexes."

Dokey snorted. "My reflexes are excellent. Where they count."

They grinned at each other and turned to enter the warehouse.

With the doors open, *DepthFinder* was visible. Her sister, *DepthFinder II,* was aboard the *Gemini,* now working the Caribbean out of Galveston. Brande was always happy when both research vessels were on contract simultaneously, making some effort to cover their costs of operation.

The early light sifted through the doorway and reflected off the submersible's waxed paint. The outer hull was composed of carbon-fiber reinforced plastic and fiberglass. On the surface of the sea, she appeared sleek, the outer hull disguising the round ball of the pressure hull. She was thirty-eight feet long, with a beam of eleven feet, and she weighed in at forty-three tons. The main hull was twelve feet high, and she towered above them.

Adding to the perceived immensity, the sail was four feet high. It was fiberglass and utile solely in preventing waves from splashing through the hatchway when she was moving on the surface. In the water, the top of the hull stood barely a foot above the surface of the sea. The transponder interrogator, a UHF antenna, and the depth sonar were mounted on the aft end of the sail. Within the enclosed sail was room for two people to stand, if they liked each other relatively well.

The outer hull was a streamlined enclosure containing the spherical pressure hull. The secondary hull contained the spherical tanks used for variable ballast, high-pressure air, hydraulic-power supplies, and fore and aft mercury trim. Forward of the pressure hull were thirty-five and seventy-millimeter still cameras, video cameras, halogen lights, ballast tanks, and the forward-looking sonar. To the rear of the pressure hull were altitude and side-looking sonars, the magnetometer gear, weight droppers, the massive propulsion motors, controller and junction boxes, and the three banks of batteries. Syntactic foam had been sprayed into all empty spaces.

Barely protruding from the lower hull were small flanged steel wheels. They kept the submersible aligned on a portable section of railroad track. It matched the tracks on the deck of the *Orion.*

While a half dozen people began moving additional sections of track into place across the dock, Brande found a ladder, leaned it against the hull, and climbed up to, and over, the sail. He opened a watertight compartment in the decking and switched off the shore-side power. When *DepthFinder* was aboard her mother ship or stranded on land, her computers and electronics were fed from outside power sources in order to preserve her batteries.

With minimal use of the electric propulsion motors and energy-consuming electrical systems, the three sets of batteries could provide 150 hours of life support. Eighty hours of time was available at normal consumption rates, and thirty-five hours was the safety limit at maximum current draw. Additionally, there was a backup system within the pressure hull, good for another five hours with minimal usage of the submersible's systems. Brande's safety consciousness, however, had dictated an MVU policy that battery packs be exchanged—one set recycling and recharging on board the research vessel—any time a submersible surfaced after more than three hours down.

He looked over the side.

Dokey looked up at him. "Clear?"

"Clear."

Dokey unplugged the umbilical to the warehouse power.

When the portable track sections were in place, everyone gathered around the submersible. Dokey pulled the chocks from the wheels, and two dozen willing hands began to push the submersible from the warehouse and out onto the dock toward the stern of the research vessel.

They eased her to a stop with her bow projecting out over the water, almost centered between the aft hulls of the ship.

The massive steel yoke above Brande started moving backward, toward him, stopping when it was almost directly above. Its two legs rotated in mounts attached to each of the catamaran hulls. Cables that were stretched to winches on the main deck controlled the forward and aft movement of the yoke. The main lift cable was suspended from the center of the yoke. The lift operator, a seaman named Del Rogers, signalled Brande, and he turned a thumb downward. The weighted cable, its length snaking through multiple block-and-tackle units, descended toward him.

Brande raised his hands to guide it aft, then leaned way over the sail and snapped it into the lifting eye. Raising his arm, he signalled reverse by circling his hand, and Rogers started it in the opposite direction.

Slowly, *DepthFinder* lifted off the tracks, then began to turn sideways. Dokey grabbed a bow line and tossed it to a woman aboard the ship, and she used it to keep the bow aligned. At full lift, Rogers braked the ascent, then started the yoke moving forward.

The submersible left the safety of the dock and

approached the ship. Brande could have sworn he felt her hull vibrating in eagerness as she returned to her proper environment.

Above the deck, Rogers lowered her, and deck-hands guided her onto her tracks. The big doors into the main laboratory were open, and a cable from an interior winch was snapped into the sub's bow eye. She could be hauled inside for maintenance if it were necessary.

While she was being snugged down to the deck, Dokey leaped to the deck of the ship and rolled a scaffolding into place against the sub's hull, and Brande crawled over the sail and descended from his high perch.

Mel Sorenson and Connie Alvarez-Sorenson were waiting on the deck with Dokey.

"For the record, Chief," Sorenson said, "I'm not happy about interrupting our maintenance schedule."

"And off the record, Mel?"

"How much longer before we get under way?" Sorenson grinned.

"Just as soon as we're stocked and all systems have been checked out."

"What's our crew complement?" Alvarez-Sorenson asked.

It was a good question. The crew makeup changed with every voyage. Scientists and engineers doubled as deckhands and galley personnel, reporting to the expedition commander in one capacity and to the ship's commanders in another.

"You just want to know who you can order around, darlin'," Sorenson said to his wife.

"We know of at least one she can boss, don't we?" Dokey said, grinning at the ship's captain.

Brande dug a Post-it note out of his breast pocket and handed it to her.

"We'll be a little light, Connie. It's a pretty straight-forward operation. Larry will handle the mapping. Okey and I will man the ROVs. In addition to the basic ship's company, I've named nine others. Mostly, they're people who haven't been out for a while. There's a couple grad students who haven't yet made a voyage. You and Mel can assign them any way you want."

She scanned the listing. "Kaylene's not going?"

"Not this trip."

"Does she know?"

"Well, uh . . ."

Connie Alvarez-Sorenson looked up at him. "Can I be here when the fireworks start?"

0845 Hours Local
San Diego, California

Kaylene Thomas turned her car into the parking lot next to the warehouse. In her rearview mirror, she saw the van-bodied truck behind her signalling for the same turn.

She took the last parking place available, shut off the engine, and got out.

The truck eased to a stop next to her, and she told the driver, "You can park on the dock next to the ship. Everything goes aboard."

"Yes, ma'am." The truck rolled forward.

As she walked around the corner of the warehouse, she noted the activity aboard the *Orion*. People moved around with purpose, carrying cardboard boxes, recoiling lines, checking fire extinguishers. There were some employees on the ship that she hadn't expected to be there, the two new interns— Bryce and Walters, for example. Connie and Mel cruised among them, supervising those with less experience aboard a research ship.

DepthFinder and *Sarscan II* were already in place on deck. *Atlas,* the small recovery robot, was in a sheath located under the submersible's bow. She supposed that a couple Sneaky Petes were lashed down in the lab. That would be all they needed for this expedition.

She checked inside the warehouse, but couldn't find Brande. Crossing the dock, she used the jury-rigged gangplank to board the ship.

He wasn't in the big lab, either. The five computer consoles lining the aft-starboard side of the lab had all been activated, and Dokey and Otsuka were going over them, double-checking their software.

"Hi, Kaylene," Otsuka said.

"Have you seen Dane, Kim?"

"In the wardroom with Larry, I think."

"You bring us nourishment?" Dokey asked.

"You'll survive," she said, turning to continue on through the lab.

At the forward end, she passed through the hatchway which led into a corridor that crossed the superstructure from one side to the other. Various companionways led to crew accommodations and engineering spaces in the twin hulls or to the deck above. Across the corridor was the open door to the wardroom which spanned the full width of the superstructure. It contained a galley in one corner, a scattering of tables and chairs, and booths along the starboard bulkhead. Oversized portholes gave diners and those off-duty a view of the seas ahead and to either side. It was a combination lounge, recreation area, and in Emry's case, office. He preferred to set up a computer terminal in one of the booths to putting up with the often hectic activity in the lab.

She found the two of them parked in the first booth. A monitor and keyboard dominated the table between them, and Emry was pecking away with the forefingers of both hands. He had never learned touch-typing, but didn't suffer much for speed anyway.

"Morning, Rae," Brande said. "You're looking vibrant today."

He had gotten up and left the condo sometime in the middle of the night. He did that frequently, when some project was on his mind. Irregular hours were normal for him.

Emry glanced up from the monitor. "Ditto."

"Any trouble provisioning us?" Brande asked.

"No. We've got a couple weeks' worth going aboard now."

"Hmm. I thought we'd settled on a week."

"And I decided that you and Avery may have underestimated the time this is going to take."

"That's nonsense, Kaylene," Emry said. "You have to remember that they've got me. Plus we have the exact coordinates from the Earthquake Center."

"MVU policy," she said, "is always to err on the side of safety. Or of hunger."

"Good point," Emry said.

Brande was watching her eyes closely. He was getting better and better at reading her moods. Almost as good as she was at reading his.

"Is something bothering you, Rae?"

"I'm assuming that John Bryce and Alicia Walters are simply helping load the ship."

"Uh, well . . ."

"As well as Cornwell, Prettyman, and Forester?"

"Well, you see . . ."

"We only settled on the number of crew last night, Dane. We hadn't talked about names."

"I kinda did that this morning," he said.

"Let me see the list."

"Connie's got it."

"Then tell me."

He rattled off the names of those he had assigned, without consulting her, above the ship's cadre.

"The kids aren't ready yet," she said. "They haven't even finished their orientation sessions."

"Oh, I think they need the trip, hon. They—"

"You conveniently left me off the manifest."

"Well, now, I know you've got a lot of work stacked up."

"It can wait. I haven't been out for over six months, and I didn't take on this job because I wanted to be stuck in the office permanently. You sure as hell aren't pinning yourself down, are you?"

"Somebody's got to watch over the shop," he said.

"Maybe I should run an errand," Emry said, starting to slide out of the booth.

"Sit, Larry," she said.

He sat.

"You've already told everyone that they're going?" she asked Brande.

"Yeah, I did."

"I won't countermand that, but damn it, if you want me to be president, let me be president."

"Sorry, Rae."

"And I'm going along."

"But—"

"Ingrid can sit in my chair for a few days, if she can find my chair. Either that, or I resign as president."

"Oh, now, Kaylene!" Emry said. "Don't do that. I like getting my paycheck on time."

"Or better," she said, "you stay behind and do the paperwork. I can handle *DepthFinder* as well as you."

"I think," Brande said, "that Ingrid would be a fine acting president."

1228 Hours Local, The Orion
San Diego, California

It wasn't until after Otsuka and Dokey had shared ham sandwiches and milk in the wardroom that Otsuka learned she wasn't on the crew manifest for this mission.

Emry and Brande were sitting in the booth next to them, and Otsuka leaned around her back cushion and asked, "Dane, what time do you think we'll get off?"

Brande looked at his watch. "Depends on the systems checks, Kim. Mel's changing out a Loran, right now. Probably around eight tonight."

"Based on past performance," Emry broke in, "add a couple hours to that."

"Okey and I will go help. The sooner I'm at sea the better."

"Uh, Kim," Brande said. "I hadn't planned on, uh, having you along this trip."

"What!"

"It's just a quickie. A few days."

"Sarscan has hardware and software that hasn't been field-tested. I had damned well better be there when something goes wrong." She felt strongly about that. They were her systems, after all. Well, Svetlana had helped with the software.

"Uh-oh," Emry said.

Dokey didn't say anything, which wasn't like him.

"Well, I don't know. Rae has the crew list. . . ."

"Then I'll talk to her."

Otsuka scrambled out of her seat and tromped across the carpeted deck toward the door. She was so small that tromping did not work well for her.

1114 Hours Local
Washington, D.C.

Wilson Overton of the *Washington Post* knocked twice on the frame of the door to his editor's office.

Ned Nelson looked up from some story he was scanning on his monitor. "Come on in, Wilson. Something up?"

"Maybe. Maybe not." Wilson took one of the plastic chairs, turned it around, and sat with his arms resting on the back. "I was over at the Navy's Research and Development Center, just poking around."

"With the Navy, isn't 'trolling' a more apt description than 'poking'?"

Overton smiled. Since his stories on the Russian missile crisis in the Pacific, when he'd come within an inch of a Pulitzer—he was certain, Nelson had pretty much given him free rein to snoop around the naval and intelligence circles of the Capitol.

"Some of these guys you've got to poke a little. Anyway, I had an ice cream cone with a bunch of junior officers who are working on some project they wouldn't tell me about. Has to do with sonar."

Nelson leaned back in his thickly cushioned desk chair. "Sonar sounds to me like a very, very dry subject."

"Bad, Ned. Bad, bad, bad. Anyway, there's a lieutenant j.g. visiting from the Pentagon, and maybe he's not paying much attention to me. I don't think he knew who I was. He wasn't giving away much, but he wanted to know about progress on this sonar system. He wanted to recommend to his bosses that it be tested in the Pacific off San Francisco."

"And they said?"

"They said, 'next year,' if they were real lucky."

"Is this going somewhere, Wilson? And if it's going toward some magnificent piece on sonar, I'll pass."

"Not the sonar, Ned. The Pacific."

"The Pacific. As in ocean."

"Right. The Navy's got something down there that they can't identify."

Nelson's eyes narrowed as he considered the implications.

"Probably just a Russian sub."

"They can identify Russian subs. You've read Clancy."

"This means your gut instincts are telling you to go to the West Coast."

"Well, yeah," Overton admitted.

"On my expense account."

"That would be best, Ned."

"Oh, hell! If you can't pin something down in five days, Wilson, I want your butt on a plane back to town."

1936 Hours Local
College Park, Maryland

It was a rare Friday for Hampstead. He had gotten away from the office at three o'clock.

He surprised Alicia by showing up early, then taking her out to a tremendous prime rib dinner. They had gotten home just in time to catch the beginning segment of another rerun of *Lonesome Dove.*

Hampstead had seen it three times before, but he couldn't yet predict when he might get tired of Gus McCrae and his fellow travellers. Alicia thought that he just liked all of that dust and dirt as a relief from salt water.

He shed his business suit and donned a jogging suit Adrienne had given him for Christmas two years before. He didn't jog, but he did wear the baggy suit. Which was not what Adrienne had had in mind, he was sure.

He got a bag of pretzels and a bottle of Michelob and the remote controls for the TV and the VCR—he was going to record it this time, for sure—and settled into his La-Z-Boy.

And the phone rang.

Alicia answered the remote telephone, then came in from the kitchen and handed it to him.

"Dane Brande," she said.

He finished chewing a pretzel and took the phone.

"This better not take long. I'm watching *Lonesome Dove.*"

"You miss it the first time, Avery?" Brande asked.

"Not the first, nor the second."

"Perhaps you were born in the wrong century?"

"No doubt about it. I know I was. Tell me about it."

"About what?"

"You've run into a little snag, right?"

Brande laughed. "Of course not. We're just getting under way. I'm calling from the *Orion.*"

"But . . . ?"

"But we need to alter our contract a little."

"I haven't even written it yet."

"That's why I thought I'd call now. Before you finished it."

"You want more money."

"When we first talked, I thought nine professional staff was going to be sufficient."

"And now it's up to . . . ?"

"Thirteen."

"Why?" he asked.

"Turns out that, since *Sarscan*'s undergoing her first sea trials, we need to have Svetlana, Kim, and Bob Mayberry along. Rae's going to help out, too."

"Sounds like a joyride to me," Hampstead said.

Brande laughed, confirming Hampstead's assessment. "It'll be a short ride, Avery. We'll be on site in fifteen or sixteen hours."

"While I'm paying umpteen thousand dollars an hour."

"But you're getting the very best, Avery."

"We can debate that later, Dane. Right now, the pigs are on screen."

After he hung up, it took him a little while to get into the movie. He couldn't decide whether he would rather be living along the Rio Grande or sailing into a starlit Pacific.

SIX

Svetlana Polodka gripped the lifeline strung between stanchions on the port-stern hull of the *Orion* as the vessel departed the harbor. Her feet were planted wide on the deck, anticipating an unexpected roll.

The seas were mild, and she barely felt the surge as the ship left the protection of the bay and turned into oncoming seas. The lights of the city began to flicker minutely as the distance increased. Behind her, off the bow of the ship, the last remnants of orange and red were following the sun below the horizon. There was a stiff breeze quartering off the bow, and it pressed the nylon of her windbreaker firmly against her back and whipped the ends of her short hair. In a few minutes, she would feel the chill.

She was happy to be accompanying the expedition, achieved after Otsuka interceded with Kaylene. There was an unrestrained air of excitement among the crew, revealed in their jokes and their eyes. All of them were elated at the prospects of even a short and minimum cruise after six or seven weeks of being landbound.

And yet, she felt melancholy. She had been thinking about Valeri Dankelov for much of the day, missing him. Though she knew she was a full member of the Marine Visions family, sometimes she felt the absence of a countryman with whom she could converse. No one aboard the *Orion* had ever experienced a Moscow winter, which could be beautiful. No one had travelled by train across the Ukraine in springtime, revelling in the rebirth of nature, lost in the lushness of greenery and the spring planting.

She thought she had detected a basic difference between the collective American and the collective Russian. Generally, Americans found thrill in the moment and in the future, while Russians often wallowed in memories. The *Rodina,* the motherland, and her history had a firm grip on them. Frequently, Polodka wondered what the history books or the storytellers a decade from now would say about the upheaval taking place in her country at the moment.

Today, she was reverting to type, recalling the warmth of Valeri's arms, bringing to mind vivid moments—at breakfast, at work—with her brother and her parents. She would write her brother and her mother in the morning.

Today, she could not quite become one with the elation being expressed by her new compatriots. For Svetlana Polodka, the future seemed indefinite.

And she was not quite so certain that the next few days or weeks would be the lark that the others anticipated.

2135 Hours Local, The Arienne
San Francisco, California

The *Arienne* was docked stern first in a visitor's
berth in the San Francisco Marina. A brisk November
wind whipping spume off the bay had driven Mark
Jacobs and his six colleagues below to the salon an
hour before. A bridge game was under way in the
banquette below the portside windows, through which
a necklace of headlights crossing the Golden Gate
Bridge could be seen. The warning lights on the
bridge towers were hazy with descending fog.

Two slips over, a loud party was under way on the
seventy-two-foot *Broker's Fee.* The band was live,
and amplified, but their music was obscure to Jacobs.

Jacobs and two of his associates, Debbie Lane and
Mick Freelander, were hunched over the coffee table
in front of the sofa, poring over the latest data to
arrive on the yacht's fax machines and modems. Jacobs subscribed to as many environmental publica-
tions as he could, but since the *Arienne* was a
transient, constantly on the move around the world,
printed material generally caught up with him out of
date. To counter that, he utilized a service which
culled the magazines and newsletters, then either
faxed copies of pertinent articles to him, or relayed
summaries to the boat's computers.

Debbie Lane was thirty-two years old, an ex-house-
wife and an ex-Floridian. Jacobs could not imagine
her as the young and vibrant suburbanite she had
once been. Her waist-length dark hair, shapeless running suit, and piercing blue eyes were the chief traits
of her elongated figure. The state of the world had

dawned on her one night in a community college class she was taking, and she had vowed to put the earth right. She left her two children with their father, packed a duffel bag, and headed for the sea. She had spent two years with several Greenpeace boats before joining the *Arienne*.

Mick Freelander, now close to fifty years of age, had left Ireland in 1972 and had never been back. He had once been an accountant, but his shaggy gray and ponytailed hair disguised that career.

Both Lane and Freelander served as Jacobs's chief advisors. Their quick minds gulped information, synthesized it, and produced concise analyses.

At the moment, the three of them were sifting through the printouts and copies for environmental problems that they might address in their particular way. Lane was jotting issues and geographical locations on a sheet of lined yellow paper. When they had completed their journey through the stack of paper, they would prioritize the listing.

The insistent buzz of the ship-to-shore telephone interrupted them.

"I'll get it," Jacobs said.

He got up and walked aft to the desk at the back of the salon where the electronics were stacked.

Pulling out the desk chair, he sat down and picked up the phone.

"Jacobs."

"Mark, this is Wilson Overton." After a few seconds, he remembered who Overton was. He didn't recall that he was on a first-name basis with the reporter.

Depressing the transmit button, he said, "With the *Post*. I remember. What can you do for me?"

Overton took a minute to digest the structure of that sentence before saying, "Actually, I was hoping you could do something for me. I know you're tuned into the gossip and rumors involving oceanographic issues, and I wondered if you had heard about anything funny going on around the Pacific."

"Funny?"

"I overheard some Navy people talking about a problem off the coast west of San Francisco. Something for which they would need special sonar equipment."

Jacobs mulled that over. He also remembered that it was Overton who had broken the story on the Russian missile crisis, so he gave the reporter a few points for credibility.

"On first sweep through my memory, Mr. Overton . . ."

"Please, it's Wilson."

"Wilson. I don't know of anything especially *funny* taking place. Let me make a couple calls and get back to you."

"I'm at the Jack Tar. Look, Mark, if you run into anything interesting and decide to go take a look, I'd like to go with you."

"Well, I don't know about that."

"I'll pay my passage."

"It's not a question of payment."

"You might get some good P.R. out of it. No guarantees, of course."

"I'll think about it," Jacobs told him, then hung up.

Lane and Freelander were watching him, waiting for a bulletin on the call, but Jacobs was thinking about the people he knew who might have more information.

He found his Rolodex in the desk drawer, and started backward alphabetically. Hap Wilson was working the *Oriental Rose* out of Seattle.

He called the marine operator and gave her the number of Hap's boat.

2310 Hours Local, The Orion
32° 33′ 45″ North, 118° 3′ 41″ West

Aft of the bridge were six small cabins used by the captain and, when they were on expedition, the senior research staff. Brande and Thomas had chosen the first cabin on the port side, then argued over who was entitled to the minuscule space in the hanging locker.

Thomas won, and Brande's extra clothing was stuffed into the drawers under the double bunk.

The shower was almost as small as the closet, and under Sorenson's restrictions relative to fresh water use, available for two minutes per person per day.

In the interest of efficiency and water conservation, Brande and Thomas showered together, using three minutes of hot water. It was close work in the confined space, but they both enjoyed it.

Brande stepped out of the stall first, grabbed a big fluffy towel, and began polishing Thomas's smooth skin. He took some time doing it, and when he reached her feet, said, "How's that?"

"You might have missed some spots. Wanna try again?"

"Sure thing."

The intercom buzzed.

"Damn," Brande said, stepping to the bulkhead. He pressed the bar and said, "Paco, this had better be good."

"Sorry, Chief. You've got a ship-to-shore call."

"Anyone I know?"

"You know Mark Jacobs?"

He knew Jacobs. Over the years, they had had a few conversations, and as far as he knew, were merely acquaintances. He respected Jacobs's stance on the environmental issues that affected the sea, but he deplored the tactics utilized by Greenpeace in many cases. Brande was just as concerned about his world, he thought, but he didn't believe that sabotage and confrontation with authorities was necessarily the best way to get it changed.

"I'll be right over, Paco."

He pulled on a jumpsuit.

Thomas told him, "I'd better not be asleep when you get back."

"You won't be for long, if you are."

She smiled at him and dove headfirst into the bunk, squirming to get under the covers.

He opened the door, slipped into the corridor, and walked forward to the bridge. Suarez came out of the radio shack to give him use of the single chair.

"Hello, Mark. Brande here."

"Sorry to call you so late, Dane. I started on the back end of my Rolodex."

"I didn't realize I was in your Rolodex."

"Just the important people are. The reason I'm calling, I'm trying to run down a rumor."

"About what?"

"About some problem—magnitude and characteristics unknown—in the ocean off San Francisco."

Uh-oh.

"Have you heard anything, Dane?"

"You don't know anything more than that? Where'd you hear about this . . . problem?"

"That's all I've got. Well, except that it must be subsurface. The Navy is talking about some kind of special sonar."

"Who told you that?"

"A reporter named Wilson Overton. You know him?"

"Never met the man," Brande said, "but yes, I know of him."

"He's written some complimentary pieces about you."

"Yes, I guess so."

Brande wasn't sure where to go with this. Hampstead had not mentioned anything about a security classification, which might be the reason that Overton had picked up on it. Reporters on a quest, however, rang little alarm bells for him. Additionally, he did not want to be hampered by environmental activists hanging around the *Orion* on the surface while they were conducting deep-submergence operations.

On the other hand, he had always avoided building a reputation for lying.

"Dane, you still there?"

"I'm here, Mark. I was trying to think if I'd heard

anything at all that fits your description. You've talked to others?"

"Yeah, a dozen people along the West Coast, but the results are zero."

Good.

"The only thing that comes to mind, Mark, is a story I heard about some kind of seabed disturbances."

"Where from?"

"I got the filtered version, but I think it originated with a seismic report out of the Earthquake Center."

"That's it? An earthquake?"

"As far as I know."

"Well, hell, I'll tell Overton to shove off."

"Do it gently, Mark. You may need a media friend sometime."

"I'll be gentle," Jacobs said and signed off.

Brande replaced the receiver on its cradle. He'd given Jacobs the basics, but hadn't been absolutely forthright in terms of MVU's role. The best outcome would be that Jacobs just forget about it, but he wondered how long it would be before Jacobs realized that the Navy didn't use sonar equipment to go hunting for seabed earthquakes.

2321 Hours Local, Submersible B-7
33° 16′ 50″ North, 141° 15′ 19″ West

The submersible broke the surface forty meters aft of the *Phantom Lode.* The seawater was still sluicing off the tiny submarine's hull when Penny Glenn undogged the hatch and pushed it upward and back. It clanged when it reached its stop.

She scrambled up the short ladder into the sail and looked around. Ten billion stars twinkled overhead. Several hundred yards to the south were the running lights of the small freighter *Island Hopper.* It was an AquaGeo leased ship, and it was carrying supplies, and especially replacement battery packs, to replenish the worn units of the sea station and its vehicles. Batteries could only be recharged so many times before they began to lose their efficiency. The submersible would assist the freighter in lowering the cargo containers to the seafloor as soon as Glenn left the sub.

"Come on, Gary!" she called down to the pilot. "Let's get a move on."

"I've got her floorboarded," he called back.

The sub crawled up on the stern of the *Phantom Lode,* and her captain and his single crewman met her at the stern boarding ladder.

Darryl Metcalf caught her canvas bag when she tossed it to him, and Capt. Billy Enders reached down to help her aboard.

"Good to see you again, Miss Glenn."

"And I'm damned glad to see you, Captain Billy."

She had not been on her boat for nearly four months, but a single glance told her that everything was shipshape. The teak decking gleamed under the lights from the cabin, with droplets of seawater beaded on it.

She leaned back over the stern to call a goodbye to Gary Munro, who had his head perched just above the sail.

"When do we see you again, Penny?"

He had a crush on her.

"Eight, nine days. I've left enough work to keep everyone busy for at least that long."

She had plotted the next exploration charges along the test tracks as well as along the course that she thought would prove most viable. And then she had decided to skip off on her own for a few days. Waiting around for test results could become quite boring.

The sub drifted away, and she headed for the cabin.

"Billy, why don't you get us under way for San Francisco. And Darryl, I'd like to have a margarita. Make a full pitcher, please."

Descending the short companionway to the salon, she turned and took the adjoining steps down to her big stern cabin. Despite the saltwater tang, everything smelled fresh. The furniture had been waxed, the carpets cleaned, the bed remade with clean sheets.

It was a complete contrast to her person, she thought. She felt mildewed and pale.

She started stripping, tossing clothing in one corner of the stateroom. She was naked by the time Darryl knocked on her door, and she opened it a crack to take the tray with the pitcher and glass on it.

"Thank you, Darryl."

The deck slanted as the Cheoy Lee sport cruiser reacted to the power on her propellers.

Glenn poured herself a drink and carried it into the adjacent bath. It also gleamed, and she relished the cleanness. Subsurface living tended to become musty, and when she returned to the surface, she wanted clean.

Skipping the shower, she took a long hot bath in

her oversized tub, soaking luxuriously and sipping her margarita. She shaved her legs, noting several bruises resulting from collisions with chairs and equipment in the sea station. She washed her hair, which brought out the traces of red among the gold. She scrubbed herself down with body lotion.

And she felt renewed.

And not at all tired.

After dressing in slacks and a heavy sweater, Glenn carried her pitcher and glass topside, passed again through the salon, and climbed the ladder to the enclosed flying bridge.

Billy Enders was in the helmsman's chair.

"Billy, you go ahead and bunk down. I'll take it for a few hours."

"You sure you ain't tired, Miss Penny?"

"I am deliriously awake. Go on, now."

When she was alone on the bridge, she refilled her glass and set it in a holder next to the helm. Dialling the radio into a Los Angeles station, she found Dean Martin singing "Houston" and decided that someday she must visit Houston.

With her feet propped on the instrument panel, to the left of the helm, she felt completely at ease.

There was nothing on the sea with her. The lights of the freighter behind had disappeared. The starshine reflected off smooth waters, which were going to get rougher according to Billy Enders's meteorological notes.

Ahead of her was an empty, lonely, and wonderful sea, as well as the beckoning finger of San Francisco.

She almost thought about the plan that she and

Paul Deride had formulated, then immediately cast it from her mind.

For the next hours, nothing was going to interfere with her holiday. Penny Glenn stared into the darkness ahead and imagined that there was nothing between her and the American coast.

NOVEMBER 15

Nuclear Detonation:
33° 14′ 51″ North, 138° 37′ 16″ West

SEVEN

Kim Otsuka was beginning to feel tired, unlike her fellow diners in the wardroom. The buzz of their overlapping conversations was loud, expectant, and cheerful. They were excited about their prospects.

Not that she wasn't eager, but she was, and always had been, an early riser. Four or five in the morning was when she felt really fresh, ready to attack problems and concepts. As a result, she was also ready for bed earlier in the evening than most of her colleagues.

Her sleep cycles did not match Dokey's because, so far as she could tell, he did not have a definable cycle. He could nap at the most inopportune moments. On the hours-long descents or ascents in a submersible, if someone mentioned the word sleep, he was gone. On the other hand, he might also stay awake for seventy hours, pursuing some elusive glitch in a computer program, machining a prototype part, or designing a dozen or so of his T-shirt messages.

Tonight, they had dined later than usual after a long workday. Brande had insisted upon double- and triple-checking every electronic, hydraulic, and mechanical system. The sea was insidious, and moisture crept into supposedly sealed chambers, attacking sensitive circuits, seals, and bearings. An unstable, salt-encrusted circuit board might fail just at the time it was most needed. Consequently, practically everyone aboard had been assigned to opening the compartments of *DepthFinder, Sarscan II,* and the two Sneaky Petes and searching for faults with the naked eye, with cotton swabs, or with the probes of digital and analog test instruments.

And after that, they had examined every corresponding system aboard *Orion* which had any major or minor connection with the diving program. Computers, fiber-optic cables, communications systems, and even the deck-mounted mechanical winches had been thoroughly probed.

Her job with MVU had provided her with skills she had never planned on having as well as a number she had never desired to have. Since everyone did everything, she had learned to be, not only a computer scientist, but also a mechanic, a plumber, and an electrician. She took her turns in the galley. She swabbed decks, and she polished brass fittings. Her resume could list experiences in geology, mapping, and oceanography. She could operate the remote vehicles, and she felt comfortable in the pilot's seat of *DepthFinder.* It was wonderful!

It was also fatiguing. The preparation for a dive was more time-consuming than the dive itself, and not only in safety and equipment checks, for which Brande was notoriously overzealous. Every minute of the dive was planned beforehand. Larry Emry had been engaged with his computer terminal all day, drawing information from databases around the world, via the satellite communications link.

Emry now had listings, graphs, or charts of prevailing weather for the dive site, expected current strength and direction at various of the known depths, and the known temperature variants. His onboard database now contained whatever maps of the seabed terrain he had been able to locate from government and private sources.

Emry and Brande had spent the late afternoon preparing a schedule of diving times and locations, and Otsuka, along with everyone else, was waiting for it to be divulged.

Paco Suarez, who had drawn duty as chef for the evening, and who had presented them with surprisingly delicious beef *chimichangas,* smothered under lettuce, tomatoes, cheese, and spicy green chili, was moving among the tables, delivering *sopapillas* when Brande stood up at the table next to hers.

"Here we go," Dokey said from his seat across the table from Kim.

"All right," Brande said, "Larry and I thought we had this thing figured out, but just after lunch, I had a call from Hampstead. We're now going to investigate an additional three sites, for a total of six. For mapping and reporting purposes, we have ingenuously decided to call them Site Number One through Site Number Six. Since we want to allow plenty of time on each site for exploration and mapping, we're going to divide the program into two dives."

"All right!" Mayberry yelped. "Do I get a shot?"

Brande grinned at him. "Yup, Bob, you do. On the

first descent, I will be the dive commander, Kim will pilot, and you'll do the monitoring."

Otsuka could not resist a smile. She had been certain she would not have a chance to dive on this trip, especially since she had more or less forced Kaylene to add her name to the manifest.

"On the second descent," Brande went on, "Rae will be in command, with Okey piloting, and Svetlana monitoring."

Polodka, sitting next to her, poked her in the ribs with her elbow. She was smiling in anticipation. Dokey grinned at the Russian woman. Otsuka suspected, of course, that Brande had assigned himself and Dokey to the two different dives because of the longtime experience each of them had had. Not that Brande didn't trust each of them, but he trusted Dokey more.

So did she.

Brande said, "Larry, fill us in on surface conditions, will you?"

Emry did not stand. He leaned back in his chair, wiped a dab of salsa from his moustache with his napkin, and said, "Fortunately, the winter storm pattern is not yet in place. Still, it's not going to be balmy. We can expect seas running at six or seven feet, temperatures in the low forties, and wind out of the northwest fairly steady at ten knots. Dress warmly, kiddies."

"And subsurface?" Brande asked.

"We're not going into a fully explored region. Our charts will show the major seamounts and some damned rugged terrain, but there are still some canyons with depths that are only estimated. Dane and

I expect that we'll be operating in a range of seventeen to twenty thousand feet of depth."

Otsuka knew the dangers of those depths. At only three hundred feet, about the maximum for a diver unprotected by a pressurized suit, the pressure was around 150 pounds per square inch. On an average man, it was similar to stacking thirty thousand pounds on him. Twenty thousand feet down, an unprotected human body would exist for perhaps a millisecond.

Of some consolation was the fact that *DepthFinder* had successfully achieved over twenty-three thousand feet during the Russian missile crisis, though not without some strain on her systems and on her crew.

Brande then briefed them on the timing, geographical coordinates, and expected depths. He outlined the responsibilities of those remaining aboard the ship. During the question-and-answer session after his briefing, they pinned down the equipment to be used as well as the types of video, film, and sonar recordings that would be made.

Brande finished by saying, "Now, we all know we have never, ever completed a project the way we planned it. Something always goes wrong, or the schedule goes haywire. The most important chore, then, is to be prepared for the unexpected. Let's stay on our toes, and let's all get plenty of sleep. And by the way, Paco, dinner was superb."

Suarez beamed.

Otsuka finished the last of her milk, then pushed her plate away.

Dokey asked, "Going up to the cabin, Kim?"

They had given up any pretense of keeping their relationship private a couple months before and were sharing a stateroom. When she had broached the subject of quarters with Kaylene, Kaylene had only said the arrangement was certainly more cost-effective.

"Not just yet. Half an hour."

He smiled. Dokey was good at giving her the time she needed to be alone.

She left the wardroom and climbed the companionway to the bridge. Fred Boberg was tending the helm, which did not require much tending when they were on autopilot. He was also monitoring the radar repeater screen and the fathometer on the instrument panel.

She was relieved to see that Boberg had the watch. Kenji Nagasaka had yet to fully understand what was happening between her and Dokey, and he could be so doting.

"Hi, Kim."

"Hello, Fred." She pointed to his windbreaker hanging on a hook on the back bulkhead. "May I borrow your coat?"

"Go right ahead."

She pulled it on, then opened the door and went out on the port bridge extension.

Gripping the railing with both hands, she leaned into it and into the stiff breeze. The stars were countless, vivid points of light in which she could become lost. Blotting them out to the east, the moon at three-quarter strength had just cleared the horizon.

The dark sea appeared smooth, but she estimated that the waves were about four feet high between troughs. The twin hulls of the *Orion* cut through them with no noticeable effect on her stability. A fan-shaped spray of phosphorescence curved out from the bow wave of the port hull, below her. Watching the patterns formed could be mesmerizing, a hypnotic soothing of the soul and the mind.

In the back of her mind, however, she was still scanning through rows and rows of computer-programming lines, an aftereffect of the two hours she had spent debugging a program for Loudspeaker, the acoustic communications system. Leaving her work behind was not all that simple; sometimes it stayed with her for hours.

She tried to suppress the numbers and the programming phrases and just enjoy the beauty and the serenity of the night.

But her effort was interrupted when she noticed the lights low on the horizon ahead. She could see both red and green navigation lights, which meant the ship was coming directly at them, bow on.

Stepping back, she pulled the door to the bridge open.

"Fred, do you see that ship?"

"Yeah, Kim, I've been following it on radar for a while. She's about six miles off, now."

"Shouldn't we go around?"

"I pulled off a couple points, earlier, but she turned with us. We'll just wait a little, and see what she decides to do. Nothing to worry about."

2031 Hours Local, The Phantom Lode
33° 1' 54" North, 133° 22' 42" West

Penny Glenn was aware of the bright blip on the matte-green background of her radar screen. She had watched it alter course toward the north, and on impulse, she had shut down her autopilot and eased the helm to the left, keeping her bow directed toward it.

"You should give them a wider berth, Miss Penny," Capt. Billy Enders had said. He was sitting in the companion seat on the other side of the flying bridge, sipping from a steaming mug of coffee and taking bites out of a bacon, lettuce, and tomato sandwich. She was certain Enders hated having her aboard, usurping his control of her boat. He didn't watch her like a hawk, but perhaps like an owl.

"You don't have any adventure in your soul, Captain Billy. Here we are, a thousand miles from anywhere, in the middle of a big, beautiful ocean, and we see fellow humans. Don't you want to know who they are?"

"I'd guess a freighter," Enders said.

"Ah, Billy, guesses are no fun. Knowing for certain is what counts."

That was one of the ways in which she assessed her job and her job performance.

The two vessels closed rapidly, and she estimated that the unknown ship was making over thirty knots, close to what her Mercedes diesels were putting out. It wasn't a freighter or a tanker. Enders, who had been watching the radar screen along with her, had known that. He was probably leery of pirates or smugglers, both of which were still strong possibilities in the twentieth century.

Once again, the unknown ship made a course correction, aiming to pass her to the north. Her running lights were clearer now, perhaps a half-mile away. Glenn watched her approach and did not turn again.

There was no sense in totally alarming the foreign captain. Or Billy Enders, for that matter.

The moon was higher in the sky, and visibility had improved a trifle, but not sufficiently to make an identification. In the rack at her right were binoculars and a military surplus Starscope. She lifted the Starscope out of the holder, held it to her eye, and leaned over the helm to train it on the other boat.

The nightscope gathered ambient light and used it to enhance images. With the clear sky and the available starlight, the image that suddenly appeared for her was clearly that of a fair-sized ship, with a greenish-tinged hull, the green tint the product of the Starscope.

No. Closer inspection revealed that there were two hulls. A catamaran. While the nightscope didn't reveal true colors, she noted that a dim band of color ran diagonally up the superstructure.

Glenn smiled to herself. She knew the ship. That is, she had seen pictures of it.

She waited until it had passed abeam, a half-mile off her port side, then spun the helm to the left, to pass behind it, cutting her wake.

"Miss Penny?" Billy Enders said, some alarm edging his voice.

"Don't you want to meet our neighbors, Captain Billy?"

2046 Hours Local, The Orion
33° 1′ 54″ North, 133° 22′ 42″ West

Brande was back in the first booth with Emry, scanning the map that Emry had composed from all of his sources and loaded into the computer. There had been some earlier concern on Brande's part that Emry's requests for information from the wide range of universities and institutes might make some people curious about their intentions, and Brande didn't want curious bystanders. Emry, however, had worded his requests to include a much larger region than they actually needed. No one would pinpoint their destination.

After compiling one master map with the details from previous explorations of the area, Emry had scanned it electronically and loaded it into the ship's computers, making a backup copy via satellite link on the mainframe computer at MVU headquarters in San Diego. The geographical coordinates Hampstead had obtained from the seismic people were indicated with red crosses and he had labelled them for the site numbers the two of them had assigned.

To the southeast was their own blip—a ship-shaped yellow symbol, imposed by a data link between Emry's system and the ship's navigation computers. Using the information on hand, the computer provided calculated information in a small box in the upper-right corner of the screen:

DISTANCE TO TARGET: 276 nm
TIME TO TARGET: 09:17:46

"With the progress we're making, let's call it oh-nine-hundred hours in the morning for the first dive, Dane. We're going to be about an hour ahead of projections, but let's use the hour for preparation."

"That's good for me, Larry."

The intercom buzzed, and Brande lifted the receiver from its cradle on the bulkhead. "Brande."

"It's Connie, Dane. Fred called me to the bridge because we have a visitor."

"They didn't phone first? How rude," Brande said.

"She just called on the radio, and *she* wants to meet you. Your fame is international."

Alvarez-Sorenson's tone suggested that this was not a good idea.

"Who is *she?"*

"Penelope Glenn, from New Zealand. That's all she said. Do you know her?"

"Never heard of . . . wait a minute." Brande flushed his memory, caught a glimmer of recognition, then framed the name, though he could not put a face with it.

"I've seen the name on some oceanographic papers delivered to conferences, Connie. I think her background is geology. Hold on, and I'll come up."

By the time he reached the bridge, Brande had also remembered that Penelope Glenn worked for Aqua-Geo, and was in fact a high-ranking executive with Deride's company. He was less certain he wanted to make her acquaintance.

He slipped into the crowded radio shack and took the microphone from Bucky Sanders. "What's the name, Bucky?"

"Phantom Lode, Chief."

He depressed the mike's button. *"Phantom Lode,* this is the master of *Orion."*

"Dr. Brande, Penny Glenn. I don't know if you know who I am?"

"I believe I do, Dr. Glenn. With AquaGeo."

"I'm flattered that you make the connection. Certainly, I know who you are, and when I recognized the *Orion,* I thought it might be an opportune time to meet you. If you can spare twenty minutes from your voyage, of course."

Brande turned to Connie Alvarez-Sorenson, standing in the hatchway to the radio shack. Behind her, others curious about the midocean meeting were gathering.

"Let's bring her to dead slow, Connie."

"Right away, Dane."

He went back to the radio. "Twenty minutes, we've got."

"I'll invite you aboard the *Lode,* but naturally I'm curious about the *Orion.*"

"By all means, come aboard, Dr. Glenn."

Brande handed the microphone back to Sanders just as Thomas arrived.

"What's going on?" she asked.

"A meeting of professionals," he told her, relating what he knew of Glenn's background.

"AquaGeo, huh?"

"Doesn't make her any less qualified, Rae. We owe the courtesy."

When the *Orion* was almost stopped, barely making headway, the smaller cruiser came alongside, and Del Rogers put the landing stage over the side with the starboard crane.

Glenn made the jump from the stern deck of her boat to the stage with practiced agility, then climbed the steps to deck level. Brande and a half dozen others, all dressed in MVU's customary jumpsuits and windbreakers, were waiting for her on the side deck.

Despite the bulky pale green jacket she was wearing, Brande could see that she was a knockout. Lots of strawberry-blond hair framed an angelic face that Brande felt for some reason could be deceiving. As she reached the deck, her eyes bored into his own, but gently, searching for his soul.

"Before we get hung up on academia," she said, "I go by Penny."

"And I'm Dane." Brande introduced Thomas, Dokey, Otsuka, Polodka, and Emry.

The group chatted with her for a few minutes on the side deck, then began to disperse.

"Would you like the quick tour?" Thomas asked.

"I'd love it!"

Brande waved toward the stern, then stepped back to let Glenn pass in front of him. Instead, she linked her arm over his forearm, quite naturally.

Thomas led the way to the stern, and they followed as a couple. Brande was half-surprised and half-amused. He suspected that Thomas was neither.

When they reached the bow of *Sarscan II,* Brande disengaged himself and found the switch for the deck lights. Glenn walked around the sonar vehicle, and then exclaiming and asking questions, skirted *Depth-Finder.*

Under the floodlights, Brande could see that Thomas's lips were set in a very stern line. When she was piqued, she reminded him of her admiral father.

They toured the laboratory next, which Glenn seemed to find impressive. Thomas explained some of the computer systems to her as well as the chemical and geologic testing that was possible with the equipment massed along the port side of the lab. Brande thought that Thomas's voice carried the slightly pedantic tone she assumed when she was addressing a seminar of graduate students.

If Glenn noticed that she was being a bit patronized, she didn't indicate as much.

The bridge and communications spaces were next, and Brande explained some of their navigational and communications capabilities. Glenn appeared to appreciate the toys that Brande had installed over the years.

He told her, "We don't keep liquor aboard, but I could offer you a cup of passable coffee."

"That would be wonderful," Glenn said.

"If you'll excuse me," Thomas said, "I'll take care of some chores."

"Certainly, Kaylene. I appreciate your time, and I've enjoyed meeting you."

Thomas spun around and left the bridge, heading for their stateroom.

Brande took his guest down to the wardroom, where a few people were still lazing around. A videotape of *Butch Cassidy and the Sundance Kid* was playing on the big monitor in one corner.

Brande filled mugs in the galley, and they sat in the booth behind Emry's substitute office. Glenn slipped her jacket off, revealing some nice curves under a burgundy sweater.

"I'm very impressed with your operation, Dane."

Brande was kind of impressed with Penny Glenn, also. He couldn't get over how intently her eyes stayed with his own when she was listening to him.

"You've been with AquaGeo for quite a while?"

"My first, and my only, job," she said. "Sometimes, though, I think I'd like to quit it and go into purely scientific exploration. I envy you that."

"It has its moments," Brande said.

"Where are you off to?"

"A government project," he said vaguely, without knowing why. "We're under contract."

She nodded and didn't pursue it. "I'm always hunting for minerals, of course. But I think that Marine Visions has a mining operation?"

"We do, though it's not an extensive or very profitable venture. It's more of a field laboratory on the seabed, where we're developing new machines and new techniques. The objective is to develop processes and equipment that extract ore without causing undue damage to the undersea environment."

"Hmmm. I'd be interested in that."

"The next time you're in the States, and I'm there, give me a call. I'll take you out."

"I hope that's a promise."

"It is," he said.

"In fact, I'm on my way to San Francisco now."

"You've crossed the Pacific in *Phantom Lode?*"

"Oh, my, no. She was in Hawaii."

"And you're going to San Francisco for the fun of it?"

"Exactly!" she laughed. "I take my vacations seriously."

Brande sipped from his mug, and he couldn't help taking a surreptitious glance at his watch.

Glenn caught him. "Ah. I'm overstaying my welcome."

"Of course not."

"I know you're on government time." She stood up, pulling her coat on.

Brande thought that the gentlemanly thing to do would be to help her with the coat, but he was too slow getting out of the booth.

Once again, she gripped his arm as he escorted her back to the side deck and the landing stage. Del Rogers was waiting, standing near his crane.

At the head of the gangway, Glenn said, "I apologize profusely for delaying you, but I'm quite happy to have finally met you."

"The pleasure's all mine."

"And I will call you in San Diego someday."

"Please do."

She waved at her boat, which was standing off the starboard side of *Orion,* and the cruiser began to move in as she went down the steps to the landing stage. She was very agile, Brande thought.

Her transfer to the *Phantom Lode* in the surging seas was acrobatic and successful. She waved again as she disappeared into the cabin.

Brande waved back.

And noticed that the yacht was beautifully built, a Cheoy Lee. For some reason, he suspected that Penny Glenn had had a hand in the design.

When he got back to his stateroom, he found it dark and found that Thomas was already asleep.

He was pretty sure she was asleep.

NOVEMBER 16

Nuclear Detonation:
33° 27′ 23″ North, 138° 52′ 21″ West

EIGHT

Penny Glenn only slept for 4½ hours, and then not very well. When she awoke, and decided she wasn't going to get back to sleep, she lay in sheets tangled by her restlessness and listened to the muted thrum of the diesel engines. The slight pitching of the yacht told her that the seas had gotten heavier during the night.

Two things bothered her. First, there was Dane Brande. She had been completely surprised by her visceral reaction to him. As soon as she had stepped on the deck of the research vessel and seen him, her stomach had begun doing flip-flops. She couldn't remember a time in her recent history when she had been so nervous. She was sure her agitation was apparent to everyone, especially to Kaylene Thomas, who acted as if she had some claim on him.

Glenn had had a number of minor infatuations in the past, always with a partner that she felt she could control, and always short-lived. Her affairs had ended, she knew, less because of her need to dominate than as a result of her focus on her career and her goals. Social and personal diversions, she didn't need.

But her initial reaction was that Brande could be different. First of all, she knew from her first meeting with him that he was an independent. He wasn't the kind to be intimidated by her money or her status, if he was even entirely aware of either. That made him the kind of challenge she relished. Secondly, some instinct told her that, with Brande, she might actually lose focus for hours at a time. Years had gone by without her once losing sight of where she was going.

Sitting in that booth in the *Orion*'s wardroom with him, it had been difficult for her to concentrate. In one dimension of her mind, their conversation had lasted hours. In another, it had been milliseconds.

She intended to meet him again and spend more than milliseconds with him. No matter what claim the Thomas woman thought she had. Like the manganese, this was a lode worth pursuing.

Conversely, there was the other bothersome aspect that had disturbed her sleep.

She threw the covers off, slipped her legs over the edge of the bed and stood up. Rummaging through her closet, she selected jeans, a black pullover, and fleece-lined, rubber-soled half-boots. Judging by the movement of the yacht, the coming day wasn't going to be tropical.

Glenn climbed the short companionway to the salon. The lights were on, and Darryl Metcalf was already at work, picking up magazines and dusting the teak coffee and end tables belonging to the twin sofas.

He looked up at her. "Did I wake you?"

"No. I've got work to do."

"You want some breakfast?"

"Sure do, Darryl. Scrambled eggs and toast. And lots of coffee."

"Coming up."

He went to the galley, and Glenn crossed the deep carpet to the navigator's desk built into the salon's aft bulkhead. She sat in the pale brown leather chair and selected the third handset hanging on the wall. It was labelled Secure, and the circuitry included an encryption device that scrambled voices before transmitting them over the satellite communications network.

The top officers of AquaGeo did not have individual telephone numbers for their cars, boats, offices, or homes. Each person was assigned a separate, single number, and the computers in the Sydney offices hunted for the person attached to the number.

She keyed in the number for Paul Deride and waited almost two minutes before he was located. A blinking light on the wall panel told her that he didn't have a scrambled phone available, and she switched the encryption circuit out.

"Deride," he said.

"Uncle Paul, where are you?"

"Washington, D.C. I'm at the Mayflower Hotel."

"You know Dane Brande, right?" He had leased some search robots from MVU, but she wasn't certain whether or not he had ever met Brande.

"I do," Deride said. "I'm buying a heavy-lift robot from him."

"Funny he didn't mention it."

"What?"

"Nothing. I met him last night."

"You did? Where?"

She told him about chasing down the research ship and going aboard.

"That's a bloody odd place to run into him."

"That's why I'm calling. He said they're working on a government contract."

"In those waters, at this time of year?"

"He didn't say exactly where they were going, but that was my thought, too, Uncle Paul. It would have to be an important contract to initiate an exploration project at this time of year."

"What was their heading?"

"I'd guess it at around two-eight-zero degrees. It was almost due west."

"You don't suppose your activities have aroused any interest?" he asked.

She knew he was being circumspect because of the unsecured channel.

"I shouldn't think so, not in any way that would alarm anyone. The United States government wouldn't add to its deficit by chasing down speculative rumors," she said.

"The taxpayers are worried about the deficit; the bureaucrats are not."

"Oh, damn. I suppose I'd better go back."

"That's probably a good idea, Penny."

0850 Hours Local, The Orion
32° 39′ 26″ North, 137° 32′ 16″ West

The research vessel was holding position in five-foot seas with the autopilot linked into the NavStar

Global Positioning Satellite system. At least three of the twenty-four satellites in the system were feeding data to the navigational computers on board, telling them precisely where she was located on the surface of the earth. Within a few feet, anyway.

The autopilot continually compared the coordinates it was programmed to maintain with the information transmitted by NavStar and made adjustments accordingly. To the uninitiated, it was often disconcerting to hear the diesel engines rev up and ebb apparently on their own as they directed power to the cycloidal propellers deployed beneath the twin hulls.

The sun had risen bright with the dawn, but within the hour, Brande expected it to be blurred by an increasing overcast. The slow front moving in on them from the northwest appeared unfriendly.

By seven-thirty in the morning, the center of activity aboard the ship had focused on *DepthFinder*. Following checklists compiled by Brande and Dokey, the people assigned to deployment activities had powered up the submersible's systems and run them through diagnostic checks. The checklists were followed religiously; no step in the process, any of which could affect safety, would be inadvertently omitted.

DepthFinder had been declared operational at eight-twenty and the assigned crew members had retired to their cabins to suit up. Brande dug into the drawers under the bunk for his subsurface wardrobe. He pulled on woolen long johns first, then topped them with the blue jumpsuit with the yellow MVU logo over the breast pocket. After donning two pairs of wool socks, he slipped his feet into soft-soled running shoes. Over the jumpsuit, he wore one of Dokey's custom sweat-shirts—this one proclaiming the formation of a work-ing shark's union. The logo was that of a Great White with a crunched boat called the *Orca* in its teeth. He found two sweaters and a pair of gloves to add insu-lation as the depth increased.

It got cold down there.

He had just folded the spare sweaters when Thomas opened the door, slipped into the cabin, and then closed the door and leaned against it.

"Be careful," she said.

"You know me."

"Redundancy is acceptable when it comes to safety."

"I preach that," he said. "You still mad?"

"She wants your body. Your mind, too, I think."

"What?"

"It's true."

"You're jumping to conclusions, Rae."

"Inescapable conclusions."

Brande had been aware of his own attraction toward Penny Glenn, but not of any overt interest on her part. He didn't know what Thomas had detected, but he had long known that women have very sophisticated sonar when it came to detecting hidden sensitivities. If he could harness and direct that power, he'd make a few billion dollars.

Hanging his sweaters over his left arm, he moved around the bunk to stand in front of her. "Don't worry about that which doesn't require worrying, Rae."

"Penny Glenn requires worrying."

"Wrong."

She shook her head. "There's something strange about her. I don't like it."

"There's something strange about everyone, Rae. People who go swimming in cold water, for instance."

She didn't respond to his attempt at humor.

Brande leaned forward, caught her chin in his right hand, and kissed her lips.

There was heat there, but he was afraid it was based in anger. She responded briefly to the kiss, but not with wholehearted abandon.

"I've got to go."

"I'll be watching," she said, suggesting today and the future.

They left the cabin together, went through the bridge, descended to the main deck, and entered the lab. Emry and Polodka had set up the control center at the first computer terminal. Four video monitors mounted on the bulkhead above the console were displaying blank pictures, waiting for digital input from the submersible. Emry could pick and choose among the data he wished to display. On the primary monitor in front of the keyboard, Emry's map of the area was shown. He would update it during the dive, adding the features picked up by the cameras or other sensors.

A smaller screen next to the primary would monitor the operational telemetry signals broadcast from the sub. The readings included depth, altitude above the seabed, direction, attitude, speed, and interior and exterior temperatures. The life-support systems, including battery charges, were also tracked, and in fact, were displayed in red letters while the rest of the data was in blue.

"Good luck, Dane," Polodka said.

"Don't break anything, please, legs or machines," Emry added.

"Count on it."

The stern door of the laboratory was open, and they passed through it to the aft deck, where almost every soul aboard seemed to be gathered, milling more or less purposely around the tall form of the submersible.

Dokey had the portable scaffolding in place next to the sub. "Come on, Chief. Kim and Bob are already aboard."

"You're getting awfully pushy."

"The sooner you're gone, the sooner you're back, and the sooner I'm gone."

"Linear logic," Brande accused.

"The only kind, when we're dealing with my time. I like the sweatshirt, by the way."

"You would."

Thomas squeezed his hand once, then Brande climbed the scaffolding and eased his legs over the sail. He squatted and handed his sweaters down through the hatch to Otsuka. Standing again, he looked to see that Paco Suarez was handling the winch controls.

Dokey released the wheel brakes and pulled the scaffold aside.

"Kick us overboard, Paco."

"*Sí, Jefe,*" Suarez said, and started drawing the lift cable taut.

The sub lifted off of her rails, and Dokey released

the line snubbed to the bow. Below him, Brande could hear Mayberry talking to Sorenson on the UHF radio, testing that surface communications link.

When he had a couple feet of clearance, Paco began to ease the yoke backward. The sub drifted away from the deck, and Dokey signalled the winch operator when the submarine's bow was clear of the decking. The sub started her descent toward the sea. While the twin hulls gave some protection to either side, Brande saw that the waves were still high, crashing into the hulls, sending spray upward. He tasted salt on his tongue, and droplets of water splashed on his face and clothing. As expected, it was cold water.

The heavy sub settled into the sea, going ever lower, until there was barely a foot of hull showing in the brief seconds when a wave wasn't crashing over it. Brande made certain that the lift hook disengaged, then waved at those on the deck, and dropped through the hatch. He did that carefully, to avoid the thick coating of grease around the perimeter of the hatchway that was used to guarantee a tight seal.

Pulling the hatch cover closed behind him, he dogged it down and watched for the green Light-Emitting Diode (LED) that told him he had a perfect seal.

He was standing on the backs of the left and right canvas-covered seats, and he turned himself in the tight space and settled into the left seat. As pilot, Otsuka was in the right seat, and Bob Mayberry, the systems monitor, was in the single backseat, which was turned ninety degrees to those in the forward location.

Mayberry and Otsuka both had headsets in place,

and the pilot was following Sorenson's directions as she backed away from the mother ship.

The sub tilted and rolled in the wave action, and though she was as high on the surface as she could be, the portholes in front of Brande were below sea level, showing him only a roiling vision of green-tinged water. Though there was little to see, it was a clear view at this level.

Mayberry handed him a towel, and he dabbed at the spots on his jumpsuit and sweatshirt where he had been splashed. He pulled on the headset hanging from his control panel.

"Larry, you there?"

"Five by five, Dane," Emry said.

"Let's go over to Loudspeaker."

"Going."

Brande gave a thumbs-up to Mayberry, who switched the communications channel to the acoustic system. Loudspeaker had been developed by a Russian ocean-ographer named Pyotr Rastonov—a friend of Valeri Dankelov's—and the technology boasted of the ability to transfer, not only voice, but digitized signals for the telemetry on acoustic wavelengths. All of *DepthFinder*'s transmitted data now utilized Loudspeaker, and one of the projects under way in San Diego involved using the technology for robotic control, to eliminate the need for tethered cables. Marine Visions had obtained the Loudspeaker design in exchange for the designs of a robotic arm and a couple of software packages.

When he came back, Emry's voice carried the echo that was characteristic of the system. "You got me, Chief?"

"Got you. We're starting down, so we'd appreciate it if you deployed *Sarscan*."

"I think I'll do that."

Under their command protocol, the mission commander—Emry at this point—made the final decisions. While Brande was in charge of the submersible, Emry was in control of the overall dive. It was never as clear as that, of course, and decisions usually evolved as compromises.

Overhead, the deck crews would be lifting the sonar search vehicle from her cradle and lowering her into the sea. She was attached to *DepthFinder* by a two-hundred-foot cable, and the submersible would tow her to the bottom.

A few minutes later, Emry reported, "She's all yours, Dane."

"Roger. We're a complete set."

"Are we ready, Dane?" Otsuka asked him.

He scanned the instrument panels, seeing all of the familiar readouts sending him a Go message.

"Take us down, Kim."

She didn't actually have a choice. While standard submarines changed depth by taking on or egesting seawater ballast, that process did not work for deep-diving submersibles because of the enormous pressures involved. *DepthFinder* did have a couple small ballast tanks, for changing altitude a few feet or controlling rates of descent and ascent, but her high-technology method of submerging involved tying lead weights to the bottom of her keel.

In two cavities on the underside of the hull—which appeared something like a tri-hull—the weights were held in place until it was time to ascend, then they were jettisoned on the bottom. Brande had once had an iffy time on the bottom when one of the weights got hung up and refused to drop off. He finally freed it by using a robot.

That experience, in fact, was the rationale for having *Atlas* along. *Atlas* was a small, tethered robot, built along the lines of Gargantua, looking like a child's snow sled with a fiberglass enclosure. Three multibladed propellers set at odd angles—aimed obliquely upward and at a forty-five degree angle across the stern—controlled its movement in the water. The ROV had two medium-sized manipulator arms, along with still and video cameras. One arm terminated in a thumb-and-two-fingered hand, and the other arm was used for tools. Currently, a cutting torch was in place. Parked in a sheath located beneath the forward bow, the ROV could be urged into action by remote controls in the sub, the signals transmitted over a 250-foot cable that unreeled from the sheath and trailed after the robot.

Inside the pressure hull, a spherical container within the fiberglass-and-carbon streamlined outer hull, the space was cramped for three humans. The hull was composed of ten-inch-thick titanium alloy in order to withstand the pressures at twenty thousand feet of depth, and the interior diameter was eight feet. The space was further compromised, however, by the equipment and instrumentation mounted behind dozens of triangular, hexagonal, and square panels that fit into the curvature of the hull. Containing gauges, cathode-ray tubes, switches, rheostats, and circuit breakers, the panels supervised systems like the central processing computer, graphic recorders, power routing, the tracking transponder transceiver, liquid coolant, alarms, sonar components, depth plotter, Doppler transceiver, main propulsion, and the altitude/depth transceiver.

There were more systems to watch, the primary responsibility of the systems monitor—Bob Mayberry on this dive. The life-support system was critical, of course. Pure oxygen was slowly fed into the sphere from external tanks, and a lithium-hydroxide blower recirculated the air while removing carbon dioxide. The system worked well, but it left the air tasting stale. After a typical nine- or ten-hour ride, aquanauts emerged from the submersible with cottony, dry mouths.

As they started down, Brande felt the slight tug as the tow cable came taut. Reading the indicators set into his control panel, he noted the attitude of *Sarscan II*'s diving and steering planes, and adjusted them slightly for downward travel with his joysticks, then trimmed them into place. He was in charge of the towed vehicle.

"Five hundred feet," Mayberry called out.

With the wave action left behind, the sub felt perfectly stable, and there was almost no sense of movement.

"Going passive," Otsuka said and started tapping pressure-sensitive switches.

In order to preserve precious electrical energy, interior and exterior lights were turned off, and motors and computers were set at minimum draw during the descent. Inside, the only illumination was provided by the dozens of red, amber, blue, and green LEDs on the instrument panels. At 1200 feet, beyond the ability of the sun to penetrate the depths, the view through the portholes was of utter blackness.

Claustrophobic people did not go well with deep-diving submersibles.

There were three portholes. One was set in the hull directly forward, and the other two were at angles to port and starboard. Directly beneath them were three video monitors used for a variety of tasks, from mapping to sonar display to repeating the video images captured by robotic vehicles.

As Mayberry called off the one-thousand-foot marker, Brande saw that his view through the portholes was diminishing. Visibility was perhaps thirty feet and very dim. A school of tiny orange-and-blue-skinned fish passed the starboard porthole.

Since they had learned from experience that changing seats in the cramped quarters, so as to relieve each other's responsibilities, was a difficult proposition, Brande and Dokey had redesigned the control panels in front of each controller seat, duplicating the controls for each position. The front edge of the horizontal panel had a cushioned lip on which the controller could rest his wrists, lessening the fatigue factor. Just beyond the lip were two joysticks and a set of slide switches used for manipulating power to the propulsion systems that provided upward, downward, sideways, and forward or reverse thrust. A master switch on each panel selected the submersible, a robot, or a robot's manipulator arms as the controlled device from either controller position.

Kim Otsuka's control panel was currently in charge of *DepthFinder.*

"Two thousand feet," Mayberry said. "Twenty-one minutes elapsed."

"I could increase the descent rate by a few more feet," Otsuka said.

"We're all right where we're at," Brande said. "No sense in pushing it."

It was going to take them three hours to reach the planned depth of 17,500 feet. There was no way to overcome those physics.

"What have we got today?" Brande asked, squirming around in his seat to get the first of his sweaters on.

"I brought along the soundtrack for *The Mikado*," Otsuka said.

Mayberry issued an anguished groan. "I have my Garth Brooks tapes."

Brande tried to settle himself comfortably in the canvas-covered seat and almost achieved it.

"What the hell," he said. "Let's start off with *The Mikado*."

Mayberry groaned again.

1015 Hours Local
San Francisco, California

Wilson Overton sat on the edge of his hotel bed, picked up the phone, and called the Greenpeace representative on his boat once again.

"Wilson," Mark Jacobs said, "we've talked three times in the last two days. That's more than in the last year."

"I know, but I just had another thought, and I

called the Earthquake Information Center in Colorado."

"What did they say?"

"About the same thing Brande told you. There have been some disturbances on the seabed. Not earth-shaking, if you'll forgive that pun. Barely touching one-point-oh on the Richter scale. They gave me the coordinates."

"And then?"

"And then I called Brande's outfit in San Diego. I talked to Dr. Ingrid Roskens, who seems to enjoy working on Sundays. She said Brande was off on some diving expedition."

"Brande didn't mention that," Jacobs said. "I didn't think to ask him where he was when I talked to him."

"And then I thought about those Navy guys. They use sonar for mapping, right?"

"That can be done."

"But do they chase earthquakes with it?"

"I don't know," Jacobs said. "Maybe they want to see if there's been any change in the seabed terrain as a result of the quake."

"Why?"

"Why?"

"That's what I asked," Overton said.

"You're assuming that Brande's going out there to do something for the Navy."

"That's the assumption. I'm reaching a little, I know. But for one thing, Mark, who gives a damn what the seabed looks like, either before or after an earthquake? Especially a tiny earthquake. For another, I ran over to the library and took a look at the Pacific maps. As far as I can tell with generalized maps, that part of the Pacific is largely unexplored. Why do it now, with winter coming on?"

"You think somebody's worried about something?"

"What do you think?"

"If, and I do say *if,* Wilson, Brande's on his way out there, then something's funny."

"Let's go look," Overton said.

"We'd probably find a wild goose."

"My instincts don't let me down often, Mark. I'll pick up your fuel costs."

Overton cringed when he said that. He hadn't checked with Ned, and he might well end up diving into his savings account for the money.

"We were looking for something to do, anyway," Jacobs told him. "I guess we could waste a week, as long as you're covering the diesel fuel."

"I'll be checked out of here in ten minutes," Overton said.

"One more thing, though."

"What's that?"

"You have to do a favor for me."

1320 Hours Local
Washington, D.C.

Paul Deride was tied up in a long meeting for the morning, which was followed by a luncheon he would just as soon have missed. When he got back to his room in the Mayflower, he called Camden.

Anthony Camden had worked for him for twenty-one years, first as an occasional contract writer, then as full-time counsel for AquaGeo. Like Penny Glenn, Camden was a multimillionaire as a result of his association with Deride, and like Penny, the lawyer had never demonstrated anything but total loyalty to Deride.

He found the man in Japan, as expected, but he was in a meeting with the Matsumoto Steel people—discussing the potential and plant requirements for expanded production—and he had to wait ten minutes for Camden to call back.

He could picture the man at work. At five two, he would fit the scale of the people he was dealing with. His steel-rimmed glasses would enlarge those big blue eyes, making him appear a little bug-eyed and perhaps less intelligent than he really was. Camden stunned his adversaries from time to time with his insights, his legal maneuvering, and his downright ruthlessness. He rarely lost a point, and when he did, it cost the opposition something—money, status, bargaining position. Deride had never seen him without a tie neatly knotted under the spread collar of his tailor-made shirt. His suits were made in England and his shoes in Italy. It was Camden who gave Deride advice on his business wardrobe.

When he called back, he said, "Yakima says he'll need to hire a thousand people, add two furnaces, and three rolling mills."

The two of them never bothered with the preliminaries of greetings or small talk.

"Is he happy about that?" Deride asked.

"Ecstatic. He'll draw up preliminary plans, so we're ready to go when the time is right. I'm also checking into leasing a refinery."

"Good. And speaking of preliminary plans, I think you should be in San Francisco."

"Problem?"

"There might be." Deride explained Glenn's chance meeting with Brande. "If the U.S. wants to raise hell about anything, I want us in a position to say 'Bugger off.'"

"Why Brande?" Camden asked.

"They use him a lot on special projects, Anthony. This reeks of special project."

"He sent your check back."

"Bloody hell!"

He had been certain that Brande, or at least Thomas, would have yielded to the power of $2.5 million. It was like a slap in the face, and no one slapped Deride and got away with it.

"Just catch an airplane, Anthony."

2020 Hours Local, DepthFinder
32° 52' 41" North, 138° 8' 21" West

Kaylene Thomas was in the left seat of *DepthFinder.* She had been there for nearly four hours, and she had enjoyed every minute. Seven months had elapsed since she made her last deep dive, and she vowed that that wouldn't happen again.

The first dive had been cancelled after an hour and forty-six minutes on the bottom when two cells in the main battery pack had indicated a malfunction. After the three-hour ascent, the crew, the film packs, the videotapes, and the battery tray had been exchanged for fresh versions, and *DepthFinder* had immediately returned to her element.

Brande's dive had located the sites of the first two disturbances. The sonar map record didn't demonstrate much since they had nothing to compare it to, but the video and camera imagery had shown two craters on the seabed. Each was approximately thirty feet deep and sixty feet across. The immediate consensus of all team members was that they were manmade. Brande and Otsuka had found nothing else in the vicinity of either crater.

Over her headphones, Thomas heard Brande's voice. He was now manning the command console on board the ship. "Svetlana, let me have a status report."

Periodically, voice reports were issued to confirm the telemetry data.

She heard Polodka changing position to relieve cramped muscles.

"Yes, Dane. The depth: seventeen thousand, seven hundred, and twenty-six feet. The altitude above seabed is nine-one-eight."

She and Dokey were attempting to "fly" the submersible about eight hundred feet above the seafloor. *Sarscan II,* trailing behind them by fifty feet, and below them by two hundred feet, captured the best imagery at that distance. While her range was limited, her power gave them good readings for a thousand feet down and three thousand feet to either side. Because they were scanning the bottom, rather than searching for a single object suspended in water, Thomas had squelched out the "ping" of sonar returns so as not to drive them crazy.

"Heading, two-eight-five," Polodka continued. "Speed, six knots."

The submersible could easily triple that speed, but the noise produced by the electric motors and the water movement against the hull added interference to the sonar vehicle's readings.

Polodka rattled off the current capacities on batteries and life-support systems.

"Roger that, Svet," Brande said. "Looking good."

Through the portholes, and despite the six million candlepower of the halogen floodlights, the view ahead was limited to about thirty feet. Microscopic bacteria lived out there, but nothing else, and the waters were clear and clean.

Thomas had put the waterfall display of *Orion*'s forward-looking sonar on the starboard video monitor, close to Dokey. It was good for about 1500 yards, but wasn't sounding any alarms. There was nothing of collision concern ahead of them.

The center monitor played the video image from *Sarscan II*'s camera, relayed over the fiber-optic cable, and under the robot's powerful floodlights, the dive team had another view of endless water.

The port monitor did have a display. The seabed, as depicted by the robot's down-looking sonar, was shown as a dark green mass across the bottom of the monitor. The irregular lines and abrupt rises in the dark green suggested a rugged bottom with large outcroppings.

It seemed to be drifting away, and Thomas checked the scale imposed by the computer on the left margin of the monitor.

"Okey, the seabed's in decline."

"I see it, Kaylene. We'll take a ten-degree dive."

Dokey eased his right stick forward, and the bow aimed downward. The twin electric motors driving the propellers forced them lower.

With her own control sticks, Thomas aimed the robot downward and watched the readout until it was showing a ten-degree negative reading.

Four hundred feet farther down, they levelled off.

Polodka, who had a chart spread over her knees, said, "We're approaching the coordinates. Okey, bear to the left two degrees."

"Done, Svet."

Thomas glanced at the magnetometer readout. They had crossed some heavy deposits of probable iron, but at the moment the sensor was not detecting anything out of the ordinary. No sunken ships full of gold and silver ingots.

Dokey reached over his head and pressed the Power On pad for the radiometer.

"We ought to see if we're getting zapped by anything radioactive, ladies."

Thomas had a quick flashback to the Russian missile recovery, with its Topaz IV nuclear reactor payload. "Why'd you bring that up," she asked.

"Just curious."

"That's bull, Dokey. You have a theory going?"

"Those holes Dane photographed look like they could have been dug with a single nuclear charge, Kaylene. They're sometimes used in mining."

"How large?"

"Not monsters. Maybe five kilotons of explosive power. Smaller than tactical nuclear weapons."

All three of them were looking up, watching the digital numbers on the radiometer.

"Levels are normal," Dokey said.

But he left it on.

"One more mile," Polodka said.

"We'll have to bear left some more," Thomas said. "I'm reading a seamount dead ahead."

Dokey glanced at his sonar readout, then eased the joystick to the left, and the sub banked slightly into the turn. They bypassed a mountain peak that rose nearly five hundred feet above their level, then straightened out again.

"Down again," Polodka said.

They descended another two hundred feet.

The first pass over the site of the Earthquake Center-provided coordinates gave them nothing extraordinary on the sonar.

Dokey turned into a spiralling descent, headed back over the area.

"We want," he said, "to get *Sarscan*-baby about fifty feet off the seabed."

"Well, slow it down some," Thomas told him.

"Slow it! Honey, we're barely making headway at this speed."

The sub was, in fact, headed into a current of about two knots, so the forward speed over the seafloor was about three knots.

"I don't want to dent anything," she told him, remembering Dane's convertible as well as the $1.5 million price tag on *Sarscan II*.

Watching the robot's sonar image carefully, Thomas increased the descent, aiming *Sarscan II* downward until the floodlights and cameras could pick up a clear view of the bottom.

"You don't have to be nervous, Kaylene," Dokey said, making her nervous.

"Shut up," she told him.

"Is there something to be nervous about, darlin'?" Mel Sorenson asked from the surface.

They had elected to keep the Loudspeaker channel open, so the ship could monitor their conversations.

"Where's Dane?" Thomas asked.

"Went to the head. You want him?"

"No."

"Here we go," Dokey said. "We've got a picture."

She glanced at the center screen. A murky bottom was showing up, growing clearer as the lights penetrated the darkness.

She began to level off the robot.

The scene on the monitor was almost that of a lunar landscape. Shades of gray and utter black shadows predominated. It was a little smoother than she had expected, but a low ridge on the north alarmed her, and she steered the robot to the left.

There were outcroppings covered with silt, though some faces of the rocks had been eroded by the current.

The seabed unrolled slowly on the screen. It started to fade away again, and she added angle to the diving planes to keep the robot heading downward.

"Crater," Dokey said.

It appeared at the top of the screen.

"Rolling camera," Thomas said, turning on the seventy-millimeter camera.

"Same as Dane saw," Dokey said. "The dimensions are the same, too, at first guess."

Brande's voice echoed on the acoustic transceiver. "Rae, do a few banks left and right."

"All right."

She worked the controller, moving *Sarscan II* left and right, to collect images on either side of the crater.

"Something there," Dokey said.

She had seen it, also. A flash from a metallic object as the lights hit it, then it was gone.

"We'll make another pass," she said.

Thrummm!

"What the hell?" Dokey said.

It was just a minute suggestion of sound. A vibration ran through the submersible.

"What was that?" Thomas asked.

"What's going on?" Brande asked.

"I don't know, Chief," Dokey said, his head wagging as he scanned the fifty-five instrument panels surrounding them. "We had a vibration and a kind of dull boom. Nothing showing on the instruments. No red lights."

"Rae," Brande said, "bring her up."

"We need to make another pass, Dane. We saw something."

"We'll work off the tapes. Up."

She was going to protest again, but realized he was right.

"Let's initiate ascent, Okey."

"Right away, boss."

"There's something else," Polodka said, pointing up at the radiometer.

Thomas followed her pointing finger.

Now they were showing above-normal radiation.

"You people want to speak in full sentences?" Brande asked. "We'd kind of like to know what's going on."

"Remember those X-ray machines in shoe stores, Chief?"

"I do, Okey."

"We're showing a rad count close to maybe four or five of them. Nothing serious."

"Hold on," Brande said. A minute later, he said, "I want you to follow the currents on the way up. Drift with them, and keep the lights and video running, as well as the radiometer. We've got a record of current direction at each level, and Mel will feed it to you."

"Do you know something we don't?" Thomas asked.

"Just a hunch," Brande said.

The problem with both Brande and Dokey, she thought, was that they both operated on gut instinct.

Worse, they were quite often right.

NOVEMBER 17

Nuclear Detonation:
33° 39′ 48″ North, 139° 9′ 57″ West

NINE

0750 Hours Local
Washington, D.C.

Avery Hampstead had been at his desk for over an hour when the phone jangled his morning nerves. Angie wasn't in yet, and normally he wouldn't answer it. That was how he got his paperwork done.

On the sixth ring, and since it was close to eight o'clock, anyway, he picked up.

"Avery, Dane Brande."

"Finished already? I told you this was going to be a quick chore. You didn't even have to go searching since I gave you the locations."

"I don't think we're done with your job, Avery. We've looked at three of the sites, up to the one that occurred last Thursday."

Hampstead felt his stomach sink. There was something wrong.

"Dokey suggests, and the rest of us agree, that they're test holes for a mining operation."

"Test holes?"

"Right. At the third site, our videotapes show what looks like a broken piece of a test probe. That's a device for pulling core samples out of the ground."

"I've seen a test probe, Dane. You mean to tell me that someone's working down there regularly?"

"Looks that way."

"So they're blowing big holes in the seabed, looking for what?"

"We're not certain yet. Dokey used *Atlas* to grab a few pieces of rock before they came up. We're analyzing those now. More important to us, Avery, is their method of conducting the tests."

"And that is?"

"Someone's in a hurry. Our best guess right now is that they're using nuclear explosives."

"What!"

"Small ones, but nuclear all the same. The appearance of the excavations suggest they were accomplished with one blast. Also, the third site had some residual radiation hanging around. Our samples are radioactive, also."

"Goddamn. Can you telex me some pictures? And the test results?"

"I'll do that. And there's something you can check for me. Call your buddy at the Earthquake Information Center and find out what time, and at what coordinates, the last disturbance occurred."

"There was another one?"

"It occurred while *DepthFinder* was on the bottom. It rocked her around a little, but there was no other damage that we've found yet."

Hampstead found that he was jotting his typically illegible notes on a legal tablet. "Anything else?"

"One more item." Brande told him about it, and he added to his notes.

"I'll get back to you, Dane."

"Soon, Avery. I may need some official guidance on this thing, much as I hate to admit that."

He hung up and called Unruh at CIA headquarters in Langley, who wasn't in, but the duty officer promised that he'd find him somewhere.

0435 Hours Local, The Phantom Lode
33° 16′ 50″ North, 141° 15′ 19″ West

When the navigational display indicated she had the proper coordinates, Penny Glenn retarded the throttles and shifted to neutral.

The *Phantom Lode* wallowed in the troughs as she slid out of the helmsman's seat.

Billy Enders hung up the acoustic telephone. "They're on their way up, Miss Penny."

"How long?"

"He said maybe two-and-a-half hours."

"All right. I'm going to take a long, hot shower and pack my bag."

"Will you be wanting us to hang around here for you?" Enders asked.

Glenn looked around at the horizons. She saw no lights indicating a ship in the vicinity. High to the east were the running lights of some airliner. Still, it wouldn't be prudent to mark the spot for anyone.

"No, Captain Billy. We want to keep the area clear. Take her to, oh, San Diego, and wait for me there."

Though he tried not to show it, Enders looked pleased at the news. He would get his boat back for a while.

And the choice of San Diego gave Glenn a reason

for visiting Brande some time in the near future. She was looking forward to that.

By the time Gary Munro brought the submersible to the surface and they rendezvoused with it, she was showered, had wolfed down some lasagna, and had packed the few things she intended to take with her. She was also impatient, and Glenn was never impatient. In was an unaffordable luxury when dealing with the sea.

The sea was becoming more unruly by the time she transferred to the sub, and she was thoroughly splashed with cold, salty water.

Without waiting to watch the *Lode* pull away, Glenn slipped through the hatch, dogged it behind her, and settled into one of the passenger seats behind the two controller seats.

In the dim light of the sphere, Munro looked back over his seat at her, infatuated silliness plastered on his face.

"Good to have you back, Penny."

"Just get us down, will you, Gary?"

He blew ballast, and the sub settled below the surface. AquaGeo's submersibles were designed with large ballast tanks and the ability to accept three sets of weights. They could make three dives before having their weights replaced, which could be accomplished from either a support ship or by one of the floor crawlers.

"Is something wrong?" Munro asked. "I didn't expect you back so soon."

Glenn had been considering her options. She could suspend activities until Brande lost interest, if indeed he had an interest, or she could continue on schedule because it was a free ocean.

"There's nothing wrong that I know about, Gary," she told him.

0725 Hours Local, The Orion
33° 14′ 58″ North, 138° 41′ 22″ West

Svetlana Polodka and the two graduate students, along with Kaylene Thomas when she popped into the lab now and then, had been conducting the tests on the samples that Dokey had brought up from the bottom.

They were not really equipped to deal with radioactive samples, but they were taking as much care as possible, having placed the four chunks of rock in a glass-fronted enclosure and handling them only with rubber gloves and tongs.

They had chiselled off chunks and soaked them in a variety of solutions, and they had run spectrographic analysis. Weights and measures. She was glad she was a computer person.

Behind them, the door to the stern deck opened and closed irregularly as people came in and went out, servicing the submersible. In the aft-portside corner of the lab, the battery chargers hummed incessantly, recharging the packs for *DepthFinder* and the ROVs.

Polodka was overseeing the kids, who knew more about what they were doing than she did, and entering the data from the tests into a report form now on the monitor of her computer terminal.

On the other side of the lab, at another terminal, Larry Emry was plotting the excavation sites on his maps. The undersea charts were becoming more detailed, now that he had the sonar and videotapes from the first two dives.

The pitch and roll of the *Orion,* with the cycloidal propellers retracted, was more noticeable as Sorenson moved them toward the next site.

Dokey strolled into the lab, carrying a mug of coffee. The mug was adorned with the legend, Carry Me Back to the Old *Lusitania.* His sweatshirt was adorned with a colorful picture of a penguin in an orange and green tuxedo and was labelled Psychedelic Penguin. In his right hand, he carried a large Danish, and he stopped to hold it over the glass box containing the samples.

"This hot enough to heat my roll, Svet?"

"I don't think so, Okey."

"Damn. I was hoping to come up with a substitute for microwave ovens."

He used his toe to snag the leg of a chair and pull it over next to her, then sat down. He looked at the rows and columns of figures she had entered into the report.

"That tell you anything?" he asked, taking a big bite out of his Danish.

"Not really."

"Me either. Dana, help us out."

Dana Fullerton, a senior at the University of Southern California, leaned over Polodka's chair and scanned the information on the screen. She was a pretty girl, and in the good old days, before Dokey had become so involved with Kim Otsuka, she would have been a target of some of his more risqué wit.

"Most of it is what we might expect to find," she said. "There seems to be a higher than normal concentration of pyrolusite ore."

"Is that significant?" Dokey asked. He was talking with his mouth full.

"This sample might be. It's loaded with manganese."

"Well, big damned deal. What am I going to do with a bunch of hot manganese?"

"Usually, they make steel with it. It's supposed to harden the steel."

"Is it rare?"

"No," Fullerton told him.

"There must be something else there," he said. "One doesn't go wasting expensive nuclear explosives on common metallic elements."

"That's all we've found, so far," Fullerton said.

"What do you think, Svet?"

Polodka thought about it. "Maybe they didn't find exactly what they were looking for. Perhaps that is why the site is abandoned."

"Good point, love. That's probably the most obvious, and best, answer."

0911 Hours Local, The Arienne
35° 22′ 41″ North, 122° 3′ 11″ West

Wilson Overton was on the ship-to-shore phone, arguing with his editor. Jacobs couldn't hear all of the words, but he guessed the subject would be money. Most people in the civilized world of business seemed to argue about money more than anything else.

There were so many more important things to debate, Jacobs thought.

Finally, Overton replaced the receiver, though with more force than Jacobs thought necessary. He walked back across the salon, a little unsteady, but that was because he was not a sailor. He had yet to learn how to time his movements with those of the sea.

Sliding into the banquette across from Jacobs, he picked up his coffee cup and drained it.

"Problems at home, Wilson?"

Overton made a face. "Damned editors sit at a desk and think they know what's going on in the world. They wouldn't know anything if it weren't for the people like me, who wear out shoe leather."

Jacobs couldn't help thinking that Overton was wearing running shoes.

"I'm sure it will all work out," Jacobs said.

"Oh, yeah, it always does. Where were we?"

"Let me fill your cup, first."

Jacobs got up and took both their cups to the small galley for replenishment. He brought them back and settled into his seat.

Overton centered his legal pad in front of him, and turned the tape recorder on.

The reporter was paying for this trip, not only with diesel fuel, but also with words. He was forced to listen to Jacobs's complaints about the world and those in it. Jacobs had agreed to Overton's caveat that nothing might appear in print, but he was keeping his discourse logical enough, and without demonstrating the rage he felt.

He was sure that some of what was going into the tape recorder would someday appear on some internal page of the *Washington Post*.

On a slow news day, perhaps.

1435 Hours Local
Washington, D.C.

Carl Unruh met with the others in a conference room at the State Department on Twenty-third Street. Since he had talked to Hampstead at nine o'clock, he had been busy trying to get this group together.

It was not the group he would have chosen, if he really wanted to accomplish something, but every time he talked to one person or another, they had suggested someone else. So the representation included the Navy, the State Department, the Justice Department, the Commerce Department, and an assistant to the Vice President—a man who was deeply interested in things ecological.

Commerce had not even sent Hampstead, with whom he could identify. Instead, an assistant to the Secretary named Porter was in attendance.

State's representative was Damon Gilliland, and Unruh wasn't sure what the man did in this building. That wasn't particularly unusual, however; he wasn't certain what most of the people at State did.

Gilliland was a dapper type, properly encased in blue wool with a regimental tie. He was of average height and had average brown eyes and hair. Remarkedly unremarkable. He could have been an agent for either the FBI or the Agency.

The woman from the Vice President's Office, Marlys Anstett, carried herself well, as if she had had graduate courses in posture. She wore a dark-cream business suit accented with a gold-and-black silk scarf at her throat. Her face was lean, barely touched with makeup, and memorable in the quizzical set of her eyebrows.

Ben Delecourt was a man that Unruh knew fairly well, the only one in the room that he had met before. The Chief of Naval Operations (CNO) had an aggressive jut to his jaw, thin gray hair, and silvery-green eyes with all the kindness of torpedoes. Delecourt didn't often send flunkies on chores that he thought important.

Obviously, this was important to him, and Delecourt was the first to speak after they sat down around the big conference table.

"I don't know who's chairing this meeting, if anyone, but Carl, I'm ready to hear more. You were a trifle brief on the phone."

Unruh had had enough time, while waiting for everyone to decide to get together, to prepare his briefing notes. He referred to them sporadically as he related the concerns of the National Center for Earthquake Information and the involvement of Hampstead and Brande.

"The last information I had, Brande had investigated the first site, some six hundred miles off the coast, and two more sites, another seventy miles to the west."

He passed around the photographs that Brande had

transmitted to Hampstead. "The oceanographers aboard the *Orion* conclude that the events were man-made and probably in pursuit of mineral deposits."

"Three miles down?" Marlys Anstett asked.

"That's right."

Damon Gilliland asked, "Isn't that a little bit far-fetched? I mean, outside of the conditions imposed on manpower, the expense of mining at that depth would be horrendous."

"They might be searching for oil," Unruh said, "and that's done all the time. In this case, Brande suggests that the profit margins would be much higher, if the developers aren't paying up-front purchase or lease costs for mineral rights. Not to mention avoiding taxes."

"We are talking about international waters, correct?" Sam Porter of Commerce asked.

"Correct."

"Does Brande have any idea who might be behind this operation?" Delecourt asked.

"He thinks," Unruh said, "that AquaGeo, headed by an Australian named Deride, is the most likely candidate. There are several reasons. One, Deride is known for his offshore mining and drilling, though this is much deeper than his normal haunts. Two, AquaGeo has the equipment and professional staff to accomplish the task. Three, Brande ran into their chief geologist in the area. And four, Deride is ruthless and greedy enough to utilize nuclear means toward his end."

"That's the main concern here, isn't it?" Delecourt asked. "The nuclear explosives. I think you estimated about a five-kiloton yield from each charge."

"At this point, yes," Unruh said, passing out more paper. "Brande's submersible collected samples from the bottom that were definitely radioactive."

"But three miles down?" Anstett said. "Surely, a five-kiloton device isn't much of a threat."

"Not to humans, Miss Anstett, no. But if you'll scan that report, you'll see that Brande's people collected data on currents and depths. The residual radiation from a detonation four days ago followed the currents and rose to a depth of around a thousand feet below the surface before it petered out."

More photographs.

"In an area of approximately three square miles, they found the dead sea life you see in the pictures. A few fish—sharks, tuna, marlin, but this is only four days after the blast. There will be other contaminated fish. And these pictures don't show the damage to plants or microscopic life, both of which are necessary for ecological balance."

Marlys Anstett's face finally developed a frown.

Unruh passed around copies of the chart.

"Dr. Lawrence Emry, the head of exploration for Marine Visions, developed this map. I marked the three sites that Brande has looked at with a yellow marker. The next three have been pinpointed by the Earthquake Information Center. Dr. Emry concurs with the Center in that the pattern appears to be following an arc toward the northwest, which will lead directly into the Pioneer Fracture Zone."

"With all of the potential that has for shaking up Californians," Delecourt added.

"What do you think, Admiral?" Unruh asked.

Delecourt's thin lips compressed even more as he

considered the question. Finally, he said, "It's possible, of course. A small atomic device, if detonated in exactly the right place, might trigger a chain reaction. Pretty remote, though, I believe. What seems more likely is the prospect of several, or perhaps larger, devices being used simultaneously should a profitable and deep deposit of minerals be located. Then, the odds go against us. I don't know what the seabed structures look like, but the scenario could be exactly what we fear."

Gilliland of State said, "What we want to do then, is stop Deride."

"If it's Deride," Unruh cautioned.

"We can't," Gilliland said. "He's operating in international waters."

"I don't think," Sam Porter of Commerce said, "that our objective is to stop his mining. Just his use of nuclear explosives."

"That would drive his costs up substantially," Delecourt said. "I suspect that he will object."

Pamela Stroh of the Justice Department, who had been silent until then, and whose white tresses reminded Unruh of a large, shaggy puppy, said, "Object or not, the man has to have some consideration for people, and for the planet."

Unruh was always less than impressed with optimistic people who didn't see the world in the same realities that were forced upon him.

"For lack of a chair," Delecourt said, "let me make some suggestions. We need to know more about AquaGeo and Deride, and whether or not they're involved. Carl, could CIA undertake that?"

Unruh nodded.

"And Mr. Porter, how about Commerce looking into Deride's business dealings, here and internationally?"

"Certainly, Admiral."

"State might make inquiries into his activities in Australia and determine what his relationship to the government there is. And some preparation might be initiated in the way of forming a complaint to the United Nations."

Gilliland said, "I'll do that."

"Miss Anstett, I would recommend that both the Vice President and the President be briefed on this. The President may want to set up a task force."

"All right, Admiral."

"I'll inform the Joint Chiefs and set up a liaison with Brande."

That would make Brande ecstatic, Unruh thought. Brande didn't care for some Navy protocols, such as the chain of command.

"What about Justice, Admiral?" Pamela Stroh asked.

"If it were me, I'd get about ten lawyers busy on a brief for the World Court."

Which was just about the way Unruh thought this thing would unravel.

Bureaucrats and lawyers.

1920 Hours Local, DepthFinder
33° 27′ 23″ North, 138° 52′ 21″ West

Brande had opted, without consulting Washington, to skip the fourth, fifth, and sixth sites, and go right for the location of the seventh detonation, a position Hampstead had verified through the Earthquake Information Center.

He, Dokey, and Mayberry were manning the submersible, over the objections of the female members of the team. They were also wearing radiation-protective gear, environmental suits that had become standard equipment on the *Orion* after the Russian missile fiasco.

He and Dokey had switched jobs four hours after deployment, to relieve the tedium. Dokey was controlling the sonar vehicle, and Brande was piloting *DepthFinder.* He kept his hands lightly on the joysticks, properly called the translation hand controller and the rotational hand controller. Directly ahead of the joysticks, beneath the port cathode-ray tube (CRT), were the primary piloting instruments, duplicates of the set in front of Dokey.

The compasses, both magnetic and gyro, defined the horizontal direction. The depth readouts kept him oriented vertically, providing distance to surface, altitude above bottom, and the rate of change. The speed was defined in knots, and tachometers monitored the speed of both electric motors.

The view through the portholes might as well have been into the black hole of space. On the center CRT was *Sarscan II*'s video view, into the same black hole even though the floodlights were activated. The port and starboard screens displayed the submersible's sonar and the ROV's sonar, respectively.

Brande shifted around in his protective suit, which was bulky. He was both cold and uncomfortable, even though none of them were wearing the hoods to the suits. They had yet to run into high areas of radiation.

He felt the sub slither to the left, and he corrected with the rotational stick.

"Current shift," he said.

"And radiation," Mayberry added. "It jumped about six percent."

"Getting close, then," Dokey said.

Two minutes later, Dokey added, "Son of a bitch! I've got a moving target."

Brande glanced across at the ROV sonar screen. A heavy mass was moving across the seabed. It appeared to be part of the seafloor.

"What's the distance, Okey?"

"Twelve hundred yards."

"Bearing?"

"Hold on . . . two-six-four degrees. It's making about six knots."

"Take her down," Mayberry commanded. "We're right on the coordinates."

"Don't lose that target," Brande said.

"Not in a million years, Chief."

Brande eased the control stick forward and the submersible nosed downward.

Altitude above bottom, 450 feet. Depth, 16,286 feet.

Minutes later, *Sarscan II*'s video lens picked up the excavation site. It appeared to be the same as the previous three. Organic rubble was strewn about the floor of the sea to the limits of the video camera. If they took time to investigate, he thought it would be like the previous sites: rubble for nearly a half-mile.

Tiny glints of some mineral reflected the floodlights back at the camera.

"Hoods, gentlemen," Mayberry said. "We're getting a healthy dose."

Brande found his hood at the side of his seat and pulled it over his head. He hated it. The loose folds felt cold on his neck and the visor restricted his vision.

"There's nothing new here," Dokey said. "Let's chase the floor crawler."

Brande eased into a left turn.

"What are you doing?" Thomas asked from the surface.

"Exploring an anomaly," Brande said. "I'd like radio and acoustic silence, please."

"Why?" she asked.

"No telling who's listening."

Mayberry switched the communications systems to passive, though Brande suspected that, if there were another acoustic system in the area, it would probably be operating on a different frequency. They had not yet heard anything interfering with their own communications.

"Bob, try scanning some of the frequencies."

"We don't have an automatic scanner," Mayberry said.

"Try it manually."

"God, what a cheap outfit."

"An acoustic scanner," Dokey said, "is something you won't find in your catalogs of electronic toys."

"We'll have to build one."

"In our spare time?" Dokey asked.

"Distance to target?"

"Six-two-four yards, four hundred feet down. Hold this level, Chief; the floor is rising on us. I'm bringing *Sarscan* up a trifle."

With only occasional glances at his instruments, Brande kept his attention on the video screen. The other two were doing the same.

"Come right a tad," Dokey said.

"What's a tad?"

"Scientific talk for one degree."

He changed heading by one degree.

The view from the ROV's video was of a mildly undulating seabed. Fissures marked the surface, and a few giant boulders appeared now and then.

There was also a dual set of tracks, like a farm road across the desert.

"Tracked vehicle," Dokey said.

"Steel treads, I'd guess," Brande told him. "Each set has about a four-foot span."

"Big mutha, then."

And it was big, when they slowly drifted up behind it. The massive tracks were raising a cloud of silt behind it, and a bank of floodlights lit the seafloor ahead of it. Above the moving tracks was a huge spherical pressure hull with a variety of appendages—manipulator arms, remote-controlled cameras, drills, and other unexplained objects. There were no markings on it.

"Do we stop and say 'howdy'?" Dokey asked.

"I don't think so," Brande said. "That hummer's going somewhere, and that's where we want to go."

"Do you suppose they go straight home when Mother calls them?"

"Let's hope so. We'll stay on this course."

"Come up a few hundred, then. Let's give these guys some clearance."

"They probably know we're here," Mayberry said. "They wouldn't dare operate down here without sonar gear."

"Which means Mother already knows about us," Brande told him.

Brande increased his altitude and his speed, and they cruised on in silence except for the drone of the electric motors. The floor crawler disappeared from the ROV's camera, sliding off the bottom of the screen.

"Damned place is getting overcrowded," Dokey said. "I don't like working around people I don't know."

"Move to the suburbs."

"I thought I was in the suburbs."

What he was looking for was farther away than he thought it would be. At their top speed of twenty knots, it took them over five hours. One hundred and twenty-four miles over the seafloor. Brande broke his communications silence three times to reassure those on the surface about their condition and to direct Mel Sorenson to bring the *Orion* along with them.

They had slowly gained altitude, and were at thirteen thousand feet below the surface when Dokey yawned and said, "Metallic mass, dead ahead, fourteen hundred yards."

Brande said, "Battery charges, Bob?"

"We're okay. Got about forty percent left."

"Well, let's go easy on the systems draw."

Brande pulled off some power, and they drifted in on the target.

Sarscan II picked up on it a few minutes later.

"Big devil, isn't she?" Dokey asked.

It was a typical arrangement for a seabed habitat at this depth, pressure hull mounted on sealegs. It was difficult to judge the size from the video image, but Brande agreed with Dokey. It was larger than he had thought it might be.

"Sub in attendance," Dokey said.

"And another crawler," Mayberry added.

Attached to the bottom of the pressure hull was the top mating hatch of a submersible, and attached to an elongated tube extending from the base of the pressure hull was another of the floor crawlers.

"Home sweet home," Brande said. "Let's get lots of pictures—video and still."

"Under way, Chief."

"You pick up anything on the acoustic, Bob?"

"Some babble on one frequency, but nothing else."

"Let me have the controls, Chief," Dokey said, "and I'll move right in and knock on their door."

"I think we'll telephone before our first visit, Okey. Let's just get our pictures and go home."

They circled the sea station slowly, snapping photographs from different angles. Brande was certain the station had sonar tracking them, but they saw no signals of greeting, nor any movement.

The station seemed innocuous enough.

And simultaneously sinister.

NOVEMBER 18

Nuclear Detonation:
34° 1′ 54″ North, 139° 36′ 17″ West

NOVEMBER '18

TEN

Except for Otsuka and Brande, everyone filtering into the wardroom appeared as sleepy as Thomas felt. Larry Emry was rubbing his eyes with gnarled knuckles. His moustache was in disarray. Polodka and Mayberry were arguing about something. As usual, Dokey was the last one to arrive. They should have named him "Pokey" instead of "Okey."

Otsuka and Brande, the two early risers, were sitting at a pair of the central tables that they had pulled together. He was munching on a thick fried egg sandwich—leaning forward so that it dripped on his plate, but though dripping egg-and-mayonnaise sandwiches were his favorite fast food, he didn't seem particularly pleased about his world this morning.

Thomas went into the galley, poured herself a tall glass of orange juice from the pitcher in the big refrigerator, turned the spigot on the famous coffee urn—the *Orion*'s morning brew was as strong as antifreeze—for a mug of coffee, then carried both back into the wardroom and sat next to Otsuka.

"You've been up most of the night," she accused Brande.

"Making phone calls," he said. "Getting people out of bed in Washington. They didn't want to get out of bed."

"And?"

"Wait until everyone gets some breakfast."

Nearly fifteen minutes went by before Dokey emerged from the galley carrying a tray heaped with burritos, pancakes, eggs, and sausage.

"I'm here," he said. "Let the games begin."

Thomas had been watching Brande closely, and she had noted the fire in his eyes. They got that glint when he became overly zealous about some project. He could become totally focused on an objective that no one else saw. Infrequently, when his dander was up, his eyes took on the same quality of hardness. The other giveaway was his mouth. It assumed a straight line that no humor or change of subject could bend.

Brande sipped from his mug—one of Dokey's, but she couldn't see the caption from where she sat.

"First," Brande said, "is something wrong, Svetlana?"

Brande still surprised Thomas at times. He noticed the little things that were going on around him, especially with his people. She had thought him so involved with his inner vision that he'd have missed Svetlana's debate with Mayberry.

"There is nothing wrong," Polodka insisted.

"The hell there isn't," Mayberry said. "She got a nine-hundred-dollar phone bill, but she wouldn't tell me about it until last night."

"How'd that happen, Svet?" Dokey asked. "You only call me a couple times a month."

"It is all right," Polodka said.

"She found herself a nine-hundred-number consultant, quote, unquote," Mayberry said.

Polodka glared at him.

"What kind of consultant?" Emry asked.

"We don't need to get into that," Mayberry said. "I told her not to pay it."

"Give the bill to our lawyer," Brande said. "We do still have a lawyer, don't we, Rae?"

She nodded. "Jim Wray. Give me the bill, Svetlana, and I'll see what we can do about it."

Thomas doubted that much could be done. "Let the buyer beware," still prevailed, even though the buyer might not fully understand or appreciate the culture or read the fine print on the TV screen.

Polodka looked a little relieved, and Brande went on, "I talked to Unruh—"

"He's that CIA guy?" Dokey asked.

"Yeah. I don't know how he wormed his way into this operation, but apparently he's fully involved, according to Hampstead. Anyway, Washington is moving at lightning speed on this thing."

"That means they set up a committee," Emry said.

"A task force, Larry, a task force. It is, however, a presidential task force, so they should have influence if not warp speed. So far, our orders are to stand by."

"We could be standing by until March," Emry told them, "and it might be a cold winter."

"True. So, while we're waiting, we want to do a little reconnaissance."

"What kind of reconnaissance?" Thomas asked. She didn't want Brande to get carried away, mounting some kind of paramilitary operation. He wasn't a fanatic about environmental and historical issues; he wouldn't go so far as to say that artifacts on a sunken ship were fated to stay sunken, though he would say they should be in the proper museums. He had never believed in sabotaging industrialists or spiking trees in a forest to prevent environmental pollution, but she knew he could be very concerned about ecological balances.

"Today, we'll go look at yesterday's blast site. I'd like to get a count on the number of floor crawlers or any other vehicles down there."

"And we stay far away from their subsurface habitat?" Thomas asked.

"Until we learn more about it, like who it belongs to," Brande said.

"My money's still on AquaGeo," Dokey said.

"Larry, you studied the footage," Brande said. "Find anything relevant?"

Emry nodded and finished chewing a piece of toast. "I think so. Starting with the station itself, I figure it at seventy feet in diameter. It could house about fifteen people on a regular basis. Perhaps a few more. And there's something you people didn't see, but I picked it up on the videotape. About a hundred yards from the station, due north, is another pressure hull, maybe twenty feet in diameter. It's connected to the main station by a thick umbilical cable laid directly on the seabed. I think it's a nuclear reactor."

"No lie?" Dokey said.

"No lie, Okey. It's a convenient and nicely portable source of energy for powering the station and re-charging the battery packs for submersibles and floor crawlers."

"I'll buy that," Brande said. "I've often thought we should develop something similar for our own use."

Thomas noticed that Mayberry wrote himself a quick note. She could anticipate that, at the next shore-side meeting, he'd have a proposal for a nuclear reactor power plant. She made her own mental note—somehow, she'd have to come up with the money for it.

Thomas saw that Dokey's face had tightened up, a sure sign that he also saw nuclear power as a challenge.

"At the top of the station is a large winch and cable reel," Emry continued. "All I saw was a thin cable headed upward, but I'd suspect it leads to a buoy that is probably retracted beneath the surface until they let it rise. It'll be their communications link."

"How about communications?" Brande asked. "You listen to the audiotapes?"

"Bucky and Paco helped me out. We didn't find anything on the recording tapes for the UHF or VHF scanners, but we think they're using a low-end acoustic transceiver for subsurface communications and possibly telemetry. The channel is, however, scrambled."

"Why would they encrypt the dialogue between the station and the vehicles?" Thomas asked.

"Maybe they don't want to reveal company secrets," Bob Mayberry put in. "Let's keep in mind that they can probably hear us, however, on the frequencies we use."

"They would not be able to read our telemetry, however," Polodka said. "Our transponders digitize the data utilizing our own codes."

Polodka and Otsuka had worked out the encoding.

"True," Brande agreed. "It keeps them from getting readouts on altitude and position directly from *DepthFinder.* They can't plot exactly where we are."

"Which may be the reason they've encrypted their transmissions," Mayberry said. "If we could tap into their telemetry, we could pretty well follow every sub or crawler they have."

"Back to the submersible," Emry said, "it is larger than *DepthFinder,* but doesn't have her streamlining. It's a pressure hull with numerous appendages, but no outer hull. There's a pair of skids on the bottom, and between the skids is a parking sheath for ROVs. In fact, I'm damned certain that the ROV in place is Sneaky Pete. I'll vote along with Okey on this outfit being AquaGeo."

"Told you," Dokey said.

"What else?" Brande asked.

"The floor crawler. She's a monster with a sixteen-foot-diameter pressure hull. Each track is four feet wide, with steel cleats that are about a foot long. The length of the surface contact for each tread is twenty-five feet, and the treads are twenty feet wide, from side to side. This baby is designed to not tip over when she's lifting a load. There is one big manipulator arm, capable of, I'd judge, ten tons of lift, and a smaller arm for tool deployment. Both the one you photographed en route and the one at the station are similar and are well used, if I go by the scratches and dings. They both had drills mounted on the tool arm, and there were additional drilling rods clipped to the side of the hull. I'd guess they could drill a forty-foot hole."

"Do you have any ideas about the size of the personnel complement, Larry?" Thomas asked.

"Difficult to tell at this point, Kaylene. If it's just an exploratory venture, they could get by with minimal manpower. That means four people for the station and two each for the crawlers and the submersible. That's ten. We don't know if there are more subs or crawlers around."

"That's what we'll try to determine today," Brande said. "We'll dive on Site Number Eight and then circle it in ever widening circles, and see if we can't pinpoint some more of their inventory."

Following Emry's recommendation, they had started numbering the locations of the exploratory excavations.

"And who's going today?" Thomas asked.

"Dokey and—"

"No."

"What?"

"You two and Bob were down for over twelve hours yesterday. Let's spread the load."

"I am well rested and well fed, Kaylene," Dokey said.

"We don't know what Washington and tomorrow will bring," she argued.

Brande looked disappointed. When he was on a project, he wanted to do everything himself.

Finally, he said, "I'm afraid you're probably right, Rae."

"Not even probably."

"I haven't been down in over a year," Emry said. "I need some sea time."

"All right, then," Brande said. "Rae, Svetlana, and Larry get the ride."

"Who's in command?" Emry asked.

"Flip a coin," Brande said.

0654 Hours Local, DepthFinder
33° 16′ 48″ North, 141° 15′ 18″ West

Svetlana Polodka drew the right-hand seat as pilot, and that pleased her. She did not have many operational hours in *DepthFinder,* far less than she had in the *Neptune*-class of MVU's submersibles.

She had bundled herself in two sets of long johns and a jumpsuit, and she carried two sweaters, but she was still cold. A light drizzle was falling from the skies when they boarded the submersible, but the wind, which was gusting to thirty knots, turned it into pelting droplets that stung the face and dampened clothing. By the time they were in their seats, with the hatch closed, the three of them were mildly soggy.

Larry Emry was in the seat behind her. He had in fact won the coin toss, but declined the commander's seat since, as he said, his submersible skills were a little rusty from lack of use.

With her wrists resting on the padded ledge in front of her, Polodka kept her thumbs and forefingers lightly clamped to the joysticks. The sticks were self-centering, and very little pressure was needed to affect changes in the submersible's attitude. It was like the power steering on her car, but much more efficient.

The depth readout read 112 feet, and she was already headed into the proper direction. They were not diving directly on the site, but aiming toward it during the descent, like a glider falling.

Mel Sorenson's voice came over the Loudspeaker acoustic system. "All right, *DepthFinder,* your sonar tow is deployed. Bon voyage."

Kaylene Thomas shifted in the seat beside her. "I have *Sarscan* under control. Take up the slack, Svetlana."

She used the twin slide switches for trim at the base of the left stick to ease in power on the electric motors, and followed that by trimming the diving planes downward. A few minutes later, she felt the tug as the towline came taut, and cut off the power. Now they were in free fall.

"Great," Thomas said. "We're on the way."

"Orion," Emry said on the acoustic transmitter, "all systems one hundred percent. We're going mute."

Brande had decided, until they knew more about who might be listening to them, to avoid chatter on the communications networks. That order was immediately void when safety was at stake.

Emry put a tape of Frank Sinatra into the cassette deck. Emry was of that era. He talked of "Rat Packs," and "Chairman of the Board," and other things Polodka didn't understand. He had told her to rent the video *Ocean's Eleven,* which she did, but she still didn't understand. Robbing a Las Vegas casino seemed to have no relationship to the song, "New York, New York."

The rate-of-change readout reported that *Depth-Finder* was falling at a rate of one hundred feet per minute. Physically, Polodka was not aware of it, but mentally, she thought of herself as a fallen leaf, wafting downward from the tree. It was much like her dreams of late.

She had talked to the psychic about her dreams of falling, and she was now very embarrassed about the way in which she had been taken. Ninety-nine cents a minute added up quickly when one did not watch the clock.

Though she was embarrassed, she still worried about her dreams and her sensation of falling.

She shivered.

Svetlana Polodka was cold and falling, and she was uncomfortable.

0727 Hours Local, SeaStation AG-4
33° 16′ 50″ North, 141° 15′ 19″ West

Her assistant sat across the round table from her and waited while she went over the last geological analyses. Bert Conroy hummed a melody she didn't know. He probably didn't know it, either.

Penny Glenn made her decision from the data spread out before her.

"Skip the next test locale, what we were calling G, and go on to the following one. It's now Test Hole G," she said. Spinning around in her swivel chair, she pointed to the position on the computer-screen map behind her.

Conroy asked, "It's looking that good to you, Penny?"

She turned back to face him. "Absolutely. If we find what we're looking for at G, we'll start mining right away."

Conroy, who was the head geologist for the station, was an old fortyish. His hair had grayed prematurely, and combined with the heavy wrinkles in his forehead and at the corners of his eyes, had added five or six years to his chronological age. He was also very conservative.

"I know the signs are good, Penny. I'd even predict as much as a half-million tons of manganese out of this site. Still, that's only breakeven when we compare the cost of deploying the equipment."

"Ah, Bert, you worry too much. This lode is going to expand, the farther north we go."

"You're relying on instinct, Penny."

"My instincts are pretty good."

"I know, I know. However, shouldn't we suspend operations for a few days, until these other people have taken off?"

Glenn had recognized *DepthFinder* on the video camera when it circled the station. She had been quite simply amazed that Dane Brande had located them with such apparent ease.

Then she had been less amazed when she remembered meeting the man and recalled his record of exploration. He was indeed intriguing.

Still, at the time, she had elected to remain silent and not give him any indication that the station was inhabited, or by whom.

And they finally went away, though she was not sure how far away.

The station crew and the vehicle crews had been edgy since the encounter, though. It was disconcerting to find unexpected humans in this environment, much as if Neil Armstrong had lifted a rock on the moon and come face-to-face with a visiting Martian.

"Like us, Bert, Marine Visions has every right to explore where they want to explore. However, we have a schedule to follow."

"You just skipped a step in the schedule."

"Because I'm certain of the trend. Don't argue with me over this."

"All right, Penny. I'll send Team Three to the site with a nuclear charge."

Team Three, headed by Jim Dorsey, was assigned to floor crawler FC-9 and was composed of nuclear experts. They performed all of the drilling, setting of charges, and detonations. The slim, stainless steel canisters that contained the nuclear charges frightened her to some degree, and all twenty-five of the nuclear devices owned by AquaGeo were aboard FC-9. Until they were revamped, they had been 105-millimeter howitzer rounds. Glenn had obtained them from a penniless, ex-East German army officer who was no longer penniless.

"What's the condition of the others?" she asked, looking up to the bulkhead-mounted monitor that was labelled Status Board.

"We've got Team One on sleep schedule, and Two is still at Test Hole F. Four is en route back from F."

"And the subs?"

"B-7 is standing down. B-12 is charging batteries, and B-3 is supervising at Test Hole F."

She knew them better by their names, *Perth, Sydney,* and *Melbourne.*

"Very well. Good. That's all."

Conroy went back to work, and Glenn spun around to her console. She flipped the switch for the buoy winch and heard it grinding above her as the cable reeled out and let the antennas rise to the surface. When the light turned green, she picked up the phone and dialled the number for Deride.

It wasn't a long wait.

"Deride." Said in the flat, positive tone with which he always answered phone calls. Glenn knew that she herself was a confident person, but she sometimes envied Deride's superassurance.

"Uncle Paul, where are you?"

"Hmmm, hello, Penny. I guess we're about a half hour out of San Francisco. I'm meeting Anthony."

"You were correct."

He laughed. "About what?"

"Brande. They found us."

"What! What do you mean?"

"I mean that *DepthFinder* paid a call on us."

"Jesus! They found the station?"

"That's right. Buzzed us a couple times and then took off. I don't know where they are now. Our sonar doesn't quite reach the surface."

"That's impossible."

"If you say so, Uncle Paul."

There was a long silence while Deride digested the information, then he said, "It doesn't change a thing."

"I didn't think so, either," she told him. "I'm proceeding with the test schedule. I want you to send me the start-up equipment."

"I've got two diggers, two conveyors, and a separator en route," Deride said. "They're only a couple days out. Two days behind them, we'll have pumps. In two weeks, we should be transporting ore."

"Good. We're starting with Test Hole D. The concentrations are sufficient to assure us a payout."

"Payout is my favorite word. One thing, though, Penny. With Brande hanging around, you tell your teams to make certain the area is clear before they detonate. Anthony assures me that our legal status is clear, but an accident might bring investigators."

"I'll do that, Uncle Paul," she said, then broke the connection.

Switching to the scrambled acoustic circuit, she said, "McBride, AG-4."

Mac McBride was piloting the submersible B-3, *Melbourne.* He responded immediately. "McBride."

Because of the combination of acoustic transmission and scrambling, his voice sounded tinny and elevated, as if he had been inhaling helium.

Her voice would sound the same to him, and sometimes it was difficult to tell who was on the other end of a transmission.

"You're aware of the presence of a Marine Visions submersible?"

"Yeah, Penny, I got that message. What's going on?"

"I assume they're interested in our activities, Mac."

"What do we do about it?"

"Nothing," she said. "We do what we came to do, and outsiders are to leave us alone."

0840 Hours, The California
Bremerton, Washington

The guided missile cruiser *California* (CGN-36) was returning to her home port after a three-month patrol cruise when the message came in. The signal officer immediately carried the flimsy to the bridge and approached Captain Harris, who was sitting in his chair watching the mooring activity on deck.

"Excuse me, Captain. This seems to be a priority."

Harris took the single page. "Thank you, Mister Evans."

Harris reluctantly looked away from the satisfying sight of his crew performing their chores flawlessly and glanced at the message:

SECRET MSG 11-76423/11/18/1321 HRS
ZULU
FR: CINCPAC
TO: COMMANDER, CALIFORNIA

CALIFORNIA ORDERED TO SEA ASAP,
ACCOMPANIED BY MAHAN AND
FLETCHER. CAPTAIN MABRY F. HARRIS
DESIGNATED COMMANDER, TASK
FORCE 36. RPT DIRECTLY TO CINCPAC.

PROCEED ON HEADING 245, CONTACT

CINCPAC 1900 HOURS ZULU FOR FUR-
THER ORDERS.

After reading the words from the Commander-in-
Chief, Pacific, who was Admiral David Potter, twice,
Harris looked up and through the windshield at the
people waving frantically from the pier, the families
eagerly welcoming their men and women home from
the sea. It was a large crowd.

And it would be a disappointed one.

Commander George Quicken, his first mate, was
supervising the mooring, and he turned away from
his post beside the helm when Harris called him.

"Captain?"

"Read this, Commander."

Quicken frowned when he was through. "Not very
timely, is it, Captain?"

"Not at all. Let's go to sea, Commander. Mister
Evans, contact the captains of the *Mahan* and the
Fletcher for me, please."

0955 Hours Local, The Arienne
32° 39′ 26″ North, 137° 32′ 16″ West

"You're sure you got the numbers right, Wilson?"
Mark Jacobs asked.

Overton flipped through his notebook and compared the coordinates written there with the readout
on the Loran.

"They're correct, Mark. One thing I always do, I
always get my facts straight."

Jacobs gave him a skeptical look.

"There'd be no reason for the Earthquake Information Center to give me the wrong coordinates."

Jacobs waved his arm expansively toward the sea outside the windows. For as far as they could see, there was only ocean, and it wasn't a particularly gentle ocean from Overton's point of view. He had a sensitive stomach when it came to oceans. Only Jacobs's seeming unconcern about the height of the waves reassured him.

They were on the bridge of the yacht, and the rain thrummed steadily on the overhead canvas. Both the glass windshields and the plastic side curtains were faintly fogged over. Visibility through them wasn't all that great, and the overcast skies and rain limited it further, perhaps to two miles, though Overton's visual perceptions got all screwy when he was the center of nothingness.

With the engines almost at idle, the pitching of the boat was more pronounced, and Overton stayed close to the passenger seat, where he could hang on to its back cushion.

"Brande's got to be out there somewhere," Overton said. "I know it."

"Uh-huh."

Overton showed Jacobs the second of the three sets of coordinates he had gotten from Golden. "Where's this?"

"North and west."

"Let's try there."

Jacobs leaned toward the Loran and dialled in the numbers. He shoved the throttles forward, and when he engaged the autopilot, the bow of the boat came around a few degrees to the north. It took several minutes to come up to speed, and then the pitching subsided.

Overton felt a little better about it.

"If we don't find him in the next couple hours, Wilson, we're going back to San Francisco."

"We'll find him," Overton said.

"It's a big, big ocean."

"I'm going down and call the Earthquake Center. Maybe they know something more."

1046 Hours Local, The Orion
33° 39' 48" North, 139° 9' 57" West

They weren't getting oral reports from the submersible, but the telemetry readouts had been telling the same monotonous story for some time. The life-support systems were all operating normally, and reserves were more than adequate. Electrical energy was in good shape. In the last couple hours, the depth had changed only a few hundred feet either way of 18,500 feet as they followed the rise and fall of the seabed. They were on the correct heading and would soon be approaching the site of the seventh detonation.

Brande had often thought that a deep dive was as tough on the support personnel aboard the mother ship as it was on the crew of the submersible. The level of anxiety, anticipating some minor or major mishap or system failure, was high. One waited in silence with mentally crossed fingers.

Worse, the monotony of sitting at the command console had given him time to think. He thought about what he had seen the day before, the people he thought were behind it, and what the future days might bring. He thought about the options he had.

And the options he *should* have.

Swinging around in his chair, he spotted Dokey at one of the other terminals, playing with the instructions for some computer program. It was one of the ways in which he passed time. Otsuka was the same way.

"Okey?"

"Yeah, Chief?"

"You want to take over here for a while?"

"Sure thing." Dokey saved whatever it was he was doing and picked up a mug sporting a picture of *Neptune's Daughter*. The miniature sub had a frown painted on her face, and she was frantically eluding an amorous whale.

Dokey stood behind him and studied all of the telemetry for a minute, to get his mind wrapped around the current status.

"Okay, got it, Chief. All normal."

"All normal," Brande repeated, rising from his chair.

Brande left the command center in the lab and climbed to the bridge where he found Connie Alvarez-Sorenson keeping an eye on both the ship and Fred Boberg.

The bridge had an overhead speaker monitoring the few conversations between the ship and the submersible, but she asked, anyway, "Everything all right, Dane?"

"Right on track, Connie. How about you?"

She smiled. "Despite the weather, we haven't drifted out of position more than ten or fifteen feet at any one time."

Brande glanced through the windshield. The wind had picked up, and the spume off the wave tops pelted the hulls of the ship. Whitecaps dotted the ocean's surface, and the lower levels of the overcast skies rolled and twisted.

"What's the prognosis," he asked.

"It's not going to get better, but I don't think it'll get a lot worse in the next twenty-four hours."

"I'll keep my fingers crossed," he said, heading for the radio shack.

Sanders was on duty.

"Bucky, see if you can't raise Bull Kontas for me."

"Coming right up, Chief."

Sanders used their satellite channel, and it only took about two minutes since Kontas was never far from his pilothouse.

Sanders exchanged positions with him, and Brande shut the door behind him and sat in the operator's chair.

"Good morning, Bull."

"Hey, Chief."

"Where are you?"

"Just left the Bay, headed for Ocean Deep."

"Precious cargo?" Brande asked.

"Buncha crates for some of the subcontractors."

"Turn her around and head in, Bull. I want you to pick up some stuff for me."

"O . . . kay, Chief. You want it out there?"

Brande gave him the coordinates. "That all right with you, Bull?"

"Damned right. I haven't been in deep waters in a long time. What'd you need?"

Brande read off the list he had formulated in his mind.

"Jesus, Chief! I know where Gargantua is, but this other crap?"

"I trust to your knowledge of the waterfront, Bull. You know the right kind of people."

"Maybe. What do you need this for, Chief?"

"I'm preparing for a rainy day. For eventualities that may never come to pass."

"How much do I spend?"

"Whatever you need to spend. You go see Ingrid for the cash, and tell her to call me if she has any reservations. Don't tell her what we're buying."

"I don't tell her what I'm spending it on?"

"You and I get along real well, Bull."

1154 Hours Local
San Francisco, California

Paul Deride had his shoes off, his feet on the coffee table, a cigar lit, a lead crystal tumbler of Cutty Sark at hand, and a fine view of San Francisco Bay from the living room of the suite in the Fairmont which AquaGeo Limited kept for him.

Anthony Camden had declined the cigar and the drink, and Deride didn't know whether or not he was enjoying the view.

"You got it down, Anthony?"

"Yes, Paul, I think so. I've got my staff preparing the boilerplate now. If anyone makes a squawk, it won't take long to fill in the particulars and get everything filed."

"In what courts?" Deride asked.

"It'll depend on where the squawk comes from. We'll be ready for anything."

"Good."

"Nothing to be nervous about, Paul."

"I'm not nervous."

"Are you hungry, then? I haven't had lunch."

"Yeah, order something up."

Camden picked up the phone from the coffee table, called room service, requested petite filets, and while they were waiting for them, the phone rang again.

Deride grabbed it before Camden could reach it. "Deride."

"Uncle Paul, there's been an accident."

ELEVEN

Angie buzzed him on the intercom. "Mr. Unruh is here, sir."

She only called him "sir," when others were present, no matter who it was. Hampstead had tried to break her of the habit when it wasn't necessary, but she would make promises, then break them as soon as he had a visitor.

"I guess we can let him in, Angie. Search him for guns and stuff, will you?"

"Mr. Hampstead!"

Grinning, he got up and went around his desk as Unruh entered his office.

"What an unexpected pleasure," he said.

Unruh smiled, though somewhat grimly. "I was getting bored, so I came over to look at your wrestling posters."

"You want coffee or something?"

"Nah, I'm coffeed-out."

He actually walked around the perimeter of the office and perused the posters. Then he sat down in one of the two cushioned visitor chairs in front of Hampstead's desk.

Hampstead sat on the corner of the desk. "You must have terrific news, to come all the way over to my place."

"I told you. I came to see the posters."

"And I believe that, of course."

"I get antsy when there's no action," Unruh said. "I spent too many years in the operations directorate."

"So nothing's happening?"

Unruh had already told him about the makeup of the task force. "I've done my part. I looked into Deride and AquaGeo."

"And found?"

"He's a hard and smart man. Came out of nowhere to make *Forbes*'s top ten wealthiest. He worked the oil fields to put himself through the University of Sydney and then Oxford, and then he worked some more. When he decided to strike off on his own, his first big project in New Zealand came up roses— million-dollar roses. That gave him the cash and leverage base he needed, and he's been hitting about ninety percent of every venture he tries."

"And that's it?"

"The Agency, nor the Bureau when I checked over there, have a great deal of interest in an Australian entrepreneur, Avery. The files are not extensive on the man as a person."

"How about his company?"

"Just about as sparse. There have been some complaints over the years, and they're mostly from people who felt they got the raw end of a deal. As far as I can tell, there's been nothing fraudulent, but there have been some sore losers. I checked out my information with what a guy named Porter in your building is supposed to come up with."

"Sam Porter?"

"That's it. Is he any good?"

"A political hack," Hampstead said. "But he knows the right people."

"He says that it appears as if AquaGeo often walks the fine lines of ethics, but they've never been in criminal court, and they've never had anything illegal proven against them. They are litigious."

"Lots of lawsuits?"

"From what Porter tells me, yes," Unruh said.

"They lose any?"

"Nope. They either win or settle out of court."

"Who's been suing them?"

"It's the other way around, Avery. AquaGeo is the first to go to court, then they draw it out for as long as possible, often for years. They sue the little guys over clauses in contracts, over the amount of royalties, over anything. They sue the big guys for the same things, as well as infringement of contractual rights. Their law-guy, name of Anthony Camden, likes to overload the system with paper, though he's rarely in court."

"What companies are involved?" Hampstead asked.

"I don't have the details. Porter gave me the gist of it over the phone, and I assume he'll have more for our meeting in the morning. The picture I get—"

Angie interrupted him. The intercom blared, "Mr. Hampstead!"

He leaned across the desk and depressed the Talk button. "Yes, Angie?"

"Dr. Brande is on the line. He says it's urgent."

Still leaning across his desktop, Hampstead punched the Phone button and picked up the receiver. "Hello, Dane. What's up?"

Brande was normally even-tempered, especially in a crisis, but Hampstead heard the rare edge of rage in his voice.

"The sons of bitches rammed *DepthFinder.*"

1104 Hours Local, SeaStation AG-4
33° 16′ 50″ North, 141° 15′ 19″ West

Penny Glenn tried to get the straight story out of Mac McBride, the wiry Irishman who was piloting B-3, the *Melbourne.* The scrambled acoustic telephone made conversation warped as it was, and McBride had probably damaged his antennas, judging from the way the transmission was interrupted or stopped altogether.

All six of the people in the station were gathered around her console, peering over her shoulder as if they would get to see some live action shots on the screen, but it was blank. She had tried to link into the *Melbourne*'s telemetry, but that was also garbled. The tension in the room was almost visible.

"I didn't get that, Mac. Repeat."

"I said . . . we went under . . . her . . . get the—"
The transmission broke off again.

Glenn spun around to Gary Munro. "Launch the *Sydney* and get over there."

Munro turned and ran for the hatch, signalling his assistant to follow him.

". . . AG-4 . . . you there?"

"I'm here, Mac. Tell me again."

Silence.

All Glenn knew from the first reports, as she had told Deride on the phone, was that the *Melbourne* had collided with the *DepthFinder* near Site F.

Jesus. All that ocean out there, and two submersibles meet each other at speed.

She felt isolated, lacking the information she needed to make decisions. McBride was able to transmit sporadically, but she wondered about the condition of Brande's submersible. At these depths, it didn't take much damage to achieve critical states.

"Bert," she told Conroy, "get on the clear acoustic and see if you can pick up any transmissions from the *Orion.*"

"Right away, Penny." He settled into a chair at the console next to hers.

"AG-4. . . ."

"I hear you, Mac."

"Told you . . . we were only . . . going . . . cut the tow."

Shit! Cut the tow!

She had to assume that the *DepthFinder* was towing some kind of robot. And McBride had taken it upon himself to sever the towline. That would be construed as an unprovoked attack. Both Deride and Camden were going to scream.

"Tell me more, Mac."

". . . came back . . . on us."

Oh, damn!

Glenn needed information, and she needed it fast. She was going to have to control the data on this, to put the best face on it.

Gary Munro broke onto the circuit. *"Sydney* here, AG-4. We're under way."

"Give me an ETA, Gary."

"We'll churn water, Penny, but it's still going to be over three hours."

"Well, hurry up, damn it! There are lives at stake."

1110 Hours Local, DepthFinder
33° 39′ 48″ North, 139° 9′ 57″ West

"Rate of ascent one hundred feet per minute, Kaylene," Emry said. "That's the max. We're two-six-hundred off the bottom."

It was dark. Thomas had shut down all of the lights and most of the electrical draw. Only a few of the crucial instruments were providing light inside the sphere. Her hands felt as if they were shaking, but they seemed steady enough on the joysticks.

"How's Svetlana?"

"Not responding," Emry said. "I think I've stopped the bleeding."

Emry was on his knees in his seat, leaning over the back of the pilot's seat to cradle Polodka's head in the crook of his arm.

Brande's voice, when it came over her headset, was confident and reassuring. "Rae, can you give me a status report now?"

Since her first report of the collision, he had been

patient—and probably frantic—while she and Emry stabilized the submersible.

"Svetlana's unconscious. Larry's stopped the blood flow."

"How did that happen?" he asked.

"We were struck on the starboard side, and she was thrown to the right. We think she hit her head on the gyro control panel. There's a long gash on her temple."

"Are you all right?"

"Yes. Larry too. Svetlana seems to be breathing normally, and her pulse rate is down, but stabilized."

"Okay," Brande said. "Now, we're showing you at maximum ascent."

"Correct. I dropped the weights immediately."

"We also show that you've lost a little over seventy percent of your available electrical capacity."

Thomas took a deep breath, trying to calculate.

Brande did it for her. "That still gives you plenty of time, if you conserve."

"I've got practically everything shut down, Dane. I'm not getting readings on amperage draw or the voltage meters."

"It looks all right from here. Don't worry about it."

"The bastard must have damaged the battery tray."

"I suspect that's the case," Brande said.

She didn't know how he could be so calm. All of her willpower was devoted to keeping her voice level; she didn't want to alarm Emry.

"How about environment?" Brande asked. "We're not getting the telemetry."

She was aware that he had worked slowly up to that

question. She knew he would be worried. Thomas and
Dokey were the only two at MVU who knew the full
story of Janelle Brande's death. She thought she knew
the agony he had gone through when he had finally
given her the last of the available air tanks and had
watched her die.

"Larry says the scrubber is still working full-time.
The flow from the external oxygen tank has decreased, but the emergency bottle is fine, and we're
augmenting from it."

"Has Larry made a calculation?"

Emry broke in. "I'm on the line, too, Dane. It's
not like I stepped outside for a smoke. Yeah, on rough
estimate, we've got a bit more than seven hours."

"Good. That's good. Any structural damage to the
pressure hull?"

"None that we can detect from the inside," Thomas
said.

"I wonder if you could deploy *Atlas* and check the
external damage?"

Thomas released the right joystick and flicked the
switch to activate the robot. Immediately, an amber
caution light flared.

She flipped the switch back.

"Not this trip, Dane. I'm getting a fault in one of
the control circuits."

Dokey was nearby, too. He said, "Kaylene, check
the ROV circuit breakers."

She had to turn on an interior light for a minute
in order to see the circuit breakers, located low on
her left.

"All of them have blown, Okey."

He thought that over for all of ten seconds. "Let's

let it be, Dane. We don't want to use up energy looking for the problems, anyway."

"It's your call, Rae," Brande said.

"We'll follow Okey's recommendation," she said.

"Next," Brande said. "We lost signals from
Sarscan. What are you showing?"

"Nothing," Thomas said, involuntarily glancing at
the monitor in front of Polodka, which had been carrying the sonar return from the search robot. It was
now blank.

"She's still in tow," she clarified, "because I can
feel the drag, but we don't have control over her."

"How much of a drag?" Brande asked. "We'd
probably better jettison her."

"It's not all that bad, Dane. We're getting full ascent
rate, and I suspect her diving planes were in the up
position when she lost power. Let's hold on for now."

"We can always recover her later," Brande said.

"We'll wait."

"Okay. Svetlana?"

Thomas glanced to her right. Emry had slipped out
of both of his sweaters and was using them to cushion Polodka's head against the side of the hull. She
released the joysticks and began to unbutton her own
sweater.

"She's the same, Dane."

"Is there anything else we can check for you,
Kaylene?" Dokey asked.

"I don't think so. We're stable, and now we just
wait."

"One other thing," Brande said. "What about the
other sub. Are you showing it on sonar?"

"I shut down the sonar, Dane."

"Try it one time," Dokey urged.

After handing her sweater to Emry, Thomas turned on the sonar, channelling the image to the screen in front of her. It took a few minutes to warm up.

When it came on-line, she noted the elongated blob in the lower-right quadrant.

The audio volume was up, and her earphones sounded off with the *ping, ping* of contact.

"Damn!"

"What!" Brande's voice now carried the higher register of his concern.

"They're right alongside us."

TWELVE

Like almost everyone else on board, Kim Otsuka had been in the lab for what seemed an eternity, waiting without patience for word from below. Without being asked, she had settled in at the computer console next to the command station, linked into the telemetry circuits for the submersible, and initiated diagnostic programs to see if the interrupted signals could be traced to shipboard equipment.

Behind her, scientists and ship's crew milled about, listening to the conversations with *DepthFinder* that were issuing from the overhead speakers. Dokey was on the computer next to her, the submersible's electronic schematic on the screen, searching for potential solutions to problems he could only guess at. Next to him, Mayberry was also on a machine, attempting to track the sub's ascent on his map by the verbal reports coming from Thomas, and calculating the rate of electrical usage.

On her left, Dane Brande, when she glanced at him from time to time, seemed close to detonation. His back was rigid as he sat on the edge of his chair, and a vein was throbbing at his temple. She was amazed that he could hold his temper in check sufficiently to maintain a level tone in his voice.

When Thomas reported the proximity of the other submersible, though, Brande came out of the chair, scattering the people standing behind him. He paced in front of the console, watching for nonexistent data on the screen, the headset's cord trailing after him.

"It's right alongside you, Rae?" he asked.

Kaylene Thomas's voice echoed on the receiver. "Not precisely, Dane. Hold on a second . . . it looks to be about six hundred feet below us and about twelve hundred feet to the north."

"Shut down your sonar, wait ten minutes, then take another reading," Brande said.

"Wilco."

The wait was interminable. Otsuka finished the last of her diagnostic checks without finding one fault in the ship's computer hardware or software.

After the designated time lapse, Thomas reported, "They've closed on us by about fifteen feet, Dane. They are using active sonar to track us."

"I don't like that a damned bit, Chief," Dokey said, though not on the acoustic telephone. He had a headset in place, but had shut off the mike.

"Tell me why," Brande said.

"The ramming had to be deliberate; with all of the space available down there, an accidental collision just doesn't happen."

"You think," Mayberry put it, "that they want to eliminate evidence? Sink the *DepthFinder?*"

"It's a damned good possibility," Dokey said.

"It's one we won't take a gamble on," Brande said. "Bob, what kind of energy can we spare?"

Mayberry leaned forward to peer at the numbers crowding his screen. "Not much, Chief. Hmmm. Go ahead and have her hit a five-minute burst at top speed. Then, I'll do some more calculations."

Larry Emry came on. "Svetlana is coming around."

"How is she?" Brande asked.

"Groggy. Give her some time."

Otsuka felt a mild sense of relief, but it was tempered by everything else that was taking place.

She tried to visualize the scene fifteen thousand feet down. The damaged *DepthFinder* rising at one hundred feet per minute, struggling to reach the surface before her electrical and oxygen reserves were depleted. And below and behind her, the unknown sub attempting to close and finish the destruction. She wanted to cry.

"Dane," Otsuka said, "I want to know what the vertical closure was."

Brande nodded at her, then turned on the boom mike of his headset. "Rae, do you know if the other sub is gaining on you vertically?"

"It was about seven feet, Dane, but we've lost some rate of ascent."

"How much?"

Emry reported, "We're now at nine-six feet per, Dane."

"Okay, that's still all right. What's your present heading?"

Otsuka keyed in the command for a spreadsheet program, and when it appeared on the screen, began entering calculations, depths, and closure rates.

"Heading one-nine-eight currently," Thomas reported. "We've been coming up in a spiral."

"Forward velocity?"

"No reading on the instruments, Dane. I judge it at about five knots."

"Go to one-eight-zero. Full power for four minutes, then change course to one-five-five for one minute, then cut the power."

"Wilco."

"Get that, Bob?" Brande asked.

"I'm mapping it. We won't lose track of her."

Brande leaned forward and tapped the intercom's button for the bridge.

"Bridge," Alvarez-Sorenson said.

"Connie, we want a heading of one-eight-zero at ten knots."

"You'll get some buffeting," the first mate replied. "We'll be taking the seas broadside."

"Just do it, please."

"Immediately."

Dokey leaned over and looked at Otsuka's screen. "I was doing that, too, but you're faster."

"What have you got, Kim?" Brande asked.

"There's a lot of variables, Dane," she said, "plus we don't know the condition of the other sub. But I think they'll catch up with Kaylene between seven and five thousand feet of depth. And that's if Bob allows two more five-minute runs at full speed."

"I can give you three," Mayberry said. "More than that, we don't get her to the surface with any power left."

"Let's all rerun the numbers," Brande said. "Double-check it. We don't want mistakes made under pressure."

They took their time on the recalculations, but both Mayberry and Otsuka came up with the same dismal results. Dokey ran his own set, but it agreed with what they already had estimated.

"Maybe," Mayberry said, perhaps to be optimistic, "the other sub is also damaged and merely trying to reach the surface as fast as possible."

Brande went back to his microphone. "Rae, take another sonar reading."

Three minutes later, Thomas said, "He's not gaining on us right now, and in fact, I widened the gap by ten yards. However, he turned to follow us when I hit him with the sonar."

Otsuka thought she detected a much higher degree of anxiety in Thomas's voice.

Brande said, "Goddamn it!" On the acoustic, he said, "Rae, jettison your tow."

"I really don't want to do that, Dane. Find me another option."

Otsuka thought about it and said, "What we have, Dane, is Sneaky Pete."

Brande considered the implications for thirty seconds. "Go, Kim."

"I'm flying him," Dokey said.

"Whatever," Otsuka told him.

Brande keyed his mike. "All right, Rae, hold on to *Sarscan* for a few more minutes. We're coming up with a possible alternative."

Otsuka moved to the fifth computer console and set it up, hooking in the joystick control board, while Dokey and a half dozen willing deckhands retrieved one of the Sneaky Petes from its cushioned shelf on the port side.

The small robot was about five feet long, and its three angled propellers made it highly maneuverable. Strictly a search vehicle, it mounted only video and still cameras, and it was controlled and powered by a thin tethered cable from the host vehicle.

"I want two reels," Dokey said.

Each reel contained five thousand feet of cable, and after one reel was emptied, operation had to be suspended while the cable from the other reel was connected.

Two people attacked the reels, which were on their own castered platforms, released their tie-downs, and started pushing them toward the big doors.

When the doors were opened, mist and spray filtered in. The sea was much louder than Otsuka had realized, and the *Orion* was pitching more now that she had changed course.

It was probably the fastest deployment the MVU crews had ever made, especially in hostile seas. Sneaky Pete was in the water, descending, within fifteen minutes.

She activated his video, and the screen filled with a greenish vista containing a school of bonito. She angled the translation stick forward, and Sneaky began his dive. She added full power, to pull cable off the reel, and turned him to the south.

Bob Mayberry had brought up the ship's sonar, and he now had a waterfall display showing on his screen. "Got Sneaky," he said.

"How about the subs?" Brande asked.

"Still way too deep, Dane."

Dokey came back in from the stern deck and stood behind her. He was soaking wet.

"I'll take him now, Kim."

"And die from cold. Go change clothes."

"Kim . . ."

"There's plenty of time."

She hoped that was true.

Dokey turned and headed for their cabin.

An hour and twenty minutes later, with Dokey seated at the controls, Brande was talking him into position using the *Orion*'s sonar, which was picking up vague and intermittent contacts with both subs, and oral reports from the submersible. *DepthFinder* had lost her ability to calculate longitude, but Thomas was giving them latitude and depth.

Otsuka sat in a chair drawn up next to Dokey and listened to Thomas's voice on the speaker. "Depth now six-one-four-four, Dane. I'd like to use the video."

"Not just now," Mayberry cut in. "You'd need the lights, and I don't want that draw."

"Try the sonar," Brande told her.

A few minutes later, Thomas said, "Not good. He's directly aft, fifty yards away."

Dokey glanced at the sonar, then at Emry's chart on the screen next to him.

"I need her to turn left, Chief. Ten degrees."

"Turn left by ten points," Dane ordered.

"Turning now," Thomas reported.

"Right there!" Dokey yelled.

The screen showed Sneaky Pete's view. It was a dark, empty sea, illuminated by the halogen flood-lights. Otsuka estimated a range of visibility of perhaps thirty yards. At first she didn't see it, but then

DepthFinder emerged from the murk, headed directly at the ROV.

"We've got you on camera," Brande reported. "Maintain your heading."

"You look good," Dokey added.

Otsuka didn't think so. As the ROV approached, quickly at a combined closure rate of fifteen knots, the lights and camera picked up the evidence of the collision. The starboard side of the sub was heavily damaged, with fiberglass chunks protruding from what once had been a sleek hull.

Dokey didn't slow down Sneaky Pete a bit. He angled back the descent and passed directly over the oncoming submersible. Her tail fins disappeared from view at the bottom of the screen, and Dokey nudged the nose down again.

Seconds later, the alien sub appeared on the screen.

"It's one of AquaGeo's," Dokey said.

"I think we knew that," Brande said.

"Yeah, but now we've got her on videotape, Chief."

"And film," Otsuka said.

"I don't think so," Dokey said. "We aren't likely to get the film back."

The AquaGeo sub, like *DepthFinder,* was not moving under power, but coasting upward on buoyancy. As they watched, the twin propellers began to rotate.

Alarmed, Otsuka said, "They're going to catch her!"

"How do you feel about a quarter-million dollars, Dane?" Dokey asked.

"Spend it!" Brande said.

Dokey picked out the port propeller as his target and dove Sneaky Pete into it.

The screen went black.

1421 Hours Local, DepthFinder
33° 39' 48" North, 139° 9' 57" West

DepthFinder reached the surface with its typical urge, as a result of her momentum, to fly clear of the surface, then bounced back.

Svetlana Polodka could tell that the weather had gotten worse since they first submerged. The forty-ton sub rocked and pitched in the waves. It made her roll back and forth in her seat.

"I want to get out," she said.

It was something she had to do.

"Won't be long now, Svet," Emry told her. "Hang on for a few more minutes. It's raining out there."

She did not really hear him. She was aware that she was not tracking well, that concentration was difficult. It seemed as if only minutes had passed since they had launched, but she knew that could not be right.

She did not worry about it.

There was something about another submersible, but she did not remember the details. It seemed strange that another submersible was on her mind. Maybe she was supposed to be aboard it.

She did know that she was sick. Her stomach was rebelling, churning. She had a terrible headache. Her head throbbed, pain racing between her temples. It was caused by the stale, dry air of the sphere's environment.

She knew that.

"I must breathe," she said.

She turned to look at Emry. "Please. I will die if I do not breathe."

Emry looked at Thomas.

Thomas's face was very white in the dimness. The dimness came and went.

"Let's just crack the hatch open," Thomas said.

"I will do it," Polodka yelped and then scrambled up out of her seat.

Emry settled back to let her pass, but held up both of his arms to steady her. She got her feet up on the back of her seat, felt Emry's hands gripping her calves. Stood up and found the hatch wheel with her own hands.

She spun the wheel, the locks released, and she shoved it open.

The wonderful ocean air rushed in. It was accompanied by big splashes of cold raindrops that felt very good on her face. Even the saltiness was welcome. She stuck out her tongue to taste it.

The sub was pitching back and forth, shunting her from side to side. She shook one foot free of Emry's grasp, got her toe hooked on the steel rung, and pushed upward.

A large waved rolled under the sub; it heeled, and she banged into the side of the hatch, spreading the sealing grease over her sweater.

Her sweater?

It was yellow. She did not recognize it.

Hooking her elbows through the hatch and on the deck, she levered herself out of the sub, got her knees under her, then stood up and gripped the edge of the sail.

God, it felt so good.

The rain pelted her, stinging a little, but she did not mind.

Below, she heard Emry telling Kaylene Thomas, "I'll go up with her."

Drinking deep gulps of the fresh air, she spun around, almost dancing. The deck bucked under her.

There was the ship.

It was so close, and getting closer.

Her vision tunnelled, and her head seemed to contract.

Darkness encroached, then ebbed away.

It was going to be all right.

1427 Hours Local, The Arienne
33° 39' 48" North, 139° 9' 57" West

Mark Jacobs was on the bridge with Overton and Debbie Lane. Dickie Folger had the helm, and Jacobs and Overton both leaned against the forward bulkhead, peering through the windshield, scanning the misty day for something.

"There!" Overton exclaimed. "Off to the left!"

Jacobs saw running lights, barely flickering in the distance.

"Come port a few degrees, Dickie," he said.

A few minutes later, the ship took form.

"That's her," Overton said, "the *Orion.*"

Jacobs recognized the silhouette. "You may have been right, Wilson."

"Of course, I'm right. My instincts are good."

Folger eased back on the throttles as they closed the distance to the research ship.

Jacobs noted that the area under the big yoke on the stern of the ship was vacant. He also saw that there were a lot of people on the starboard and aft decks. They were all concentrating on something forward and starboard of the ship.

He followed the track of their interest and soon spotted the small submarine bouncing in the troughs.

"Let's stay back a little, Dickie. It looks as if they're about to recover their submersible."

"Sure thing, Mark," Folger said and took a slight turn to the north.

"There's somebody on top of the sub," Overton said.

Jacobs could make out the yellow-clad figure. It seemed to be weaving about, but that might have been the result of the rough seas and the way the submersible was being tossed around.

And as he watched, the figured slumped, pitched forward, and went over the sail. The body bounced once on the deck, and then slid into the sea.

1441 Hours Local, The Orion
33° 39′ 48″ North, 139° 9′ 57″ West

The minute he saw Polodka collapse forward onto the sail, Brande ripped off his slicker.

When the submarine lurched and threw her over the sail, he stepped over the railing, leaned forward, and dove into the sea.

Otsuka yelled behind him, "Dane!"

It wasn't one of his best dives. He hit the surface of the sea almost flat, and an oncoming wave slapped him off course, rolling him sideways. He went under only a few feet, kicked his shoes off, and emerged on the surface swimming hard, knifing his hands into the water, pulling until his muscles hurt. His feet flailed behind him.

The water was cold, but after a few seconds, the sensation died. The sub was twenty yards in front of him, but Polodka had slipped off on the opposite side, and he angled to the right, to pass around the bow.

His clothing was immediately waterlogged, and he fought their weight as well as the eight-foot-high waves. The sub appeared and disappeared as he rose and fell in the troughs, struggling his way up to a crest, then falling over it. The rain peppered the surface, and his mouth filled with water when he breathed. He spat it out and concentrated on making his strokes as powerful as possible.

It took him three minutes to reach the *DepthFinder,* and he swam clear of the bow, twenty feet away, so as not to be smashed up against it.

On the other side, he found an empty, tempestuous sea.

Mayberry was up in the sail now, and he yelled, "Over there, Dane! She went down there!"

Brande aimed for the spot where Mayberry was pointing. A wave rolled over him, shoving him toward the sub.

He kicked hard, pulling water with his hands, fighting for a clear breath. Forty feet took forever to traverse.

"There! There!"

Brande filled his lungs, ducked his head under, rolled his legs up, and dove.

Without a mask, his vision was blurry. The overcast day didn't allow much light to penetrate.

He kept kicking, driving himself downward, looking to his left and right.

She wasn't there.

Driving downward.

Svet. Come to me, sweetheart.

Down.

And at last, he had to reverse direction. He bobbed to the surface, gulping air.

Then dove again.

He went as deep as he could go ten times, but he never saw her again.

NOVEMBER 19

Nuclear Detonation:
34° 25′ 19″ North, 140° 1′ 3″ West

THIRTEEN

0300 Hours Local, The Orion
33° 39′ 10″ North, 139° 10′ 4″ West

Okey Dokey had deployed their second Sneaky Pete from the *Orion* in the search for Svetlana Polodka, but the results were negative. It took too much time to retrieve the cable attached to the first Sneaky Pete. Or which had been attached. The first ROV was gone, cleanly amputated from the cable, and most likely mangled in the propeller housing of the AquaGeo submersible.

No one on board the *Orion* had worried about AquaGeo's vehicle. It had slipped off their sonar, headed for the bottom of the ocean.

In the rough seas, it had taken them over two hours to recover both *DepthFinder* and *Sarscan II*, utilizing every available hand.

Brande was worried about both Thomas and Emry. Rae wouldn't admit it, but he thought she was suffering from some degree of shock. He had ordered her to bed—orders that she didn't accept very well, but she went up to the cabin after a short argument. He doubted that she slept much. With his own adrenaline levels, he hadn't slept at all.

Emry was blaming himself—he should have done this, he should have done that. Brande's and Dokey's consolations and rationales didn't seem to help him at all.

A long, hot shower and a fresh set of clothing had taken care of Brande's immediate physical needs— the bone-deep cold to which he had subjected himself, but he too felt extreme anguish over Polodka's loss.

And he couldn't help but blame AquaGeo.

As well as himself. He should have exerted his macho side and not let the women make the dive.

God, he could have lost Rae.

The more he stewed over it, the higher the rage built. Brande was not quick-tempered, or even one to harbor anger for lengthy periods, but occasionally some inequity or injustice caused him to build a slow head of steam. He didn't normally share his ire with anyone else. At the moment, he wished that Bull Kontas would move a little faster.

Most of the crew and mission members had spent the night evaluating the damage to *DepthFinder,* which had been wheeled inside the lab and which dominated the space available.

Brande had spent the night in the wardroom's first booth, utilizing Emry's computer terminal to compose reports and angry letters to the Maritime Commission, the United States Department of State, the Coast Guard, and the Australian government. He had been about to ship them off when he reread them and decided they were first drafts.

He grabbed the phone off the bulkhead.

"Suarez."

"Paco, get hold of Hampstead for me."

"*Sí, Jefe.*"

When Hampstead came on the line, he said, "You're damned lucky I came into the office early, Dane."

"Not so lucky, Avery."

"Yes. That's why I came in early. Didn't sleep too well, either, as a matter of fact. What more have you learned about the collision?"

Brande recounted the events of the previous day.

"Jesus Christ! Svetlana's dead?"

"We haven't recovered the body."

"Oh, shit! What about the other sub?"

"We haven't looked for it. And I'm not going to look for it."

"It's evidence, Dane. It's evidence."

"To hell with it. I'm going back to that subsurface station and—"

"Ease up, Dane. Tell me what happened again. On the bottom."

Brande took a deep breath and recalled what Thomas had told him. She had been shaky, and it had taken some time to get it all from her.

"Rae had the command. She was approaching what we're calling Site Number Eight, the November seventeenth detonation. They had already recorded heavy traces of radiation, and Rae had both a floor crawler and the other sub on the sonar. Two hundred yards from the site, the AquaGeo sub turned toward them. Larry tried to raise it on the acoustic phone, but didn't get a response."

"None?"

"Not verbal. The sub nosed around a little. They looked at each other with the video cameras."

"Did Kaylene see them? The operators?" Hampstead asked.

"Vaguely, through their ports. Two males, she thought, but she didn't have a clear view."

"And then what?"

"The AquaGeo sub went after the tow cable. Rae wasn't sure what was going on, but she felt the jolt when it hit, and she turned back hard, trying to put slack in the cable. The AquaGeo sub turned into her and slammed into the right side of *DepthFinder.* Rae immediately dropped the weights and began the ascent."

"Damn."

"They tried to stop her, Avery. Chased her most of the way up."

"You're sure?"

Brande told him how they had used Sneaky Pete to stop the pursuit.

"We've got evidence, Avery. We've got the videotape recorded from Sneaky Pete."

"Which shows that you attacked their sub, right?"

"It also shows that they were in pursuit," Brande insisted.

"Maybe. For the time being, just keep that tape to yourself, will you?"

"For what reason?"

"I want to check with some of the others involved."

"Svetlana's dead, Avery."

"Christ, Dane, I know that! I'll get on the horn and get somebody in gear. What else are you doing?"

"I wrote some letters."

Hampstead was silent for a few minutes, then said, "Hold off on the letters, too. File your required reports about a death at sea with the appropriate agencies. Send me a copy I can give to the task force."

"I can't be objective about this, Avery."

"Try, please. Give me a chance to work out something on this end."

Brande sighed. "Two more things, Avery."

"There would be."

"There was another detonation in late afternoon. Mel got the direction and range pretty well pinpointed with the ship's sonar."

"I'll check with Golden. What else?"

"The *Washington Post* is here."

"You're shitting me."

"Not at all. Wilson Overton is on board a Greenpeace boat a half-mile off our starboard."

"You didn't talk to him?"

"No. I've refused three requests for interviews, but he knows that something is going on. They saw Svetlana fall into the sea, and they saw our rescue efforts. Mark Jacobs brought his boat in close and offered to help."

"What about the other stuff, the encounter? Does Overton know about it?"

"I don't think so. It was all subsurface. But if Mark Jacobs learns what's going on, he could call in some friendly environmentalist buddies, and we might end up in a real brouhaha."

"This is getting out of hand, Dane."

"It's past that," Brande said.

After he hung up, he called up to the bridge on the intercom.

"Bridge," Mel Sorenson answered.

"Mel, where are we?"

Sorenson gave him the coordinates. "We've been holding station where we picked up *DepthFinder*."

"Let's get on a northwest heading and look for Site Nine, the one you picked up yesterday. Contact Bull Kontas and let him know about our position and course."

"We're continuing with this, Dane?"

"If *DepthFinder* is repairable at sea, I'm damned sure going to find out what's going on."

0450 Hours Local, The Orion
33° 39′ 52″ North, 139° 12′ 14″ West

Kaylene Thomas didn't sleep, though she stayed in her bunk for six hours. When she got up and showered and checked the mirror, she saw the black smudges under her eyes. She had done some crying, too.

There was a void in her life.

She and Polodka had not been particularly close, but they had been friends. She had respected Svetlana's mind and abilities. Like others, she had been amused and empathetic as she watched the Russian woman learn about Western culture. Most of Thomas's night had been spent with recriminations. If she had exhibited some leadership, told Svetlana to stay put, told Larry to hold on to her, done almost anything. . . .

The tears began to well in her eyes once again.

Wiping her eyes with a towel, she dressed in long johns and a jumpsuit. It took a few seconds to locate her running shoes, which she had kicked into two different corners of the cabin. Had he known, the admiral—her father, would have raised hell about the sloppy behavior.

She went down to the wardroom for coffee, stopping on the bridge for long enough to find out that Brande had told Sorenson to get under way. The *Orion* had her bows into the waves, and the deck felt more stable. It had stopped raining, but in the darkness beyond the windshield, she detected low-hanging clouds that were blotting out the stars.

"The *Arienne* is still with us, darlin'," Sorenson pointed out.

She saw the navigation lights off to the starboard by a quarter-mile.

"Reporters are tenacious, Mel."

"Not to mention Greenpeace people."

In the wardroom, she found Brande stretched out on one of the bench seats in the first booth, his long legs hanging over the end. He was sound asleep, and she nearly woke him in order to find out what he had been doing all night.

Instead, she filled a mug with coffee and carried it across the corridor to the lab.

The submersible nearly filled the lab. The top of her sail was within six inches of the overhead, and her broad hull didn't leave much room for people to move between the sub and the computers and workbenches. One had to be careful to dodge the tie-downs; someone was always tripping over them.

She saw that somebody had mopped the deck of the

water that had dripped from the sub, and someone
else had used a power saw to cut away the ripped
fiberglass on the starboard side. She moved around
the hull to her left and peered into the exposed cavity.

Dokey was sitting in a castered chair backed up to
a computer console, studying the inside of the hull.
He didn't look happy.

"What have we got, Okey?"

He pulled another chair over for her to sit in and
turned so that their knees almost touched. He searched
her eyes.

"How are you doing, Kaylene?"

"I'll be fine."

"That's what all the old hands say."

"Really."

"Just remember that the Fates are involved, love.
Not much you can do to change their minds."

She gave him a weak smile. "I'll remember."

"All right, then. Back to your question. We've got
a mashed submersible, and that pisses me no end."

"Can we make her operational? And safe?"

"I'll know in a little while. The main concern is
the pressure tank for the oxygen. I've got a couple
of the guys testing it for integrity right now. It was
shoved sideways a couple inches, but I think the oxy-
gen-feed problem you encountered had to do with a
crimped supply line to the main pressure hull. That,
we can replace easily. The tank, we can't."

"Batteries?" she asked.

"Not as bad as I thought. The starboard battery
tray was mangled, along with the cells of seven batteries. The center tray was bent up a little, and we
lost a couple batteries there, too. Mainly, the cable

connections were snapped, and that's why you lost so much of your electrical reserve."

"I know we've got replacements for the batteries. What about the trays?"

"That grad student, Alicia Walters? You ought to see her at work with an acetylene torch. She's a sculptress."

"Sculptor."

"Not in my world," Dokey said.

Thomas had to grin at him. "Oh, hell! All right."

"Then, there are the other little things."

"Such as?"

"The impact must have been a hell of a lot stronger than I imagined. We've got some electronic components inside the hull that were damaged by vibration or overloaded when an electrical surge hit. That's why so many of the circuit breakers tripped. We're checking out each, and we may not have replacements for everything."

"We won't deploy unless every system is perfect, Okey."

"That'll be up to Dane, love."

"Not necessarily," she insisted.

"Up to Dane and you and me, then."

"That could come up two votes to one, Okey."

"That's the way it might be, yes."

0875 Hours Local, The Arienne
33° 39′ 52″ North, 139° 12′ 14″ West

"Damn it, Ned, that's all I've got for now."

Overton's editor said, "An unidentified person fell

into the sea and was not rescued. Man or woman, Wilson?"

"I couldn't tell at that distance." Overton shifted the phone to his left hand.

"We don't have much here," Nelson said. "Try to talk to Brande, again."

"He's adamant. No interviews."

"We can't go with what we've got."

"You've got the fact that MVU is diving on a Pacific site that the Navy's interested in—"

"From unspecified sources."

". . . and at a time of year that's not normal for deep-submergence expeditions. Plus, there's the hard data from the Earthquake Center. Brande's going to have to file a report on the accident with some agency. Send someone out to check on that."

Overton heard Nelson's pencil scratching on paper. "What do you think is down there, Wilson?"

"I don't have the foggiest."

"It's too thin. I need a kicker."

Overton hesitated. "I've got one, but I want to save it until I know more."

"What?"

"The *DepthFinder* was heavily damaged. When they lifted it out of the water, we saw that the right side was caved in."

"You get pictures?"

"Not good ones, what with the weather, but yeah, I did."

"Fax me the pictures."

Overton hung up and looked over at the banquette. Debbie Lane and Mick Freelander were leaning over a map with Jacobs. Dickie Folger was in the galley making up another big pot of coffee. He made lousy coffee.

Overton crossed the deck uneasily because of the sway and pitch and stood beside the table, gripping its edge and watching them. Lane's long, dark hair kept falling on the map, and she kept shoving it back over her shoulder. She was pretty good-looking, Overton thought, but too intense.

The map had a series of crosses marked on it, derived from the five coordinates that Overton had gotten from the Earthquake Information Center. Looking at them on a map for the first time, Overton was aware of the shallow arc they made.

"That doesn't happen in nature," he said.

Jacobs looked up at him. "No, it doesn't. What do you think, Wilson?"

He slid into the booth next to Lane. "Man-made."

"But why?" Freelander asked.

"I can't answer that," he admitted.

"Here's something else," Jacobs said, moving the point of his stubby pencil to a spot on the map north and west of the last X.

"What's that?"

"That's where we are now. Or were, until the *Orion* started moving again, and we decided to follow along."

"That's only where the submersible surfaced," Debbie Lane said. "There's no telling where it first dove."

"Except," Jacobs said, moving the pencil northward on his map, "if they went down about here, it would be in line with the arc."

"You're saying," Overton said, "that there's been

another earthquake we don't know about, and that Brande was investigating it."

"Perhaps."

"And these earthquakes are man-made."

"Perhaps."

"And that Brande's sub ran into something he didn't know was there?"

"Or ran into an earthquake," Freelander said.

"Or ran into somebody," Debbie Lane said.

1020 Hours Local
San Francisco, California

"Have you got the *Melbourne* back, Penny?" Paul Deride asked. "That's an expensive piece of machinery."

"Munro's still towing it back and is about an hour out," she told him. "There's some damage to the bow, the antenna system, and one of the propulsion units, but McBride and his assistant are all right."

"It's repairable?"

"Yes, damn it!"

"Well, that's what counts. Those hummers are too bloody expensive to replace every day." Deride glanced over at the suite's dining room table, where Anthony Camden was on another phone. The top of the table was littered with stacks of paper, most of them drafts of legal documents.

"What do we do about Brande?" Glenn asked.

"Nothing. I expect he got the message that he's not to intrude on our operations." He put his booted feet up on the coffee table and leaned back on the couch.

"He's bound to report the incident."

"So what, Penny? We're within our rights to protect our site. Hell, for all they know, we could have been planting another explosive charge, and old Mac was warning them off. And if Brande makes a big stink in any of the international organizations, we'll just sue. We've done that before."

"What if they get some kind of injunction or mount an investigation?"

"You've been through this before, Penny. Anthony will have them tied up in court for ten years, and by the time there's a judgement, we'll have played out the vein and be on our way. Don't you worry your sweet head about it."

"So I can proceed with the program?"

"Certainly. You do what you do best, and Anthony and I will take care of the odds and ends."

"Then that's what I'll do, Uncle Paul."

Deride thought she sounded awfully relieved. There were still some things she had to learn about dealing with people in business, but she was coming along.

He replaced the receiver in its cradle and got up to refill his coffee cup. Then he sat down at the table opposite Camden and waited for the man to finish his conversation.

When he finally finished talking to Harriet in the Sydney office, Camden hung up and said, "They're making inquiries about us, Paul."

"Who are 'they'?"

"American agencies. The State Department, the Commerce Department, the CIA."

"CIA? That's a first."

"Also, we've got a letter requesting information about our activities and intent in the Pacific. That's from the Vice President's Office."

"I wouldn't bother responding," Deride grinned. "Hell, if they can't get the President involved, it's nothing to get excited about."

"I suspect the State Department will put pressure on the Australian government, too."

"Big deal. We're still operating offshore."

Camden leaned forward and put his elbows on the table. "We can't stonewall for too long. At some point, we should make our position clear."

Deride thought about that. "Okay. File for a bloody injunction against Brande. He's interfering with our work."

"Good. I'll do that."

1430 Hours Local
Washington, D.C.

Now, he was getting some action, if inaction could be considered any movement at all.

Carl Unruh thought it was damned unfortunate that it took a death to do it.

After a dozen phone calls—some people were reluctant to call him back—he had the same task force group gathered in the same conference room at State, and they all looked rather glum after his recitation of the events leading to Svetlana Polodka's death.

Marlys Anstett's quizzical eyebrows were raised even higher. "It was a drowning?"

"Prompted by an overtly offensive action that induced a brain concussion," Unruh told her.

"We'd have a hell of a time proving that, Mr. Unruh, if we don't even have the body. I don't see Justice taking a position on this. We will need much more."

"Well, Jesus H. Christ!"

"The best we can do right off, Carl," Admiral Ben Delecourt said, "is a show of strength. The *California* and her escorts will be on the scene shortly. They can watch over any future dives."

"If Brande can even get his submersible repaired sufficiently to make another dive," Sam Porter said. "Perhaps the presence of warships is a moot point?"

Unruh wasn't going to argue with the man from Commerce. If he wanted information from Commerce, he'd ask Hampstead.

"We sent a strongly worded letter by fax to the AquaGeo offices in Washington and San Francisco, as well as their headquarters in Sydney, over the Vice President's signature," Pamela Stroh said. She shook her white tresses sadly. "We haven't yet received a response."

"That's it?"

"These things take time, Mr. Unruh."

"What about State?" Unruh asked.

"We asked some questions of the Australian foreign affairs department, and they were congenial enough, but they also declined to become involved in entrepreneurial disputes," Damon Gilliland said.

Gilliland was wearing the same blue wool suit, Unruh noted, but his tie now belonged to a different regiment.

"So," he said, "in two days, no one has accomplished anything. That about sum it up?"

Delecourt said, "We've had more seafloor detonations. Have you been following them?"

"Yes. And there's now a change in the pattern," Unruh told him.

"What kind of change?" Anstett wanted to know.

"They're still following the same trend line, Miss Anstett, but where the first six events took place about thirty to forty miles apart, the last two have been eighty to ninety miles apart."

"So they're moving faster," Delecourt said.

"It looks that way, Ben, yes. From our perspective, it looks more ominous. The Earthquake Center, without wanting attribution, just in case they're wrong, suggests that a likely trigger area would be in the vicinity of thirty-six degrees, fifty-eight minutes north, one hundred-forty-one degrees, twenty-eight minutes west."

"Is the energy output for the devices still the same?" Gilliland asked.

"They seem to be larger, perhaps in the ten-kiloton range," Delecourt said. "The Navy intelligence analysts think that they might be going deeper. Whatever they're looking for may be farther down than they expected."

"Are they actually drilling wells, or are they mining?" Porter asked.

"Not on any of the sites Brande has explored, beyond the hole they drill for the explosive," Unruh said. "He does think they might be going after manganese since the samples he took off the bottom show a strong concentration. If that's the case, Brande thinks they'll start with the earlier sites, maybe Site Number Four, bring in their equipment and set up shop. They'll then continue moving the equipment northeast as they follow the vein."

"What's the likelihood of that, Carl?" Delecourt asked.

"One of my people did a worldwide search on AquaGeo ships," Unruh said. "There are three freighters at sea, out of New Zealand, headed in the right direction. We're trying to find out if their cargoes might be mining equipment."

"And this pattern you see," Anstett said. "What if it continues?"

Unruh looked at his watch. "Let's see. Today is Wednesday, the nineteenth. On Monday, November twenty-fourth, California goes into the sea."

FOURTEEN

The research vessel had her cycloidal propellers extended and was gripping her place on the watery earth with dedicated tenacity. In the cloudy, cold, and damp mist that swirled over the stern deck, Brande and Dokey toured the exterior of the submersible.

DepthFinder wasn't as pretty as she used to be. The gaping hole in her right side, which had been nearly nine feet wide and six feet high, had been covered, but it had been covered with what they had on hand, which were clear plastic panels. The panels were only thirty mils thick, so they had bonded four layers in place, butting the 3- x 4-foot panels to each other and overlapping them for strength. The thickness of four sheets created an opacity that prevented a clear view into the hull, though the ragged edges of the covered hole were apparent.

Additionally, three twelve-foot-long, three-inch angle irons had been bolted and bonded in place horizontally across the damaged region to provide additional rigidity to the outer hull. The sub's original sleekness had disappeared in a matter of hours.

Checking to make certain that Thomas wasn't within earshot of them, Brande told Dokey, "Ingrid wouldn't approve of this, would she?"

"Hey, Chief, she goes about these things like a damned structural engineer. You and me, we're from the duct-tape generation. Can you imagine a NAS-CAR stock-car race being completed without forty rolls of duct tape?"

They ducked under the bow line and walked around to check the port side.

"If we're photographed," Dokey said, "make certain you present your good side to the camera."

"Will do, Okey."

The comment made him take a glance at the *Arienne*. She was still trailing along, though as soon as they had stopped, she had moved closer and was now standing off the stern by about two hundred yards. With the low visibility, he couldn't identify any of the figures aboard, but he saw shadows moving in the cabin and on the flying bridge. Overton had radioed them a half hour earlier, seeking another interview.

Again making sure that Thomas wasn't close by, Brande asked, "You comfortable with the systems check?"

"Ah, hell yes. Sometimes the technology just gets in the way, Dane. You have to remember what we first started diving with. That was a Model T, compared to the Saturn."

On the decision to proceed with the dive, he and

Dokey had voted Thomas down. They had felt they could get by quite easily without a few of the backup systems and still cameras they had been unable to repair. The important life-support, control, and propulsion systems were, if not in A-1, at least in A-2 condition. Dokey called them A-1b.

With their physical inspection completed, Brande ordered all of the access hatches closed, and the deck crew rushed in to batten them down. They stepped back into the lab to doff their slickers and pull on sweaters.

Otsuka was waiting in the crowd gathered there, already dressed for the dive. Mayberry had wanted the third seat, but Otsuka had forced a coin flip and won.

"Ready, Kim?" Brande asked.

"I still think I got screwed," Mayberry said. "We'd better flip again."

"No," she said. "It is my turn."

Thomas stood to one side, watching him with disapproval. Brande thought she was going to protest again, but she kept her disenchantment to herself.

He moved over in front of her. "We'll be back in a few hours, Rae."

"This isn't a run to the grocery store."

"Think of it that way," he said.

Reluctantly, almost, she took his hand. "If anything at all looks bad, you'll abort the dive?"

"Of course."

She squeezed his hand once, and then Brande, Dokey, and Otsuka trotted through the stern doors out into the mist and scampered carefully up the rain-slickened scaffolding, reaching for the submersible's sail.

1735 Hours Local, The Arienne
34° 25′ 19″ North, 140° 1′ 3″ West

Jacobs, along with Overton and everyone else on board, watched from the stern well deck as the submersible was lifted from the deck of the *Orion* and lowered into the sea. Jacobs held a pair of 7 x 50 binoculars to his eyes, and when *DepthFinder* twisted on her suspension line toward him, noted the repairs made to the right side. Even in the dim light of the overcast evening, the sheen of the patch appeared inadequate. Spray quickly coated the lenses and blurred his view.

Debbie Lane noticed the repair, also. "That doesn't look very professional to me."

"What? What?" Overton asked.

Jacobs handed him the binoculars, but the sub had already settled into the sea.

He wondered if Lane was thinking along the same lines that he was. He asked, "Debbie?"

"I think it's strange that they're diving with an obviously badly damaged submersible," she said. "We're pretty sure the depths here are extreme, and therefore, the risks greater. Wilson made a good point, first of all, about diving in this region at this time of year. If, as he suspects, the Navy is involved with this, then someone, somewhere, is worried about something."

"What would it be?" he asked.

"A nuclear submarine that's been lost?" she said. "Brande rescued one of those a couple years ago, didn't he?"

"That was the *Los Angeles*," Overton said. "But here, we've got all these seismic disturbances. I don't think it has to do with a sub."

Overton's source at the Earthquake Center had given him the coordinates of two more disturbances, but according to the Loran readings, the Marine Visions people were diving in a new location right now. Jacobs felt certain, however, that when they checked Colorado again, they would find that a new disturbance had been recorded.

Freelander suggested, "Maybe it's a plane that went down. Spy plane with all kinds of secret stuff on it. They'd want it back pretty bad, wouldn't they?"

"You'd think there'd be a lot of military hanging around if that was the case," Lane said.

Jacobs looked around at the horizons. His range of visibility was limited to perhaps a mile. "There's certainly no Navy presence."

Overton seemed to have not heard him. He had a firm grip on the railing that ran along the stern gunwale. The pitching of the deck had made him a little pasty-faced.

"Brande's always been good about talking to me in the past," Overton said. "The fact that he won't talk now is suspicious in itself."

Jacobs recalled his earlier conversation with Brande. "I don't think he lied to me, either. He just didn't give me everything he knew. We need more information, and we need it right away."

"I'll call the Navy," Overton said. "If I ask a direct question, they'll have to answer."

"And then I'll call Hap Wilson on the *Oriental Rose,*" Jacobs said. "Hap has some expertise in subsurface issues."

0015 Hours Local
College Park, Maryland

Avery Hampstead had watched the second part of *Lonesome Dove,* and his dream was pleasantly nostalgic until it was jarred by the ring of the telephone. There shouldn't be telephones in West Texas.

Muttering to himself, and trying not to wake Alicia, he rolled his legs to the floor and fumbled for the receiver in the blue light of the radio dial on the nightstand.

"Hampstead."

"Avery, this is Kaylene Thomas."

"Kaylene." He forced the sleep out of his voice and eyes. "Is something wrong?"

"No. I needed someone to talk to."

Hampstead sighed to himself and decided not to tell her that it was after midnight in Maryland.

"Let me get to another phone," he whispered.

He shoved the telephone under the pillow and walked to the kitchen to pick up.

"I'm here."

"Sorry for waking you up. I tried to call Adrienne, but she wasn't back at her hotel, yet."

Hampstead felt a kinship. Whenever he was troubled, he called Adrienne, too.

"Where's Dane?"

"They're about an hour away from reaching Site Number Ten. After they come back up, I want you to talk to him."

"About what, Kaylene?"

"About Svetlana. I think he's very angry, deep inside, and I think he might take some unnecessary risks."

"I don't know what I could tell him, Kaylene."

"For one thing, you could tell him that revenge belongs to the Justice Department."

"Uh . . ."

"Uh, what, Avery?"

"Well, so far, Justice has declined to act."

"What!"

"It has something to do with a lack of sufficient evidence," he said.

"Evidence! Damn it, Avery! I was there. I know. I'm an eyewitness, for God's sake."

"Well, there's the matter of intent, Kaylene."

"Goddamn it, Avery! I know they intended to ram us, and they did."

"Kaylene, dear, listen. I know—"

She hung up on him.

Leaving Hampstead with the thought that he wasn't very good at solace, not like Adrienne was. And wondering what might happen if he ended up with a whole bunch of Marine Visions scientists mad at *both* AquaGeo and their own government. After a trip to the bedroom to hang up the other phone, he called information and asked for the number of Adrienne's hotel in Seattle.

2032 Hours Local, The DepthFinder
34° 25′ 19″ North, 140° 1′ 4″ West

"I've found a signal," Otsuka said.

"What kind of signal?" Brande asked her from his place in the left controller seat.

"I was scanning the acoustic spectrum. I've located the frequencies on which they're transmitting, but all of them are scrambled. However, on another frequency, I also hear a steady Morse code transmission. I think they've planted a signal device."

"Locator beacon," Dokey said. "I'll bet it's a homing device."

"For construction or mining crews, you think?" Brande asked him.

"You give me the odds, I'll tell you whether I'd bet on it or not, Chief."

"I'll pass, Okey."

Brande leaned forward to peer through his port. Without *Sarscan II* in tow, they were able to "fly" closer to the bottom terrain. Dokey was piloting, using the forward-scanning sonar and the six-million candlepower floodlights, which gave them about fifty feet of visibility, to warn him of imminent obstructions. The audio output from the sonar was linked into Dokey's headset.

They were twenty feet off the bottom, following a down-sloping ridge, moving along at nine knots. Under the lights, the seafloor looked barren and lunar. The projections of rock created utterly black shadows that would have been excellent hiding spots, if there were any living organisms which wanted to hide from them. At 18,600 feet of depth, though, anything living that was large enough to see would be in a pressure hull.

The whole panorama was stark and gray.

"We should see something in a couple minutes," Otsuka said. "We're coming up on the coordinates."

They had descended from the surface in a wide spiral, finding the bottom several miles east of the location of the seabed disturbance. The compass showed that they were aimed along a 281 degree axis.

"How we doing, systems-wise, love?" Dokey asked.

"Everything in the green. She is staying together quite well," Otsuka told him.

Brande felt pretty good about the repairs they had made, though he found himself scanning the readouts more frequently than he normally would and eyeing them with suspicion. He felt they were more untrustworthy than they were supposed to be. He felt colder than usual, too.

"What's the temp, Kim?"

"Balmy, Pacific day, Dane. Thirty-eight degrees, Fahrenheit."

"I was thinking about shedding a couple of these sweaters."

"Uh-uh, Chief. No floor shows, please."

"You can give them to me," Otsuka told him.

Changing clothes would be awkward. On top of their warming layers, they were each wearing a white antiradiation suit. The suit was bulky and hampered movement.

Brande glanced at Dokey. His concentration seemed almost total. He was relatively relaxed in the controller seat, and his gloved fingers gripped the joysticks with apparent tenderness, but his eyes flicked rapidly between the port view and the sonar readout on the center monitor.

DepthFinder rose and fell with the terrain, a roller coaster going downhill. . . . Until a tall escarpment abruptly showed itself on the screen, long before they would have had visual contact.

"The top of that thing's about three hundred feet above us," Brande said.

"The mother of all obstructions," Dokey said, but he already had turned left, and hauled the diving planes into the extreme up position.

The sub spiraled upward, climbing, and had achieved sufficient altitude by the time Dokey returned to his original heading.

Having topped the blockade, the sonar was able to pick out a moving blob.

"Floor crawler," Brande said. "I'm going to release the guard dog."

"Go," Dokey said.

"Let's put the hoods on," he said.

"Sadist."

The radiation hoods of their suits were made of coated fabric, and they had clear Plexiglas visors, but once in place, peripheral vision was restricted. Brande felt like he was turning his head on a lazy Susan to keep himself aware of the instrumentation and other activities.

Brande had already set the switches for control of *Atlas,* and he used the left stick to ease in propulsion for the ROV. He flicked on the robot's video camera and put the image on the left monitor, then turned on *Atlas's* floodlights. He had a view of the underside of *DepthFinder* for a few seconds until the ROV moved out of her sheath and took flight on her own. A quick look at the monitor gauge told him that the tether was unreeling freely behind the robot.

"Find that acoustic channel they're using for voice, Kim," he said. "We won't know what they're saying, but maybe you can tell if the tempo picks up."

"I've got it," she said.

Brande's and Dokey's headsets were tuned into the ship-to-sub channel on the Loudspeaker system, though they had not utilized them in the last hour. Otsuka was listening in on AquaGeo's frequency.

"Sonar shows no subs in the area," Dokey said. "If you don't count us."

"I don't know how many they had available before," Brande said, "but we know for damned sure that they're short one, right now."

Dokey put the bow down, and they glided. A few

minutes later, the huge excavation appeared in the ports. Both the left and right edges of the hole were invisible, hidden by the darkness creeping into their lighted field of view. The far side wasn't yet visible to them, either.

"Larger than the last one," Dokey said.

"They're using more horsepower in those nuclear charges," Otsuka guessed.

"Which is just what we didn't want them to do," Brande said. "I wonder if anyone from Washington is actually talking to anyone from AquaGeo."

"I'd bet it's still in committee, Chief."

Dokey sailed over the near-side lip of the excavation, heading directly across it. Several seconds went by before they saw the other side.

And the floor crawler.

It was parked right at the edge, its manipulator arm fully extended as it gathered rock samples, lifting them into a collector basket mounted on the front of the crawler, between the tracks.

If they had been so busy with their chores that they weren't watching their sonar, the crewmen inside were now aware of them. As he watched, the manipulator arm retracted and the crawler backed quickly away from the lip of the hole, turning away from them.

Dokey went into a right bank, aiming to circle around and come in behind the crawler.

Brande had discussed their tactics on the way down, allowing Otsuka to overhear. He had worried that she might object, but she had wholeheartedly endorsed the strategy Brande and Dokey had devised.

"He's going to hightail it," Brande said. "Headed for the garage."

"The garage is damned far away," Dokey said, straightening out his sticks and bringing *DepthFinder* into line directly behind the scampering crawler.

The crawler dodged around a giant outcropping, but returned to a course of 205 degrees.

"His heading is directly toward that sea habitat," Otsuka said.

"He's making fourteen knots," Brande told Dokey. "I'd guess that's his top end on the level."

"I can outdrag him."

The submersible was making sixteen knots, her twin electric motors spinning fast enough to create a whining vibration in the hull.

Brande watched through his port and saw the back end of the crawler drawing closer. It was in silhouette, outlined by the powerful lights on the front end. The view was hypnotic. He felt as if he could reach through the porthole and touch the crawler. Small clouds of silt rose behind each of the massive tracks as they spun their way across the seabed.

And ahead of him by thirty feet, *Atlas* shot along above the seafloor, responding instantly to the signal inputs of the joysticks.

"He's watching us," Dokey said.

On top of the crawler's spherical hull was a nest of antennas and a remote-controlled video camera. The camera was aimed at them.

"Be careful of the antennas, Dane," Otsuka cautioned.

"Roger, Kim."

Brande didn't intend to damage their communications ability. He wanted them to be able to get a message out. They could send for help, but the message was important, too.

The gap between them closed.

Brande switched his attention to the view on the screen from the ROV. *Atlas* had closed to within ten feet of the crawler, which was bouncing up and down as it traversed the rugged terrain. On the screen, he watched it jolt into a large depression, then bounce back out of it. The ROV slid along smoothly behind it, disappearing into the cloud raised by its passage.

The monitor view was hazy for a moment as *Atlas* passed through the roiling silt. The ROV advanced on the center of the crawler, between the tracks, and the view cleared enough to show him the big induction motors mounted low and behind the crawler's hull, between the tracks. Each motor drove a transmission attached to it that directed power to each of the tracks.

"See anything vulnerable, Okey?"

After a quick look at his screen, Dokey said, "I'd try for those armored cables coming out of the motors, Chief. You only need one, and he goes in circles forever."

"We're going to have to change our design-thinking in the future," Brande said. "We didn't anticipate trying to maneuver both *Atlas* and her manipulator arm while on the move."

"We don't usually go after moving objects," Dokey said. "Not too many objects move down here."

The crawler driver decided to participate in his own destruction. Apparently worried about his exposed rear, he slammed on the brakes and went into a left turn.

Dokey reversed motors so as not to overshoot him, and Brande turned the ROV to follow the crawler, slowed her to a stop, and shifted his hands to the manipulator controls. On the screen, he saw the arms shoot out directly ahead of the robot, into the video camera's field of view.

He quickly eased in power, moved the robot ahead, went back to the manipulator, and clamped the thumb-and-two-fingered hand over the thick cable exiting from the left motor. It was only about two feet long, reaching from the motor into a control box.

With the hand clamped in place, the crawler would never lose him now. As long as Brande wanted, *Atlas* was now a trailer for the floor crawler. He glanced out the port and saw the crawler's video camera moving frantically, attempting to angle down, trying to see what was happening.

The crawler driver threw power to the right track, spinning in place, trying to move his own manipulator into position to protect himself.

"Somebody's talking up a storm on their acoustic channel," Otsuka reported.

Dokey backed away from the crawler and its flailing manipulator arm, but *Atlas* hung on to the aft end.

Brande watched his screen and extended the tool hand. It had a cutting torch in place.

He fired the torch.

Reached out, put the flaming torch next to the armored cable, and watched as flexible metal turned molten, superheated, then frozen white in the chill of the sea. Big droplets of shapeless metal dripped slowly out of the camera's view.

The crawler stopped turning.

The cable parted.

"Good show," Dokey said.

Brande released the robot's grip, then backed her away, making certain he kept the ROV clear of the machine's big manipulator.

The crawler tried to go somewhere. It started and stopped, but only the right track would move, and it spun in place, like a child's broken toy. And no one was going to get out and change the tires.

"You suppose he's cussing us, Chief?"

"He would be," Otsuka said, "if I could interpret the acoustic channel."

"The best part, Okey, is they're going to have to bring in support ships and raise him to the surface to make repairs. That takes time."

"Talk about cost-efficiency," Dokey said. "These accidents are going to eat into their profit margins."

"What now?" Otsuka asked.

As an answer, Brande activated his headset. "Larry, you standing by?"

"Got me," Emry said. "How's it going?"

"Quite well."

"See anything interesting?"

"Only that they seem to be using larger explosive devices. They're leaving bigger holes behind."

"And more radiation," Otsuka said after checking the radiometer.

"That's not good," Emry said.

"Maybe they'll change their minds. Anyway, Larry, take a look at your chart."

"I'm looking."

"You see a pattern there? In the distance between detonations?"

"I do."

"Where do you think the next one will take place?"

"Oh. Hold on. I see what you mean."

A few minutes later, Emry continued, "There's not an exact spacing, Dane. But if I follow the arc, I would expect to see something happen between eighty and a hundred miles northwest of where you are now."

"Give me a heading."

"Ah, Dane, hang on a minute. Someone else wants to get in a word while we've got you on the line."

"What do you think you're going to do?" Thomas asked.

"Preventative medicine," he replied.

Before she could respond to that, a new voice broke into the channel. "Brande, what are you doing?"

"Ah, Penny," he said. "How nice to finally hear from you."

2054 Hours Local, SeaStation AG-4
33° 16′ 50″ North, 141° 15′ 19″ West

"What have you done to my crawler?" Glenn asked.

She was furious, and the fury edged her voice.

"Crawler?" Thomas asked.

"I believe," Brande said, "that the vehicle may have had a malfunction. You ought to send somebody out to check on it, Penny."

"Damn you! You're interfering with a legal enterprise, Brande. I want you to stay away from my operations, and I want you to do it . . . now!"

"It's a free ocean, Penny."

Abruptly, she cut off the circuit and turned to Conroy. "What have you got?"

"They lost control of one track, Penny. We're going to have to send someone out to tow them in. We'll also have to raise it for repairs, no doubt."

"Damn, damn, damn!"

The *Outer Islands Lady,* AquaGeo's surface maintenance ship was already en route. She had ordered it away from its station off Alaska as soon as she knew they would have to raise the *Melbourne* to replace the propulsion unit.

Every contact with Brande had resulted in delays.

She was losing equipment so fast she'd never complete the program in time.

Time was the problem. She was closing in on Deride's final solution, and she was going to run out of time before it was achieved.

"What about *Sydney,* Penny?" Bert Conroy asked. "In another couple of hours, she'll be ready to supervise Team Three's placing of charges. I'd better recall her and send her to watch over the crawler."

Glenn had heard Brande talking to Emry on the *Orion.* She knew he was going to go searching for Site I.

He might even find it before the charge was set off.

Or just as it was set off.

God, and he was such a find, too.

"Bert, you just let *Sydney* and FC-9 do what they're supposed to do."

"Penny."

"All right, send *Sydney.*"

2217 Hours Local, The California
34° 25′ 19″ North, 140° 1′ 3″ West

An Airborne Warning and Control (AWACS) aircraft en route from Japan to Travis Air Force Base had helped them out a little by making an earlier radar contact, and the *Orion* and some other, smaller vessel had appeared on the *California*'s radar screens about forty minutes before.

Commander George Quicken, who had the conn, was standing on the port side of the bridge, scanning the angry seas with binoculars.

"There we go, Captain Harris," he said. "Four points to port."

Mabry Harris trained his own binoculars in the direction indicated and saw the two vessels. Their navigation lights made it possible to discern them through the scud that clung to the surface of the sea.

"All right, Commander. We'll want to take up a position south of them."

"Aye aye, sir."

"Mister Evans," Harris said.

"Sir."

"Message to CINCPAC. We have made visual contact with the *Orion*. Awaiting further instructions."

Harris didn't know why he was there, and he wasn't sure that Commander, Pacific Fleet did, either. Maybe someone in Washington had a clue.

But he doubted it.

NOVEMBER 20

Nuclear Detonation:
34° 50′ 2″ North, 140° 21′ 2″ West

FIFTEEN

For the last two hours, the seabed had been steadily rising, but not so much that anyone on the surface would know, or maybe care. Brande had been feeding altitude data into the submersible's onboard computer, thereby updating Emry's current mapping information on the *Orion* via the Loudspeaker telemetry data link.

On the left monitor, Brande had a copy of Emry's map, with *DepthFinder*'s current position superimposed as a yellow square. On the small keypad, he tapped in the current depth reading: 18,214 feet. It was a pretty dismal map, showing almost no prominent features for the surrounding twenty miles of its scale. There was one seamount which rose to within fourteen thousand feet of the surface. If one could see through transparent water, looking down on its top would be similar to viewing one of Colorado's "fourteeners" from sea level at Los Angeles. Colorado peaks were impressive, but they were normally seen from the spectator's stance, which was already at least a mile up.

On the feedback link, Brande also had *Orion*'s position shown as a yellow circle; she was some fifty miles behind them on the surface. Mel Sorenson was staying way back, so that his location didn't necessarily betray that of the submersible. He was constrained to a degree by the range of the Loudspeaker acoustic system. They had voice over a longer range, but lost data-transfer capability at around fifty-five miles.

Over the last six hours, they had steadily moved north-northwest, travelling at a conservative cruise speed of ten knots in order to preserve their battery charges. Kim Otsuka had passed around their lunch boxes, and they had consumed every last bologna sandwich, potato chip, and apple. Brande was getting hungry again, but he suspected it would be another six hours before they resurfaced.

He was also certain they were on the right course. Over an hour before, they had detected the high-speed cavitation of propellers on the sonar, and Dokey had immediately settled *DepthFinder* on the seabed and shut down the lights and noisemaking systems.

Brande had gone passive with the sonar to avoid giving away their location, but not before determining a bearing on the alien sub. After waiting twenty minutes, he activated the sonar briefly and took another reading on the sub, which was then six thousand yards behind them. From the two readings, he extrapolated its heading and track.

"If it were up to me, Okey, and if that thing was coming from where we're heading, I'd want to bear right a trifle, to a heading of three-two-five."

"Those guys will be going to help out a floor crawler, I'd bet, and they're flat moving out," Dokey had said. "Roughly, I calculate their speed at fifteen knots."

"Given their lack of aerodynamics, that's probably their top end, Okey."

Now they were approaching their projected target range of eighty to a hundred miles from the last detonation site, Number Ten.

Under the six-million candlepower floodlight glare ahead of them, Brande saw the seabed abruptly disappear. One second it was there; the next, they were floating over an abyss without an apparent bottom.

He tried the sonar, which was displaying its readings on the center monitor.

"Rather a sharp drop-off, Okey. I show bottom four hundred feet down. Let's go take a look."

"Going, Chief."

The sub nosed downward and glided at a slower pace as Dokey retarded the motor controllers. Soon, the seafloor gleamed in the floodlights once again, and Dokey made his glide path shallower.

"I'm hungry," Otsuka said.

"Go back to sleep," Dokey told her. "That way, you can at least dream about a steak."

Brande extended the range on the sonar and aimed the antenna downward. He found nothing but undulating seabed.

"No contacts," he said.

"They've got to be somewhere out there," Dokey said.

"Why?" Otsuka asked.

"Dane and I think they have to work in teams of

a sub and a crawler. The crawler will have to drill the hole and set the charge since the subs don't have manipulator arms."

"So we're looking for a floor crawler?"

"Right on, doll."

"And what then?"

"We'll try to disable it, just like we took care of the last one."

"And what if our timing is absolutely perfect?" Otsuka asked.

Dokey and Brande both looked back at her. In the dim illumination from the cabin lights, her face was creased with concern.

"Meaning?" Dokey asked.

"We could find the site just as they detonate a nuclear blast."

Brande switched his gaze to Dokey.

"The lady has a point," Dokey said.

0521 Hours Local, The Perth
33° 16′ 50″ North, 141° 15′ 19″ West

Paul Deride stood on the upper hull of the *Perth,* only partially protected from the spray by the sail. Fine droplets pelted his face and upper torso.

He took another deep breath and scanned the horizon. The Canadair seaplane was on its takeoff run, its hull bouncing from the wave tops. As he watched, it clawed its way into the air, then quickly disappeared into the overcast. The pilots had been overly anxious about making the landing in the first place, and Deride had to admit it had been a harrowing experience. He had given them permission to return to San Francisco, rather than wait it out on the surface.

To the east, he saw the hazy silhouettes of the three freighters they had circled before landing. They were still moving east, and he knew they were loaded with the specialized equipment required for mining at depth. There were three more submersibles, six more floor crawlers, a living module, and a nuclear power module along with the excavators, conveyors, and power washers. Two days from now, two more freighters would arrive with supplies and high-pressure pumps on board. There was, he estimated, a half-billion dollars sitting on board those fragile ships. His equity, of course, was as small as he could make it. The bulk of the investment, and the risk, was in the hands of the international bankers who had learned that Paul Deride delivered on his promises.

Once they were on station above Site D—where Penny had decided to initiate the mining phase, it would take eight to ten days to get everything set up on the bottom. In another six days, the refiner ship, *Dolly Cameron,* would be in place, accepting the crushed-rock sludge pumped up to her from below, and performing the first rough culling of the ore. With the content readings that Penny Glenn had been reporting, Deride expected that they would extract a quarter of a ton of manganese-rich ore from each ten tons pumped from the seabed. Over nine tons of rubble would be dumped back into the ocean; there was no economic sense in transporting the raw ore to Japan. The next stage of refinement, conducted in Japan, should produce roughly two hundred pounds of pure manganese. The ratio promised to get better and better as the mining operation moved north, following the trail Penny was preparing.

He fully expected that within two weeks he would be seeing the first shipment of partially refined ore on its way to the more sophisticated processing center. Within a year, he projected, Matsumoto Steel would be undercutting the hardened steel price worldwide. Two years after that, Matsumoto and Deride would own the world's steel market.

The anticipation of that event almost made him forget that he was about to go where he didn't want to go.

With a final deep breath of salt-laden air, Deride hunched his shoulders against the cold and his mind against the coming confinement, slipped down the ladder, and slammed the hatch behind him.

The pilot came halfway out of his seat, his eyes automatically darting upward to check the seal of the hatch as he extended his hand.

"Welcome aboard, Mr. Deride."

"Who are you?"

"My name is Jerry Tompkins, sir. Pilot of the *Perth*. Hyun Oh, here, is copilot."

Deride didn't bother shaking hands. He nodded curtly to Oh, who appeared to be Korean, then flopped heavily into one of the four rear seats.

Tompkins twisted his way back into his seat, and soon, the submersible began to settle below the surface. The smoothness was comforting, though it couldn't override the building anxiety he felt about losing touch with the surface.

Penny's summons—she wouldn't talk about it on the phone—had damned bloody well better be worth the discomfort he was undergoing.

1032 Hours Local
Washington, D.C.

As soon as Pamela Stroh had hung up, Carl Unruh dialled Hampstead's number.

The secretary put him right through.

"Hello, Carl. You inviting me to lunch?"

"It's not a lunch-type day, Avery. We've got legal problems."

"We? In what way?"

"I just talked to Pam Stroh at Justice. I called her to see what they were doing about Brande's claims against Deride."

"And?"

"It's gone the other way around. AquaGeo has filed briefs and lawsuits at the Maritime Commission, the World Court, and in U.S. District Court. The Maritime Commission has already issued an injunction."

"What in the hell are you talking about?"

"Of immediate concern," Unruh said, "is that Brande, Marine Visions, and any sponsoring organization, has been enjoined from interfering with the mining operations of AquaGeo Limited. That's pending a hearing, probably to be set for January, Stroh said."

"You're not kidding, are you?"

"Hell, no. They've also asked for copies of all contracts between Marine Visions and its sponsoring organizations. You happen to have a contract, Avery?"

"Actually, it's right in front of me. I'm just now working on a few of the clauses. I'm adding a compensation paragraph for the robot they lost. You and the Navy are paying for it."

"What?"

"You've got to live with it, Carl."

"Oh, hell. Yeah, I'll live with it."

"Anything else you think I should put in?"

"You mean this contract's not even signed yet?"

"Brande and I trust each other, and if you'll recall, everyone involved was in a big hurry."

"Shit. Ms. Stroh is going to come unhinged."

"Who is this Stroh?" Hampstead asked.

"Our attorney."

"I don't get a choice? I'd prefer F. Lee Bailey or Melvin Belli or the guy from Jackson Hole, Wyoming. You know, somebody who can win."

"Don't joke, Avery."

"So what do we do?"

"Send me any notes you have about the contract, as well as what you have of it. Then, get on the phone and tell Brande to back off."

"Until when? I thought we were worried about earthquakes and such. You did mention something dire about the twenty-fourth of the month, didn't you? That happens to be four days away from us."

"We can't do a damned thing until we can get this settled in the courts, Avery. Justice and State have both convinced the Vice President that we're a law-abiding nation. Ben Delecourt is issuing new instructions to his ships on the scene. You have to tell Brande to suspend operations."

"You can't mean we're going to sit on our asses and actually wait for the courts to decide something, Carl? Do you think Deride will wait around?"

"Stroh is going to file for an injunction preventing further exploration by AquaGeo until they satisfy environmental and ecological concerns."

"Good luck."

"I don't know what else we can do. The Attorney General is crying because we have to do this much."

"Christ. They wouldn't even pursue the matter of one Svetlana Polodka, Carl."

"The AG is, I'm sure, getting pressure from the Vice President's Office on the environmental side, or we wouldn't be contesting AquaGeo at all."

"And the Navy?" Hampstead asked.

"Stroh was going to talk to Delecourt some more, so I don't know their reaction beyond a policy of noninterference. When we get down to it, though, Commerce, CIA, and the Navy are all contractual partners with MVU. We'll have to get our acts together."

"That's going to be like asking a convention of Christians, Jews, Muslims, Hindus, and Buddhists which religion God prefers," Hampstead said.

0540 Hours Local, The Orion
34° 26′ 24″ North, 140° 15′ 42″ West

Kaylene Thomas took Hampstead's call on the scrambled satellite channel in the radio shack.

"Injunction!"

"I haven't seen it yet, Kaylene, but CIA says we should suspend your operations."

"Just the CIA?"

"I suspect the Justice Department, my bosses, and the White House would back them up."

"I can't reach Dane just now, Avery."

Hampstead cleared his throat patiently. "And why is that, Kaylene?"

"He's imposed radio silence."

"I see. Radio silence."

"AquaGeo transmits on a scrambled acoustic frequency, so we can't understand them. And we don't want them overhearing what we're talking about."

"This isn't a war," Hampstead said.

"Tell that to Svetlana. If you can find her," Thomas said. Her own fury was close to the surface.

"Ah, Kaylene. I know. Still, you have to call Brande back."

"I'll think about it."

"Please take action. There's something more. I got a call from the *Washington Post,* and I had to admit that MVU is under contract to the Commerce Department. I've been able to stall on the reasons, but the reporters are on to something."

Thomas almost made a suggestion, then thought better of it. Recommendations made to Washington ended up in committee for twelve weeks.

"I'll think about it," she said again, then hung up.

She did think about calling Brande for nearly five seconds, then cast it aside. He had made the decision on radio silence, and she wasn't going to overrule him. Instead, she picked up the microphone, dialled the UHF set to channel nine, the international hailing channel, and pressed the transmit stud. *"Arienne,* this is the *Orion."*

Whoever was on the radio came right back to her, and she asked for Wilson Overton. It took a few minutes to get him to the radio.

"Dr. Thomas? This is Wilson Overton."

"How would you like to join me for breakfast?" she asked.

"What? I'd like that."

"If you don't mind joining us by way of a breeches buoy," she told him.

"What's that?"

"Don't worry about it, and plan for eight A.M. You'll enjoy the ride."

She was halfway through the communications compartment hatchway to the bridge when another voice came over the UHF radio.

"Orion. Mighty Moose calling *Orion."*

She went back and picked up the mike. "Bull, this is Kaylene. Where are you?"

"About half-a-mile off your stern, missy. I'm ready to link up with you."

What the hell?

"I've got your supplies," Kontas went on. "It'll take awhile to transfer them in this weather. You want to tell Del Rogers to get on one of your cranes."

"What supplies?"

"I don't think, missy, that we want to talk about it on the air."

"Bull!"

"The torpedoes and stuff," he said.

0745 Hours Local, The California
34° 26′ 24″ North, 140° 15′ 42″ West

In the late afternoon of the preceding day, CINCPAC, Vice Admiral David Potter, had signalled the *California* and her escorts, *Mahan* and *Fletcher,* that their mission was simply to make their presence known and to stand by the *Orion* should any ship of a foreign flag harass her.

Mabry Harris had thought at the time that it would have been helpful if he had known just what the *Orion* was doing that required the support of a naval warship. Obviously, it was something on the bottom, which was some three miles down at this point. It was also something important enough to garner Navy interest.

And the interest of Greenpeace, since the *Arienne* hadn't been out of sight since their arrival. If the people on the Greenpeace boat knew more about this than he did, he wouldn't be surprised.

He *would* be irritated.

And was beginning to become so. At 1800 hours the night before, he had sent a request to CINCPAC, asking for a briefing on the mission of the Marine Visions craft. So far, he hadn't received a response.

Captain Harris usually took the morning watch since mornings at sea were his favorite times, and this morning only he, the helmsman, and a radar officer were on the bridge when the chief petty officer from communications entered.

"Permission to come on the bridge, sir?" he asked from the hatchway.

Harris signalled him in and took the flimsy he handed to him.

"Give me the gist of it," Harris said.

"Uh, sir, we're to make certain that the *Orion* doesn't launch her submersible."

Harris involuntarily glanced through the windshield toward the research vessel and her bare stern deck.

Without intending to speak audibly in front of enlisted personnel, Harris said, "Somebody in Washington is totally fucked up."

"Yes, sir," agreed the chief petty officer.

0755 Hours Local, The Adrienne
34° 26′ 24″ North, 140° 15′ 42″ West

Some sailor on the much higher deck of the research vessel fired a small cannon at them.

The pilot rope leaped from a coil on the deck, arched over the water, and across the rear deck of the *Arienne.* Mick Freelander grabbed it, then began towing in a heavier rope sliding off the deck of the research vessel.

Overton held firmly to the railing along the gunwale. Both the larger ship and the yacht were bouncing high on the waves and out of synchronicity with each other. The sea conditions had determined that he would go visiting aboard the *RV Orion* by this primitive method.

He wasn't looking forward to it. He was wearing Levi's and a sweatshirt. His parka held his camera and his tape recorder. And over that, he was wearing bulky weather pants and a slicker that felt as if they were made of the same stuff as his mother's breakfast tablecloth.

Freelander secured the heavy rope to an anchor point on the deck, and the breeches buoy came sliding down the rope from the other ship. It dipped into the sea, splattering water, before Freelander hauled it aboard.

"In you go," he said, grinning hugely.

Clumsily, Overton stepped into the two holes for his legs. The slack came out of the ferry rope, and he was jerked off his feet. The sailors on the research ship began pulling on the second line, and he had to lever his legs up to clear the gunwale as he went overboard. He grabbed the rope above him with his hands, but nearly got them run over by the pulleys from which the breeches buoy was suspended.

As he had feared, when the ship and the boat passed each other in their up-and-down journeys, the rope slackened, and he went into the water.

Not far. His feet got wet, and his face was splashed by icy droplets.

Then four welcome hands on the ship were grabbing him, helping him out of the contraption.

He stood weakly on the side deck before one of the men said, "I'm Del Rogers. If you'll follow me, Mr. Overton."

The sailor walked with a wide stance, absorbing the shocks and sway of the deck with seemingly elastic knees. Overton tried to emulate him, but wasn't very successful. He lurched about like a drunk.

It was much warmer inside the superstructure, and he shed his foul-weather gear in a large corridor, then went into the wardroom Rogers pointed out for him.

There were a half dozen people present, finishing their morning meals. He saw Thomas, whose picture he had seen before, sitting in a booth with an older, bald-headed guy with a big moustache. Also in the booth, unaccountably, like an amiable meal companion, was a computer.

The two of them got up as he entered and came across the deck to meet him.

"Hello, Mr. Overton. I'm Kaylene Thomas, and this is Dr. Lawrence Emry, Director of Exploration. I'm happy you could join us."

They all shook hands, and Overton kept his suspicions to himself. Brande had denied him an interview three times, but now he was suddenly being welcomed with open, cuddly arms. Everybody wanted something; his boat ride with Jacobs was going to cost him a couple of articles. There were no free lunches. Or breakfasts, either, for that matter.

He shrugged out of his parka and dropped it on the bench seat of the booth.

Thomas led them into the galley, and they loaded plates from a warming rack of scrambled eggs, bacon, sausage, and biscuits. With heavy mugs of coffee, the three of them went back to the booth with the computer in it. Thomas scooted a chair over and sat at the end of the table, and Emry sat in front of the computer monitor, which displayed a confusing array of numbers, turned slightly away from Overton. Emry seemed to know what they meant, and every few minutes, he glanced at them. So did Thomas.

They made it through the eggs on small talk, and they all got down to first names. Then Thomas said, "One thing that's always mystified me about the media, Wilson, is its penchant for trying court cases in print and on the TV screen before the legal system is done with them."

"The philosophy is that the public has—"

"I know what the rationale is," she said, "and the more sensational, the better."

Was this going to be an inquisition of his profession? Overton had a whole list of questions he wanted to ask, and the tape recorder in his parka just itched to be placed in the center of the table. But, he had been invited, and he waited, though perhaps not as patiently as normal.

"Would you like to take notes?" Thomas asked.

Overton dug out his notebook and recorder from the parka beside him.

"What subject am I taking notes about?" he asked.

"Do you know why we're here, Wilson?"

"I only know about the seabed disturbances." He told her what he had learned from the Earthquake Information Center.

"I got caught in the L.A. earthquake," she said.

"Cost her a damned good Pontiac," Emry broke in.

"And I didn't like it one bit," she went on. "The property destruction was probably typical, but the effect on people was appalling. I saw people who were injured very badly, some who died, a little girl trying to be brave, administering first aid to her mother."

Overton jabbed a finger downward. "Do you think that's what's happening down there, something that will affect people?"

He couldn't help sounding dubious.

"I think it could, yes."

"That why the Navy's here?"

"I don't know why the Navy is here," she said.

Overton had to smile. "Tell me, why am I here?"

"Because I've had a change of heart. I have a case I want to try in the media before it gets to the courts. I thought you'd like that."

0845 Hours Local, SeaStation AG-4
33° 16′ 50″ North, 141° 15′ 19″ West

Right after Deride arrived, Penny Glenn spent twenty minutes briefing him on what had taken place at Test Hole H.

They sat in the control room, Deride in his normal safari gear and an additional sweater, and Glenn in a heavy jumpsuit. He was nervous, and trying not to show it, but Glenn had always known he was uneasy with subsurface. Her account of the disabling of the floor crawler had made him furious.

Deride got up and began to pace around the table. "That son of a bitch! He's coming after us, isn't he?"

"It was a deliberate act, Uncle Paul."

"He's mad about the woman."

"Woman? What woman?"

"The one that drowned."

"Paul, I don't know what you're talking about."

"It was in the papers. The reporter that saw the *DepthFinder* surface damaged, saw the woman—some Russian name—fall overboard."

Glenn hadn't known about that. She was saddened to some extent but reminded herself that there were always casualties in dangerous ventures. Deride certainly knew about casualties in the minerals industry.

"Anthony has heard that Brande is blaming the accident for her death, and all kinds of U.S. agencies are probing into AquaGeo affairs," Deride said.

That was all right. Glenn didn't care about that. If the timing were right, it would be helpful.

"It *was* an accident?" Deride suddenly turned to look directly at her.

"You can talk to McBride, Uncle Paul. He's here in the station."

"I'll do that."

Glenn had already prepped McBride on what to say to the CEO, and she was about to call him on the intercom when one of the technicians at the bulkhead consoles pulled his headset off and said, "Penny!"

She spun around in her chair to look at him.

"Dorsey wants to talk to you."

Jim Dorsey headed Team Three, and he was aboard the floor crawler FC-9 at Test Hole I. She scooted her castered chair over to the console, flipped the speaker switch so that the conversation would come over the ceiling speaker, picked up the microphone, and said, "Yes, Jim?"

"We've got a glitch."

"What's that?"

"I've got the charge set, and I'm ready to blow it, right? So we take one last look on the sonar, and there's a sub hanging around. I know it ain't Munro, 'cause I just talked to him at Test Hole H."

She told Deride, "It has to be Brande."

"Goddamn bloody hell!"

She keyed the mike. "Have they located the charge?"

"Nah, not even close yet. But they're getting there. What I need to know, Penny, is do I go ahead and blow it, or do I try to warn the sub off? Do you want me to try to raise them on the acoustic?"

"What do you think, Jim?" she asked.

"I don't really want to get too close to the sub. Look at what happened to Eddie when they went after him."

The technician was following the conversation closely, looking back and forth between Glenn and Deride. It was important for Glenn that he be aware of the dialogue and who said what.

She asked, "Uncle Paul?"

Glenn knew that Deride was still angry about the damaged floor crawler, about the damaged sub, and about how much those repairs were going to cost in time and money.

"Jesus Christ!" he said. "I suppose we ought to give them some kind of warning."

"I can reach them on their acoustic frequency," Glenn told him. "It would certainly be more than they did for Eddie and Hank when they attacked FC-4."

"That's true," Deride said.

"Then again, Brande's violating the injunction you just told me about."

"That's also true."

"And we may go a day or two over schedule on the project. You realize that?"

Deride nodded.

"The *Outer Islands Lady* will be here shortly, to make repairs on *Melbourne* and FC-4. The loss of those vehicles has also eaten into the project schedule," Glenn reminded him.

"How much?"

"It'll go over a million."

"To hell with Brande," he said. "Blow it."

SIXTEEN

A ridge six hundred yards ahead effectively blocked the scan of the forward-looking radar. It looked like a solid granite wall on the waterfall display, like that of a prison, Otsuka thought.

She was perched on the edge of her seat, leaning forward against the back of Dokey's and Brande's seats. They were at 18,900 feet of depth and twenty-five feet off the bottom. Through the portholes, the seabed appeared forlornly beautiful, almost a Japanese rock garden in monochromatic grays. The floodlights made the rock sentinels stand out in stark poses of military attention. The silt swooped up against their bases on the north sides, pushed there by the strong current that flowed north to south.

She could tell that Dokey was fighting the current, leaning into it, by the position of the controller handle under his fingers. Occasionally, the submersible felt as if it were sliding to the left.

"Kim," Brande said, "do me a favor. Check on the times of the detonations."

"Time of day, Dane?"

"Please."

She leaned back against the seat cushion and swivelled the keyboard mounted to the chair arm into place in front of her. With a few keyed commands, she linked into Emry's mapping program, peering across Brande's face at the display on the left monitor. The detonation locations were indicated on the map, with the coordinates printed alongside each. Emry had also stored the times in his database, though they were not shown on the display. She called up the file, losing the map for the time being.

After a quick search, she found the subfile, then keyed in the command to display the time of detonation alongside each coordinate.

The map reappeared on the screen, and she pushed the keyboard out of the way and rested her elbow on Dokey's seat as she studied the screen.

"We want to climb this ridge, Chief?" Dokey asked.

Brande was scanning the map, also. "We're ninety-two miles from the last site, Okey. I'd have thought we'd run into a floor crawler by now."

"Maybe on the other side of the ridge."

"Let's go over. I read it as three hundred and twenty feet high."

Dokey eased the bow up with the joystick, and *DepthFinder* began to rise.

"Dane," Otsuka said, "I don't see a pattern, as far as time of day goes. There's been a detonation almost every day, but they have taken place anywhere from four in the morning until nine-thirty at night."

"I was afraid of that," Brande said. "It doesn't leave us a way to predict the future."

"Just whenever they reached the site and got their charge buried," Dokey said.

Otsuka felt her level of anxiety increasing. If they were in the right area, something devastating could happen at any moment.

Dokey had gone into a right turn, climbing along the face of the cliff which was now in the fringe of the floodlights and visible on their left. It appeared massive and strong. Both Brande and Dokey were leaning forward, close to the ports, to examine the rugged face.

Otsuka switched her attention to the sonar display. The top of the ridge was coming up. The crest was saw-toothed, with lots of depressions and rises. Her eyes were drawn to an especially strong return hidden in one gulch along the lip of the ridge. Automatically, she switched on the magnetometer.

"Dane! We're showing a heavy magnetic field!"

Brande glanced at the readout. "Where?"

She reached between the seats and tapped a finger on the screen.

"Probably the floor crawler," Dokey said.

"He's protected himself well," Brande said. "Gotten down in the rocks. Oh, shit! Dive, Okey!"

Dokey didn't ask for reasons. He slapped the stick forward and ran the electric motors up to full power.

The submersible nosed over and headed for the bottom.

And they almost reached it before the concussion wave hit them.

And this time she heard it, a crescendo of deep-throated thunder that hit in one loud clap.

DepthFinder rolled over.

Otsuka was tossed out of her seat, hitting the overhead, bouncing into Dokey.

For some reason, she recalled how idyllic and sun-filled her days at Stanford now seemed.

0903 Hours Local, The Orion
34° 21' 10" North, 140° 20' 3" West

"Nuclear detonation," Emry said calmly.

Thomas rose from her chair involuntarily. She rushed across the lab and leaned over Emry's shoulder.

"Where, Larry?"

"Same coordinates."

He didn't have to say, "Same as *DepthFinder*'s."

Mayberry, at the next console, said, "We've lost the telemetry."

The others in the lab abandoned what they were doing and hurried to gather around Emry's console.

Without asking permission of anyone, Bull Kontas reached around Emry and picked up the microphone. He had been aboard for several hours, after transferring his six huge crates and the robot Gargantua from the *Mighty Moose* to the research vessel. His crewman was keeping the workboat in trail a few hundred yards behind the *Orion*.

Nobody had bothered telling Kontas that radio silence had been imposed, and no one was going to tell him now. He keyed the mike. "*DepthFinder,* this is *Orion.*"

Released the Transmit button.

Dull undertone of static.

"Hey, Chief, come back to me, damn it!"

Nothing.

Kaylene Thomas collapsed onto her knees next to Emry's chair.

"Could be anything," Emry said. "Electromagnetic Pulse, EMP. Might have knocked out the electronics."

"Goddamn," she said.

"Take it easy, Kaylene," he said, putting an arm around her shoulders. "Give us some time."

She reached over and pressed the intercom's button.

"Bridge," Connie Alvarez-Sorenson said.

"Full speed, Connie. Heading two-two-five."

"Full turns coming up," she said.

Mayberry got out of his chair, got his hands under Thomas's arms, and eased her up into the chair.

She couldn't believe it had ended so abruptly.

She felt dead inside.

0912 Hours Local, The California
34° 21′ 10″ North, 140° 20′ 3″ West

The missile cruiser had her engines at dead slow, the screws turning just enough to maintain her heading into the oncoming seas. Life aboard had been dead slow, too, for almost eight hours now, since they had located the research ship. Not much had changed in that time, including the fact that Mabry Harris had not yet received his requested briefing from CINC-PAC relative to his mission.

During the night, they had received a message from Naval Intelligence that some twenty boats had departed Seattle, San Francisco, Los Angeles, and San Diego, all on headings that would intersect his position. Several of the boats were painted in the Green-peace scheme, and NI's analysis was that Mark Jacobs had called them out.

The *Arienne* had moved away from the *Orion* after retrieving the passenger they had sent over earlier in the morning, but they were still matching the speed of the incongruous fleet. *Mahan* and *Fletcher* were a half-mile off to either side of the *California*. An old tugboat, obviously belonging to Marine Visions because of its color scheme, was stationed astern of the research ship.

The intercom buzzed and Commander George Quicken answered it while Harris continued his pacing of the bridge. He knew his back-and-forth journey was getting on the nerves of his subordinates.

Quicken turned to him, "Captain, we've detected a large explosion on the seabed."

"Nature?"

"Unknown, sir."

The petty officer on the helm interrupted, "Captain, the *Orion* is on the move."

Harris spun around and saw that the vessel had indeed picked up speed. She was climbing a long swell, with the froth produced by her propellers spreading out behind her.

"Commander, we'll want to stay with her. Notify our escorts."

"Aye, aye, sir."

Harris took Quicken's place at the intercom and buzzed the communications compartment.

"Sir?"

"Priority message to CINCPAC. Explosion of undetermined origin on seafloor—get the coordinates from the Combat Information Center. *Orion* apparently en route to position, Task Force 36 following. Paragraph two. Submersible still not recovered and may be involved in explosion. Paragraph three. No further contacts with additional vessels. Paragraph four. Urgently request response to message, eleven-dash-nineteen. Get that right off, please."

"Aye, aye, sir."

The deck of the bridge tilted slightly as the cruiser got under way. Harris crossed to stand next to Quicken.

"What do you make of it, George?"

"I hate working in the dark, sir. Obviously, whatever is taking place is at extreme depth, or the powers-that-be would have sent a submarine to play guard dog. I'm assuming that we were sent originally to watch over the *Orion,* but that she's now in disfavor."

"Bit of a seesaw, George?"

"I've tried to never question my orders," Quicken said, "but sometimes I think naughty thoughts about politicians and admirals."

"You and me both," Harris told him. "How strong was this event?"

"It was quite impressive, Captain. It would take a hell of a load of conventional weapons to produce the shock wave we picked up."

"You don't suppose Research and Development is conducting some secret weapons program? Perhaps out of sync with one treaty or another?"

"I really don't know, sir. Do you really think this could be nuclear?"

"Possible, isn't it?"

"I suppose so," Quicken said.

"And accidents happen. That submersible could be vapor right now, drifting to the surface."

0930 Hours Local, SeaStation AG-4
33° 16′ 50″ North, 141° 15′ 19″ West

Paul Deride had stayed close to the control center for the last several hours, awaiting word on the test hole. Penny had gone to the deck above, to take a nap. She said these things were routine by now.

They weren't routine for him, though. This was the first project on which they had used nuclear mining techniques, and he had never been present during an operational blast. That was Penny's job.

Dorsey, on board FC-9, had reported a successful detonation at three minutes after nine. He was now making a circuit of the area prior to collecting samples, and he had said it would take some time because he was in rough terrain, at the top of a mesa. To get to the bottom, he had to drive some sixteen miles over tortuous seabed.

Deride tried to imagine what the seafloor looked like over there, but had difficulty doing so. Their equipment was not capable of transmitting video from the subs or floor crawlers to the sea station. Because he so detested being subsurface, he had never taken an intense interest in what it looked like, beyond the fifty or so feet surrounding the habitat since it was visible on the overhead video camera. Penny was the one who loved this kind of high-technology, high-risk exploration and really revelled in it. He was content to give the orders and let others take care of the tasks.

"AG-4, Dorsey," the transponder blurted over the speaker system.

Bert Conroy was monitoring the console, and Deride grabbed a castered chair and slid it across the carpeted deck to sit down next to him.

"AG-4," Conroy said. "What you got, Jim?"

"That submersible? I can't see it, but I've got it on the sonar."

"What's the condition? Can you tell?"

"Not from my image. She's about three hundred feet above the ridge, drifting slowly upward. I don't detect any noise, either from motors or the interior. You want to bring *Sydney* in to look her over?"

Conroy looked to his boss.

Deride said, "Let's get on about our business. Right now, that means collect the samples."

Camden's injunction was no longer necessary, and that was all right with Deride. Cheaper, that way.

* * *

0935 Hours Local, The DepthFinder
34° 50′ 1″ North, 140° 20′ 29″ West

Brande said, "I think I'm going to bill Hampstead for the cost of all our replacement electronics."

"Why not send a nicely overstated statement to Deride?" Dokey asked.

"He won't be able to write the check when I'm done with him, Okey."

"Valid argument."

Brande was shaken, but was trying not to give it away. He was disoriented, frightened, and totally aware of the unwelcome silence of the capsule. The air was stale, dry, and it tasted funny.

He reached back in the darkness, found Otsuka's hands clutching her knees, and squeezed them lightly. She was shivering almost uncontrollably.

"We're doing all right, Kim," he said.

"Of course," she said. It came out squeaky. Her teeth were chattering.

"Are you hurt?"

"B-bruises. Everywhere."

"Okey?"

"Most of my pieces are in the right place, Chief. By my watch, if I remember the time, and if the damned thing's working, I was blacked out for at least twenty minutes."

"Same here."

"I think we went completely upside down," Dokey said. "Like a big bowling ball. I wouldn't have thought it was possible to turn this hummer over."

"It is my firm belief," Brande said, "that the detonation took place on top of the ridge. We were pretty well protected from the direct blast."

"How much is pretty well?" Dokey asked.

"Good question."

It was completely black inside the pressure hull. They had no instrument panel lights, and the exterior floodlights had also been extinguished. The monitor screens were dark. When he had first come to, Brande had been surprised that he was breathing, then amazed that he was sitting more or less upright in his seat.

"Any idea where we are, Okey?"

"I think we're on ascent, but the rest is a blank. You ready to try the systems?"

"Let's do. I wish we had a flashlight."

"J-just a minute," Otsuka said.

He heard her fumbling around with her clothing, then a small stab of light erupted from the backseat.

"Wonderful, Kim."

She handed him the small penlight, and he slowly worked its beam around the interior. There was no obvious damage. Bits of mud and dust from the flooring could be found lodged in odd places. The wrappers from their box lunches were spread around, also.

"We did turn turtle," he said.

"At least this turtle found her legs again," Dokey said.

"All right," he said, "environmental systems first."

He turned halfway around in his seat and held the light beam on the circuit breaker panels for the life-support systems at the rear of the hull, near Otsuka's legs. All of the breakers had blown.

"Go ahead, Kim. Oxygen, first."

She tried the switch tentatively. It held in the closed position, and the gauge above it immediately blinked itself to life.

"We have oxygen flow," Brande said.

"In that case, I'm going to take my first deep breath," Dokey told them.

"Lithium-hydroxide blower, Kim."

She closed the switch, and the minor hum of the motor sounded blissfully in his ears.

"Let's open up the emergency oxygen bottle for a while, until the main system stabilizes," Brande told her.

She reached under her seat, and under the guiding light of the penlight, found the valve for the backup oxygen bottle. Watching the gauge at the top of the bottle, she twisted the valve a half-turn.

Twisting back into his seat, he trained the light on the center control pedestal.

"I think the weights are next."

"I think you're right," Dokey said. He reset the circuit breaker on the weight monitoring readout. It blinked, then showed them one Locked and one Clear indication.

"We lost one weight when we did our somersault, Chief."

"Let's lose the other."

Dokey thumbed the switch for the portside weight, and a green light immediately flared, and the digital readout changed to Clear.

"Weight dropped. We're on the rise."

Brande couldn't feel the movement, but he had to trust history. In the past, when they dropped weights, they went up. If nothing major had altered their buoyancy configuration, it had to work the same way again.

Panel by panel, they slowly went through each system of the submersible. It took them a half hour, and when they were done, they had recovered only about twenty percent of the operating systems. Some light was coming from the panel dials and readouts now. None of the Loudspeaker components—data or voice—would come up. Sonar, video, and altimeter transponders were inoperative. They had no idea of their position, longitudinally, latitudinally, or relative to the ocean surface.

"I think we got a dose of EMP, Okey."

"You're right. Those systems that have elaborate electronics in the circuit are the ones we've lost."

"The rad-radiometer reading is dropping," Otsuka said.

Brande looked up at the gauge.

"Do you remember how high it went, Kim?"

"No. I looked, but it was too dark."

"Well, it's low enough to shed this damned hood," Dokey said.

Brande ripped the Velcro closure and shrugged his way out of his hood. The freedom of movement helped immensely, and the cold air of the interior seemed to spark his energy. He hadn't realized how his confined body heat had warmed his face.

"I wish we could see the exterior, to see if there's any physical damage," Dokey said.

"Try *Atlas.*"

The robot was still in her sheath, but wouldn't respond to inputs from Dokey's controls.

"So much for that. How's the atmosphere, Kim?"

"Coming back to normal," she said, the edge of fear somewhat lower in the tone of her voice. "I'm going to shut down the emergency supply now."

"Fine." Brande knew she wanted to conserve it in case they lost the main source again. He didn't blame her.

"The others will be worried about us," she said.

"I know, dear. We'll just have to surprise them when we pop out."

"We can't give them a locator beacon, Dane. It's not working, either."

"I'll bet Mel's already pinpointed us," Dokey said.

"Trust to fate, Dokey, and Mel Sorenson, honey."

"All right."

Both of the chronometers on the panel were working again, but Brande didn't know how far they had risen from the seabed. He figured they had at least a couple hours to wait, and probably more.

"Anyone for three-handed bridge?" he asked.

"No cards," Otsuka said.

"I wish I'd saved my apple from lunch," Dokey said.

After some debate, Dokey got them playing a verbal trivia game which lasted for forty minutes, until the lithium-hydroxide blower shut down.

SEVENTEEN

1020 Hours Local, SeaStation AG-4
33° 16′ 50″ North, 141° 15′ 19″ West

A short nap was all it took to revive Penny Glenn physically. She had a small, Spartan cubicle of her own on the bunkhouse deck, barely five feet by six feet, and when she rolled her legs out of the bed, they almost hit the opposite wall. She got up, donned heavy undergarments and a jumpsuit, made the bed to military standards, and went down the corridor to use the communal bathroom.

She wasn't exactly revived mentally. The decision—made by Deride—to eliminate Dane Brande had both relieved and repulsed her. On one side of that issue, she would be allowed to complete her program without interference. On the other side, there was no reason now to visit San Diego—she could order the *Phantom Lode* back to Hawaii. She was afraid that that was going to be her loss. She had never before had the feeling—as she had with Brande, that something positive could come out of a relationship. She was deeply saddened.

Trying to set aside those feelings for the time be-

ing, she descended the spiral staircase to the main
deck, got coffee and a Danish from the galley
counter, and carried them into the control room.

"Good morning, Uncle Paul."

He was sitting at the big table in the center of the
room, surrounded by reams of report folders and geologic samples tagged in plastic bags. They were
heaped in an untidy array all around him. He had a
plastic coffee pitcher and a mug in front of him, and
she could see the stains where coffee had been spilled
on the tabletop and a few of the papers.

Two technicians were manning two of the consoles,
and she automatically checked the status monitor
which told her where all of the undersea vehicles were
located. They were about where she expected them to
be. The technicians went about their chores quietly
and competently. If they had reservations about the
events of the last few days, they weren't saying much
about them. In fact, she thought, there wouldn't be
one employee on AquaGeo payrolls who would voice
a complaint about Dane Brande or Marine Visions.
Because of the harsh environment in which they
worked, they were all hard and tough men, and they
were paid exceptionally well. To them, Brande had
only been an impediment to payday.

"Hello, Penny." Deride's smile was dour.

"You've been reviewing the reports, I see." She sat
down opposite him.

"Yes, I have. They don't bloody well tell me what
they've been telling you."

She wasn't too worried about that. Beyond the
amateur sense, he was not a geologist.

"Oh? In what way, Uncle Paul?"

"Test Hole D, where we're deploying a half-billion dollars of equipment? This report says the manganese content in the ore is less than five percent."

She took the page from him, turned it around, and glanced at the heading.

"Because, Uncle Paul, you're reading the assay from the seabed surface. The report from the bottom of the test hole is significantly different. That is, after all, why we dug the test hole."

"Ah, I see. Well, I'm not too good at this crap, Penny. That's why I have you."

She smiled at him. The truth, of course, was that the bottom of the hole tested out almost exactly the same as the surface of the hole.

"How much longer is the testing going to go on?" Deride asked her.

"We're close to the end of the blasting phase," she said. "Four more to go."

She dug through two of the stacks of paper before she found what she was looking for. He had completely messed up her paper organization, and probably, when she went to check on them, her files. He was better on a drilling rig or in an office making decisions. When he got his hands into areas he didn't understand, chaos resulted.

"Here." She handed him the revised blast schedule, which she had practically memorized.

Test Hole A: 32° 39′ 26″N 137° 32′ 16″W Completed
Test Hole B: 32° 45′ 15″N 137° 50′ 34″W Completed
Test Hole C: 32° 52′ 42″N 138° 8′ 23″W Completed
Test Hole D: 33° 14′ 51″N 138° 37′ 16″W Completed

Test Hole E: 33° 27′ 23″N   138° 52′ 21″W   Completed
Test Hole F: 33° 39′ 48″N   139° 9′ 57″W   Completed
Test Hole G: 34° 1′ 54″N   139° 36′ 17″W   Completed
Test Hole H: 34° 25′ 19″N   140° 1′ 3″W   Completed
Test Hole I: 34° 50′ 2″N   140° 21′ 2″W   Nov 20
Test Hole J: 35° 21′ 13″N   140° 45′ 16″W   Nov 21
Test Hole K: 35° 50′ 2″N   141° 2′ 7″W   Nov 22
Test Hole L: 36° 17′ 52″N   141° 16′ 31″W   Nov 23
Test Hole M: 36° 58′ 12″N   141° 28′ 10″W   Nov 24

"So," he said, "four more to go after today."

"That's correct. We'll be doing Test Hole J in the morning."

"Well, that should get some people off our back, we get finished with the blasting."

"Have you talked to Anthony?"

"Yes. There's been no response from anyone relative to the court filings. And the injunction is a bit of a moot point, now, wouldn't you say?"

She felt a tiny stab, a pinprick, to her heart. "I suppose so."

"The most important thing, Anthony says, is that we had the injunction on record before Marine Visions barged in on our operation."

Marine Visions?

She hadn't been thinking in terms of the company as an entity, only of Dane Brande. There was every chance in the world that he hadn't been piloting *DepthFinder* himself. It could have been anyone.

Perhaps Kaylene Thomas.

Penny Glenn felt much better.

1215 Hours Local, The Arienne
34° 50′ 14″ North, 140° 20′ 30″ West

Mark Jacobs had spent the morning on the flying bridge, alternating with Freelander, Lane, and Folger on the helm, staying close to the *Orion*. It was something of a relief to get away from Overton for a while; he had been uncommunicative since returning from the research ship. He had told Jacobs he could read it after he had written it up.

And he had been banging away on a typewriter in the salon all morning.

About nine o'clock, the *Orion* had taken off like a bat out of hell, and Jacobs had engaged his own propellers, slammed the throttles to the forward stops, and pursued. He wasn't alone, the American warships were right with them, as well as the tugboat that had shown yesterday.

It wasn't raining anymore, but visibility was still limited to about a mile by fog and overcast, and the seas were running at around ten feet. Several times, he had lost sight of his quarry, panicked a little, then found her again.

A couple times, when he had gone below for coffee, Overton had complained about the stability of the yacht; he was having difficulty typing. At Jacobs's suggestion that he phone it in, he had bristled. This was his story, he was writing it his way, and he would fax it.

Freelander was at the helm now, and they were making small talk when the *Orion* suddenly cut power.

"Hey, Mick, back off," he said.

Freelander eased off the throttles.

It appeared as if everyone on board the research ship was now on the deck. They were standing on all sides, and there were people on the bridge extensions as well as two standing atop the bridge, hanging on to antennas. They were all scanning the ocean forward and to their sides. Many of the observers clutched binoculars to their eyes.

"Debbie," he said, "go down and get Overton."

A few minutes later, Overton climbed from the ladder hatch and said, "What's going on?"

"You tell me." Jacobs pointed toward the *Orion*.

"Jesus. They lost something."

"The submersible," Jacobs said.

"In these seas, she's going to be awfully hard to spot," Lane said.

"I'd guess they don't have radio contact with the sub," Jacobs said. "Mick, let's go right and put on some power. Debbie, get everyone up here to help look."

Before she had a chance to go below, the radio sounded off on channel nine.

"Orion, this is the *California."*

A few seconds elapsed.

"California, Orion here. Captain Mel Sorenson."

"Captain Sorenson, I am Captain Mabry Harris. We have your submersible on our radar. Your heading three-four-one, two-and-a-half miles."

"Captain Harris, I am much obliged."

"Is she in trouble?" Harris asked.

"We don't know, Captain. We lost voice contact several hours ago."

"We wish you well, and if you need assistance, call on this channel."

"Thanks, Captain."

The *Orion* got under way again.

"Hit it, Mick," Jacobs said.

In the pitching of the sea, they were almost on top of the *Orion,* fifty yards off her starboard side, when they finally spotted the sub.

Freelander eased off the power as the research vessel closed on the submersible. Taking a look through the starboard windows, Jacobs saw that the Navy ship was still with them. A group of officers stood out on their port bridge wing, brandishing binoculars.

The sub disappeared, dropping low in a trough.

When she reappeared, riding the crest of a wave, there was a figure standing in the enclosure of the sail.

"That's Brande," Overton said.

Brande waved lazily at the *Orion* and gave a thumbs-up signal.

The people crowding the deck cheered loud enough to be heard across the windswept gap between the vessels.

"What the hell is going on?" Jacobs asked Overton.

"It's a long story. Come on downstairs and I'll let you read it."

"Below, Wilson."

"What?"

"We go below, not downstairs."

"Whatever."

1720 Hours Local
Washington, D.C.

Angie poked her head through his open doorway.

"You find Unruh yet?" Hampstead asked.

"I've left messages everywhere, boss. He's bound to run into one of them sometime."

"Okay, go on home."

"Night-night."

Hampstead called Alicia and told her he would be late, then frustrated, he looked up the number in the government directory and called Pam Stroh at Justice.

She was in.

"Miss Stroh, I'm Avery Hampstead, in the Commerce Department."

"Yes, Mr. Unruh has mentioned your name. What can I do for you, Mr. Hampstead?"

"I've tried to reach Carl, but in lieu of finding him, I thought I'd better call you. We've got a bit of a situation with Brande."

"Describe it to me, please."

Unruh had characterized her to Hampstead as a shaggy dog, but she sounded fairly alert to Hampstead. He gave her the gist of the report he had had from Brande.

"What? Are you saying they set off an atomic bomb on the *DepthFinder?*"

"It's not a bomb, Ms. Stroh. But Brande is certain that the people in the floor crawler would have had the sub on their sonar. They knew what they were doing."

"You're telling me it was attempted murder."

"Yes, I guess I'm telling you that."

"Brande wasn't supposed to be there," she said. "There's the injunction."

"Brande didn't know about it."

"Oh, damn. I've got to talk to some people."

She hung up on him.

1303 Hours Local, The Orion
34° 50′ 14″ North, 140° 20′ 30″ West

After he had called Hampstead, and after they spent several hours assessing the damage to *DepthFinder*— Brande especially recalled Dokey's contorted position on the floor as he repaired a damaged electrical circuit for the lithium-hydroxide blower, Kaylene Thomas had ordered Brande, Otsuka, and Dokey into hot showers, so Brande figured she had overruled Sorenson's time-limit ordinance, and he took a five-minute shower. It felt damned good.

He emerged to find her waiting for him with a salami sandwich on rye and a tall mug of hot chocolate.

"Drink this," she ordered.

He drank it down.

"Eat this."

He took a bite out of the sandwich. "You know just what I need, don't you?"

"You need some common sense."

"I thought I was pretty common."

He settled naked onto the bed, and Thomas sat beside him, snuggled up against him as he finished his sandwich.

"You also need sleep," she said.

"We've got a lot of work——"

"It doesn't matter. We've been enjoined from further dives."

He pulled his head back and turned to look her fully in the eyes. "Tell me about it."

She related what Hampstead had told her of Aqua-Geo's injunction.

"What the hell's going on, Rae?"

"I'm not sure. I've been thinking about it, Dane, but the only motive I can read into it is greed."

"It's got to go beyond that."

"Perhaps not. Deride has a timetable, and if we interfere with it, it costs him money."

"He could damned well wait a few days. He could talk to people."

"And have some international organization eventually stop his use of nuclear charges? That costs him more money," she said. "It might be enough to close down his project."

"I don't know why he's so bent on making all of these tests," Brande told her. "He hasn't even started mining the sites we've seen."

"That we know of."

"True. Maybe we should go back and check the earlier sites."

"We're not going anywhere. Except back to San Diego, maybe."

He didn't feel like arguing with her. Not for the moment, anyway.

Thomas said, "Deride has a reputation for this kind of strategy, you know."

"What kind of strategy?"

"He ties his opponents up in court cases that last

years, milks the resources he's after, then settles out of court, if at all."

"Where did you learn that?"

"Unruh told Hampstead."

"Unruh, huh?"

Brande didn't have a high opinion of Carl Unruh as a result of some of the decisions that had been made during the Russian missile crisis, when he had first learned of the CIA man's existence.

He finished his salami.

Thomas stood up and slipped out of her jumpsuit.

"What are you doing?"

"Helping you sleep."

"I need all the help I can get."

He slid back on the bed, shunted the blanket and top sheet aside, and made room for her. Neither Brande nor Thomas slept right away.

After they made love, Brande held her close to him, her head on his arm, and twirled a lock of her blond hair with his forefinger.

"You worry me, sometimes," she said. "A lot of the time, actually."

"Not intended, love."

"I know. But you get so intent on a project that other things—like me—get pigeonholed."

"May I remind you that that trait is part of your psyche, also?"

"Maybe," she said, wincing at the criticism, "but it's not so pronounced."

"All right, hon, I promise—"

The intercom buzzed, and when Brande got up to answer it, he found Emry on the other end.

"Dane, I made the projections you asked for."

"What did you come up with, Larry?"

"My best guess—and it's only a guess, but it coincides with the best guess of the seismic people at Golden and Scripps—is that a trigger could be found in the area of thirty-six degrees, fifty-eight minutes north, one-forty-one degrees, twenty-eight minutes west."

"And where are they now?"

"At the rate they're going, and with the current spacing of test shots, four more will do it. Call it the twenty-fourth of November."

"Monday."

"Monday's the day."

1320 Hours Local, The California
34° 50′ 14″ North, 140° 20′ 30″ West

Rear Admiral David Potter, CINCPAC, finally came through with a Top Secret message for Mabry Harris. The captain of the missile cruiser could imagine that David Potter had had some long and involved telephone discussions with Admiral Benjamin Delecourt, the CNO.

The long message outlined the concerns of several government agencies with seabed disturbances, the contracting of Marine Visions to investigate them, the probable discovery that AquaGeo was behind them, and the subsequent injunction barring Marine Visions from interfering with AquaGeo operations.

Harris read the message in his cabin, then used the intercom to summon Commander Quicken.

When he arrived, Harris waved him to a seat on the bunk and handed him the three-page message.

"Read that, George."

Quicken took his time going through the pages. "So that's what it's about."

"I suspect we were sent to intimidate any interference by AquaGeo vessels with Brande's examination of the bottom. No one seemed to think it would go beyond that."

"Except that, AquaGeo's presence must be all subsurface, sir. We can't very well intimidate people who don't even know we're here."

"That's very likely true, George."

"It also explains the presence of the Greenpeace people. However they got wind of it, they're not apt to take kindly to radiation poisoning of the sea."

"I can't say that I don't agree wholeheartedly with them," Harris said.

"And in the meantime, AquaGeo went to court. So, what do we do, Captain?"

"Just as it says there, George. We stand by. We don't allow Brande to deploy the sub again."

"And if Brande ignores us?"

"Why don't you give him a call? Let's make certain we're all operating by the same rules."

"May I be sympathetic to his cause, sir?"

"Yes. But be firm, will you, George?"

1915 Hours Local
Washington, D.C.

Carl Unruh and his peers in the operations, science, and administrative directorates had been tied up most of the day in a long meeting with the Director of

Central Intelligence and his executive director. They ate dinner amid a flood of paper, and with all of the issues facing the agency, the problem in the Pacific was only summarized briefly for the others by Unruh. No one, much less the DCI, Mark Stebbins, bothered going into depth on it.

When he got back to his office, he found another flood of paper, most of it telephone messages from Hampstead. Tossing his coat on the sofa, he leafed through the rest of the call-back slips while dialling Hampstead.

"You're putting in awfully long hours for a commerce person, Avery."

"Where in the hell have you been?"

"This is Washington, remember? Where else but committee meetings?"

"That's right, of course. Look, if this were LBJ's time, we'd be saying the war is escalating."

"What happened?"

Hampstead told him about *DepthFinder*'s encounter with a nuclear blast.

"Jesus, Avery! Are they all right?"

"So far as I know. A lot of the electronics on the sub were damaged, but her hull is fine. I talked to your gal Stroh a couple hours ago, and she called back, let's see, twenty minutes ago. Justice is spending the night preparing a stack of briefs, and in the morning, they're sending out a platoon of lawyers to counter AquaGeo's legal claims. The first thing will be to lift the injunction. Plus, she hinted at some other tactics they have in mind, but she wouldn't elaborate."

"I'll bet the Oval Office is now involved," Unruh said.

"That was my thought, too. The Vice President probably got through. However, Carl, all of this court action may not be soon enough."

"I know. Monday, the twenty-fourth."

"Not only that," Hampstead said. "You know Brande. The guy's had one of his people die—however that might have occurred, and he's just been socked by a nuke. I suspect he won't wait around for the niceties to be finalized."

Unruh thought about that. Brande did have a proclivity for ignoring the regulations when he thought ethics, morality, or justice was being subverted by the unscrupulous in this world. The fact that he was usually right didn't enter into it, when bureaucracies were involved.

"Let me hunt down Delecourt and see what the Navy's up to, Carl."

"Then call me back, will you? I hate being left in the dark."

"You're not the only one."

Delecourt was at his home in Virginia, the duty officer at the Pentagon told him, and Unruh reached him there.

"Yeah," Delecourt said, "I heard about Brande's intimate knowledge of nuclear events from Pam Stroh. The *California* got a reading on it, and after analysis, our people judge it at twelve kilotons of output."

"That's getting too damned big, Ben."

"A typical tactical nuke is twenty kilotons."

"Want to make a little wager, Ben? That the next one will be larger yet?"

"My betting money is already in Las Vegas, Carl."

"What else are you doing?"

"We were trying to be circumspect about this, but I finally had CINCPAC give Harris all the details."

"Who's Harris?"

"Commander of the *California*. Mabry Harris. Another thing, I put a P-3 Orion up, and I've got them orbiting the area. The weather's not too hot, and they're high, but they have reported activity at Site Number Four."

"What kind of activity?"

"Three large ships have maintained station there for about the last ten hours."

"Do your analysts say anything about that?"

"We'll do a flyover at first light in the morning, Carl, but the estimate suggests that they're delivering mining or drilling equipment."

"So, Deride's starting mining operations on the southern end?"

"While continuing to blow up the northern end," Delecourt said. "However, it all indicates that he intends to follow through with his mining. That might stand him in good stead in any hearing."

"Shit. Can we stop the mining or drilling?"

"On what grounds? He's legal all the way, Carl. And we're at a standstill because of the injunction."

"Let's put the evil eye on him."

"I could send the destroyer *Maher* south to watch the freighters," Delecourt said. "I don't think it would do any good, however."

"Probably not. Anything else I should know?"

"I don't think . . . oh, you know about the environmental activists?"

"No."

"There's twenty-seven yachts, tugboats, houseboats, and rowboats on their way to the scene. They'll be a few hours out, yet."

"Damn. That's a replay of the Russian thing."

"Think on the positive side, Carl. They may be able to do more than we're doing."

2219 Hours Local, The Arienne
34° 50′ 14″ North, 140° 20′ 30″ West

Wilson Overton had faxed his story to Washington in midafternoon, and Ned Nelson had faxed back a simple statement: "Hot damn!"

Nelson had also confirmed that Brande's outfit was under contract to the Department of Commerce, and that the Navy was involved in some way. Both confirmations supported and gave independent collaboration to claims Overton made in the article. Nelson was trying to run down a rumor that the CIA was involved, and he had put two reporters to work checking the backgrounds of high-level AquaGeo people.

Overton was seated in the banquette in the salon with Jacobs, Freelander, and Lane. Lane had cut her hair; it now only fell halfway down her back, and Overton thought it looked much better.

"You'd think a floating palace like this would have some scotch hidden somewhere," Overton said.

"We don't drink at sea," Jacobs told him.

"You read my story. Don't you think that's worth celebrating?"

"You might celebrate, Wilson. It's rather discouraging to us," Jacobs said.

"I'm trying to help you. Look at the P.R. you'll get when that bomb hits tomorrow."

Jacobs smiled. "One, then. Debbie, do you want to see what you can find?"

Lane got up, found bourbon and scotch in a lower cabinet in the galley, got some ice from the refrigerator, and poured out four drinks for them.

Overton sipped his, knowing he was going to nurse it for a long time. Jacobs could be stingy.

"Can you believe that?" he asked. "Intentionally irradiating the ocean? Emphasis on *intentional*."

"I believe," Jacobs said, "that you're finally coming around to our way of thinking, Wilson."

"Hey, Mark, I've never been too far away from it. We'll get the bastards," Overton promised.

NOVEMBER 21

Nuclear Detonation:
35° 21′ 13″ North, 140° 45′ 16″ West

EIGHTEEN

1244 Hours Local, The Orion
35° 10′ 11″ North, 140° 29′ 45″ West

Bull Kontas was proud of his acquisitions. He was grinning widely when, with a crowbar, he popped the cover on a wooden crate with its stencilling blacked out, and stood back so Brande could marvel.

"A torpedo?" Brande asked.

"Got two of 'em, Chief. They're old Mark 43s, and they're electric powered, and they're slow as hell, but they can do a job. Damn things weigh two hundred and sixty-four pounds. I think they were destined for Nicaragua, but, you know, money talks."

Brande had no idea in the world what he was going to do with two torpedoes except, like Bull, be the proud owner. Located on the deck next to the battery chargers, the crates were about nine feet long, and the seven-foot, eight-inch torpedoes were cradled lovingly inside each box.

"Damn, that's great, Bull."

Okey Dokey tested the Cosmoline protectant with a forefinger. "Greasy mutha."

With his back to Kontas, Dokey looked at Brande

and rolled his eyes. "I don't know, Dane. Control and ignition might be a problem."

"Got the manuals, too," Kontas said.

"That's all we'll probably need," Brande said. "I sure didn't expect you to find torpedoes, Bull."

"We're in the underwater business, right? I thought they were damned appropriate," Kontas said, his weathered face creased into an uncharacteristic smile.

Brande hated to wipe away that smile. "I thought you'd be lucky to get the mining explosives and grenades. You did get the grenades?"

"Oh, yeah. A hundred of them, most of them fragmentation, and a few phosphorous. Guaranteed to be good."

Brande was certain the torpedoes would be useless at eighteen thousand feet of depth. They just weren't designed for it. The grenades, however, were already densely compacted, and could take the pressures.

"How about the magnets, Bull?"

"No sweat there, Chief."

Dokey grinned. "Now it dawns on me. We're going to build our own mines."

"What do you think, Okey?"

"It's far better than using a cutting torch on a manipulator arm."

"My original thought," Brande said, "was to plant a few of these things around, disable their equipment, and slow down the march. Mark Jacobs would probably approve."

"We won't tell him, though, I trust."

"I don't believe so."

"You don't like the torpedoes?" Kontas asked.

"I want to keep those in reserve, Bull. We'll go

after the floor crawlers, first. If they attack us with subs at shallower depths, we'll have those as a surprise."

Kontas grinned yet again.

The three of them conducted their conversation scrunched into the starboard-aft corner of the lab. *DepthFinder*'s bulk was again taking up most of the space, her innards being explored and tested by a gaggle of technicians and scientists, a few of whom had seen the torpedo and were probably wondering when they'd signed up for military service. The empty cardboard boxes and protective plastic bags for dozens of replacement circuit chips were spread all over the deck.

Not part of their group, but listening intently to them, Rae Thomas leaned against the side of the submersible. She had a look on her face that was wavering between complete amazement and stark disapproval.

Brande was doing his best to avoid her eyes.

"Bull can help me," Dokey said, "and we'll start building us a few Marine Visions Unlimited Mark One, mod one, deep-submergence mines."

"The hell you will," Thomas told him.

Which stifled the activity around them.

Bob Mayberry, standing near a workbench with an opened black box for the forward-looking sonar resting on it, said to the grad student interns, "Come on, people, back to work."

"Why don't we put the lid back on this thing, Bull," Brande said.

He knew that, within seconds, everyone on board would know that the *Orion* was now an armed vessel, and he didn't think that most of them would appreciate the change of status.

Brande and Kontas replaced the lid on the crate, and Kontas picked up a hammer to drive the nails back home.

"Are you listening to me?" Thomas asked.

"Rae, let's you and I go get a cup of coffee," Brande suggested.

He reached for her arm, but she shrugged it out of his grasp.

"Please."

She wasn't happy, but she followed him out of the laboratory, across the corridor, and into the wardroom. Otsuka was there, gathering a box of soft drinks for the people working on the sub.

"Hi," she said brightly. Brande thought she was looking at life a little differently now, like he was.

"Kim," Thomas said, "do you really want Okey to blow himself up?"

"What? Of course not."

"Go talk to him."

Otsuka left them alone in the wardroom.

"You're not happy, I guess," Brande said.

"I'm upset about Svetlana, yes. I'm upset about you taking Okey and Kim into an area where you *knew* there could be nuclear activity. And, you're damned right, Dane, I'm unhappy about you ordering up all this armament without telling me. We're not fighting this war alone."

Thomas's eyes seemed to be firing tiny sparks at him.

"I'm incensed about Svetlana myself, Rae. And my run-in with the nuke only convinced me that Deride won't be stopped. Not at any cost. Sure, it's a war. You tell me what Washington is doing about it. If it shows, I don't see it."

"It's not up to us."

"It *is* up to us. We're the ones on the scene, and we're practically the only outfit available that's capable of *reaching* the scene."

"You're so certain," she said, "that you speak for the company. You're putting others at risk without asking them, Dane."

He was taken completely by surprise. She was correct, and he knew it.

"Come on, then," he said. "I'll ask them."

He started for the door, but she stopped him with, "You won't even talk to Deride."

He hesitated and turned back to her. "We've tried a couple of times."

"Try again."

"All right, I'll do that first."

Brande decided to use the acoustic phone in the laboratory, and he went directly to the command console, where Emry was sitting, fiddling with the map he had on the screen. Thomas trailed along.

"Larry, let me on the Loudspeaker a minute, will you?"

Emry looked up. "Sure thing."

They exchanged places, and Brande tried first on the frequency they normally used. There was no international convention for a hailing channel on acoustic transmissions, but Glenn had called them once before, so it was possible that she was monitoring them.

"AquaGeo habitat, this is the *RV Orion*. Come in, please."

He tried three times before he got a response.

"Orion, this is AquaGeo SeaStation AG-4."

Even with the warbled acoustic characteristics, he could tell that it was a man's voice, but not one that he knew.

"Dane Brande calling for Paul Deride or Penny Glenn."

He didn't know whether or not Deride would be aboard the habitat.

"Hold on a minute."

Dokey, Otsuka, and Mayberry came over to stand beside Thomas and Emry.

It was Deride who finally responded. "What do you want, Brande?"

"Let's talk about what you're doing."

"Let's not. We're pursuing a perfectly legal activity, and you're interfering with it, Brande. You have been enjoined from doing so, and if you want talk, talk to my lawyer."

"Deride, I don't give a damn about your mining. You can dig for gold anywhere you want. My concern is your methods and how they endanger both the ocean and the West Coast of the United States."

"My methods are my business. Stay out of the way, and you won't get hurt. Goodbye, Dr. Brande."

Brande sat back. "We probably should have sold him Gargantua. Maybe he'd be nicer to me."

"I wouldn't count on it," Emry said.

He looked up at Thomas. "I tried, Rae."

She appeared to be as frustrated as he felt. "Yes, you tried."

Brande stood up and went to the head of the laboratory. He didn't have to call for attention; all eyes were on him. There were fifteen people present, all gathered around the bow of *DepthFinder*. All of them depended upon him for their livelihood as well as competent decisions. He felt the weight.

"We'll get involved with a little democratic governance," he said. "Everyone knows what's been taking place. According to Larry's projections, if AquaGeo continues its current pattern of blasting, we've got three more days, including today, and three more detonations before they're interfering with some delicate structures in the Pioneer Fracture Zone. We don't know the probabilities of a nuclear detonation triggering earthquakes, but as long as it's possible, I'm concerned. On top of that, their activities are leaving behind a lot of ecological damage. You've seen the videos of dead and irradiated sea life.

"My intention would be to delay them as long as possible, until the legal eagles have a chance to act."

Brande saw a few affirming nods in his audience.

"On the other side of this coin, we'd be defying some legal restrictions ourselves." He aimed a thumb to starboard. "There are three Navy ships out there, and I suspect that they're going to be determined to uphold the law. They'll tell us 'no.' "

Brande took a deep breath. "I'm probably going to break the law. But you don't have to break it with me or assume the risks. Bull has the *Mighty Moose* nearby, and we'll transfer anyone who wants to return to San Diego."

"Not me," Kontas said. "Someone else can captain her."

"Nor me," Dokey said.

"I'm staying with my ship," Mel Sorenson said over the intercom's overhead speaker. He had been listening to Brande's speech from the bridge.

Connie Alvarez-Sorenson spoke over the intercom, "It's my ship, too."

"Let's see some hands," Thomas said. "Who wants to go back?"

There were no raised hands.

"All right, Dane," she said. "We stop AquaGeo, but I want a say in the tactics."

"What do you suggest, Rae?"

"We've been chasing after the problem, trying to anticipate the next nuke event, and look where it got you. We're on our last set of replacements for the submersible, and she may be close to the envelope of safety. The hull may have suffered stresses we can't find. If Ingrid were here, doing a competent structural analysis, I'm sure she wouldn't allow us to launch again."

She was probably correct. Ingrid Roskens was even more conservative than Brande in safety matters.

"We don't know for sure," Thomas went on, "where the next charge will be placed."

"I've got a damned good idea about that, though, Kaylene," Emry said.

"Give or take a few hundred yards, Larry. But we do know the exact coordinates of the root cause of our problem."

"The seabed habitat?" Brande said.

"If you want to risk riding out another subsurface hurricane looking for floor crawlers to disable, Dane, you can do it by yourself. If you want to confront the real problem, which is people, I'll dive with you."

The fire was back in her cheeks, and Brande thought she had made her determination.

Brande crossed the deck to Emry's monitor. He checked the symbols indicating the known locations of test sites. To the south-southwest was the square designating what he now knew Deride called SeaStation AG-4.

"Mel, you still listening?" he asked in the direction of the intercom.

"Got you, Chief."

"Let's come to a heading of one-ninety."

"Coming to one-ninety. Aye, aye."

The deck heeled slightly to port as the ship began to come about.

Brande turned to the others. "Anyone else have another good suggestion?"

Otsuka, standing next to Dokey, smiled at him. "The next time, Dane, that you order bomb materials, consult with me first. I'd have chosen better components."

Thomas shook her head in resignation.

1415 Hours Local, The California
34° 57′ 27″ North, 140° 41′ 42″ West

A seaman second brought the visitors to the officers' wardroom, showed them in, then closed the door behind them. Captain Mabry Harris and Commander George Quicken were waiting for them.

Harris walked around the table, smiled, and extended his hand.

"Dr. Thomas, I'm Captain Harris. This is Commander Quicken."

"I'm pleased to meet you, Captain," she said, shaking his hand firmly. She introduced Dr. Lawrence Emry.

"I'm sorry Dr. Brande couldn't join us," Harris said.

"As I told you on the radio, Captain, he's extremely busy with the repairs to the submersible."

She had been forthright, and perhaps justifiably angry, in her description of the maelstrom to which the sub had been subjected.

They took seats around the table, and a steward served coffee and rolls. The rolls went untouched.

"I asked for this meeting," Harris said, "because I thought it was time to discuss several issues."

"What's on your agenda, Captain?"

She was a striking woman, Harris thought. He had expected that the president of Marine Visions would be, somehow, more severe. He also noted some subtly recognizable features—the color of her eyes, the shape of her nose, the jutting of her chin.

"Are you, by any chance, related to Admiral Charles Thomas?"

"He's my father," she said.

"A terrific man and commander," Harris said. "I served with him in the Med."

"Stubborn and irascible, too," she said.

He grinned. "Yes, there were times. At any rate, I feel we need to talk about, first of all, this injunction."

"We've turned off-course, Captain."

"Yes, I noted that, though you haven't turned back to San Diego."

"We want to remain in the area, should we be needed when the legal matters are ironed out. Our contract is still in effect, so far as we know."

Was she being overly optimistic? Given the normal speed of the courts, Harris thought so.

Emry dug into a large plastic envelope he had placed on the table and came up with an oversized chart. He handed it to Quicken. "That's a map we've compiled of the test sites. You're aware of the implications?"

Quicken scanned it quickly. "We're aware, Dr. Emry. This is a nice chart. There are structures we weren't aware of."

His first mate handed it to him, and Harris looked it over. Their own computers had stored the detonation sites, but this map also detailed a great many seabed features.

"It's yours," Emry said.

"Thank you. Let me say," Harris said, "that I'm completely sympathetic to your cause. Conversely, my orders are to be certain that you comply with the injunction. For however long it is in place."

"You don't care about what Deride's doing down there?" Emry said.

"I care. Still, we live in a civilized world."

"It's a free ocean," Thomas said. "We—"

"I believe that's the argument AquaGeo's attorneys are making, Dr. Thomas," Harris remarked.

"We can still go where we want to go."

"My concern is with the heading you've taken."

"Why is that?"

"A hundred and twenty nautical miles south, on your present heading, you will run into the *Outer Islands Lady*."

Thomas's surprise appeared to be valid.

"I don't know anything about her."

"She's AquaGeo's submersible maintenance ship, and she arrived in the area this morning. Along with her is a freighter that, until yesterday, had taken up a station a couple hundred miles to the east. I'm suggesting that the *Orion* steer clear of her. Just to avoid potential unpleasantries."

"I'll bring the subject up with Dane when we go back," she said.

"Good. Now, you can imagine that the information I get has been filtered through Washington and a few other commands. Would you be so good as to provide Commander Quicken and myself with a firsthand account of what has taken place to date?"

Thomas quickly told them of her own encounter with the AquaGeo submersible—he hadn't realized that she was also a qualified diver—and of Svetlana Polodka's death. She also seemed convinced that the AquaGeo people knew that the *DepthFinder* would be endangered when they set off the charge at Site Number Eleven.

Quicken was taking shorthand notes of the testimony.

If her version of the facts was correct, Harris would agree that Paul Deride's people had shown extremely reckless disregard for human life. If she were unbiased. Sometimes, though, the cold, objective scientist's view could be slanted. So far, though, Harris didn't think there was anything provable, in the matter of intent.

"Is there anything else?" Quicken asked.

She glanced at Emry, but was apparently not going to say anything.

Emry did. "We, ah, happened to disable one of their floor crawlers."

"I see," Harris said. "How did you do that?"

"Brande and Dokey cut a power cable to one of the tracks. Keeps them moving in a circle."

"Without endangering anyone?"

"The crew could be picked up."

"I might also suggest that similar sabotage in the future won't be conducive to resolving the issues," Harris said, though he had to suppress an urge to grin.

"You ought to get the CIA or someone to brief you on Deride's history," Thomas said. "He won't be trying to resolve any issues but his own."

Once again, Harris felt a bit deprived of information. Everyone around him seemed to know more than he did. It left him at a disadvantage.

"Okay, there's one more thing, Dr. Thomas."

"Of course there is."

"George?"

Quicken passed each of them copies of the faxed articles from the *Washington Post*.

He waited while they read the Wilson Overton-bylined story, then said, "That hit the street this morning."

"I think he got it mostly right," Thomas said. She was smiling.

"I assume that you're the unnamed source from Marine Visions."

"Since I was a little kid, I've always wanted to be an unnamed source," she said.

"This is damned good, Kaylene," Emry told her.

"I understand your point, naturally," Harris said. "You can't get the legal system to move, so you went to the public with the story."

"It nearly worked for Ross Perot," she said. "In fact, there are changes being made directly as a result of his concern for the involvement of people in the political process."

"Not that I don't understand your motivation," Harris said, "but this article is already having some drastic response."

"Such as?"

"The White House and the Pentagon are swamped with telephone calls and wires, for one thing. Protestors are lined up on Pennsylvania Avenue and in front of the state capitol in Sacramento."

"For another," she said, "I'll bet you heard from your bosses."

"I did, as a matter of fact," Harris admitted. The Chief of Naval Operations, Delecourt himself, had blistered his hide for a half hour on a scrambled radio frequency.

Harris had taken it stoically. He didn't know what he could do about changing freedom-of-the-press rules. There was no declared war or hostilities involved here.

"Of concern to the people in Washington, Dr. Thomas, are the mounting number of protests. AquaGeo's offices in Washington and San Francisco are being protected by police. There's a flotilla of environmental activists on its way here. Someone is bound to get hurt."

"And what's Deride doing?" she asked.

"Ah, as far as I know, and I may not know very much, Deride's doing very little."

"You must have an eye on the *Outer Islands Lady.*"

A P-3 Orion was flying an orbit that encompassed both the maintenance ship and the two freighters holding station above what Emry's map described as Site Number Four.

"We do."

"And what is happening with her?"

Harris didn't have a security classification to fall back on, so he said, "The ship has retrieved a submersible. Our recon photos show that it's severely damaged."

"One of the propellers?"

"Yes."

"That's the one Dokey took out," Emry said. "Cost us a quarter-million-dollar robot to do it."

"And the freighter?" Thomas probed.

"They seem to be off-loading additional submersibles and floor crawlers."

"Damn," she said. "They've got reinforcements, Larry."

"How many did you see?" Harris asked.

"We were figuring two subs and three floor crawlers, with one of each out of commission," Emry said. "But if Deride's bringing in more, then surely you know that he's not going to listen to any reason that doesn't have a dollar amount tied to it."

Harris thought that Emry made a good argument, but he said, "Our hands seem to be tied. The Chief of Naval Operations would like to do more, but the directions are apparently being devised by the Justice Department."

"Don't you get overwhelmed by the bureaucracy?" Thomas asked him.

"I try to do my job, Dr. Thomas."

"What's your job going to be when San Francisco and Carmel slide into the sea?"

1620 Hours Local
Washington, D.C.

Avery Hampstead asked Brande, "Who leaked this thing to the press?"

Their scrambled communications circuit caused voices to echo, ebb, and rise.

"An unnamed source, as I understand it," Brande said.

"Well, it's got people riled up. When I talked to Unruh last, they had just called an emergency meeting of the task force. He said that a whole fleet of Justice Department lawyers had just sailed for the courts of prominent jurisdiction. Plus, they're digging into every on- and offshore permit and license issued to AquaGeo. They're going to dig until they find something."

"Good. Maybe a little blackmail is in order, Avery."

"How about you?"

"We're just hanging around. The Navy made it clear to Rae, without saying so, that one massive missile cruiser will get in our way if we don't stick to the rules."

"And will you stick to the rules?"

"You know me, Avery."

"That's the problem. I do know you."

"So where are we?"

"Our contact at Justice, one Miss Pamela Stroh, tells me that AquaGeo, through its counsel, Mr. Anthony Camden, has denied any wrongdoing on the part of the company. He said they'd alleviate any concerns at the hearing before the Maritime Commission."

"And when is that?" Brande asked.

"Camden asked for a continuance, and that's being considered."

"When is the hearing scheduled, Avery?"

Hampstead cleared his throat. "Ah, the sixth of January."

"Shit!"

"Well, they're getting some pressure now, as a result of the publicity, and I think they'll try to move it up."

"If it's not held within the next two days, it's too damned late."

"I'm aware of that, Dane. So are others."

"Go out and buy yourself an electric cattle prod, Avery. Try that on them, will you?"

1705 Hours Local, SeaStation AG-4
33° 16' 50" North, 141° 15' 19" West

Deride took the call at the console on the far end and bent over the countertop, trying to keep his conversation confidential.

"Tell me that again, Anthony."

"There's FBI agents and Justice Department lawyers invading every operation we've got going in the States, and within the offshore limits."

"Bloody hell! What are they looking for?"

"Anything, I imagine, Paul. There will be some loopholes, some *t*'s that we forgot to cross. As soon as they find one, they'll close us down."

"Damn it!"

"I told you this morning that the newspaper story was going to hurt."

In all of its years of operation, AquaGeo had never had a single adverse article appear in the media. Their success had been derived from staying in the fringes and out of the limelight. As much as he hated working below the surface, Deride enjoyed working in the dark.

"We've got five San Francisco cops outside the office door here," Camden said. "There are a dozen protestors in the hallway with all kinds of derogatory placards, and when I look down on the street, I can see another hundred or so."

"These people don't scare me."

"Nor me, Paul. However, our revenues could be drastically affected if Justice convinces the Environmental Protection Agency or the Bureau of Land Management or some other agency to suspend our permits pending hearings."

"We're getting to trade-off time," Deride said.

"I think so, yes."

"I'll talk to Penny."

1851 Hours Local, SeaStation AG-4
33° 16′ 50″ North, 141° 15′ 19″ West

Glenn had concerned herself with logistics for most of the day. From the mining operation at Test Hole

D, she had diverted two subs—the *Brisbane* and the *Canberra*—and three floor crawlers to the sea station. The sub maintenance ship was now in position and had hoisted the *Melbourne* aboard, though the technicians said it would require two to three weeks to make the required repairs. They were going to have to ship a new motor out of Sydney, as well as fabricate a new housing. The damaged floor crawler, FC-6, was still being towed back.

Deride had wanted to talk to her earlier, but she had put him off for a while. She had too much to do.

Hitting the transmit switch, she said, "FC-9, AG-4."

"Dorsey here, Penny."

"What's your status?"

"Joey and I got us a couple hours' worth of nap," he said. "But the drilling's done, and next, we'll place the charge. Maybe another hour."

"And your power supplies?"

"Oh, another seventy hours, easy."

"Good. You go straight through with it, Jim, then set out for Test Hole K."

"You don't want us to collect samples?" he asked.

"No. I'm sending McBride with *Canberra* and one of the new crawlers."

"Roger, then. We're off."

She closed the circuit and updated her status board which was actually on the computer. Discounting two crawlers—the tower and the towee—for the time being, she had four crawlers available. She would keep one here, and send the others out after briefing the crews on Brande's imaginative use of a cutting torch. That wouldn't happen again. One of the new subs should be sent to cover Dorsey's Team Three. Team Three was composed of her two nuclear experts, and she didn't want Brande getting near them.

The fact that Brande was alive had thrilled her. There was still a future beyond the immediate future. But she had been busy enough that she hadn't had time to consider all of the implications.

Something would work out. Give it a week, when it was all over, and she would devote some time to R & R and planning in some warm place like Acapulco.

But now, the goal was in sight, and she couldn't afford to lose her concentration.

"Penny, we've got to talk."

"Sure, Uncle Paul. Sit down."

He pulled up one of the chairs and sat close to her for privacy. The sea station was currently overflowing with fresh bodies, the crews who would man the vehicles coming down from the freighter. They milled around the lounge and the control room, simultaneously nervous and excited. There were four women among them.

"I talked to Anthony a little while ago."

"How is Anthony?"

He told her about the siege of the American offices and the FBI investigations.

That alarmed her a little. "How did that happen?"

"Brande spilled it all to the press. We're being crucified. Anthony says he's been contacted about an appearance on *Nightline*. He declined."

"Are we going to let a bunch of environmental zealots dictate how we conduct business, Uncle Paul? We never have in the past."

"That's what I want to talk to you about, Penny. What if we'd suspend operations farther north until this all settles down?"

"We've got four more locations to go," she said. "If we suspend for a month or so, then start up again, they'll be all over us for breaking our word. Wouldn't it be better to press forward, to stonewall them for another four—now three—days, then quit entirely?"

He thought about it for a few seconds. "That's all there is? Four more?"

"That's it. But if you're worried about a bunch of tree freaks, why we can . . ."

"No. Let's just get it over with."

"I knew you'd come up with the best decision, Uncle Paul."

She had counted on it, in fact.

His decision.

1920 Hours Local, The Orion
33° 37' 15" North, 140° 37' 46" West

Connie Alvarez-Sorenson, who was on the bridge, had altered course several hours before at Brande's direction.

He wanted Harris on the *California* to be reassured that the *RV Orion* wasn't seeking out the surface ships above the sea station. He was, in fact, certain that Harris didn't know the exact coordinates of the sea station. As far as the local Navy knew, only the surface ships were worrisome.

Or worrisome, if the *Orion* approached them. Therefore, she would not.

In the lounge with Thomas, Emry, Otsuka, Dokey,

Sorenson, and Mayberry, Brande wolfed down egg-and-sausage sandwiches that Fred Boberg had con-cocted. He was facing forward, and in the failing light of day, he could see a sea that was becoming almost as angry as he was. Waves were running at fifteen feet, and a darkly slanting rain obscured the lights of the *Mighty Moose;* she was now running ahead of them.

On the starboard, the *Arienne* was still present, and Brande had turned down two additional interview re-quests from Wilson Overton. The man was ecstatic about the stateside reaction to his articles.

The Navy ships were still with them, also. Harris had reported earlier that several boats operated by marine activists were closing to within a hundred miles of their position. By morning, it was going to get crowded, and the Navy captain wasn't happy about the prospects.

Emry had dumped the sausage and eggs out of his sandwich and was eating them with a fork, the way he claimed civilized people did. "You sure I can't go along, Chief?"

"Need you on the command console, Larry. With-out encouraging your ego, I want someone level-headed there."

"You don't think I'm levelheaded?" Otsuka asked, holding her chin out, to level her head.

"Of course. You're Larry's backup. Let's not argue this anymore, huh? It's Okey and Rae and me."

And he wasn't happy at all about Rae, but she had prevailed in their private argument. By way of black-mail. She had insisted, and he had believed her, that she would call Captain Harris in and spill the plot if she wasn't allowed to go along with them.

DepthFinder had been moved out of the laboratory and to her customary position on the fantail, primarily to reassure the watchers aboard the *California*. She was in relatively good shape, with most of her electronic components changed out for fresh units. Ninety-eight percent pure, Dokey said, downgraded only to A-1c.

Atlas, with a long series of electronic problems, had been removed from the submersible's parking sheath.

In the growing dusk, and with the deck lights extinguished, she would slowly disappear from observation into the gloom and the rain.

Dokey took a gargantuan bite out of his sandwich and chewed mightily and happily. He was wearing a recent creation, a sweatshirt with a piranha eyeing a barracuda, and captioned, "Who's Your Dentist?"

With his mouth full, Dokey said, "The best part about this location is that we don't have to wear the damned radiation suits. Everybody gets to wear ten Dokey sweatshirts."

Brande had one of his on already, and he had decided against the protective suits on the assumption that AquaGeo wouldn't store, much less detonate, one of their nukes in the region where they were headed.

"Mel," he said, "any questions?"

"I don't think so, Chief. We've been holding ten knots for the last three hours, so we don't scare the naval types. I don't like launching you at speed, but I think you're right. We go any slower, they're going to get suspicious."

"Kim, how about you?"

"None, Dane. I gave Dokey the black box, and he's already installed it in *DepthFinder.*"

She had designed, and encased in black plastic, a remote detonator utilizing an acoustic signal generator that would utilize some existing telemetry circuits. This was in addition to the twenty-five receivers she had built for the acoustic signals. Her hands were stained with etching acid, and she had a burn from a soldering iron on one wrist.

Mayberry said, "No more than eighty hours, Dane. I'm going to be firm about that."

"That's a promise, Bob."

"Anyone else? Okay, then, let's get suited up."

They were, in fact, already suited up. As a group, they quickly finished the remnants of their meals, Dokey grabbed four boxes of foodstuffs he had prepared for the trip, and they walked aft.

The lab was in semidarkness, with light shining from the computer monitors. A blackout curtain had been rigged across the stern doorway, so that light wouldn't spill out when the door was opened.

Brande, Thomas, and Dokey gathered up their spare clothing, slipped into ponchos, and slid through the hatchway.

The designated deck crew members went with them, everyone feeling their way carefully in the darkness and hard, slanted rain of the stern deck. As Brande had ordered, the deck crewmen clipped on lifelines as soon as they left the safety of the superstructure.

Brande took Thomas's hand and led her through the blackness until his left elbow bumped into the scaffold. Cautiously, he urged her upward, and she climbed swiftly to the top, then over the sail.

As soon as Brande and Dokey reached her, she opened the hatch, and one after the other, they slipped aboard. Dokey closed the hatch and dogged it, but not before they had shipped a fair amount of rainwater.

There would be no UHF transmissions, for fear of the Navy overhearing, and the acoustic system didn't operate until they were in the water.

They had timed the launch, instead.

Dokey flopped in the right-hand seat, saying, "Zero plus ten seconds."

Zero hour began with the closing of the hatch.

Brande took the left seat, and Thomas settled in the back position and began flipping switches.

At zero plus fifteen seconds, Dokey powered up the instrument panels.

By four minutes after the hatch closed, all of their systems were up and operating. At five minutes, Brande had the option of opening the hatch to abort the dive.

He didn't.

At six minutes, he felt the submersible lift from her deck rails.

"Here we go," he said.

"Betcha this is a rough bounce, Chief," Dokey said.

"Rae?" he asked.

"I'm ready."

With no deck lights, it was difficult to tell when they dropped below deck level. He thought he saw a paleness through the driving rain that was the port hull.

When the sub hit the water, she immediately skewed to the right, throwing Dokey toward him.

Then she surged upward, riding a wave.

Then the winch line was released, and they bobbed in the wake of the research vessel.

"I suggest we head for the bottom," Dokey said.

"Execute your suggestion, Okey."

A few seconds later, they were stable, and the fury of the storm was behind them.

Dokey worked his control sticks, finding the direction he wanted.

"I'm on two-five-five, descent rate eighty per minute. All right with everyone?"

"Sounds good to me," Brande said.

"Kaylene, honey," Dokey said, "if you look in the top box there, you'll find a burrito. I'm hungry."

NOVEMBER 22

Nuclear Detonation:
35° 50′ 2″ North, 141° 2′ 7″ West

NINETEEN

0016 Hours Local, The DepthFinder
33° 22′ 15″ North, 141° 6′ 26″ West

Two hours before, they had received a coded one-word signal from Emry on the Loudspeaker acoustic voice system. They were not transmitting telemetry data on the system since AquaGeo or even the Navy might pick up on the transmission and because Dokey and Otsuka had requisitioned some of the circuits. It left the command center aboard the ship in the dark as to their condition, and they had agreed to send an hourly report via an oral code word.

Only Thomas, who was wearing a headset, heard the signal from the surface.

She tapped Brande hard on the shoulder. "Larry says 'barbeque.' "

"Barbeque? That means they set off another nuke."

"Three to go," Dokey said. "I hope to hell the Navy is keeping track."

"They can have the U.S. lawyers complain to the AquaGeo lawyers," Brande had said. "That should stop it."

Other than that information from the surface, the descent had been uneventful. Thomas was wearing three sweaters and feeling as bulky as a kid about to head out into a wonderful snowstorm. Dokey kept the submersible in a steep glide, aimed in the direction of the sea station. Brande's Nana Mouskouri cassettes played on the tape deck. Thomas could tell he was in a melancholy mood because he had played "Even Now" three times.

She thought he was thinking of Svetlana, much as she had been. So much potential lost. Thomas knew that Brande had personally called Valeri Dankelov with a private obituary, and she knew that would have been difficult for Brande.

"Position check," Brande said.

They were relying on the internal Inertial Navigation System (INS) since they had foregone, in favor of stealth and ordnance, the data link to *Orion*'s connection with the NavStar satellite constellation.

Dokey said, "I've got us eighteen nautical miles out, Dane. Still on a heading of two-five-five. Forward momentum reads out at eleven knots."

Brande had the mapping program up on his monitor, and he keyed the new data in.

"We're on track," he said, "but you know we still have some time to change our minds."

"Second-guessing yourself, Chief?"

"If I don't do it for myself, someone else will do it for me, Okey."

"If you're worrying about me, Dane," Thomas said, "don't do it."

"Kaylene," Dokey said, "before I forget, I appreciate the position you took back on the ship."

"You do?" She was halfway surprised.

"Sure. You're president of the company. You couldn't do any less."

In the semidarkness, she saw Brande turn his head back toward her and smile. He snaked his hand between the seats, found her knee, and squeezed it lightly.

Her residual anger at him dissipated, though her anxiety level didn't lessen a bit.

Five minutes later, after Nana got through "Danny Boy," Dokey said, "Chief, I suspect we ought to unleash Gargantua, and make sure we're talking on the same line."

"I'm greatly reassured by your confidence in your ROVs, Okey."

Brande activated his panel, switched the controls to the robot, and flipped on the exterior lights. Through the portholes, Thomas saw the ultrablackness at the end of the visibility range. Over time she had become inured to that nothingness.

Brande gripped the joysticks lightly, eased in power, and Gargantua, who was too large for the sheath, and who had been in tow, slowly emerged from under the bow into their field of view. Dokey flicked a switch and put the robot's camera view on the center monitor.

Trailing the fiber-optic tether like a lazy eel, the ROV moved out ahead of them, then turned to face the sub. Brande slipped it into reverse power to keep it backing in position. Retarding the throttle momentarily, he let Gargantua close in on the center port, until they were staring at it from about five feet away. The view under the halogen lights was stark and bright, as if the brightness control on a television set was out of adjustment.

The monstrous robot appeared to be almost an inquistive sea creature, perhaps a whale. With his floodlights illuminated, he had very bright eyes.

The video view from the ROV gave them a picture of themselves, peering intently from the submersible's portholes.

Beneath Gargantua's "chin" was a wire basket used for holding samples or relics from undersea wrecks. It was crammed with the crude packages that Dokey and Otsuka had devised. Each fragmentation grenade had had its pin pulled and replaced with a fusible link attached to a nine-volt battery. Applying power was supposed to melt the fusible link, allowing the grenade to perform the action for which it had been designed. The circuit was controlled by a coded signal from the sub, utilizing revamped circuitry in the telemetry system. The black box Dokey had plugged into Loudspeaker mounted a rotary switch for selecting up to twenty-five grenades whose receivers were controlled by discrete codes, an arming switch, and a push button.

The problem was a matter of selection.

Selecting number nine, if number nine were still in the basket, arming it, and firing it, would blow Gargantua into tiny bits and pieces.

For that reason, the operators had to visually check each "package." As she watched, Brande activated the manipulator arm. It extended slowly, then reached back underneath the robot. The thumb and fingers parted, reached into the basket, and clamped on one of the packages.

"Light touch here would be nice, Chief."

"I know I don't have your sensitivity, Okey."

The robotics engineer was capable of tying a shoe-lace neatly or hoisting a full fifty-five-gallon drum with the same manipulator.

When the arm pulled out of the basket, Thomas saw that it was gripping the awkward-appearing, plastic tape-wrapped bundle. The handle of the grenade was exposed, and in this case, because of the way Brande had grabbed it, upside down. Each unit contained a grenade, a receiver, a battery, and a magnet. The ROV's fingers and thumb had been changed out, switched to a reinforced carbon-carbon (RCC) set so that the magnet would not adhere to them. A big white vinyl number was glued to each package.

"For our test shot," Brande said, "I happened to draw number eight from the lottery basket."

"Looks like an eight to me, too, Chief."

"Damn, I hope so. You put the numbers on."

"I tried not to lose track," Dokey said.

Thomas's anxiety increased dramatically. She leaned forward between the seats and watched Dokey as he fiddled with the black box resting in his lap. He clicked the rotary dial until he found number eight and lined it up under an arrow etched into the box.

"The next time," Dokey said, "Kim and I will make this digital."

"There's never, never going to be a next time," Thomas told him.

"Right. I forgot. Okay, number eight."

"Nine hundred and twenty-five feet above the sea-bed," Brande said. "You want me to drop it before you arm it?"

"Damned right. This is all new technology, Chief."
Brande released the black bundle.

It dropped away slowly, spinning away from their view.

Dokey counted aloud, "Five . . . four . . . three . . . two . . . one, armed."

"Didn't hear anything," Brande said.

"Good. You're not supposed to. Five . . . four . . . three . . . two . . . one, *boom!*"

The concussion, from probably a hundred yards away, was only enough to slightly rock the sub. Thomas heard a mild thud as the shock wave slapped the sub.

"Registered on the sonar," Dokey said. "Test one hundred percent successful."

"You only get a score of zero or one hundred on this test," Brande told him, then added, "Damn, Okey. This seems kind of haphazard."

"It's definitely a Rube Goldberg getup," Dokey said. "I hope to hell they all work."

Which didn't help Thomas's anxiety in the least.

0025 Hours Local, The Orion
33° 2' 15" North, 141° 21' 26" West

Kim Otsuka sat at the computer console next to Emry, who wouldn't give up his spot, with her feet up on the desktop. She had wrapped an old comforter around her legs.

Some of the crew members and scientific personnel had headed for their bunks, but most were gathered in the lab waiting for something, anything, to happen. An odd collection of chairs drawn from the lab and the wardroom were aligned randomly behind Emry's command console.

Through the porthole above the console, Otsuka was shocked to suddenly see stars. It was a brief glimpse, then the hole in the cloud cover closed up, and they were gone.

"I wonder if the weather is lifting, finally," she said to Emry.

"Doubt it, with my luck," he said. "I'm supposed to be in Tahiti."

She glanced at his screen. With no telemetry feedback, he seemed like a lost man. He had his map on the screen, and he was adding a dotted line to it for *DepthFinder*'s projected course. It was mostly guesswork.

"How long do you think, Larry?"

"I'm estimating them twenty-five nautical at the moment. Couple more hours, Kim."

She wondered if they had conducted the ordnance test yet. The more she thought about it, the more she worried. What if she had put the dash under the *nine,* rather than the *six?* Was *sixteen* really *nineteen?*

She couldn't remember, and it bothered her that such simplistic math was so troublesome when she could remember the exact sequence of numbers in a three-line, fifteen-element computer instruction.

She knew it was just her nerves.

Had to be.

She stared out the porthole, hoping against hope to see more stars.

And the night suddenly erupted in white glare.

"Goddamn!" Emry yelped.

"What's that!" she chimed in.

"The damned *California* has put her lights on us," he said, scrambling out of his chair.

"What are they going to see?"

"That's not the problem, Kim. It's what they're *not* going to see that's the problem."

0535 Hours Local
Washington, D.C.

Carl Unruh was on his way to work, sailing along a nicely auto-free George Washington Memorial Parkway in a light snowfall when his cellular phone buzzed.

He figured the news wasn't going to be good as he searched for the phone with his free right hand, found it, and clicked it on.

"Unruh."

"Ben Delecourt, Carl."

"What's up, Admiral?"

"Not up. Down. I just got word from the *California* that Brande's submersible, along with a large robot that was in a cradle, have disappeared from the deck of the *Orion.*"

"Maybe they pulled it inside?"

"Captain Harris talked to Lawrence Emry, who said he could not tell a lie—the *DepthFinder* was undergoing tests on its repaired systems."

"Sounds logical to me, Ben."

"In the middle of the night, where they are? Damn it, Carl, you know Brande as well as I do. He's not above telling the Navy, or even the President, to go to hell if they interfere with his concept of what's right or wrong."

"Is he wrong on this, Ben? I mean, you and I and Avery put him out there in the first place. Time's running out." Unruh took the exit for CIA Headquarters, slowing rapidly as he realized that what looked like clear highway was black ice. His Dodge did a little tango dance which he corrected with his left hand.

"I'm on his side," Delecourt said, "but there are just a few problems. State and Justice say we do it right, through the courts. Plus, I don't know what the hell he's got planned. I hate it when I don't have all the data."

"If we continue to follow the lawyers' advice, Ben, we'd better notify the governor of California to start evacuating the state."

"Isn't Justice cracking down on Deride?"

"I talked to a couple FBI supervisors last night," Unruh said. "Sure, they're trying to pressure Deride, but both of them told me it would be weeks before they sifted through all of the paperwork. And they both expect Anthony Camden and his legal staff to be filing counterclaims against the government this morning, or at least on Monday. No one's heard directly from Deride."

"So what do you suggest, Carl?"

"Me?" Unruh asked as he showed his ID to a guard and pulled into the parking lot. "I'm thinking of taking a couple days' vacation."

"And let Brande go?"

"You told me he's already gone."

"The President has told me to uphold the law,"

Delecourt said. "I've got to order the *California* to protect AquaGeo's assets against anything Brande might do."

"All you can protect are the surface ships, Ben. You haven't got anything in your inventory that will reach the submersible."

"If he comes shallow enough, we could put a couple Asrocs into him."

Unruh didn't think that two or three antisubmarine rocket torpedoes would deter Brande very much. The man was amazingly resilient.

He pulled into his slot, slapped the gearshift into park, but left the engine running for the heat.

"Tell me something, Admiral. If you were in Deride's chair, and you saw the whole damned American government mad at you, turning your American assets upside down looking for incriminating evidence, threatening your income, would you persist in blowing a few more test holes?"

"If it were my money, I sure as hell wouldn't, Carl. What are you saying?"

"I think there's another motive," Unruh said. "We were quick to attribute it to Deride's natural greed, but if that were the case, to protect what he's already got, he should suspend the Pacific operations. He doesn't appear to be doing so."

The Chief of Naval Operations thought that over. "You think maybe he's looking specifically for an earthquake trigger?"

"I spent last night poring over the papers from his previous lawsuits. A hell of a lot of them involved litigation with California companies. What if he just decided to dump all those bastards in the ocean?"

"That's weak motivation," Delecourt said.

"I'm looking for anything beyond greed. Look at that pattern of detonations, Admiral."

Again Delecourt paused, probably trying to refresh his mind. "No one really knows where a trigger might be, or if there is one, beyond an educated guess. Do you think he's just walking across the sea bottom, hoping to hit it?"

"I don't know what to think," Unruh confessed. "If that's the case, I don't think he's thought out the backlash. If he were successful, accidentally or not, I think he could be banned by the business and industry community. No one would buy from him. He'd be persona non grata in practically every country in the world. He initiates an earthquake along the West Coast, and he's dead meat."

"In the meantime, what do we do?"

"I'm beginning to think that sometimes no decision is the best decision," Unruh said. "Let Brande go. Hell, for all we know, Ben, the next nuke sets off the chain reaction."

0058 Hours Local, The Arienne
33° 2′ 15″ North, 141° 21′ 26″ West

Wilson Overton wasn't sleeping well.

He wasn't much of a sailor, he knew, and the tossing of the yacht kept him awake as much as did his continual review of the success of his story.

He thoroughly enjoyed writing articles that had impact, that inspired people to action. It meant that he had influence in his world. The stuff that Thomas had given him—Paul Deride's use of nuclear explosives, the alleged attacks against Marine Visions, the man's disregard for ecology and the environment, the possibility of initiating massive earth tremors, and the way he hid behind the law—was the kind of thing that spurred people to action.

And things were happening. People were yelling, especially those who lived along the San Andreas Fault. A protest of some sort was scheduled for this afternoon in Sacramento. And while the governments—both federal and State of California—appeared stalemated, his feedback from Washington had indicated that the Justice Department was at least investigating Deride and AquaGeo. Last night, three boats out of Seattle had joined up with them. A crowd was gathering.

The only drawback, as far as Overton was concerned, was his entrapment. He wasn't in his normal habitat, and he couldn't chase down Washington bigwigs for their "no comments." And though he was on the scene, Brande and Captain Harris on the *California* had all denied him interviews. Thomas wasn't going to tell him anything more.

The bunk heaved under him, and he rolled onto his side and pulled the pillow over his head. There was just the smallest inkling that his stomach might rebel.

On second thought, he tossed the pillow aside and sat up. If he kept his stomach lower than his head, he might keep it under control.

He became aware of a soft rapping on the louvered door of his small cabin.

"Yes?"

The door eased open, and Debbie Lane poked her head inside.

Well.

His successes were mounting.

"Wilson," she said, "I hope I didn't wake you."

"I was just lying here, thinking about you."

"Mark wants you to come topside." She backed away and closed the door.

Oh.

Overton slipped out of his bunk and pulled on his pants and shirt. He had to turn on the overhead light to find his shoes and socks.

The salon was darkened when he went through it to the ladder to the bridge. Climbing quickly, he emerged on the flying bridge to find Jacobs, Freelander, and Lane. They were all scanning the ocean through the windshield.

"Is something wrong, Mark?" he asked.

"The *California* is gone."

"Gone?"

"Just disappeared, along with the destroyers."

"What about the *Orion?*"

Jacobs pointed to a blob in the night. "Still there. So is the tugboat."

"You think something's happened?" Overton asked.

"If not, it's about to happen."

0106 Hours Local, The DepthFinder
33° 16′ 50″ North, 141° 15′ 19″ West

"We've probably been in their sonar range for about fifteen minutes," Dokey said.

"Then they should have the red carpet rolled out soon," Brande told him.

"I'll give you this," Dokey said, "you've got her down in the carpet."

Brande and Dokey had switched jobs, and Brande was flying *DepthFinder* less than twenty-five feet off the seafloor. The forward-looking sonar picture was displayed on the center screen, with Thomas monitoring it closely. The left screen held the imagery captured by the submersible's video camera, and the right CRT, which Dokey refused to look away from, was the view seen by Gargantua, some two hundred feet ahead of them as an advance guard. Both the sub and the ROV had about fifty feet of visibility under each set of floodlights.

The seabed was relatively level here with only mild rises and falls, probably the reason that Deride had selected the area as his base of operations.

"More tracks," Dokey said.

Brande glanced at the starboard monitor. A pair of floor crawler tracks had appeared in the robot's camera view.

"Busy place," Brande said.

At five miles out from the station, they had started seeing the tracks more and more frequently. They testified to the use the crawlers were getting.

"Oops," Dokey said. "I got a little close. The seabed's climbing, Chief."

"Gotcha."

Brande eased back on the right control stick and followed the terrain as it increased altitude.

"Let's back off on the speed, Okey."

"Six knots good by you?"

"Seems prudent."

Together, they reduced speed from the ten knots they had been holding for both vehicles.

Through the porthole, Brande's view was of rock sentinels and heavily silted sea bottom. Another set of tracks, this one older judging by the way the ocean current had drifted silt into it.

Then two more tracks, converging on each other, and following the direction they were heading.

"Another set of tracks," Dokey said. "This is turning into a regular Chisholm Trail."

Abruptly, the seabed levelled again.

"I've got them on the sonar," Thomas said.

Brande looked at the waterfall display. As soon as they had topped the ridge, the sonar had found what they were looking for. The station was apparent on the screen, balanced on its thin legs.

"Two subs," Thomas said, "and three floor crawlers."

"I don't suppose," Dokey said, "you'd want to circle around and sneak in from the back side."

"Is there a back side, Okey?"

"As soon as we came out of the sonar shadow, they picked us up," Thomas said.

"You sure?" Dokey said.

"I'm sure. They're coming after us."

TWENTY

Stretched out on her bunk fully clothed, Penny Glenn had been napping when the buzzer of her wall-mounted intercom sounded off. She rolled over and hit the Talk key.

"Yes?"

"Penny, it's Bert. Can you come down here?"

"On my way."

The tinge of panic in Conroy's voice urged her to speed, and she went through her doorway and down the spiral staircase at a trot.

In the control room her eyes immediately checked the status board: *Canberra* was on the way to Test Hole J to collect samples. *Perth* was at Test Hole K. *Melbourne* was on the surface for her extensive repairs. *Sydney* and *Brisbane* were nearby, their crews sleeping aboard. There were three floor crawlers parked in the vicinity. FC-6 had been towed back from where it had been disabled and was in the process of being raised to the surface for replacement of her motor control cable aboard the *Outer Islands*

Lady. Team Three was on the site of Test Hole L, drilling the hole for the explosive charge.

In the subsection of the status board for activities at Test Hole D, she noted that the sea station had been lowered to the seafloor, but was not yet anchored or manned. The nuclear reactor power supply was to be lowered today.

"What do you have, Bert?" she asked, taking a chair next to him at the main console.

He laid a forefinger against the upper-right corner of the sonar display on his screen. "Right there, Penny."

The elongated shape was moving slowly in the direction of AG-4, which was displayed as a gray circle in the center of the screen.

"Sub?"

"But it's not one of ours. It appeared just a few minutes ago."

"Well, then, it's got to be our friend Brande. Go wake up Mr. Deride."

As he got up, Conroy said, "I've already alerted the sub and crawler crews. They're taking up positions around the station."

A defensive posture. AquaGeo Limited had never, and Penny Glenn had never, been anything but aggressive in their corporate and personal lives. She didn't know why she should start changing now.

"Have you heard anything on their frequency, Bert?"

"Not much," he said, heading for the doorway. "About an hour ago, there was a one-word message, 'Glorify.' "

" 'Glorify'?"

"Right. Some kind of code, I figured."

She checked the station monitors and got a sense of Conroy's paranoia. He had turned on all of the banks of exterior floodlights. The overhead camera was turning lazily in a circle, but not capturing much beyond the sixty feet of space illuminated by the lights. As she watched, the camera got a glimpse of the top of one of the floor crawlers, just starting to move. A few seconds later, it caught *Sydney* rising a few feet from her resting spot on the bottom. The monitoring video camera mounted outside the air lock showed *Brisbane* disengaging from the station.

Switching the acoustic transponder to the frequency utilized by Marine Visions, she pulled the desk microphone close and pressed the Transmit button.

"*DepthFinder,* this is AG-4."

The response was immediate, and even with the distortion of the acoustic system, she knew the voice was Brande's.

"Dr. Glenn, I presume?"

"Are you snooping again, Dane?"

"I'm watching you," he said.

She liked the thought of that—it set up a tingle of anticipation for the future, but she said, "You're not supposed to be here."

"Penny, I don't know what topics the legal artists are toying with, but I like my ocean the way it is. Irradiating it or blowing up sensitive geologic structures is not my idea of progress."

"We'll have to talk about progress sometime, Dane. For the present, though, I don't think you'll find much change in *your* ocean."

"Have you measured the radiation?"

"Nothing there that won't dissipate in a short time," she said.

After a momentary pause, he said, "This could all be resolved easily if you'd shut down your operation for a few days."

"That can't happen, Dane. We don't have all that taxpayer-supported scientific money to rely on; we have to stay on schedule."

"Whose schedule?"

"My boss's, of course. Everybody has a boss."

That was good. She wanted to get that statement on the record, and she was certain that *DepthFinder* and *Orion* were recording this conversation.

"I'll have to stop you, Penny."

That wouldn't happen, either, she knew.

"I suspect, Dane, that if you try, Uncle Paul will sue you out of your beautiful ship and submersible. Look, this will be over in a few days, then I'll come to San Diego, and we can laugh about our differences."

"I'm not laughing, Penny."

"You will," she said. "Bye for now."

Glenn immediately switched over to the scrambled frequency for Team Three.

"Dorsey, you there?"

She had to try twice before he answered.

"You always catch me when I'm trying to get a few winks, Penny. What's up?"

"You're on site?"

"You bet. After we rest, we'll start drilling."

"I want you to skip Test Holes K and L. Go right onto M."

"Are you sure?"

"Yes, I am. And, Jim, go now. I want that hole done today."

"Hey, Penny, we're getting into some rugged terrain. It's going to take twelve hours or more to get there, and some of our reserves are getting low."

"Then you'd better get under way," she said. "I'll send out a sub with fresh batteries and an oxygen recharge."

"Please do," he said. "I hate running this low."

She signed off just as Deride arrived in the control room.

"It's the middle of the night, Penny," he said. "Something wrong?"

"Brande's out there."

"Bloody hell! You talked to him?"

"I tried," she said, and left it ambiguous.

0114 Hours Local, The DepthFinder
33° 16′ 50″ North, 141° 15′ 19″ West

"Deride's a stubborn man," Dokey said.

"There is something definitely wrong with that woman," Thomas said.

"That's jealousy talking," Dokey told her.

"Go to hell, Okey."

Brande was reminded of family gatherings when he would get into arguments with a female cousin he couldn't stand.

"Now, children, as my grandma Bridgette would say, let's stop the bickering."

Dokey and Brande had brought *DepthFinder* and *Gargantua* to a standstill as soon as Glenn had contacted them. When he checked the sonar, he saw that they were still nine hundred yards from the station. The movement that Thomas had noted was still taking place; a sub had detached itself from the station. Another sub was moving toward them, but slowly. It was barely making five knots. The three floor crawlers were sidling away from the station in three different directions, protecting all of the flanks.

Dokey looked over the image on the screen.

"Any idea, Chief, how we go about fighting another submersible?"

"None, Okey."

"We don't ram it," Thomas said.

"The veteran knows something we don't," Dokey said.

"Judging by the one we saw up north," Brande said, "I think we can outrun it."

"But we don't want to run."

"Not just yet."

"Both of you listen up," Thomas said. "Let's not start ad-libbing right off the bat. We developed a strategy before we left the surface; stick to it."

"You're right, Rae," Brande told her.

"Communications first, then," Dokey said.

"Let me get a mine," Brande told him.

"Keep the nomenclature pure, please," Dokey said. "That's a Marine Visions Unlimited Mark One, mod one, deep-submergence mine."

"I thought that's what I said," Brande told him as he worked Gargantua back toward them, into their lighted field of view.

It only took a couple of minutes to pick a mine out of the basket and determine its number.

"Number fourteen," Brande said.

"Fourteen," Dokey echoed, setting the rotary dial on his detonator. "That's in his left hand."

"Remember that, if you don't mind," Brande said, switching to the right manipulator controls and picking out a second grenade.

"Number Three," he said.

"I wish you could pick up these things in sequence," Dokey said.

"Somebody could have packed them in sequence," Brande said.

"Picky, picky."

He eased in the rotational stick, spun the robot on its axis, then drove forward, bringing the ROV's bow down as he added power. That was one thing Gargantua could really boast. He had power to spare.

The center screen, with the ROV's view, showed a heavily tracked and yet relatively smooth seabed. Brande dove almost to touchdown, then levelled off, keeping the robot barely five feet above earth level. He extended both arms until they showed in the video eye.

"That's the heading you want?" Dokey asked.

"For the time being."

"Then I'll go three points port."

"Fine."

Dokey moved the power switch forward, and the submersible eased ahead, then left the track of the robot, moving divergently away to the left. They could only go so far with the tactic, until they reached the limit of the 250-foot tether.

The idea, of course, was to present the AquaGeo defenders with a major sonar target that would catch their attention and perhaps raise their adrenaline levels. If by chance, they happened to miss the significance of the smaller sonar target, the robot, so much the better.

Thomas called out the range. "Eight hundred yards to target."

Brande saw the opposing sub picking up speed. "I'm going to call that first sub Alpha," he said.

"How military," Dokey said.

"Alpha's making nine knots, heading directly toward us."

"Five-fifty yards to Alpha," Thomas said.

Brande was a little surprised at how calmly Thomas was taking this. It may have been a residual effect of her harrowing experience after the collision, or it may have been her deep-seated anger over Svetlana's death, or it may have been the result of her resolve, once the vote had been taken by the MVU employees. Whatever it was, he was proud of her, and he loved her all the more.

He even felt twinges of guilt at even considering a dalliance with Penny Glenn. Though he had just spoken to her, he now found it difficult to remember the details of what she looked like, or why he had found her so attractive.

He divided his attention between the robotic view and the smaller sonar shadow of Gargantua on the sonar. When the spread between them reached two hundred feet, he turned the ROV to parallel the course of the submersible, staying far out to the right.

He kept the robot as close to the seafloor as he dared. With any luck, the opposing sonars wouldn't pick it up, or at least notice it, until it was too late.

"Making twelve knots," Dokey said.

"Range to target, six hundred yards," Thomas said.

"Alpha is three-twenty out. The other sub, Beta, I guess you want to call it, is coming on strong now. A bit over five hundred to Beta."

On the sonar screen, the Alpha target closed on them quickly. Time seemed to go into hyperwarp.

"Two-fifty," Thomas said.

"You ready for this, Okey?"

"Better than ballroom dancing, Chief."

When the Alpha sub passed under a hundred yards until closure, Dokey slammed the motors into reverse, bringing *DepthFinder* to a halt.

Brande abandoned the robot's view and switched to the sonar. With the joysticks, he banked the ROV into a left turn and headed for the track of the Alpha sub, leading its forward progress by a wide margin. On the screen the intersection tracks looked perfect.

The pilot of the AquaGeo sub seemed surprised by their abrupt halt. After a few seconds, he reduced power to his own propellers.

Brande corrected the flight path of Gargantua to account for the now slower-moving sub.

Then the pilot became aware that he was being attacked from his left side.

He tried for altitude.

But Brande had him visually now, in the glaring eye of Gargantua.

And in the lower quadrant of that eye, the ROV's arms were extended, reaching out for the alien submersible.

Brande quickly tried to determine a target, and just as quickly settled on the same one Dokey had used with the earlier sub.

He aimed the robot's arm toward the portside pro-

peller housing, and just before it touched, released
the grip on the mine, then aimed Gargantua upward,
sailing high over the submersible.

The sub was out of the camera view too soon.
Brande didn't see where the mine went, or if its magnet had been attracted to the housing.

"Nearing the end of my tether," he called out.

"Going," Dokey said, applying power so that the
tether wouldn't go taut on them.

"Turning starboard," Brande said.

"Ditto," Dokey said.

On the sonar the ROV's signal pulled away from
the Alpha sub to the right, and *DepthFinder* followed.

The hostile pilot, not yet figuring out what had
happened, seemed confused. He had slowed yet more,
and he had turned to the left in his eagerness to
dodge the robot.

"I think now," Thomas said.

Dokey flipped the arming switch and hit the detonation button.

A couple seconds later, the dull thud reached the
hull of the submersible.

"Worked," Dokey said.

"But did we get him?"

"Look at the sonar," Thomas said, "He's going in
a circle . . . now he's stopped. We got something vi-
tal."

"Damned sure he's telling his pals about it," Dokey
said. "I'll give you a million to one odds that these
good old boys didn't expect to run into boxes that
go boom in the dark."

Brande saw that the Beta sub had begun to slow
down abruptly.

The Beta sub turned completely around and headed back toward the station.

"Full speed," Brande said.

"You're still going to get there before I do."

"Four hundred to target," Thomas said.

The distance fell away rapidly.

"Floor crawler in our path," Thomas said.

"What do you suppose the reach of that manipulator is, Okey?"

"With the crawler, maybe twenty feet off the seabed."

"Go to forty feet."

"Gone."

The robot, leading by two hundred feet, and the submersible both rose higher to avoid the manipulator on the front of the floor crawler.

"Two hundred yards," Thomas intoned.

"Beta's been ordered to defend, at all costs," Dokey said.

Brande glanced at the monitor. The sub had once again turned toward them.

"I wonder how brave they are?" he asked aloud, but the question was directed more to himself.

"I'm dropping number three," he said, signalling Gargantua's thumb to open.

"Five . . . four . . . three . . . two . . . one," Dokey intoned, then added, "armed, blown."

The thud of detonation sounded a moment later, and Brande worried about shrapnel from the blast—which hopefully had occurred on the seabed—severing the robot's tether.

He wiggled the controls, and Gargantua responded immediately.

Brande had to force himself to not worry about power usage. With the big ROV operating continuously, and despite his internal power supply, the battery drain on the submersible was substantial.

The Beta sub immediately turned off course. The opposition had no way of knowing how many bombs the robot carried. They probably thought they had just narrowly escaped death.

But Gargantua was unarmed now, though only in a manner of speaking. He still had his arms, and they were extremely powerful ones.

"Slow it down some, Okey."

"Roger, Chief. Coming back to five knots."

The robot was slow enough by the time the station came into its view that Brande had a chance to select his targets. He applied power to the forward up-thruster, and the robot raised his blunt nose, his video camera aiming upward toward the top of the sphere.

He steadied the flight.

Identified the sonar antenna, the acoustic antenna, and the winch that unreeled the surface antenna array.

"All stop," he ordered.

"All stop," Dokey echoed.

Slowing the robot to a crawl, Brande moved him in on the antennas, reached out, and found a grasp on the base of the sonar antenna. He ran in upthrust, and the powerful motors surged, struggling with the anchoring point of the antenna. He rocked the right joystick back and forth, and the ROV responded, shifting left and right.

The antenna base snapped.

He dropped it, moved Gargantua slightly to the right, and gripped the acoustic antenna. If anything,

the base broke more readily, but he had to back off
six feet in order to snap the cable.

Using both manipulators, Brande grabbed the
winch cable in two places, some eight inches apart.
With Brande rocking the arms in opposing directions,
it took less than thirty seconds to part the cable.
When he released it, the cable leading from the surface immediately surged upward and out of sight.

"That was pretty good," Dokey said with admira-
tion. *"Atlas* couldn't have done that."

"That should make them feel isolated," Brande
said. "They've lost their ears and their sonar."

"What about their eyes?" Dokey asked, pointing to
the video camera on its rotatable tripod. It was now
aimed at them.

"Let's leave it."

"Here comes Beta," Thomas said.

"And away we go," Dokey said.

The two of them went to full speed, headed directly
west, and within five minutes, had outdistanced the
pursuing submersible, which finally turned around
and went back.

"Now the nuke plant?" Dokey asked.

That had been Thomas's suggestion in their planning phase, and she said, "Now the nuclear plant."

0123 Hours Local, The California
33° 16′ 50″ North, 141° 15′ 19″ West

"Bridge, CIC."

Harris moved to the intercom and pressed the button. "Bridge. Go."

"We've detected two small detonations on the bottom. Type and strength are unknown."

"Thank you." Harris released the button and stood back.

He looked through the port-wing window at the freighter and the maintenance ship that were holding position some two hundred yards away. The starboard crane of the maintenance vessel was lowering a gigantic seabed crawler to its well-lit deck. A dozen seamen swarmed around it.

"These guys work around the clock," Commander Quicken noted.

"And force us to do the same, George."

The *California* had been with the AquaGeo vessels for several hours now. Harris had mounted additional lookouts on his rainswept decks, keeping an eye out for Brande's submersible. His best sonarmen were manning the warship's sonars, told to look and listen for anything in the world that sounded suspicious. Even whale contacts had been reported, and there had been three of them.

He didn't think that Brande would attack the surface ships, but he also didn't *really* know what to expect from the marine scientist.

"Two explosions," Quicken said.

"Yes. I don't imagine there's been an accident, do you, George?"

"I doubt it, sir. Where the hell would Brande get explosives?"

"Maybe it's AquaGeo's people. They'll have mining supplies."

"I hope they didn't get Brande."

"Me too, George. But I've got to report this to

CINCPAC and Washington, and they may be hoping for the other outcome."

0125 Hours Local, The Orion
33° 21' 41" North, 141° 5' 59" West

"There went the first two," Otsuka said.

She typed in X's next to the items on her checklist. As with all of MVU's expeditions, they had set up a planning checklist, and she had been eyeing it on the monitor for quite some time.

"They're about an hour ahead of my predictions," Emry said. "I must be getting old."

"Nonsense, Larry. Your mind's just on Tahiti."

"Not on Tahiti, Kim. On those grass skirts."

"Quiet, please," Bob Mayberry said, "I'm trying to hear."

Mayberry was at the command console, a headset in place.

After a few minutes, he said, "There it is. Code-word 'Cranapple.' Phase one complete, everyone's in one piece."

Otsuka felt a little bit better about her numbering system on the mines. Or maybe they hadn't selected nine or nineteen yet.

She wanted to go on the acoustic and talk to Dokey about it, but Mayberry and Emry would think she was worrying needlessly.

"Go ahead and give 'em a try, Bob," Emry said.

Mayberry tried the UHF and HF radios, then several frequencies on the acoustic, asking for AquaGeo's SeaStation AG-4, but he got no reply.

"Either they aren't answering, or they're off the air," Emry said.

"Let's hope it's the second option, Larry," Mayberry said.

"I want to talk to *DepthFinder,*" she said abruptly.

Emry and Mayberry exchanged a knowing look.

"Worried about your boyfriend?" Emry asked.

"I need to talk to him."

Mayberry shrugged. "Fifty-fifty chance the station will never hear us, though the vehicles are probably still receiving."

"Go ahead, Kim," Emry said.

She leaned over and grabbed the mike, then depressed the Transmit stud. "Okey?"

A few seconds went by before he replied, "Kim?"

"Don't use six, nine, sixteen, or nineteen."

"Got ya, babe."

0132 Hours Local, SeaStation AG-4
33° 16′ 50″ North, 141° 15′ 19″ West

Paul Deride felt steel bands clutching his heart, slowly squeezing it. The sweating dampness of the interior was stifling him. His forehead felt as if it were caressed by frozen ice one moment, burning heat the next.

He and Penny Glenn, along with Bert Conroy and the four others currently aboard the station, had watched in almost rapt fascination as Brande's submersible ripped out their communications and sonar antennas.

A panicky Conroy had grabbed the controls of the overhead video camera and kept it trained on the robot—Gargantua, as Deride had recognized it—while the remote-controlled machine destroyed the antennas.

Several attempts had failed to produce any contact with the surface ships or with the subsea vehicles. He had tried to phone Anthony Camden to tell him to get the Navy—get somebody—in here to stop Brande.

Almost unbelievably, Deride had found himself unable to talk to his trusted advisor, to reach out to the world.

The station had closed in on him immediately.

He was pacing in a continuous circle around the worktable in the center of the control room.

Trying to keep his voice level, Deride said, "All right, give that one to Brande. Penny, get the subs in here to take us off."

"We can't talk to them, Uncle Paul."

"Use the goddamned floodlights. Blink Morse code at them, for Christ's sake!"

Conroy appeared immediately relieved at that suggestion, as did the others milling around in the room.

"It would depend on whether they're close enough to see the lights," she said.

The relief on Conroy's face was short-lived.

"Besides," she went on, "you heard Gary Munro before we lost the acoustic. *Sydney*'s out of the picture. She's lost all propulsion, and he's dropped weights. She's already on her way to the surface."

"Son of a bitch!" Deride yelped.

He thought he was yelping. He couldn't help it.

"It'll be all right, Uncle Paul. Brande's just trying to scare us, and damn it, I won't be scared off."

"Fine, Penny, that's just fine. You all can stay here. In the meantime, get that other sub in here. I'm going to the *Outer Islands Lady* so I can use a bloody damned telephone. I'll have Anthony screaming so loudly at them, the whole bloody damned world will hear."

"Bert," she said, "blink the exterior lights and see if you can catch the attention of someone on the *Brisbane*."

Conroy went to do that, and Deride felt better. He decided right then that, after he reached the surface, he was never again leaving it.

0637 Hours Local
Langley, Virginia

Jesus. These calls always came in the early morning.

Unruh had planned to sleep in, something he hadn't done in months, but Ben Delecourt got him out of bed.

"The *California* says what, Ben?"

"They think there's maybe a miniwar taking place on the bottom, Carl. Harris talked to the captain of the *Outer Islands Lady,* but the captain says he can't reach the station on the seabed. Captain Harris is a little miffed at us. CINCPAC forgot to tell him there was a habitat on the bottom. Harris also tried the *Orion,* but somebody named Alvarez-Sorenson told him that communication with the submersible was sporadic. Also, Harris has requested permission from the Joint Chiefs to seize the *Orion.*"

"Whatever for?" Unruh asked.

"Violation of the injunction."

"Is that legal?"

"Hell, who knows? I've got the Navy legal department looking into it, but the first question the guy asked me was, 'Did the *Orion,* or did the *DepthFinder* make the violation?' He thinks we could seize the sub, but not the research vessel. Only we can't find the damned sub."

"Let's get back to this miniwar of yours, Admiral. What's that about?"

"California has heard explosions. They think someone is attacking someone else."

"All those billions we've spent on satellites and high-tech intelligence gathering don't seem to add up to much, do they, Ben?"

"Carl, we'd better get the task force together, and damned fast."

"What will we ask them to do, Ben? And, better yet, what will they do?"

Delecourt thought about that for a second, then said, "Go back to bed, Carl."

0210 Hours Local, The Arienne
33° 20' 21" North, 141° 6' 47" West

The *Orion* had startled him when she heeled to the right and added power. By the time Overton voiced his observation, Mark Jacobs had already replaced Mick Freelander at the helm and shoved his throttles in.

Behind them, in a dismal gray night and high waves, eight boats of varying description fell into line and picked up speed. Behind the research vessel, the white-and-yellow tugboat was struggling to keep up.

"Where in hell do you suppose she's headed, Mark?"

Jacobs shook his head. "As a guess, I'd think they're about to recover their submersible again."

"Well, damn it! This time, Brande's going to tell me what he's been up to."

"Good luck, Wilson."

Overton grabbed their coffee mugs and took the ladder down to the salon.

Freelander was there, frying himself an egg.

In the back corner, the fax machine was chattering, so Overton went to check on it.

It was directed to him, from Ned Nelson, and he read it as it came off the machine. When he could rip the page off, he refilled the mugs and carried them back upstairs.

Excuse me. Topside.

When he handed Jacobs his mug, the Greenpeace leader said, "What do you have there?"

"Bios on the execs at AquaGeo."

"Anything interesting?"

"Not much on first reading, except for the Glenn woman."

"Who's she?"

"A geologist and, according to this, the heir apparent of the corporation. Hold on."

Overton read through Glenn's report a second time.

"This is kind of strange, Mark."

Jacobs rode the slight bounce of the helmsman's chair and just looked at him.

"Glenn's more or less an adopted daughter of De-

ride. He put her through some good schools, took
care of her from age twelve on. Made her a honcho
in his company, and according to rumor, pays her
millions."

"The man may have the hots for her, Wilson. Nothing strange about that."

"Yeah, but back in 1971, it was Deride that aced
her parents out of their mining company. Practically
stole it from them, and made his first million with
it."

"What happened to the parents?" Jacobs asked.

"They died. Double suicide, it says here."

0234 Hours Local, DepthFinder
33° 16′ 50″ North, 141° 15′ 19″ West

They rested on the bottom for nearly an hour, not
only to relax themselves, but to hopefully build anxiety and dread in their foes. The Beta sub passed close
to them a couple of times, but didn't locate them.

"According to my trusty checklist," Dokey said,
"it's time to go."

"Let's go then," Brande said.

He hadn't relaxed much. He was keyed up, eager
to get it over with, and that wasn't good. That was
when mistakes happened.

Rae Thomas had actually slept for forty minutes.

Dokey had eaten two of his meals. No doubt, he'd
be bargaining with Brande and Thomas later for the
eating rights to their desserts.

"This one's on the floor bed," Thomas reminded
them. "That will mean the floor crawlers will have
a chance at us, depending on where they are."

As the submersible and Gargantua rose from their resting places and Dokey switched the sonar on, he said, "These guys strike me as dummies. They won't know what we're after."

However, once they were within a thousand yards of their target, Dokey changed his mind.

"Damn. Two crawlers, friends. The bastards knew we were coming."

TWENTY-ONE

They paused to reload Gargantua, and the first grenade/mine that Brande selected from the robot's basket was number nine.

"Throw it away," Dokey said.

"Do you really think Kim mixed the numbers?" Brande asked.

"We'll never know, and that's going to drive her batty, but let's humor her, Chief."

Brande dropped it, then picked up twelve and ten. After the visual verification, he turned the robot and moved it out two hundred feet ahead of them.

With Gargantua leading the way, they made their attack run toward the habitat from the west, moving at ten knots.

Thomas was analyzing the imagery on the sonar screen. "It looks to me, Dane, as if the Beta sub is mated with the habitat."

"Good. That's what we wanted."

"But it means they'll have use of the sub's communications," she said.

"That's why the crawlers are in place," Dokey said.

"And we'll have to live with it for a few minutes," Brande said. "This won't take much longer."

"No more than a couple, three hours," Dokey clarified.

"Pessimist," Brande told him.

"Five hundred yards," she said.

He removed his hands from the joysticks for a few seconds to flex his fingers, then replaced them. He listened as Thomas read off the descending numbers, and as Dokey ordered a change in heading, but he kept his eyes on the multifunction screen displaying the ROV's view of the sea bottom. The monotonous terrain unrolled before the camera, a backdrop to the outstretched manipulator arms. He had to trim in additional downthrust on the aft end of the robot in order to balance the weight of the extended arms.

The seabed was ten feet below the robot, according to the readout on his panel. The darkness ahead steadily gave way to the floodlights.

"One hundred," Thomas said.

"Go to fifty feet," Dokey told Brande.

"Climbing."

He eased back on the right stick, and the seabed fell away, nearly disappearing from the field of view.

"Two knots," Dokey said.

"Two," he repeated, backing off on the forward speed. "Where's the sub, Rae?"

"Still at the station."

The first floor crawler appeared on the screen. They had seen Gargantua's lights, and their video camera was trained on the robot. The crawler's manipulator arm waved back and forth, a cobra ready to strike.

But the robot was out of reach, and the snake was impotent.

Brande sailed Gargantua slowly over the crawler, aimed the ROV downward so he could maintain his camera view, aligned the left manipulator arm, and released the mine.

It drifted downward with apparent nonchalance, found the right-hand track, and clicked into place, its magnet enchanted with the steel tread. As it fell, the crawler's video camera tracked it, and as soon as it locked in place, the operator panicked and slammed power to the treads.

They began to move, kicking up a fog of silt.

"Three . . . two . . . one," Dokey said as Brande threw upthrust into the ROV, moving it out of range.

He didn't get to see the explosion since Gargantua's lights had gone out of range, and inside the submersible, they were barely aware of it.

"The other crawler is scrambling," Thomas said.

"Where to, Rae?"

"Anywhere but here, I think. They're headed south."

"Let's go back down and check our work," Dokey said.

Brande lowered the ROV, and they soon had a view of the floor crawler. The left track had parted and been spun off its sleepers by the sprockets. It lay, half-twisted, under the canted crawler like a steel-encrusted eel. A thick cloud of silt was just beginning to settle.

Brande turned the ROV slowly in place. The camera picked up the nuclear plant's dome, some forty feet to the north.

"I hope that thing will shut itself down," Brande said.

"Has to," Dokey reassured him. "Basic safety design."

Turning the robot back to the east, Brande dove it toward the seafloor and coasted until he picked up a view of the thick umbilical cable resting on the seabed.

"That's the honey, Chief."

It was armored cable, and the magnet of the mine snapped into place easily. Brande backed Gargantua out of range, and Dokey detonated it.

When the robot approached the cable again, Brande saw that it was neatly severed.

"I should think the station would be on emergency power now," Thomas said.

"And its inhabitants should be reevaluating their alternatives," Brande added.

"Do you like legs, Chief?" Dokey asked.

"I like legs."

"Let's go find some."

0246 Hours Local, SeaStation AG-4
33° 16' 50" North, 141° 15' 19" West

When the power went, there was a momentary blackout before the emergency battery system cut in. It was eerie for those few seconds—blower motors that were always chanting in the background shut down, the hum of electronics evaporated.

When the power came up again, Glenn was aware of the reduction. The overhead lights were dimmer. The computer screens displayed garbage. The sonar was automatically recycling, as it had been doing since Brande destroyed the antenna. She shut it down.

She felt deaf and mute, entirely alone.

She spun around and left the control room, passed through the lounge, and descended the spiral stairway to the reception chamber.

Paul Deride was there, waiting to board the *Brisbane*. In contrast to the brief blackout, his face was pasty-white. He was seated in a chair, and he didn't look good at all. She wondered if he was on the verge of a heart attack.

"Are you all right, Uncle Paul?"

"I think so, yes," he panted. "What happened?"

"What I feared might happen. They cut off our power supply."

"Bloody hell! Are we . . . are we—"

"We're fine. There's a three-day supply of energy. However, I think we'd better evacuate the station until we can make the repairs."

"Goddamn it! We're letting Brande drive us out."

"Only for the moment, Uncle Paul. There's always tomorrow. Or the day after. It's going to take some time for the *Outer Islands Lady* to raise the crawlers."

"How long, Penny?" Some of the color was returning to his face.

"A week, perhaps. Ten days."

His lips sagged, and she knew he was counting the cost.

He looked so pathetic, sitting there. Scared to death. Helpless. His decisions didn't matter much.

She didn't want him to die, not like he had forced her parents into their mutual suicides by stealing from them everything they owned and believed in.

She wanted him to live to suffer the ridicule and ostracism of an entire world when that world realized he was responsible for the devastation of the American West Coast. She wanted him to know that, for the first time, he had been conned. Soon, she would tell him that the manganese samples were doctored to show higher contents. He would learn that the written and recorded records would show that every decision had been his own.

That would still happen. Jim Dorsey and Team Three would see to it.

She turned to a visibly shaken Bert Conroy. "Bert, let's get everyone off. It's going to be crowded in the sub, and it'll be a long ride, but I don't think we have a choice. Start shutting down the systems."

0251 Hours Local, The Orion
33° 16′ 51″ North, 141° 15′ 18″ West

DepthFinder was using her acoustic voice system freely now, and Kim Otsuka was thrilled to hear Dokey's voice.

"You didn't use . . ."

"Hey, babe, we're skipping your magic numbers."

Brande came on. "Kim, get on the horn and call the *Arienne,* will you?"

She jotted down the message Brande wanted to pass on, then called the Greenpeace ship on UHF

channel nine. Wilson Overton must have been right
next to the receiver.

"Let's see," he said, "you're Kim Otsuka?"

"That's right."

"I keep running into new names. I don't suppose
Dr. Brande is available?"

"Not just now, but he has told me to tell you that
he'll talk to you in the morning."

"It's morning now."

"Later in the morning. Right now, he'd like to
know how many boats you have in your group."

"Boats? I don't . . . well, I think there's maybe
eight, nine with us. There's more coming."

"All right," she said, "here's the deal. . . ."

0258 Hours Local, The DepthFinder
33° 16′ 50″ North, 141° 15′ 19″ West

"I should have rigged up something to make these
things go simultaneously," Dokey said.

"You don't think it'll work?" Thomas asked him.

"Well, it should work out okay, but it's a hell of
a lot of wear and tear on my finger, pressing the
button three times when one would do it. That's what
we computer people are all about, Kaylene. Avoiding
repetition of simple tasks."

Thomas shook her head in resignation. Brande and
Dokey seemed entirely too glib sometimes, especially
in crucial situations. She supposed it was a male reaction to stress, but she just wanted to get it over
with.

"They're slow as hell, aren't they, Chief?" Dokey asked.

"It may be time to spur them on, yes."

The Beta sub was in view of Gargantua's camera, still mated to the station's port on the bottom of its sphere. They couldn't tell what was taking place inside the station or the sub, but she could tell that Brande was getting impatient.

"Let's take it out, Okey."

"Back off then."

Brande reversed the ROV out of range, and Thomas saw the station's leg, with four grenades adhered to it, slip out of sight. One of the grenades was number nine. Dokey didn't know whether or not it would go off in sympathetic detonation, but he had suggested that the attempt was his contribution to Thomas's cost-efficiency program—"I don't know how much you paid for that grenade, Kaylene, but we'll try to make use of it."

He spun the rotary dial three times, armed each charge, and set it off. The series of explosions came to them in small vibrations against the hull.

Then Brande eased in power, and Gargantua closed in for an evaluative look at the stainless steel leg of the station. Dokey followed with the submersible, and the station was visible through the ports. It appeared to tilt slightly.

The leg was buckled, but not entirely severed.

"Going to take one more," Dokey said.

"I hope we don't run out of Mark One, mod one's," Brande told him.

Dokey brought the submersible in closer, and while the two of them set up the ROV with two more grenades, Thomas watched the station on *DepthFinder*'s camera view.

The explosion and sudden settling of the station had prompted the people inside to greater speed. As she watched, the Beta sub released its grip on the mating collar and backed away from the station.

"She's going," Thomas said.

The two men stopped what they were doing to watch, and possibly, to make certain the sub didn't counterattack them.

She didn't. After reversing clear of the habitat, she dropped her weights and began to rise.

"That's something of a relief," Brande said.

"Let's just get on with it, please," she said.

It took them forty minutes to cut all three legs, and when they were done, the sea station had settled partially on its side, moving slightly in the bottom current.

"By the way she's moving around," Brande said, "I think she's as close to neutral buoyancy as we'd hoped."

"Twenty minutes," Dokey said, "and we'll know for sure."

"Optimist," Brande accused Dokey this time.

Brande brought Gargantua back toward them, then raised the ROV to sail above *DepthFinder*. The robot's video picked out the four folded rubber bladders secured to the afterdeck of the submersible.

Because it required his precise hand on the manipulators, Dokey said, he and Brande exchanged piloting chores. Still, it took nearly an hour for Dokey to release the bladders, one by one, from the sub and attach their securing lines to anchoring points on the sphere. When all four were in place he moved Gargantua from one to the next, pulling the release valves on the stainless steel bottles of carbon dioxide. The bladders filled infinitely slowly, Thomas thought, but knew that if they just got a little upward movement going, the bladders would get larger as the exterior pressure on them lessened.

Dokey finally brought the ROV back, reeled in his tether, and parked him near the sheath.

"How's the power supply, Rae?"

"We've been using it up fast, Dane, but we're still in the green."

They waited.

And ever so slowly, through the portholes, they saw the habitat begin to right itself.

Then there was a foot of space between it and the seabed.

Then two feet.

Then ten.

Brande keyed his headset microphone.

"Bull, are you listening?"

"Got me, Chief."

"What are you going to be doing in, say, six hours?"

NOVEMBER 25

TWENTY-TWO

1112 Hours Local
San Francisco, California

Paul Deride and Anthony Camden had ordered a large brunch delivered to the suite in the Fairmont. The remnants of scrambled eggs, bacon, sausage, oranges, and pineapples dried on their plates as they sat at the dining table and attempted to calculate the damages.

The reports were still coming in by phone and fax, and it was taking an effort on Deride's part to assimilate them. He had left the area of the sea station by way of his Canadair almost as soon as the *Brisbane* had surfaced after a three-hour, intensely uncomfortable ascent, but the effects of the experience would be with him for a long time.

"The Justice Department has said nothing yet, Paul."

"But they will."

"Yes. I suspect they'll find where we've made some shortcuts. There's the wetlands we filled in in Oregon, the unreported spills in the northern Pacific . . ."

"Don't catalog it for me, Anthony."

"It'll take some time to recover," the lawyer said. "These cases will be with us for years."

"Hell, we don't care about that, do we, now? The longer, the better."

The telephone buzzed.

He picked it up. "Deride."

"Hello, Uncle Paul."

"Good morning, love. Are things looking better this morning? Something for which to give thanks?"

"We've lost FC-9 and Team Three."

"What?"

"I'd forgotten they were low on life-support reserves. Or maybe they lost electrical power, I don't know. But they're way past their check-in. We're certain they're both dead by now."

"Jesus." Deride knew what it might be like, to die down there. Several times, he thought he had.

"They've got six nukes on board," she said.

"Which we'll never use now."

"Unless you find them, no."

There was something wrong with that statement, and he was about to say so, but she went on.

"Plus, there's another setback, Uncle Paul."

"I don't know why I expect this," he said.

"I took the *Brisbane* down early this morning, to survey damage."

"And?"

"AG-4 is no longer there."

He couldn't believe that. "Not there?"

"Gone. We searched fifty square miles, but it's gone, Uncle Paul. I think Brande took it with him."

"That's impossible!"

"For Brande, perhaps not."

"Damn! What do we do now?"

"Whatever you want, I suppose. At this point, I think you've got about three hundred million tied up in this project."

"I think that's about right," he said.

"I'd write it off," she said.

"You'd . . ."

"There's not enough manganese to justify the mining," Penny Glenn said. "That's because the testing results were only what you wanted them to be."

That steel band clutched his heart again.

"Penny, what are you saying? What do I do?"

"You might use a gun, like my daddy did. I quit."

"Penny, you can't—"

She hung up on him.

1520 Hours Local
Washington, D.C.

"Hello, brother dearest."

"Adrienne!" Hampstead said. He gripped the phone tighter. "Where are you?"

"I just got into town. I'm letting you take Alicia and me to dinner tonight. Some place expensive, naturally."

The last episode of *Lonesome Dove* was scheduled for tonight, but he'd missed most of them this time, anyway. "Certainly."

"And I want to come up right now and talk to you about the Marine Visions contract we have yet to see."

"Well, I . . ."

"There's the matter of a robot, a Sneaky Pete, that you should reimburse us for."

"I already wrote . . ."

"And hazard pay. I think there should be a clause inserted, just in case any of the participants run into something unexpected, don't you?"

"Adrienne. . . ."

"And legal expenses. The Navy, the Commerce Department, and the CIA should foot the bills there for any hearings or procedures that may come up in the near future. That's only understandable, isn't it?"

Hampstead didn't think he was going to enjoy dinner.

1317 Hours Local, The Orion
32° 36′ 19″ North, 135° 45′ 29″ West

The seaplane with the AquaGeo Limited logo on its fuselage had flown over them twenty minutes before, and Brande was expecting a phone call at any minute.

His little fleet was moving at a snail's pace, and San Diego was still ten hours away, but he felt good. He was warm again, he had dined on Paco Suarez's famed culinary delights, and he was standing on the bridge of the *Orion* with Rae Thomas at his side.

Mel Sorenson and Connie Alvarez-Sorenson were arguing over who had the watch.

The seas hadn't gotten much better, and the skies were a slate gray, but the weatherman out of Los Angeles was promising a brighter day tomorrow.

The *Orion* was leading the flotilla. To port and starboard, in a protective screen, were seventeen boats belonging to friends of Mark Jacobs. The Greenpeace leader and Wilson Overton were on the bridge of the *Arienne,* immediately to port. Every once in a while, Overton waved happily at them. In exchange for the escort of environmental activist vessels, Brande had given him a story that would last him for a few weeks.

Trailing the fleet was the *California* and her two escorts. Captain Mabry Harris had insisted on accompanying them, just in case AquaGeo ships tried to get in their way.

Directly astern of the research vessel, a grinning Bull Kontas piloted his *Mighty Moose.* Kontas was, in fact, the reason for their reduced speed—the tugboat was towing the habitat that had once been known as AG-4.

"I'm about ready for a nap," Thomas told him.

He put his arm around her waist. "I'll join you, love, but in a little while. I'm expecting a call."

She pouted a little, but waited with him.

When it came, he went into the radio shack and picked up the receiver.

"Hello, Deride."

"Brande, you've got my sea station."

"That's incorrect. I've got my sea station."

"Bullshit!"

"It was abandoned at sea," Brande told him. "I salvaged it, and it's now mine. Reread your salvage law, Deride. Or have your lawyer do it for you."

"You forced us to leave it," Deride complained.

"Sue me. Somebody will settle it in a few years, no doubt."

**FOR THE BEST OF THE WEST, SADDLE UP WITH
PINNACLE AND JACK CUMMINGS . . .**

DEAD MAN'S MEDAL	(664-0, $3.50/$4.50)
THE DESERTER TROOP	(715-9, $3.50/$4.50)
ESCAPE FROM YUMA	(697-7, $3.50/$4.50)
ONCE A LEGEND	(650-0, $3.50/$4.50)
REBELS WEST	(525-3, $3.50/$4.50)
THE ROUGH RIDER	(481-8, $3.50/$4.50)
THE SURROGATE GUN	(607-1, $3.50/$4.50)
TIGER BUTTE	(583-0, $3.50/$4.50)